The
MX Book
of
New
Sherlock
Holmes
Stories

Part XLI – Further Untold Cases
(1887-1892)

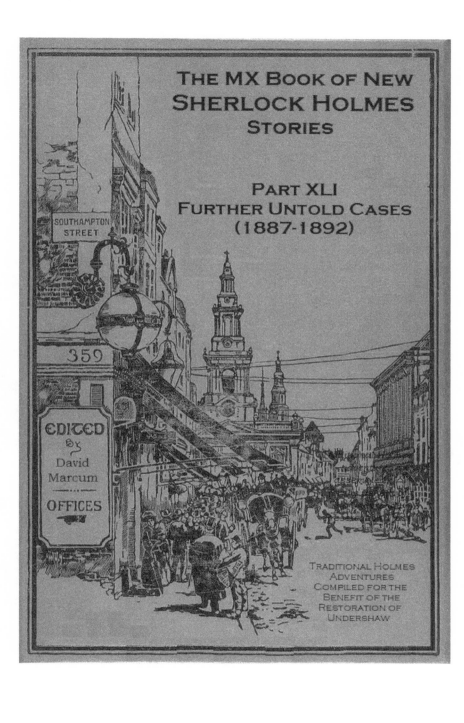

THE MX BOOK OF NEW SHERLOCK HOLMES STORIES

PART XLI
FURTHER UNTOLD CASES
(1887-1892)

SOUTHAMPTON STREET

359

EDITED
By
David
Marcum

OFFICES

TRADITIONAL HOLMES
ADVENTURES
COMPILED FOR THE
BENEFIT OF THE
RESTORATION OF
UNDERSHAW

ISBN Hardback 978-1-80424-361-9
ISBN Paperback 978-1-80424-362-6
AUK ePub ISBN 978-1-80424-363-3
AUK PDF ISBN 978-1-80424-364-0

Published in the UK by
MX Publishing
335 Princess Park Manor, Royal Drive,
London, N11 3GX
www.mxpublishing.co.uk

David Marcum can be reached at:
thepapersofsherlockholmes@gmail.com

Cover design by Brian Belanger
www.belangerbooks.com and *www.redbubble.com/people/zhahadun*

Internal Illustrations by Sidney Paget

CONTENTS

Forewords

Adventures

(Continued on the next page . . . .)

(Continued on the next page . . . .)

(Continued on the next page . . . .)

(Continued on the next page . . . .)

PART V – Christmas Adventures

(Continued on the next page . . . .)

(Continued on the next page . . . .)

The Unwelcome Client – Keith Hann
The Tempest of Lyme – David Ruffle
The Problem of the Holy Oil – David Marcum
A Scandal in Serbia – Thomas A. Turley
The Curious Case of Mr. Marconi – Jan Edwards
Mr. Holmes and Dr. Watson Learn to Fly – C. Edward Davis
Die Weisse Frau – Tim Symonds
A Case of Mistaken Identity – Daniel D. Victor

PART VII – Eliminate the Impossible: 1880-1891
Foreword – Lee Child
Foreword – Rand B. Lee
Foreword – Michael Cox
Foreword – Roger Johnson
Foreword – Melissa Farnham
Foreword – David Marcum
No Ghosts Need Apply (A Poem) – Jacquelynn Morris
The Melancholy Methodist – Mark Mower
The Curious Case of the Sweated Horse – Jan Edwards
The Adventure of the Second William Wilson – Daniel D. Victor
The Adventure of the Marchindale Stiletto – James Lovegrove
The Case of the Cursed Clock – Gayle Lange Puhl
The Tranquility of the Morning – Mike Hogan
A Ghost from Christmas Past – Thomas A. Turley
The Blank Photograph – James Moffett
The Adventure of A Rat. – Adrian Middleton
The Adventure of Vanaprastha – Hugh Ashton
The Ghost of Lincoln – Geri Schear
The Manor House Ghost – S. Subramanian
The Case of the Unquiet Grave – John Hall
The Adventure of the Mortal Combat – Jayantika Ganguly
The Last Encore of Quentin Carol – S.F. Bennett
The Case of the Petty Curses – Steven Philip Jones
The Tuttman Gallery – Jim French
The Second Life of Jabez Salt – John Linwood Grant
The Mystery of the Scarab Earrings – Thomas Fortenberry
The Adventure of the Haunted Room – Mike Chinn
The Pharaoh's Curse – Robert V. Stapleton
The Vampire of the Lyceum – Charles Veley and Anna Elliott
The Adventure of the Mind's Eye – Shane Simmons

PART VIII – Eliminate the Impossible: 1892-1905
Foreword – Lee Child
Foreword – Rand B. Lee
Foreword – Michael Cox
Foreword – Roger Johnson
Foreword – Melissa Farnham

(Continued on the next page . . . .)

(Continued on the next page . . . .)

The Lambeth Poisoner Case – Stephen Gaspar
The Confession of Anna Jarrow – S. F. Bennett
The Adventure of the Disappearing Dictionary – Sonia Fetherston
The Fairy Hills Horror – Geri Schear
A Loathsome and Remarkable Adventure – Marcia Wilson
The Adventure of the Multiple Moriartys – David Friend
The Influence Machine – Mark Mower

Part X – 2018 Annual (1896-1916)
Foreword – Nicholas Meyer
Foreword – Roger Johnson
Foreword – Melissa Farnham
Foreword – Steve Emecz
Foreword – David Marcum
A Man of Twice Exceptions (A Poem) – Derrick Belanger
The Horned God – Kelvin Jones
The Coughing Man – Jim French
The Adventure of Canal Reach – Arthur Hall
A Simple Case of Abduction – Mike Hogan
A Case of Embezzlement – Steven Ehrman
The Adventure of the Vanishing Diplomat – Greg Hatcher
The Adventure of the Perfidious Partner – Jayantika Ganguly
A Brush With Death – Dick Gillman
A Revenge Served Cold – Maurice Barkley
The Case of the Anonymous Client – Paul A. Freeman
Capitol Murder – Daniel D. Victor
The Case of the Dead Detective – Martin Rosenstock
The Musician Who Spoke From the Grave – Peter Coe Verbica
The Adventure of the Future Funeral – Hugh Ashton
The Problem of the Bruised Tongues – Will Murray
The Mystery of the Change of Art – Robert Perret
The Parsimonious Peacekeeper – Thaddeus Tuffentsamer
The Case of the Dirty Hand – G.L. Schulze
The Mystery of the Missing Artefacts – Tim Symonds

Part XI: Some Untold Cases (1880-1891)
Foreword – Lyndsay Faye
Foreword – Roger Johnson
Foreword – Melissa Grigsby
Foreword – Steve Emecz
Foreword – David Marcum
Unrecorded Holmes Cases (*A Sonnet*) – Arlene Mantin Levy and Mark Levy
The Most Repellant Man – Jayantika Ganguly
The Singular Adventure of the Extinguished Wicks – Will Murray
Mrs. Forrester's Complication – Roger Riccard
The Adventure of Vittoria, the Circus Belle – Tracy Revels

(Continued on the next page . . . .)

Part XII: Some Untold Cases (1894-1902)

PART XIII: 2019 Annual (1881-1890)

(Continued on the next page . . . .)

PART XIV: 2019 Annual (1891 -1897)

(Continued on the next page . . . .)

(Continued on the next page . . . .)

The Adventure of the Headless Lady – Tracy J. Revels
Angelus Domini Nuntiavit – Kevin P. Thornton
The Blue Lady of Dunraven – Andrew Bryant
The Adventure of the Ghoulish Grenadier – Josh Anderson and David Friend
The Curse of Barcombe Keep – Brenda Seabrooke
The Affair of the Regressive Man – David Marcum
The Adventure of the Giant's Wife – I.A. Watson
The Adventure of Miss Anna Truegrace – Arthur Hall
The Haunting of Bottomly's Grandmother – Tim Gambrell
The Adventure of the Intrusive Spirit – Shane Simmons
The Paddington Poltergeist – Bob Bishop
The Spectral Pterosaur – Mark Mower
The Weird of Caxton – Kelvin Jones
The Adventure of the Obsessive Ghost – Jayantika Ganguly

Part XVII – Whatever Remains . . . Must Be the Truth (1891-1898)
Foreword – Kareem Abdul-Jabbar
Foreword – Roger Johnson
Foreword – Steve Emecz
Foreword – David Marcum
The Violin Thief (*A Poem*) – Christopher James
The Spectre of Scarborough Castle – Charles Veley and Anna Elliott
The Case for Which the World is Not Yet Prepared – Steven Philip Jones
The Adventure of the Returning Spirit – Arthur Hall
The Adventure of the Bewitched Tenant – Michael Mallory
The Misadventures of the Bonnie Boy – Will Murray
The Adventure of the *Danse Macabre* – Paul D. Gilbert
The Strange Persecution of John Vincent Harden – S. Subramanian
The Dead Quiet Library – Roger Riccard
The Adventure of the Sugar Merchant – Stephen Herczeg
The Adventure of the Undertaker's Fetch – Tracy J. Revels
The Holloway Ghosts – Hugh Ashton
The Diogenes Club Poltergeist – Chris Chan
The Madness of Colonel Warburton – Bert Coules
The Return of the Noble Bachelor – Jane Rubino
The Reappearance of Mr. James Phillimore – David Marcum
The Miracle Worker – Geri Schear
The Hand of Mesmer – Dick Gillman

Part XVIII – Whatever Remains . . . Must Be the Truth (1899-1925)
Foreword – Kareem Abdul-Jabbar
Foreword – Roger Johnson
Foreword – Steve Emecz
Foreword – David Marcum
The Adventure of the Lighthouse on the Moor (*A Poem*) – Christopher James
The Witch of Ellenby – Thomas A. Burns, Jr.

(Continued on the next page . . . .)

Part XIX: 2020 Annual (1882-1890)

(Continued on the next page . . . .)

The Adventure of the Matched Set – Peter Coe Verbica
When the Prince First Dined at the Diogenes Club – Sean M. Wright
The Sweetenbury Safe Affair – Tim Gambrell

Part XX: 2020 Annual (1891-1897)
Foreword – John Lescroart
Foreword – Roger Johnson
Foreword – Lizzy Butler
Foreword – Steve Emecz
Foreword – David Marcum
The Sibling (*A Poem*) – Jacquelynn Morris
Blood and Gunpowder – Thomas A. Burns, Jr.
The Atelier of Death – Harry DeMaio
The Adventure of the Beauty Trap – Tracy Revels
A Case of Unfinished Business – Steven Philip Jones
The Case of the S.S. Bokhara – Mark Mower
The Adventure of the American Opera Singer – Deanna Baran
The Keadby Cross – David Marcum
The Adventure at Dead Man's Hole – Stephen Herczeg
The Elusive Mr. Chester – Arthur Hall
The Adventure of Old Black Duffel – Will Murray
The Blood-Spattered Bridge – Gayle Lange Puhl
The Tomorrow Man – S.F. Bennett
The Sweet Science of Bruising – Kevin P. Thornton
The Mystery of Sherlock Holmes – Christopher Todd
The Elusive Mr. Phillimore – Matthew J. Elliott
The Murders in the Maharajah's Railway Carriage – Charles Veley and Anna Elliott
The Ransomed Miracle – I.A. Watson
The Adventure of the Unkind Turn – Robert Perret
The Perplexing X'ing – Sonia Fetherston
The Case of the Short-Sighted Clown – Susan Knight

Part XXI: 2020 Annual (1898-1923)
Foreword – John Lescroart
Foreword – Roger Johnson
Foreword – Lizzy Butler
Foreword – Steve Emecz
Foreword – David Marcum
The Case of the Missing Rhyme (*A Poem*) – Joseph W. Svec III
The Problem of the St. Francis Parish Robbery – R.K. Radek
The Adventure of the Grand Vizier – Arthur Hall
The Mummy's Curse – DJ Tyrer
The Fractured Freemason of Fitzrovia – David L. Leal
The Bleeding Heart – Paula Hammond
The Secret Admirer – Jayantika Ganguly

(Continued on the next page . . . .)

Part XXII: Some More Untold Cases (1877-1887)

(Continued on the next page . . . .)

(Continued on the next page . . . .)

Part XXV: 2021 Annual (1881-1888)

(Continued on the next page . . . .)

The Switched String – Chris Chan
The Case of the Secret Samaritan – Jane Rubino
The Bishopsgate Jewel Case – Stephen Gaspar

Part XXVI: 2021 Annual (1889-1897)

Foreword – Peter Lovesey
Foreword – Roger Johnson
Foreword – Steve Emecz
Foreword – Jacqueline Silver
Foreword – David Marcum
221b Baker Street (*A Poem*) – Kevin Patrick McCann
The Burglary Season – Marcia Wilson
The Lamplighter at Rosebery Avenue – James Moffett
The Disfigured Hand – Peter Coe Verbica
The Adventure of the Bloody Duck – Margaret Walsh
The Tragedy at Longpool – James Gelter
The Case of the Viscount's Daughter – Naching T. Kassa
The Key in the Snuffbox – DJ Tyrer
The Race for the Gleghorn Estate – Ian Ableson
The Isa Bird Befuddlement – Kevin P. Thornton
The Cliddesden Questions – David Marcum
Death in Verbier – Adrian Middleton
The King's Cross Road Somnambulist – Dick Gillman
The Magic Bullet – Peter Coe Verbica
The Petulant Patient – Geri Schear
The Mystery of the Groaning Stone – Mark Mower
The Strange Case of the Pale Boy – Susan Knight
The Adventure of the Zande Dagger – Frank Schildiner
The Adventure of the Vengeful Daughter – Arthur Hall
Do the Needful – Harry DeMaio
The Count, the Banker, the Thief, and the Seven Half-sovereigns – Mike Hogan
The Adventure of the Unsprung Mousetrap – Anthony Gurney
The Confectioner's Captives – I.A. Watson

Part XXVII: 2021 Annual (1898-1928)

Foreword – Peter Lovesey
Foreword – Roger Johnson
Foreword – Steve Emecz
Foreword – Jacqueline Silver
Foreword – David Marcum
Sherlock Holmes Returns: The Missing Rhyme (*A Poem*) – Joseph W. Svec, III
The Adventure of the Hero's Heir – Tracy J. Revels
The Curious Case of the Soldier's Letter – John Davis
The Case of the Norwegian Daredevil – John Lawrence
The Case of the Borneo Tribesman – Stephen Herczeg
The Adventure of the White Roses – Tracy J. Revels

(Continued on the next page . . . .)

Part XXVIII: More Christmas Adventures (1869-1888)

(Continued on the next page . . . .)

Part XXIX: More Christmas Adventures (1889-1896)

Part XXX: More Christmas Adventures (1897-1928)

(Continued on the next page . . . .)

Part XXXI: 2022 Annual (1875-1887)

Part XXXII: 2022 Annual (1888-1895)

(Continued on the next page . . . .)

Part XXXIII: 2022 Annual (1896-1919)

(Continued on the next page . . . .)

(Continued on the next page . . . .)

Part XXXVI: "However Improbable . . . ." (1897-1919)

(Continued on the next page . . . .)

(Continued on the next page . . . .)

Part XXXIX: 2023 Annual (1897-1923)

The following contributors appear
in the companion volumes:
The MX Book of New Sherlock Holmes Stories
Part XL – Further Untold Cases (1879-1886)
Part XLII – Further Untold Cases (1894-1922)

Further Untold Cases – Parts XL, XLI, and XLII of
The MX Book of New Sherlock Holmes Stories
are dedicated to

Kelvin I. Jones

I first became aware of Kelvin in the early 1980's, when I managed to obtain a number of his expert Holmesian monographs. Little did I know that one day I'd be able to be friends with him (even if we haven't met in person) and that he would continue to contribute so ably. The world – Sherlockian and otherwise – is a richer place because of him.

Editor's Foreword:
Untold Infinite Possibilities
by David Marcum

In 1932, Edith Meiser did an amazing thing: By way of her Sherlock Holmes radio show starring Richard Gordon and Leigh Lovell as Holmes and Watson respectively, she related one of Holmes's *Untold Cases*. I may be wrong – I claim no expertise in Sherlock Holmes radio and film history, other than having a lot of reference books – but I think that this was the first time that anyone had done this – told an *Untold Case* – in any format.

For those who don't know what an *Untold Case* is, or believe that any post-Canonical Holmes adventure is an *Untold Case*, the term refers specifically to those *other* cases that Holmes solved (or some with which he was at least involved) that are mentioned in passing in The Canon. There are around 130 of them, some more famous than others, and – as seen with a few stories in this collection – other Untold Cases are being identified and related all the time. (More about that in a minute.)

I've been collecting and reading and studying Holmes's adventures since 1975, both those known as *The Canon* – those pitifully few sixty tales that came to us by way of the First Literary Agent's desk – and all the others that have been pulled from Watson's Tin Dispatch Box since then. And I'm pretty sure that "The Giant Rat of Sumatra", possibly the most famous of the Untold Cases, was the first one of those that were shared with the public. It was transcribed by Meiser from Watson's notes and broadcast on April 20th (although some sources say June 9th), 1932, and again on July 18th, 1936; and then on March 1st, 1942 (this time with Basil Rathbone as Holmes). Sadly, all of these versions are apparently lost, although I'd dearly love to hear – and read – them! (According to one source shared with me, Meiser's script for "The Giant Rat of Sumatra" is held within the Sherlockian collections at the University of Minnesota, but my attempts to see this – or any of her scripts that are kept there – have been unsuccessful.)

Meiser's "Giant Rat", though the first related Untold Case, wasn't her first post-Canonical tale. After numerous Canonical broadcasts, she approached the Doyle Heirs, who were in a non-litigious mood that week, about doing something different, and she was then allowed to present other Tin Dispatch Box-sourced adventures. The first of these was "The Hindoo in the Wicker Basket", broadcast on January 7th, 1932 (although one source I've seen shows some sort of Holmes *Christmas Carol* on

1

December 23rd, 1931.) During early 1932, there were a few more Canonical broadcasts – "The Yellow Face", "The *Gloria Scott*", and a six-part version of *The Hound*, but there were also a few others that people hadn't heard of before, such as "Murder in the Waxworks", "The Adventure of the Ace of Spades", "The Missing Leonardo da Vinci" – and then "The Giant Rat".

I would give much to hear (or read) some of these lost adventures (although some of the scripts aren't "lost", just hidden away). And of course there are many other cases from the Tin Box out there, also lost, would be just as interesting to read, see, or hear. Meiser wasn't the first to pull non-Canonical adventures from the Tin Box. For instance, not counting parodies, Kowo Films, a German concern, might have been the first, producing nine post-Canonical Holmes films between 1917 and 1919. (Apparently being on the losing side in an ongoing World War couldn't prevent the production of Holmes films by a German company about one of their enemy's greatest heroes.) These were fascinating titles like *The Earthquake Motor*, *The Indian Spider*, and *The Fate of Renate Yongh*. One of them, *The Cardinal's Snuff Box*, might possibly maybe could-have-been the actual first portrayal of an Untold Case – *The Sudden Death of Cardinal Tosca* – but as of now, we cannot know.

Now, assuming that one gives Meiser due credit for being the first to relate an Untold Case (as far as I can tell) with her version of "The Giant Rat of Sumatra", some might be inclined to think that she had staked that one as her own claim, and that there would be no need for someone else to find and publish an alternate version of "The Giant Rat". After all, Meiser had brought it forward first, and there's no reason to suppose that what she presented wasn't perfectly fine. But in truth, there have been lots of versions – all very different indeed – of this particular Untold Case. Over two-dozen of them, in fact, not counting irrelevant parodies, science fiction and fantasy attempts, and versions where the true Holmes is not present.

"The Giant Rat" is mentioned Canonically in "The Sussex Vampire":

> "Matilda Briggs *was not the name of a young woman, Watson,"* said Holmes in a reminiscent voice. *"It was a ship which is associated with the giant rat of Sumatra, a story for which the world is not yet prepared.*

That, and the fact that Morrison, Morrison, and Dodd said that Holmes's action in the case of the *Matilda Briggs* was successful, are all we officially know about the Giant Rat. We can speculate a few other things: Morrison, Morrison, and Dodd specialized in the assessment of machinery – and yet they were somehow involved in the matter of the Giant Rat enough to know of Holmes's successful action. The fact that Holmes has to explain that the *Matilda Briggs* was a ship and not a young woman implies that Watson doesn't know about it – and that possibly this case occurred during some period when Watson wasn't involved in Holmes's cases – perhaps before they moved to Baker Street in January 1881, or during a period when Watson was married and living elsewhere. And we know that it was especially serious, and of a nature that might cause panic or with a solution that might stretch credulity. The world is not yet prepared. *The whole world? Not prepared?* That implies something that's seriously disturbing.

Or perhaps someone else might read this short description from "The Sussex Vampire" and interpret it an entirely different way. In fact, many have. Many of the different versions of "The Giant Rat" never even mention involvement of any sort by Morrison, Morrison, and Dodd. Instead of Watson being ignorant of details, all versions involve Watson right alongside Holmes. And he knows about the *Matilda Briggs* – except in some iterations, where the *Matilda Briggs* isn't mentioned at all.

The fact that there are so many versions of "The Giant Rat" might be a source of consternation for some, who think there can only be one, and that all others are simulacrums and distractions of greater or lesser quality. Just as some might think that because Edith Meiser was the first to describe Holmes's connection with the Giant Rat, and therefore no other descriptions are valid, others might prefer a different version. My personal favorite is the late Rick Boyer's *The Giant Rat of Sumatra*, published in 1976, one of those first post-Canonical adventures to ride the initial wave propagated by Nicholas Meyer's *The Seven-Per-Cent Solution* in 1974, beginning a Sherlockian Golden Age that has never faded since.

If I were to decide that my favorite "Giant Rat" by Boyer was the *only* "Giant Rat", I would have cheated myself of over two-dozen other versions, equally good in their own ways, and also any others that have yet to be revealed.

I play *The Game*, wherein Holmes and Watson are recognized as historical figures who lived and died – Yes, they're dead now, and have been for a long time. When doing that, one might be a bit wobbly when trying to figure out how one charmed and famous lifetime and notable career could have included over two-dozen encounters with a Giant Rat. Nearly everyone who has ever lived has never met a single Giant Rat. The easy answer is that these are all different encounters, and there just happened to be a lot of Giant Rat crimes across the decades between when Holmes commenced his career and when he and Watson discussed the Giant Rat in "The Sussex Vampire. It isn't as if Holmes solved the case with a specific set of individuals, places, and circumstances, and then the deck was somehow cosmically reshuffled and the game replayed with the same individuals, places, and circumstances proceeding along different lines, (as were the characters in two Stephen King back-to-back companion novels, *The Regulators* and *Desperation*, both published on the same day in 1996.) The Giant Rat adventure related by Boyer is vastly different than the ones rescued from the Tin Dispatch Box by Paul Gilbert, Hugh Ashton, Amanda Knight, Alan Vanneman, David Stuart Davies, and many others.

And the Giant Rat is just an example, used because it is the Untold Case that has been related in the most versions. There are so many others that have also been told in multiple ways. The peculiar persecution of John Vincent Harden in 1895? Just keep in mind that there were a *lot* of tobacco millionaires in London during that time, all being peculiarly persecuted – but in very different ways – and Watson lumped them in his notes under the catch-all name of *John Vincent Harden.* Huret the Boulevard Assassin? There have been a number of different narratives telling how Holmes caught Huret – all completely different from one another, and all accurate and true and part of *The Great Holmes Tapestry*, that amazing mix of Canonical adventures, serving as the main cables, and the thousands of post-Canonical tales that make up fibers in between that fill in the details and provide all the color and nuance. The explanation for so many Huret narratives? There was a whole nest of Hurets to be rooted out in 1894, and each separate story relates how Holmes did it is just part of the bigger tapestry.

Since Meiser brought us the first Untold Case, there have been many others – far too many to list here. In *The MX Book of New Sherlock Holmes Stories*, we've had several volumes of them. In 2018, we presented Parts XI and XII – *Some Untold Cases*, and then in 2020, Parts XXII, XXIII, and XXIV returned to that theme with *Some More Untold Cases*. In the initial 2018 set, I required contributors to let me know beforehand which Untold Case they were going to choose, so that no one would provide more than one of them, and there would be no duplication. I only made one exception: Nick Cardillo had already signed up to bring us his version of "The Giant Rat" when Ian Dickerson made available the 1944 "Giant Rat" radio script written by Leslie Charteris and Denis Green – Rathbone and Bruce's *second* time telling that story, in a completely different script and investigation from the one by Edith Meiser which had been broadcast two years before. This worked out okay, because the 1944 script was set in the 1880's and included in Part XI, and Nick's story occurred in the 1890's and was in Part XII.

For the 2020 set, I had no requirement that anyone had to sign up and reserve an Untold Case. I was happy for people to send whatever Watson recorded, as long as it was traditional and Canonical. This was fortunate, because every story was excellent, even if there were some duplications of Untold Cases. For example, the matter of the Two Coptic Patriarchs occurs on a specific date in July 1898. Three contributors – John Davis, DJ Tyrer, and Harry DeMaio – all told versions of the Two Coptic Patriarchs, and since these books are arranged chronologically, these three stories were all presented side by side. There was no contradiction – they all told about different cases with Two Coptic Patriarchs that came to a head in that moment. (And of course, there have been a number of other narratives about these same Patriarchs in other books. Two, as a matter of fact, were by John Linwood Grant and Séamus Duffy and included in other parts of the MX Anthologies.)

In these new volumes, there are several versions of old intriguing favorites – *The Addleton Tragedy. The Sudden Death of Cardinal Tosca. The Most Repulsive Man. The Paradol Chamber. The Grosvenor Square Furniture Van* – all different, and all wonderful. Strangely, for all that I've mentioned it here, this time no one chose to provide any new revelations about one of the Giant Rats that Holmes faced during his career. But there are a few of Untold Cases described in these volumes by Alan Dimes and Chris Chan (and me) that no one had previously thought to add to the list. (My friend, the late Phil Jones, had a special passion for Untold Cases, and he would have been thrilled to see these.)

If you read Holmes adventures for very long – novels, themed or un-themed collections by one author or many, single magazine stories – chances are that someone will soon be telling you an Untold Case. And with so many of them, and with their mysteriously intriguing but often vague descriptions, one never knows what in what directions they'll jump.

In *The Valley of Fear* and "The Norwood Builder", Holmes used the phrase *"infinite possibilities."* In "Wisteria Lodge" he also used the phrase *"a perfect jungle of possibilities"*, and in "The Six Napoleons" he mentioned that *"There are no limits to the possibilities . . . ."*

Possibilities are what to expect when beginning any new Holmes adventure – reading one or writing one. As I've stated before, these can leap in any direction. One might find a comedy or a tragedy. A police procedural or gothic horror. The story might be set early in Holmes's career, or very late. It could be a city adventure or a country tale. Watson might be the narrator, or it could be Holmes, or someone else, or it might even be related in third person. And it might be long or short, taking just what it takes to tell what happened.

5

You may have read other versions of some of these Untold Cases before, and you may have favorites, but keep in mind that just because one version occurred in Holmes and Watson's life doesn't mean that it was the *only one* and that another didn't. They're *all* true, and they fit together like a most-intricate and complex puzzle, and in a vastly entertaining way.

In "The Sussex Vampire", Holmes states that Watson has *"unexplored possibilities"*. This, as well as *"infinite possibilities"*, is a good description of what one can expect when finding new adventures within Watson's Tin Dispatch Box – and also in the case of these volumes of *Further Untold Cases.*

* * * * *

"Of course, I could only stammer out my thanks."
– The unhappy John Hector McFarlane, "The Norwood Builder"

As always when one of these collections is finished, I want to thank with all my heart my incredible, patient, brilliant, kind, and beautiful wife of thirty-five years, Rebecca – Every day I count my blessings and realize how lucky I am! – and our amazing, funny, creative, and wonderful son, and my friend, Dan. I love you both, and you are everything to me!

With each new set of the MX anthologies, some things get easier, and there are also new challenges. For several years, the stresses of real life have been much greater than when this series started. Through all of this, the amazing contributors have once again pulled some amazing works from the Tin Dispatch Box. I'm more grateful than I can express to every contributor who has donated both time and royalties to this ongoing project. It's amazing what we've accomplished – over 860 stories in 42 volumes (so far), and over $116,000 raised for the Undershaw school for special needs children!

I also want to give special recognition to the multiple contributors of this set: Arthur Hall, Tracy Revels, Dan Rowley, Susan Knight, Alan Dimes, Brenda Seabrooke, Barry Clay, Ember Pepper, and Tim Newton Anderson. Finally, I cannot express how thankful I am to all of those who keep buying these books and making them the largest and most popular Sherlockian anthology ever.

I'm so glad to have gotten to know so many of you through this process – both contributors and readers. It's an undeniable fact that Sherlock Holmes people are the *best* people!

I wish especially thank the following:

- *Tom Mead* – Tom has burst on the scene as the new face of locked room mysteries in the best Golden Age style. We are all very fortunate that he's writing these type of stories, and also that we live in an age where social media, for all of its evil problems, also allows us to be in contact with authors in real time. When preparing these books, I realized that I wanted very much for Tom to be part of them. I'm still trying to recruit him to write a Holmes story – and what a Holmes story that would be! He's interested, but he's also very busy! – but in the meantime, he immediately agreed to provide a foreword to these latest books. I'm very grateful for that, and also the opportunity to have "met" him (though not yet in person) at the start of what promises to be his long and wonderful career. Thanks Tom!

- *Steve Emecz* – From my first association with MX in 2013, I observed that MX (under Steve Emecz's leadership) was *the* fast-rising superstar of the Sherlockian publishing world – and ten years later, that has not changed. Connecting with MX and Steve Emecz was personally an amazing life-changing event for me, as it has been for countless other Sherlockian authors. It has led me to write many more stories, and then to edit books, along with unexpected additional Holmes Pilgrimages to England – none of which might have happened otherwise. By way of my first email with Steve, I've had the chance to make some incredible Sherlockian friends and play in the Holmesian Sandbox in ways that I would have never dreamed possible.

  Through it all, Steve has been one of the most positive and supportive people that I've ever known.

  From the beginning, Steve has let me explore various Sherlockian projects and open up my own personal possibilities in ways that otherwise would have never happened. Thank you, Steve, for every opportunity!

- *Roger Johnson* – From his immediate support at the time of the first volumes in this series to the present, I can't imagine Roger not being part of these books. His Sherlockian knowledge is exceptional, as is the work that he does to further the cause of The Master. But even more than that, both Roger and his wife, Jean Upton, are simply the finest and best of

7

people, and I'm very lucky to know both of them – even though I don't get to see them nearly as often as I'd like. I look forward to getting back over to the Holmesland sooner rather than later and visiting with them again, but in the meantime, many thanks for being part of this.

- *Brian Belanger* –I initially became acquainted with Brian when he took over the duties of creating the covers for MX Books, and I found him to be a great collaborator, and wonderfully creative too. I've worked with him on many projects with MX and Belanger Books, which he co-founded with his brother Derrick Belanger, also a good friend. Along with MX Publishing, Derrick and Brian have absolutely locked up the Sherlockian publishing field with a vast amount of amazing material. The old dinosaurs must be trembling to see every new and worthy Sherlockian project, one after another after another, that these two companies create. Luckily MX and Belanger Books work closely with one another, and I'm thrilled to be associated with both of them. Many thanks to Brian for all he does for both publishers, and for all he's done for me personally.

And finally, last but certainly *not* least, thanks to **Sir Arthur Conan Doyle**: Author, doctor, adventurer, and the Founder of the Sherlockian Feast. Honored, and present in spirit.

As I always note when putting together an anthology of Holmes stories, the effort has been a labor of love. These adventures are just more tiny threads woven into the ongoing Great Holmes Tapestry, continuing to grow and grow, for there can *never* be enough stories about the man whom Watson described as *"the best and wisest . . . whom I have ever known."*

David Marcum
October 4th, 2023
The 123rd Anniversary of
the first day of
"The Problem of Thor Bridge"

Questions, comments, or story submissions
may be addressed to David Marcum at
thepapersofsherlockholmes@gmail.com

8

Foreword
by Tom Mead

It is perhaps notable that I'm writing this on Arthur Conan Doyle's birthday, and so I am thinking now about Conan Doyle as a man – as a human being, rather than a mere name embossed on leather spines. My image of him will always be the one conjured by John Dickson Carr in his excellently readable biography. Carr was a fervent Sherlockian, not to mention a *pasticheur* – his *The Exploits of Sherlock Holmes* collection, co-authored with Adrian Conan Doyle, is such a fascinating curio. So it's through the lens of Carr's admiration that I have recently revisited the Holmes stories.

My very first experience of Sherlock Holmes came courtesy of Basil Rathbone. They used to show those movies on Channel 5 here in the UK, padded out with commercials for a ninety-minute runtime. This was in the mid-to-late '90s, and I'd get my mum to record them on VHS while I was at school, to watch repeatedly at my leisure. To begin with, Holmes signified *adventure* rather than mystery: Espionage, the *Pursuit to Algiers*, the hunt for *The Scarlet Claw*, Gale Sondergaard as *The Spider Woman*.

Thus, when I actually sat down and *read* my first Holmes tale, it was certainly an eye-opener. It was the fabled "Adventure of the Speckled Band", not only a great mystery but a great *locked-room* mystery, a subgenre which has had a profound influence on my own writing – and which fascinates me still.

It was a slim illustrated edition with a colourful painted cover that completely gave away the solution to the mystery. But even that could not impair my enjoyment. The book was somewhat out of place on the shelf in my primary school's library – it was bigger than the other books (not thicker, but taller), and of course it had that weird title. What was a *speckled band*? The first image in my head was a marching band.

And the next Holmes I read was *The Hound of the Baskervilles*. Perhaps unsurprisingly, I was more interested in the hound when it was an entity of uncanny origin. And yet I remained enthralled by Holmes's unorthodox detection – his elaborate chains of deduction, his disguises which fooled Watson every single time.

I did not *devour* the Holmes stories the way I did those of other authors – Agatha Christie, for example. Rather, I eked them out over the

9

years, and as I matured so did my appreciation of Conan Doyle's momentous accomplishment.

I read "The Man With the Twisted Lip" at university and found it to be a vivid, gothic portrait of psychological schism akin to Poe's "William Wilson". I read "The Red-Headed League" and found it to be a marvellous logic puzzle. And when I reread *Baskervilles*, I was surprised to find it was folk horror masquerading as detective fiction – a tale of rationality clashing with superstition in an uncertain world.

Now more than ever I see what a glorious sparkling gem each tale is, and what a towering figure Conan Doyle has always been. To have redefined a genre, but also to have gifted so many talented writers with so much scope to develop, to reimagine. I suppose you could say it took me a while to fully immerse myself in Conan Doyle's literary world – the world of the stories, which transcend the countless cliches they have spawned. I had to "find my way in", so to speak. But now I'm here, I have no intention of leaving any time soon.

Tom Mead
May 22nd, 2023

10

"What Is It That We Love in Sherlock Holmes?"
by Roger Johnson

Edgar W. Smith asked that question back in April 1946. It's the first line of his editorial in the second issue of *The Baker Street Journal*. The founder of the Baker Street Irregulars was, of course, Christopher Morley, but it was Smith who ensured the BSI's stability and viability. He was one of the great Holmesian scholars and commentators, so his creation and editorship of the *Journal* was surely natural.

I don't intend to discuss Edgar Smith's answers to his own question, except to say that they are intelligent and wise. (The two don't always go together.) [1]

However, it seems to me that the Great Detective is, on a superficial level, much easier to respect than to love. He can be remarkably churlish to those whose intellects are, by his standards, inferior to his own – particularly his professional rivals in the police, and on occasion he is more than waspish to the man he considers his only friend. Read "The Disappearance of Lady Francis Carfax" again, and note the words exchanged after Holmes has rescued Watson from his attacker:

> *"I cannot at the moment recall any possible blunder which you have omitted. The total effect of your proceeding has been to give the alarm everywhere and yet to discover nothing."*
>
> *"Perhaps you would have done no better,"* I answered bitterly.
>
> *"There is no 'perhaps' about it. I have done better."*

Watson has every right to be bitter. In his admirable book *The Curious Case of 221B: The Secret Notebooks of John H Watson, MD*, Partha Basu imagines his unspoken response:

> *"It was I who tracked Lady Frances; it was I who discovered the Shlessingers, and their hold on her and the fact that they spirited her away to London. I did not raise any alarm with the Shlessingers or with Lady Frances because they had already left the Continent when I happened onto their trail. You, on the other hand, ignored my accurate deduction that*

the three were in London and not in Montpellier where you
landed up in your ludicrous disguise . . . ."

Nowhere in the Canonical sixty records, fortunately, is Holmes's asperity as bluntly expressed as in one of the movies starring Basil Rathbone and Nigel Bruce. The exact context escapes me, but I remember the line exactly: *"No, no, Watson! D'you have to be so stupid?"*

Holmes's lack of manners and of friends does not inspire our affection, though it may amuse us. And, after all, that isn't the complete picture.

In "The Dying Detective", we learn that the faithful Mrs Hudson *"was fond of him . . . for he had a remarkable gentleness and courtesy in his dealings with women. He disliked and distrusted the sex, but he was always a chivalrous opponent."*

There are numerous instances throughout the Good Doctor's chronicles of Holmes's respect for women – or, more accurately, for those women who deserve his respect, from Mary Morstan to the tragic Eugenia Ronder. He even, most unexpectedly, refers to the wife of the missing Mr Neville St Clair as *"this dear little woman"*, and he treats Irene Adler with great respect, even while working against her. He is polite but cold towards Mary, niece of the unfortunate banker Alexander Holder, and he is necessarily harsh in dealing with Susan Stockdale and her employer Isadora Klein – though his manner towards both is naturally different.

After their first meeting with Mary Morstan, Watson exclaims, *"What a very attractive woman!"* To his surprise, Holmes languidly replies, *"Is she? I did not observe."* His friend's response is, I suspect, largely responsible for the image of the Great Detective as a man devoid of human emotions:

> *"You really are an automaton – a calculating-machine!"* I
> cried. *"There is something positively inhuman in you at*
> *times."*

In fact, however he might appear to the average person, Sherlock Holmes is one for whom Walt Whitman's famous words might have been written:

> *Do I contradict myself?*
> *Very well then I contradict myself,*
> *(I am large, I contain multitudes.)* [2]

Holmes is not a superhero. He is more intelligent than most, and he has developed his talents to an unusually high degree, but they are human talents, and he is a human being, who makes the occasional mistake. If we were to dedicate an immense amount of time and concentrated effort, a select few of us might actually be able to be something very like him. Would we really want to, though? Most of us, I suspect, would rather be a Watson – and in reading the accounts of Holmes's adventures, whether for the first time or the hundredth, we can effectively place ourselves in the Good Doctor's rôle, accompanying the Great Detective in his investigations, sharing the danger and the excitement, marvelling at his perspicacity and the almost magical moment when he reveals the truth, and perhaps relaxing with him afterwards, discussing the case over a glass of brandy and a cigar.

That is what we love in Sherlock Holmes!

Roger Johnson, BSI, ASH
Editor: *The Sherlock Holmes Journal*
September 2023

NOTES

1. If you don't have a copy, you can read the editorial online at: *https://www.blackgate.com/2015/11/16/the-public-life-of-sherlock-holmes-edgar-smiths-the-implicit-holmes/.*
2. "Song of Myself", Section 51, from *Leaves of Grass*, first published in 1855.

An Ongoing Legacy
for Sherlock Holmes
by Steve Emecz

Undershaw
Circa 1900

With over five hundred Sherlock Holmes books, it's been a fantastic fifteen years publishing novels, short story collections, graphic novels and more. *The MX Book of New Sherlock Holmes Stories* remains our greatest program and achievement – made possible by the authors, the editor, and the fans who support the series. The total raised for Undershaw school for children with learning disabilities has now passed $116,000.

In 2023, every book bought on our website means we donate a meal to a family in need through ShareTheMeal from The World Food Programme (WFP). I am proud to have been a member of the external advisory council and a mentor with the WFP for several years, and part of the team in 2020 that was awarded the Nobel Peace Prize.

You can find links to all our projects on our website:

https://mxpublishing.com/pages/about-us

As long as the fans want more Sherlock, we'll be here to publish it.

Steve Emecz
September 2023

The Doyle Room at Undershaw
Partially funded through royalties from
The MX Book of New Sherlock Holmes Stories

A Word from Undershaw
by Emma West

Undershaw
September 9, 2016
Grand Opening of the Stepping Stones School
(Now *Undershaw*)
(Photograph courtesy of Roger Johnson)

"Find a voice in a whisper."
– Martin Luther King, Jr.

Why is it so important to us that our students have a "voice" at Undershaw?

It seems like an obvious question, but all too often the very people for whom a school exists are not heard when it comes to decision-making. A healthy, inclusive, and inspirational seat of learning should have a whole-school approach to listening to the voices of everyone in the school community, including our children.

Our students offer us a unique insight into what it is like to be a learner at Undershaw and thus, involving them in the decision-making process makes perfect sense. We have made significant improvements to the curriculum, the pastoral care, and the learning environment over the last academic year. These evolutions often come about by listening to our

16

children. We are here to ensure they have meaningful opportunities to share their views and their input features in every corner of our school life.

Our school vision clearly puts the child are at the heart of everything that we do, so what better way to achieve this then through listening to their voice.

> *Undershaw is an inclusive school where the best interests of the child are at the heart of everything that we do.*
> *Undershaw is a school where we empower students to aspire and achieve.*
> *Undershaw is a caring and safe environment which allows students to thrive and flourish, and prepares them to be socially and economically engaged in the future.*

If we are ever in doubt of our ethical centre, it is this. Our vision guides us, shapes us, and holds us to account. It is our conscience and our true North. Undershaw is a thriving centre of learning, friendships, noise, and bustle . . . and we will always strive to find a voice in a whisper.

As ever and on behalf of all our voices, my heartfelt thanks for being by our side during all of our evolutions. We have such a vibrant community here and we are very fortunate to have such a committed band of friends and supporters. Undershaw and MX Publishing have a friendship that spans a decade, and for that we are all incredibly grateful.

Until next time . . . .

Emma West
Headteacher, Undershaw
October 2023

"Undershaw," Hindhead. Conan Doyle's House.

Editor's *Caveats*

When these anthologies first began back in 2015, I noted that the authors were from all over the world – and thus, there would be British spelling and American spelling. As I explained then, I didn't want to take the responsibility of changing American spelling to British and vice-versa. I would undoubtedly miss something, leading to inconsistencies, or I'd change something incorrectly.

Some readers are bothered by this, made nervous and irate when encountering American spelling as written by Watson, and in stories set in England. However, here in America, the versions of The Canon that we read have long-ago has their spelling Americanized, so it isn't quite as shocking for us.

Additionally, I offer my apologies up front for any typographical errors that have slipped through. As a print-on-demand publisher, MX does not have squadrons of editors as some readers believe. The business consists of three part-time people who also have busy lives elsewhere – Steve Emecz, Sharon Emecz, and Timi Emecz – so the editing effort largely falls on the contributors. Some readers and consumers out there in the world are unhappy with this – apparently forgetting about all of those self-produced Holmes stories and volumes from decades ago (typed and Xeroxed) with awkward self-published formatting and loads of errors that are now prized as very expensive collector's items.

I'm personally mortified when errors slip through – ironically, there will probably be errors in these *caveats* – and I apologize now, but without a regiment of professional full-time editors looking over my shoulder, this is as good as it gets. Real life is more important than writing and editing – even in such a good cause as promoting the True and Traditional Canonical Holmes – and only so much time can be spent preparing these books before they're released into the wild. I hope that you can look past any errors, small or huge, and simply enjoy these stories, and appreciate the efforts of everyone involved, and the sincere desire to add to The Great Holmes Tapestry.

And in spite of any errors here, there are more Sherlock Holmes stories in the world than there were before, and that's a good thing.

David Marcum
Editor

Editor's Note:
Duplicate Untold Cases

In some instances, there are multiple versions of certain Untold Cases contained within this volume. Each of these are very different stories and do not contradict one another, in spite of their common jumping-off place. As explained in the Editor's Foreword, no traditional and Canonical versions of the Untold Cases are the definitive versions to the exclusion of the others. They simply require a bit of additional pondering and rationalization to consider what was going on in Watson's thinking, and why he chose to present them in this way.

In this volume, the reader will encounter several versions of The Old Russian Woman, The Grosvenor Square Furniture Van, The Amateur Mendicants, The Paradol Chamber, The Most Repulsive Man, the Blackmail Case (from *The Hound of the Baskervilles*), The Addleton Tragedy and the British Barrow, The Sudden Death of Cardinal Tosca, The Service for Sir James Saunders, and the interesting cases brought to Holmes by his brother Mycroft and Stanley Hopkins.

Enjoy!

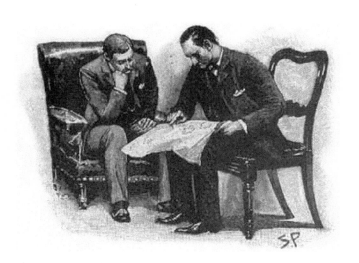

Sherlock Holmes (1854-1957) was born in Yorkshire, England, on 6 January, 1854. In the mid-1870's, he moved to 24 Montague Street, London, where he established himself as the world's first Consulting Detective. After meeting Dr. John H. Watson in early 1881, he and Watson moved to rooms at 221b Baker Street, where his reputation as the world's greatest detective grew for several decades. He was presumed to have died battling noted criminal Professor James Moriarty on 4 May, 1891, but he returned to London on 5 April, 1894, resuming his consulting practice in Baker Street. Retiring to the Sussex coast near Beachy Head in October 1903, he continued to be associated in various private and government investigations while giving the impression of being a reclusive apiarist. He was very involved in the events encompassing World War I, and to a lesser degree those of World War II. He passed away peacefully upon the cliffs above his Sussex home on his 103rd birthday, 6 January, 1957.

Dr. John Hamish Watson (1852-1929) was born in Stranraer, Scotland on 7 August, 1852. In 1878, he took his Doctor of Medicine Degree from the University of London, and later joined the army as a surgeon. Wounded at the Battle of Maiwand in Afghanistan (27 July, 1880), he returned to London late that same year. On New Year's Day, 1881, he was introduced to Sherlock Holmes in the chemical laboratory at Barts. Agreeing to share rooms with Holmes in Baker Street, Watson became invaluable to Holmes's consulting detective practice. Watson was married and widowed three times, and from the late 1880's onward, in addition to his participation in Holmes's investigations and his medical practice, he chronicled Holmes's adventures, with the assistance of his literary agent, Sir Arthur Conan Doyle, in a series of popular narratives, most of which were first published in *The Strand* magazine. Watson's later years were spent preparing a vast number of his notes of Holmes's cases for future publication. Following a final important investigation with Holmes, Watson contracted pneumonia and passed away on 24 July, 1929.

Photos of Sherlock Holmes and Dr. John H. Watson courtesy of Roger Johnson

The
MX Book
of
New
Sherlock
Holmes
Stories
Part XLI – Further Untold Cases
(1887-1892)

He Was . . . .
by Kevin Patrick McCann

Murder took root at conception,
Obscenely it swam through his veins,
Nurtured his twisting perceptions,
Tightened its darkening skein.

A child alone with his shadow
Gazing for hours at the sky,
Under the sinuous willows
Enmity flared in his eyes.

Jack haunted Whitechapel
Orbed in a halo of mist,
His hands would silently throttle,
Next his knife would kiss their cold lips.

Death was his true friend and mentor,
Revenge for his mother, the lie,
Under the cover of darkness
Insanity flared in his eyes.

The butcher of five drowned himself in the river:
The myth he conceived will rebirth forever.

J.H.W.

The Case of the
Trepoff Murder
by Stephen Herczeg

"Hello, Mrs. Hudson."

"My word, Dr. Watson!" The look of surprise and glee on my former landlady's face made my journey to Baker Street already worth my while. "It's always nice when you visit."

"I've just finished with a patient nearby in Dorset Street, and felt I simply had to make the time to drop by."

"Oh, very good to see you as always. How is married life treating you?"

I knew I smiled widely at that point. "I am so happy, Mrs. Hudson. Mary is the light of my life." I began to extol the virtues of my new world, but I realised I must have carried on for quite some time because even someone as delightful as Mrs. Hudson couldn't disguise a need to retreat back inside. Finally, I stopped talking and took a breath.

Without missing a beat, Mrs. Hudson brought Holmes into the conversation. "He's upstairs, and he'll be so glad to see you. It's been ever so quiet around here without you, and I do worry when that happens."

"Let me see if I can't bring him out of any *ennui* he has allowed to settle over him."

My hostess stepped back and disappeared into her rooms, possibly preparing some refreshments for us. I watched her vanish before turning my attention to climbing the steps that separated me from my former lodgings.

Standing on the landing before Holmes's door, I stopped and drew breath for a moment. In all honesty, I was unsure what I would find behind there. When I had vacated Baker Street, a small part of me began to worry about leaving Holmes unattended, and in my quiet times, I often pondered what he was up to.

Bucking up my courage, I knocked.

"Come in, Watson, there's a good chap." Only slightly shocked, I turned the knob and stepped back into my old life. The rooms looked almost the same as when I left. There were quite a few more files, folders, and papers scattered around, a hint that Holmes had been occupying his time, but hadn't been overly concerned with maintaining a modicum of tidiness.

Smiling as I found my good friend reclining in his chair by the window and smoking a pipe, I said, "Good morning, Holmes. Still as sharp as ever."

"Yes. Having heard you traipse up that flight time and time again, it wasn't hard to recognise it once more."

"Very good. I would expect nothing less." Shrugging off my coat, I hung it on a nearby hook and strode across to greet Holmes, throwing my hand out and shaking his effusively. "I had a gap in my day, and was nearby, so thought I'd take the chance you were in."

"No worries there. I've kept myself quite active. When I'm not on a case, I continue with my research into all things." His face showed no signs of prolonged boredom, but I could detect a slight waver in his voice, which told me his story was not always the way. There was no evidence of his other distractions, and no sign of his little Moroccan leather case in the immediate vicinity, which lifted my heart slightly.

I sat down in the vacant chair next to his own and breathed a sigh of relief. Nothing really to do with Holmes, just a sudden overwhelming feeling of tiredness from my morning's activities and a dire need to rest my feet.

"I might suggest that I should be the one concerned about you," he said. "Our adventures never left you in such a breathless state – or is it that you lead a more sedentary existence in your own house and practice, which has left you slightly bereft of fitness?"

"Perhaps," I said, a smile playing on my face. The familiarity of the room penetrated my thoughts and brought a type of warmth to my body as well as my mood. "I will admit that I haven't had the need for rigorous excursions of late. They're something that my body probably misses more than my mind."

"Oh, I'd like to think that you miss the stimulation of our adventures, if not the intrigue and danger."

Chuckling, I replied, "You might be right." Changing the subject from myself to Holmes, I added, "Speaking of your past adventures, I spent a few nights collating my notes, and came across a memo to myself from a while back that mentioned some of your adventures abroad without me. I never had the chance to ask, but you visited – What was it? Sri Lanka? Holland? Ukraine?"

Leaning back in his chair, Holmes steepled his fingers and thought for a moment. "Ah, yes. That *was* a while ago, but I did have the opportunity to journey to some far-flung places – all work, no real pleasure, though."

"I know you, Holmes: Your work *is* your pleasure. I would have loved to join you on some of those adventures. What were they for? Holland was for the Dutch Royal Family, wasn't it?"

"Ah, yes. Now that was a matter of some delicacy, and I'm afraid I'm bound to keep my silence on that one. I do apologise. I know how much you love to document my cases, but for now, there are many high-level aristocrats who would react quite dramatically to any word leaking about that one." He touched his nose with his forefinger. "In time, things may change."

It was at that moment that the sitting room door opened, and Mrs. Hudson entered carrying a tray of coffee and cakes. "I thought you two might need something to eat and drink while you visit."

I stood and took the tray from her, catching a wink as she handed it over. Nodding, I replied, "Thank you, Mrs. Hudson, for your kindness."

Placing the tray on the little table, I doled out the coffee and sat back, sipping the brew and sending more questions Holmes's way. "I'm intrigued by your trip to Sri Lanka, but also of the one to Odessa."

"Ah, yes, Sri Lanka was a simple matter of brothers coming to a shared tragedy due to their own ineptitude. My journey to Odessa was both intriguing and parlous, although the denouement was unexpected."

"Do tell," I said, sitting back and pulling out my little notebook.

Holmes shared a wry smile and nodded. "Yes, you can take notes on this one – though I would ask that you not publish the details for some time yet. As the story unveils, you'll understand why."

"Very intriguing."

"The tale begins in late January two years past – you must remember the deep snow that lay about, surely."

"Yes. Quite extraordinary, but it eased up in February."

"True. Well at the time, I was quite unoccupied. It seems the extreme cold, mixed with snow, slows down even the most notorious of villains. Except, it seems, across the channel."

"Odessa?"

Nodding, he answered, "Yes, we'll get there. But first, around the 26th, I received a telegram from my brother Mycroft. A simple message to meet him at the Diogenes Club, in the Stranger's Room. There was no real surprise at the location. Mycroft isn't one for any excursions outside of his regular haunts at the best of times. In the middle of such a cold winter, I was surprised that he'd even set foot in the club. It was obvious that he wanted to talk. Pulling on my warmest clothing, I set off into the street and managed to flag down a lone hansom. I found Mycroft quite comfortable in the warmth of the Stranger's Room, alone as well. It turns out he had requested it of some other guests, who were only there because the rest of the club was quite well attended."

"What did you discuss?"

"Patience, Watson. As you should know, a good story is in the telling." Holmes drained his coffee and replenished it before continuing. "Even though he looked relaxed, and had been provided with brandy and cigars to elevate his comfort, I could tell from his eyes and manner that he was slightly agitated."

"How so?"

"A twitch of the fingers holding his glass, the disturbed line of smoke rising from the cigar in his other hand. Small signs, but there all the same. As I greeted him and sat, he placed his glass down, picked up a small folio, and glanced at it once before dropping it on the table before me. From the external markings, I could tell it was official Government business, but rather than immediately snatch it up, I simply poured myself a brandy and sat back . . . .

"Sherlock," Mycroft began, "First, thank you for attending on this vile sort of a day." He shook his head slightly and picked up his glass, draining it in one long swig before replenishing. "There are times, I'm afraid, that I come to my wit's end with the business I am in."

"And what business is that?" I asked, smiling to myself. "As you've since learned, Mycroft tends to be very cagey about the scope of what he actually does for Her Majesty's Government. I'm always hoping for a snippet of information, but once again I was disappointed."

"Never mind. To be perfectly honest, if you undertake my request then you may gain a little more knowledge on that aspect than I've ever provided you in the past."

"What is it you wish of me?"

Mycroft studied me for a moment, as if summing up whether to go through with his request, or simply take back the folder and be done with it. He sighed once and then began. "One of the main tasks of any Government is to safeguard our sovereignty, and with it, the borders of our country. We do this through the employment of a Defence Force, and also through more covert means. That is, the gathering of information and intelligence, from and about our possible enemies."

"And even our friends, I have heard."

"Yes. True." He took a long pull on his cigar and blew a line of smoke away from us. The tang of its smell told me it was a La Intimidad from Cuba, not one of the standard Partagas typically on offer at the club. Mycroft must have brought them with him. Sensing my interest, he pulled a small case from his pocket and held it towards me. A single cigar

remained inside. Realising that it was possibly needed to calm my brother during the rest of the afternoon, I simply held up my hand and said no. Instead, I pulled out my cigarette case and lit one of my own in response.

Replacing the case, Mycroft continued with his story. "I can't remember, but have you been to Ukraine?"

I shook my head.

"Pity."

"Why?"

"Some knowledge of the area would prove very useful. Regardless, as I was saying, our government, from time to time, feels the need to seek information about our potential enemies."

"Russia?" I said, putting together several facts.

"Yes. Russia."

"Why Ukraine?"

"The security prevalent in Mother Russia is much more entrenched into the souls of the populace than in its neighbour. The people are very dedicated to their Tsar. Even though we have perceived several groups that are fomenting unrest, the average Russian has as much love for Nicholas as our citizens have for the Queen."

I nodded wondering where this was all going.

"For many years, we have placed members of our bureaucracy in positions within the borders of Greater Russia, to observe and report back regarding the feelings of the populace. They aren't there to assist with any instability. Only to witness and scrutinise."

"Has one gone missing? Or perhaps dead?"

"Very astute, but yes, precisely that. One of our agents, for want of a better word, has indeed gone missing."

"Where in Ukraine?"

"Odessa – a thriving seaport on the Black Sea."

"I'm aware of that," I replied.

"From our observations," Mycroft continued, "the place simply yearns for Western freedoms, but is held back under the yoke of Imperial Russia."

"What can I do? I'm not a spy."

"No, and that is precisely why I need your services." He reached into his coat once more and withdrew a thick paper envelope, which he tossed onto the folder. "I have been asked by my superiors – Yes, I do have superiors. – to investigate the disappearance of one of our operatives using the name 'Nikolai Trepoff'."

Intrigued, I picked up the envelope and peered inside. It contained a sizeable pile of pound notes and other currencies from across Eastern Europe.

39

"A substantial fee for your services, and more to cover any expenses." I didn't wish to appear so gauche as to pull the wad of bills out and count them, but even looking at the thickness and the top denomination, I deemed there to be around five-hundred pounds. It struck me that this Trepoff fellow held something of very high import to Her Majesty's Government.

"It isn't just this Trepoff's location you're after, is it?"

A frown crossed Mycroft's face for a moment before it eased, and he replied. "No. Trepoff is simply the conduit for information. He hasn't been in contact for a good two months now. The trail is probably very cold, and we can't be seen sending in agents, left, right, and centre, to investigate. Most of them are well buried in their own little stories, which would be fractured if the local authorities connected them to Trepoff. That's why we need someone like you."

"Or you," I suggested. "Your deductive reasoning and intelligence are equal, if not far superior, to mine. You've proved that on multiple occasions!"

Mycroft chuckled. "Yes, but I'm far from what you would consider a field agent. You've kept yourself at the peak of your physical condition, while I, shall we say, have rather enjoyed life."

"Quite, so. I can only assume that you wish to establish if this Trepoff fellow has been removed by the authorities, and whether he had any vital information in his possession."

"Exactly, though I have expressed to those that have requested your services that this could all be a fool's errand. The trail is long and cold, and we haven't picked up any sniff of repercussions from the Russians. I half-expect that Trepoff has simply grown bored of his life, found himself a local wife, and gone native. If you track him down, he'll possibly be living in a small yurt on a cattle farm in the depths of Ukraine."

At that, I had to let out a small chuckle. "Does that happen a lot?"

"You'd be surprised. Send a red-blooded man into the wilds of some far-flung exotic country for a year or two, and they develop a taste for the environment and culture. The local females become enamoured by his strange accent, or his physical differences when compared to the local chappies, and anything can happen. Most men in the world aren't like you and me, Sherlock. Their sense of duty and diligence in their work is merely a façade that can easily be broken by the slightest hint of the simple life of hearth and home."

"You sound like that is something you've long thought about," I said, half in jest, drawing a slight sigh from my brother.

"I feel that is far beyond me. I have signed up for a life of duty to Her Majesty, and I cannot fathom anything else."

40

At that point, I moved the envelope of money aside and picked up the folder. Opening it, I found it thick with handwritten pages. A quick scan revealed that most of them were transcripts of reports from Trepoff. The earliest was from two years earlier.

Closing the folder, I leaned back and sipped at my brandy. "I'm intrigued – though I will stress once again that I am no spy."

"That's for the best. Your task is simple: Travel to Odessa and look into Trepoff's disappearance. That file contains much about Trepoff's cover. His real name was Archie Brand, born and bred in east London, though he did have parents from Eastern Europe, Hungary, I think. You'll be Alexandr Trepoff, his brother. There are identity papers in there, but I suggest you derive a story for yourself. Find some other place of birth, one that you're familiar with. Much easier to keep to the facts if you have prior knowledge . . . ."

"As Mycroft relaxed back into his seat and went silent, I took his attitude to mean no more information would be forthcoming. I wasted little time on trivialities, promptly finished my cigarette and brandy, and bade my leave, taking the file and envelope with me. Back here in Baker Street, I read through the folio. There was little detail about what Trepoff was investigating or being asked to keep an eye on, except for a line which stated: *Ensure to view the docks and harbour area for military activity.*"

"Military activity?" I asked.

"Yes, the Russian Navy regularly sends ships through the Bosporus Strait and into the Mediterranean. This avenue is controlled by Turkey, but there is a long-standing convention that applies between the Black Sea countries and Turkey over its use. Odessa, being one of the largest cities on the Black Sea, is a perfect spot for military activity, especially from the Russian forces controlling the city."

"What was your plan?"

"I quickly arranged transport to Dover, and onwards to France. If I could catch the Orient Express in Paris, I could make it to Bucharest. From there I planned to stay for some days and gain some familiarity with the area and provide details for my cover story. I was to become Alexandr Trepoff, a simple clerical worker from Bucharest in Romania. Nikolai and I had been separated in our childhood, but I had found some records relating to him and wished to reconnect. Our father had recently died, and there was a bequest for both of us, but I needed Nikolai to witness the documents. It took me a few days to get there but was worth the trip."

"Simple, but ingenious. If there was money involved, then it would shift suspicion away regarding any espionage."

41

"My thoughts as well. To ensure to enhance the authenticity, I found a small solicitor's office, and convinced him, with the addition of a small amount of money, to draft a will and other papers."

"But you don't speak Romanian, do you?"

"I didn't. As I said, I had several days to learn. My knowledge was still rather rudimentary but serviceable. I didn't think I'd need an extensive vocabulary for the first part of my journey. My Russian is functional, so I also brushed up a bit on that, and hoped it would see me through in Odessa itself."

"Very good."

"Indeed. From Bucharest, I travelled by slower train to Varna on the shores of the Black Sea. From there I was able to procure passage on a steamer north to Odessa. A journey that took another three days."

"A very mixed journey, and long."

"Admittedly, yes. But straying from my cabin on the steamer, I was able to practice my Russian with some of the other passengers. Some were from Odessa, while others were only passing through."

"What did you converse about?"

"I wanted to understand the temperament of the locals in the town. From a couple of older Ukrainians, I caught a sullen undertone of repressed belligerence towards the Russians. The Ministry of Education in Moscow had recently begun to remove the teaching of the Ukrainian language. Only Russian was being taught. At one point, one of my acquaintances let loose a string of obscenities against that, before being quietened by the other."

"Hmm. Perhaps something that this Trepoff fellow may have been keeping an eye on."

"Perhaps. By the afternoon of that third day, we docked in Odessa. I spent an hour familiarising myself with the area and created an escape plan in case it was needed. Finding a modest hostel, I booked a room for several nights, then made my way back to a stable I had seen earlier. There I bought myself a horse."

"Bought? A horse?"

"Yes. The sum that Mycroft gave me was quite substantial. My emergency plan was for a quick exit from the city. A horse would provide that transport. I hoped that if I didn't require it, I could sell it back to its original owner. It didn't worry me even if I had to give it away. I paid for several days stabling for the nag, and then proceeded to a nearby market where I procured some food and then headed back to my hostel room until nightfall."

Holmes stopped and again refilled his coffee cup. I was happy at that moment as it gave me time to add some more details to my notes. As he sat back and sipped, I took the opportunity to refill my own cup. This story was getting intriguing, and it had only just begun.

"Now, that first night was interesting. I had no compunction to play the tourist, and I simply ate and bathed to remove the indications of travel from my body before donning a costume I had prepared for just that purpose. I chose a style of clothing mostly worn by members of the merchant craft that plied the waters of the Black Sea, providing me with an immediate alibi or excuse if cornered and questioned. My outfit was also of the darkest blue, rather than black, I wished to blend into the shadows and avoid any attention. I set off through my second-floor window and kept to the rooftops. The town was mostly one- and two-storey buildings, but packed very closely together, making traversal much easier. When I had to cross an avenue or street, I climbed down to the road level and skulked across in whatever shadows I could find. Unlike London, there was very limited lighting, which made my journey much easier.

"I finally found myself in Pastera Street. Trepoff's rooms were located on the second floor of a small building near the centre. As I walked along the dim boulevard, I heard the noise of voices coming from a brightly lit building across the way. I found out later that it was the Odessa Music and Drama Theatre. I had arrived on the scene just as the performance was concluding. Quickly pulling away the scarf that I had wrapped around my face and head, I strode quietly and confidently, mingling with the audience as they left the building, and found the entrance I required. The denizens of that port city aren't as concerned with burglary as ours, and I found the main doors unlocked."

"Nikolai's front door was another matter. It wasn't only unlocked, but the entire locking mechanism was broken off. I found it lying on the floor in some detritus beside the external wall. As you can imagine, I was alert for anything else untoward."

"Why didn't you just leave and return in the daylight?"

"At that point, I was intrigued and needed to see the inside of Nikolai's apartment. Even in the dim light afforded by the dull gas lamps in the hallway, I was able to examine the door. The lock had been broken away by several whacks with a large sharp object, probably an axe. From what I could see, I suspect the assailant wasn't trying to be subtle. A crack in the door at about knee height indicated that he had attacked the lock until it was damaged enough to fall off, followed by a swift kick or two to finish the job."

"Surely that would have aroused others in the building?"

"Ah, that I can assure you did happen, and I'll get to that later. I pushed the door lightly and it swung inwards, with only the slightest squeal from the old hinges. They were rusted, rather than damaged. With luck, I found a shelf just inside which held a small candle and matches. I had brought my own just in case, but that made it much easier to investigate. Stepping inside, I quickly lit the candle and shed light on the area."

Holmes stopped for a moment and took a long drink from his coffee. It seemed he was steeling himself for the next part of the tale.

"Now, Watson, you and I have seen some horrors in our time, have we not?" I nodded in agreement as several incidents flashed past my eyes. "What greeted me in that place was possibly one of the worst sights I had seen."

"What was it?"

"Blood. The place was covered in it. It had dried to a dark brown stain, but even in that dim light, I could tell it was blood. From puddles to pools, to splashes and trails. From where I stood, I simply pieced together what I could see. Whoever was inside when the assailant burst in tried in desperation to race out of the only available exit: The lone window. It yawned wide open, filling the room with the frigid intensity of the deep winter outside, and snatching away any scent from the terrible display before me. It has surprised me, in hindsight, how I couldn't smell the blood, but on reflection, the chill breeze that entered probably accounted for that."

"If it was as cold as you say, then the blood was possibly frozen as well."

"Yes, markedly so."

"Sorry, I broke your train of thought. You were piecing together the crime."

"Yes, thank you. As I said, I stood on the threshold and viewed the area as best I could. The largest pooling or splashing occurred at the window. Assumedly, the assailant caught the victim as he probably tried to escape out the window. Later examination proved me right. There were deep wounds in the windowsill where several blows had missed the victim but landed in the wood. Even now I can't be sure how many rained down on the poor unfortunate, but it must have been at least a couple of dozen, such was the extent of the crimson tide."

"That sounds like a crime of passion, more than an execution."

"My thoughts exactly. Scanning the immediate area confirmed that as well. I found three sets of boot prints, all of which were stamped as if inked by the victim's lifeblood, and all of which led from the room. That told me that three men entered, possibly at different times. The assailant's boots led from the very depths of the blood. Several tracks showed where he stepped during the ordeal, and where he dallied over his handiwork. His trail led away in a series of staggered steps, as if in a slunk posture, almost as if he was overcome with grief after the adrenaline had dispersed. The second and third sets were more straightforward, as if the owners had simply moved into the room to pick up something, then leave."

"How could you tell that?"

"Because one set was reversed at the exit. It looked like two people walked side by side, about six feet apart, and then one turned and exited backwards. I found traces of bloodied footprints in the hallway that confirmed my suspicions. Their footprints were quite pronounced, which would be indicative of them having carried something heavy – say a body."

"The victim?"

"I can only assume. There was no evidence of the body in my line of sight and, given there were no immediate signs that it was located elsewhere, it can only have been moved out through the front door or pushed out of the window. I decided to check on the second location once I left the apartment complex."

"Did you work out whether it was this Trepoff fellow?"

"Not at first. Until I had more evidence, it was all simple supposition. My first task was to establish that Trepoff was the most likely occupant of the apartment at the time. My second was to uncover any information that he had documented during his observations of Odessa. With an eye on the first, which would require the discovery of identity documents, or unearthing a witness or two, something I would attempt in the morning, and a keen sense of the second, I moved into the apartment, carefully avoiding the splatters and pools of blood. It was then, in that dim candlelight, that I realised whoever appropriated the victim's body had also returned to investigate the apartment."

"How so?"

"There was more evidence of footprints, mostly partial, but some led through the more far-flung blood spatters and tracked the crimson marks further through the rooms. It was also, at that point, that I noticed several drawers in the nearby bureau were partially opened, or dislodged from their track, as if hurriedly opened and closed with some force. Looking through some of them revealed nothing of import remaining, but it did give me cause to believe that the second set of visitors had a far different motive than the first."

"Police?"

Holmes nodded. "Or worse."

"Worse? What do you mean *worse*?"

"The Russians employ a covert squad that belongs to the Department for Protecting Public Security. Colloquially they are known as the *Okrana*. Ostensibly, they are a police force interested in espionage or terrorist activities in and outside of Russia, though I have heard they can be employed for more ruthless activities."

"My word. Would they have been responsible for this apparent murder?"

"That occurred to me, but I dismissed it at the time, as the evident ferocity of the attack would only be used if they were trying to send a loud message. That didn't seem to be what had happened, because they would most likely leave the body behind as a form of punctuation."

"Hmm." I was starting to become happier that I hadn't been involved in Holmes's little trip to Ukraine. "What did you do next?"

"The signs that I could discern indicated that the second visitors moved from the main room into the adjoining rooms. Stepping carefully and as close to the perimeter wall as possible, I moved into the small adjacent bedroom. It only took a momentary glance around the area to see that it had been visited with less care than the main room."

"How so?"

"The sheets had been ripped from the bed. The stained mattress was slashed open. Its innards were torn out. The drawers in the little bedside had been pulled completely out, their meagre contents strewn across the floor. The small robe lay open, and the clothing snatched from the hooks before joining the detritus upon the floor. Any boxes, or bags, had suffered a similar fate. Someone was in a desperate need to find whatever Nikolai had secreted away in that apartment."

"Do you think they found it, whatever it was?"

"At that point I was unsure. All I could conjecture was that Trepoff had been tasked with observing and documenting the Odessa port. If he had taken notes, then there would need to be a notebook, or papers, or perhaps a diary, of some kind. I took up the search, mostly to convince myself that whatever evidence existed had been found or didn't actually exist."

"He could have simply held the facts in his memory before communicating them."

"True. After a thorough search, I decided to leave. It was growing late, and I didn't think I could garner any more information in the dim light. The scene was far too sullied for that. I made my way downstairs, stopping and noting the name on the last door. The name *Tsyganov* was written on a small card by the door. Underneath I deciphered that he was the building superintendent. I would make my way to see him first thing in the morning. A quick trip to the side alley proved slightly fruitless. In the darkness, I could neither see any evidence of bloodstains nor marks from where a body would have landed. I mapped the route back to my hostel via the alleyway so that I could conveniently retrace my steps and investigate in the light."

"What were your thoughts at that stage?" I asked. The evidence so far presented left me quite puzzled, and I hoped that Holmes could help me add some context to the tale at the point in time of his story.

"To be honest, without any contradictory evidence, I simply saw a case of murder, or at least heavy violence, against the person posing as Nikolai Trepoff. Whether that violence came from the authorities, a robbery attempt, or some other intervention was unclear. What was apparent was that someone was intent on finding an item or items amongst Trepoff's possessions. Whether they had or not was another matter. And even with my exertions over the last few days, I slept rather fitfully that night, cogitating on all that I'd seen."

Holmes picked up his cup and, noticing it was empty, reached for the pot. When that too was bereft, he simply huffed, placed it down and pulled out his cigarette case. As he withdrew one and lit it, I quickly read through my notes, hiding my eagerness for more of this story. When I raised my eyes towards him once more, I caught him looking at me, with that little smile. He had been waiting until I was ready before continuing.

"That next morning, I ate a light breakfast in the small room on the ground floor, set aside for such, before donning clothes more suited to blend in with the local population and once more set off for Trepoff's apartment building. It was retracing my steps through that side alley that my intrigue was quite piqued. As I had noticed from my cursory examination the night before, there was no blood to be seen, and any indentations in the dull dirt and mud had been extinguished by recent rains. But," he held up a finger, snatching my attention, "I found the weapon."

My eyes grew wide at that fact, and I simply stared at him in fascination, almost forgetting to take notes.

"Lying in a small patch of weeds growing against the wall of the neighbouring building was a small hatchet. The blade, though sharp, was pitted with small dents and nicks as if it had been used on the toughest materials. The head and handle were covered in sparse spatters of dried blood, though there was an indication from some streaks that most had washed away. Instead of taking the object with me, I found some scraps of material and wrapped it, secreting it behind some cast aside boxes, ready to be retrieved if required."

"It could have just been a coincidence."

"My thoughts exactly. That was why I wanted it available at a later date. My next destination was this Tsyganov fellow, the superintendent. Within a moment of my knocking, I heard him banging around and yelling coarse insults towards me. It was obvious he didn't relish his lot in life. As the door opened, I was greeted with the large frame of a man in his fifties, dressed in little more than a dirty undershirt and pants. He looked me up and down and a sneer came to his lips.

"'What you want?' he asked.

"In my broken Russian, I told him I was Nikolai's brother from Bucharest. His face dropped in fear, and I thought he was about to shoo me away. Instead, he simply pointed to the stairs and I caught the words, 'First floor, number eight,' before the door slammed shut."

"Surely he knew of the state of the place?" I asked.

"From his expression, I could only imagine he knew something. Regardless, I took his reaction as permission to enter the apartment unfettered, and that was exactly what I did. As expected, nothing had changed, but I was able to see more of the carnage. The attack appeared even more unhinged than I had previously deduced. The hatchet had found its mark on several occasions, but on many more, it had left dents and cuts in the furniture, walls, and window frame. I felt a little sorry for Trepoff. Nobody deserved to leave this world through such a violent act, even one undertaking covert work for his government."

"But you couldn't be sure that was the reason for the attack."

"True, and I didn't know that Trepoff was the victim. For all I could construe from the evidence, Trepoff might have been the perpetrator, or what was done may have been in self-defence. Brushing aside such confused thoughts, I revisited my search from the early morning and was a little disappointed to unearth only cursory items. Some paper, several pencils, and one blank notebook, but nothing that contained Trepoff's observations. I did, however, find something that the previous seekers had missed."

"What?"

"A small hidey-hole in the bathroom. It was tucked down beneath the bath. Two of the ceramic tiles had been loosened and a small hollow had been formed beneath. The contents surprised me, though upon examination I realised it proved that Trepoff had been there."

"What was it?"

"The first was a Webley Mark IV revolver – standard issue for the English Army. It had either been left by a previous foreign office employee, or by Trepoff himself. His file mentioned that he spent several years in the Army. Perhaps it was brought along in much the same way that you or I bring our own revolvers. It was fully loaded, but there were no other bullets, so I decided to take the pistol with me. If Trepoff was gone, he wouldn't be needing it. If not, then hopefully I could have it returned to him. The second item was a buff-coloured envelope, filled with bank notes in a mix of notes and denominations. Mycroft's envelope held a similar mixture. From the amounts in the envelope, it appeared that Trepoff had been given enough currency to see out the better part of a year. It was obvious that this place had remained hidden. Even the most diligent policeman wouldn't leave a gun and a wad of money, like that, lying in wait for the owner to return."

"Wasn't the cavity big enough for a diary or notebook?"

"Yes, it was, but again, I can only suppose about its use and contents. Trepoff may have only used it for the gun and the money. I pocketed the revolver and envelope and, as I pondered my next move, a knock came from the open main entrance. Stepping through to the bedroom to investigate, I found an old man standing at the entrance. His watery eyes fell on me as I moved towards him. He appeared to be in a slightly agitated mood and beckoned towards me.

"'*Gospodin*,' he said, his head turning to look over his shoulder. '*Okrana.*'

"I realised he was warning me of the approaching secret police.

"'The superintendent?'

"I can only assume he had called them. As I reached the exit, I heard voices from the ground floor and heavy boots heading up the stairs. The old man stood in the doorway across the corridor. Fearing detection, I started towards him. As I moved, I spied a cup sitting on a small table. I picked it up and threw it towards the open window, it broke against the glass pane, shattering the window and sending shards into the street outside. I quickly fled and rushed inside the old man's apartment. He threw the door shut and stood with his finger to his lips. My new comrade and I stayed still, listening to the approaching footsteps and voices.

"'*Okno!*' a rough voice shouted, before other shouts of '*Snaruzhi!*'

"The booted feet retreated. My rudimentary Russian translated the words *window* and *outside*. My ruse had worked. The *Okrana* had a ghost to chase. I began to speak to my host, but he put a finger to my lips. The heavy footsteps returned. From the sound, I determined a lone figure stepped into the apartment and rummaged around for what seemed like hours before another pair stomped up the stairs and fired off a stream of Russian to the first person. Finally, both men retreated downstairs, and all fell quiet once more."

"Good Lord, Holmes! What would you have done?"

"Pleaded my case. I was simply looking for my brother. I had the fake documents. If worse came to worst, I had the revolver."

"What happened then?"

"After another few minutes, the old man let out a long sigh of relief. I pointed towards the apartment and spoke Trepoff's name. The old man nodded, then ran a finger across his neck. That told me almost everything

I needed to know about Trepoff's fate. I then said '*Okrana*'? To my surprise, he shook his head. I asked who, to which he replied, '*Dmitry*'. When I asked who Dmitry was, he gave a simple two-word answer – '*Rosanna's father*' – before pushing past me and moving to a nearby rolltop desk. He bent over and wrote on a small piece of paper before returning and handing it to me. It was an address. I recognised the street. It was only two away from where we stood. The name *Rosanna Kravchenko* was written above it."

"What did you make of it all?"

"After the old man ushered me out of his apartment, shutting the door, and from the noises behind locking it several times, all I had was the name and address."

"Was that your next destination?"

"Yes. I made a short stop at the superintendent's apartment. The look on his face when he answered the door told me everything I needed to know about the visit from the *Okrana*. As there was nothing more to find in Trepoff's apartment, I knew I wouldn't be returning, so merely nodded towards the man before turning and leaving. I assumed that he would send word to the police again as soon as he was able, so hurried off towards Sadova Street, the address given to me by the old man."

Holmes took a drag on his cigarette and blew out a long line of smoke before proceeding. . . . .

It was Rosanna that opened the door, a puzzled look tinged with fear on her face. She was young and quite attractive, but her eyes were haunted by some tragedy. I simply said Nikolai's name and any hint of courage left her. Shuffling her distraught and weeping figure inside, I scanned the street, fearful of any witness by police or nosey neighbours. Luckily, the area was deserted, so I took the poor woman into a small reception room and bade her sit down. I found an open bottle of vodka on a nearby shelf and poured her a small measure. Offering her the glass, she downed it in one gulp. The calming effects were almost immediate. She wiped the tears from her eyes before holding the glass up towards me. The second helping went down slower and enabled her to address me.

"Who are you?" she asked.

"Alexandr Trepoff. Nikolai's brother from Bucharest."

"He never mentioned you."

"We have not spoken in many years. Our father has died, and I am here to settle some legal issues over the will."

"He didn't mention his father either."

"Let us say that Nikolai and our father did not see eye to eye." I *broached my next question carefully, but fully expected the reaction. "Can you tell me where Nikolai is?"*

As the tears flowed, I brought another glass of vodka and waited for the sobbing to subside. It proved to me that she knew of Nikolai's fate, or at least the rumours of his fate.

"Is he dead?" A drop of the head, a slight nod and more crying. "Was it the Okrana*?"*

At that, she looked up. Shaking her head, a confused look crossed her face. "No. Why would the Okrana *care?"*

"Who was it? Do you know?"

"My papa. He came home and the neighbours told him about Nikolai. He . . . he . . . went crazy. He burst in here yelling and screaming at me. Then he snatched up the hatchet we use to cut wood and looked at me with such rage in his eyes. I ran into my room and locked the door. I was so afraid. I've never seen him like that."

"Do you know why?"

"No. I heard him come home. There were noises of rage and sobbing. I stayed hidden until all went quiet, and then I crept out and found him asleep in that chair. He was covered in blood, and there were two empty bottles on the floor. I almost screamed when he spoke in his sleep. Nasty words – about foreigners, about me. I was so worried about Nikolai. I left and raced to his house, but all I found was blood, but no Nikolai."

"Did you go inside?"

Shaking her head, she said, "No. I stood in the doorway. I listened, but it was quiet. I didn't want to see him like that."

"You believe your father killed him?"

More tears ran down her face. "Yes. He told me the next day. He said I was never to love a stranger, only a Ukrainian. As he left to go back to his fishing boat, he turned and said if he caught me with a stranger, then my fate would be worse than that of my former lover's. He slammed the door and I haven't seen him since."

"What did you tell her, Holmes? No one should have to live under such threats, even from a parent."

Holmes shrugged. "I can only agree with you, but this was a foreign country, with their own traditions. Who was I, an Englishman, masquerading as a Romanian, to advise the young woman? I simply told her to go to the authorities and report her father for murder. At that, she simply shook her head and said they would be worse. It was at that point that I brought out Trepoff's money and handed it to her. I said that if she felt she was in danger, then she could use the money to leave Odessa and set herself up somewhere safe. Her face showed confusion until she saw the money, and then her eyes simply grew wide as she considered everything I had said."

"Do you know what she did?"

"No. I was near the end of my quest. I only had one more question for her, and that was whether Nikolai had given her anything that he wished to keep safe. Rosanna immediately leapt from her seat and disappeared into a room at the rear of the apartment. She returned, her demeanour thoughtful. She considered the small item in her hands. I believed she wanted to keep it as the only memory she had of Nikolai, but finally, she held it out towards me."

"It was a small diary. She said that Nikolai left it there, and would return when Rosanna's father was away and fill it with words. She mentioned that she couldn't read any of the strange writings. The words were not of her language."

"I took the book and flipped through it. It was indeed a diary, full of notes, diagrams, times, and dates. From my quick reading, it appeared to track the movements of ships berthing in Odessa. Trepoff had catalogued the cargo loaded and unloaded. Signs of any troops disembarking. It was everything that Mycroft had hoped for."

"Good Lord! What did you do next?"

"What more was there for me to do? I thanked the young woman and wished her luck with whatever choices she decided to make and then I fled into the streets. Once back at the hostel, I had the uncomfortable feeling of many pairs of eyes staring at me. Several of the guests sat around the reception area, feigning interest in their papers or books, but when I shot glances in their direction, there was a distinct rustle of items and faces disappearing behind them. Even the manager had a strange demeanour about him. Back in my room, I quickly packed. I believed that I had overstayed my welcome and attracted the wrong kind of attention. It was the shouts and whistles from the street that spurred me into real action."

"What was it?"

"The *Okrana*. Like the superintendent at Trepoff's apartment block, one of the other guests must have informed them. Rather than leave through the ground floor or my window, I tracked my way down the second-floor corridor and exited via a window at the end of the hall. I had examined it the day before for just such a contingency. It overlooked the neighbouring roof and allowed me easy access. Within a matter of minutes of scaling across the rooftops, I dropped down to the cobbles outside of the stables where my horse was stalled. The stable-master helped me harness my horse to the cart and gave me a wink, pointing to a nearby corner that ran behind the stables. He told me to head that way for a mile before turning back and heading out on the other street that led out of Odessa. He was obviously not one of the cowed citizens under the oppressive yoke of the secret police. I thanked him and spurred my horse onwards."

"As I fled past the buildings, I caught sight of agitated people and dark-clad men, whom I could only assume were the *Okrana*. Whistles and shouts accompanied the heavy footfalls of boot-clad feet. Within a few minutes, all went silent except the clopping of my horse's hooves on the cobbled streets, and soon we had left Odessa behind."

"That must have been a relief."

"Yes, it was, though I would have liked to have learned more about Trepoff's murder, and the interest that the *Okrana* had in him. I could only assume that it was they who stole away with his body, possibly in the hopes of examining him further, or finding some evidence on his person, or to hold onto it in the hope of unearthing more of our agents."

"But he wasn't killed because he was a spy."

"No. Although it was obvious that Trepoff was of interest to the Russian secret police, his demise came down to a simple case of maddened xenophobia. A father, desperate to keep his daughter under his control, and scared of any stranger wishing her away."

"Do you think she took your advice?"

"I can't say. When I handed the journal over to Mycroft, I asked him to send word to Odessa to have the welfare of the girl investigated, but he simply laughed off my suggestion and implied that I'd gone a little soft and been overly influenced by you."

"And what is the problem with that?"

Holmes smiled. "I must admit that I have missed that influence and am happy you came here today. I hope my little tale has whetted your fervour for more adventures to document."

Looking down at my copious notes, I smiled and replied, "Yes. I think this will keep me quite busy for a while. A strange little case, and one I'm actually happy I wasn't involved in."

The little mantel clock struck twelve. Holmes glanced towards it and smiled before standing to retrieve a bottle of brandy with two glasses. As he poured, he said, "I may have only spent a few days acting as a sailor, but I believe that the sun is over the yard-arm, so it must be time for one of these."

Sitting, we clinked glasses and enjoyed a middle-of-the-day refreshment.

I heard some vague account of his doings: Of his summons to Odessa in the case of the Trepoff murder . . . .

– Dr. John H. Watson
"A Scandal in Bohemia"

The Strange Case of the Disappearing Factor
by Margaret Walsh

The year of 1887 was one of strange and unusual cases for my friend, Mr. Sherlock Holmes. No case was stranger than the case that took us north to Scotland in late September that year.

We had been visited in Baker Street by no less a person than the Duke of Hamilton. The dukedom was a reasonably rich one – at least, where land was concerned. It was one of his pieces of land that brought him to Holmes.

"Amongst my holdings, Mr. Holmes," the Duke said, "is the island of Uffa. It came into my family when one of my ancestors served the Norwegian king, Haakon Haakonsson. He gave land grants to three of his local supporters. Bute was given to Ruadhri, Arran to Murchad MacSween, and Uffa to my ancestor. It isn't much of a place. I have three tenant farmers on it. However, with the rise in interest in such activities as fishing, hunting, and sailing purely for leisure, I have been thinking about cancelling the leases and building a fine lodge on the island."

"Such an undertaking would be expensive," I observed.

His Grace nodded. "I agree, Doctor. However, I believe it would pay for itself in the long run. The money I make from the leases is minimal. I could earn the entire year's rent for the island in three months with a comfortable well-run lodge."

"As interesting as this is," Holmes said, "you still haven't told us what brought you to our door."

"My apologies, Mr. Holmes," the Duke said. "Six days ago, I sent my factor, Gabriel Grice Paterson, and his son, Joseph, to Uffa to check suitable sites to build a lodge." He paused. "They were also to find out what compensation would be suitable for the three tenants. I am not a heartless man, gentlemen. I would see that they receive adequate compensation to allow them to start their lives afresh somewhere new. Apart from one letter, I have heard nothing. I sent another of my men to Uffa to investigate, as I had to come to London. He sent me a telegram from Glasgow."

"And?" Holmes asked.

"The Grice Patersons are missing," the Duke replied. "Gone as if spirited away. The tenants believe – " He stopped.

"The tenants believe what?" Holmes asked.

The Duke of Hamilton gave us a sombre look. "The tenants believe that the Grice Patersons have been abducted by the selkie folk."

The selkie folk, commonly just known as "selkie", were shapeshifters who walked on land in human form, but took the form of seals in the sea. Legend had it that the selkie took their sealskin off when they came ashore to frolic. The selkie were believed to be very attractive, and there were many tales of men stealing a skin so that a female selkie must remain on land so that they could claim her as a bride.

"Will you investigate for me, Mr. Holmes?" the Duke asked. "I cannot believe that such a creature even exists, let alone that it has spirited away my factor and his son. I fear foul play."

Holmes looked thoughtful. "It is an interesting case you have brought me, your Grace. I shall be pleased to help." He turned to me. "Fancy a trip to Scotland, Watson?"

"Of course," I replied.

It took several days to sort out the details, but we were soon on our way to Glasgow by train. The trip was long, and it was a relief to debark at Glasgow Central Station. We were met by a tall, dark, dour man who introduced himself to us as Inspector Archibald Kerr. "But call me Archie, gentlemen. Only my mother, God rest her soul, ever called me Archibald."

Inspector Kerr had been assigned to assist us, as he was from Arran originally. "Meaning I have a little more knowledge of Uffa than any other officer," he told us. "Not that it means much. I know *of* the families on Uffa, but do not *know* them."

"Who lives on Uffa? Holmes asked.

"The Gibbs at Arden, the Fullartons at Corriemains, and the McBanes at Carracuil. When I was a lad, it was the McDonalds at Carracuil, but old man McDonald died in an accident and his son didn't wish to remain on Uffa. McBane took over the tenancy. He married the Fullarton lass, or so I am told."

"And they are all farmers?" I asked.

"Aye. Small time, you understand. The land won't stand for more. Sheep for wool, mostly. A few cows for milk for themselves, and they grow corn and potatoes. There is also fishing. It was a fishing accident that did for old McDonald. You will see a number of fishing boats around Uffa."

"How do we get there?" I asked. I very much doubted that there was a ferry service.

"We will take the ferry to Arran," Kerr replied. "After that, I have arranged for Tommy McBane to take us across."

The island of Arran was strikingly beautiful in a raw, bleak manner. There were both highlands and lowlands, small lochs, rivers, and beaches – all of this on an island that was roughly twenty miles long and ten miles wide. It isn't without cause that the island is often referred to as being "Scotland in miniature".

The ferry came into the village of Brodick. Brodick Castle, which Inspector Kerr pointed out to us, was the seat of the Duke of Hamilton.

From Brodick, a pony-and-trap took us to the exposed end of Arran. There, at a distance of perhaps two to three miles, we could see the bulk of another, much smaller island. It was rugged and forbidding. Rising from the centre were two knolls that Inspector Kerr informed us were called Beg-na-sacher and Beg-na-phail. Between the two islands lay a strip of water that looked anything but calm. The water seemed to boil and froth as if someone had lit a fire beneath it.

"That, gentlemen," Inspector Kerr said, "is the Roost of Uffa. One of the most dangerous pieces of water you will ever meet. Even the Vikings had trouble with it. They called it Aegir's Ketill, or kettle. Aegir was a sea giant who hosted parties for the Norse gods. Legend has it that one of the party sites was below the Roost. According to the legend, if the Roost is rough, then Aegir has set his kettle to boil. If a ship was wrecked in the Roost, it used to be said that the captain and crew had been invited to attend the party. It was one invitation that you couldn't refuse."

Inspector Kerr grinned at us. "But come, gentlemen, Tommy McBane should be waiting for us. The Roost is relatively calm today, so there should be no danger of unwanted party invitations for us."

Tommy McBane turned out to be a man in his mid-forties, with skin beaten dry and hard by the elements. His fading blonde hair and blue eyes spoke of more than a little Viking blood in his family.

Few words were spoken as we made our way across to Uffa. It wasn't until we reached McBane's mooring at Carravoe that the man even spoke to us. "You'll no be coming to the house tae talk tae the family," he said firmly. "They saw nothing of the Duke's men. They were staying with mae wife's auld man at Corriemains. I fetched them frae Arran as I did ye, but I didnae speak with them. My wife and I, we cannot help ye."

"What about the other family?" Holmes asked. "The Gibbs?"

McBane shrugged. "I dinnae know about that. Ye will be having to ask them."

"You knew why the Grice Patersons were here?" Inspector Kerr asked.

"Och!" McBane replied. "Ye'd have tae be daft not tae work that out."

"You weren't upset at possibly having to leave Uffa?"

McBane shrugged again. "That's how it is. I understand from auld Fullarton that the Duke was going to gie us a goodly sum. I only came here twenty year ago. I am no as attached tae Uffa as the others are."

"What about your wife?" I asked.

"Minnie's a good lass. She'll do what I tell her. And if that means leaving Uffa, then that's what she'll do." He pointed towards a house a short distance away. "That be Corriemains. Fullarton's expecting you." With that, he walked away and left us standing beside the boat.

"Welcome to Uffa," Inspector Kerr said dryly.

He led the way across the heather towards the house that McBane had pointed out. As we got closer, I could see an old man standing at the door, watching us.

"You'll be the men come from Arran?"

"A bit further than that," Kerr replied. "The Duke asked for these men from London to search for the Grice Patersons."

"They'll no find them." He turned and went into the house, gesturing to us to follow.

"Why not?" Kerr asked, as we entered.

"The selkie folk took them. They'll no give them back."

"How do you know they were taken by the selkie folk?" Holmes asked softly.

"Because I have seen them with my own two eyes."

"You saw the Grice Patersons taken?" I couldn't quite comprehend what I was hearing.

Old Man Fullarton shook his head. "Nae, nae. I have seen the selkie folk upon the beach at night." He pointed to a small door. "The Grice Patersons' belongings are in there. I have nae taken anything. Not so much as a farthing."

Holmes gestured to me to follow him, and we went into the small room, leaving the door open.

I heard Inspector Kerr cheerfully telling the old man that no one would accuse him of theft.

Holmes sorted swiftly through the few possessions that the Grice Patersons had brought with them. It was nothing more than a few changes of clothing, some under clean under-garments, a bag containing some fishing line and hooks, and a Bible."

"I cannot see that anything is missing," I stated.

"Can you not?" was Holmes's response.

"What is it that I'm missing?"

"There are no outdoor things. I would expect to find an ulster at the very least – though a Mackintosh is more likely given the weather here and on Arran. Mr. Fullarton has an old Inverness cape hanging by the door, but that is the only outdoor clothing here. The Grice Patersons were obviously wearing their coats when they disappeared."

We went back out into the main room.

"Mr. Fullarton," Holmes said, "what can you tell me about the history of Uffa?"

"The history, eh?" Fullarton shook his head. "It's no very exciting. None o' the three families knew who was here first. There's no legend about that."

"What legends are there?"

"Ye have heard the Roost called Aegir's Ketill?"

"We have. Inspector Kerr told us of that before Mr. McBane brought us across from Arran."

"But did he tell you of Halfdan's Treasure?"

"He did not."

"To be honest," Inspector Kerr said, "I didn't think of it."

"Uffa sits close by what was a trading route for the Vikings," Fullarton began. His tone was almost hypnotic, as if he had learned the story by rote and was repeating it verbatim. "Coming and going from Ireland and Scotland and the lands o' the north. The legend has it that any longship passing through the Roost had tae pay a toll tae Aegir, by throwing something of value that had been taken in the raid, be it gold, gems, or a slave, into the water for the giant. There was one Viking leader, Halfdan Knutsen, known as Halfdan Hardfist, for he kept a closed fist around his money chest and wouldnae part with his wealth if he could help it. Halfdan and his crew had raided a monastery. Some say it was St. Blane's on Bute. Others that it was in Ireland. The ship came away with a king's ransom in gold plate and jewelled boxes." Fullarton broke from the story to comment, "Though I have nae idea why monks would need jewelled boxes."

"They were called reliquaries," I said. "They were used to hold the relics of saints. Scraps of clothing, teeth, even bones, were sealed in gold-and-silver boxes decorated with gems."

Fullarton nodded. "Anyway, Halfdan decided to go through the Roost, but didnae give a toll to Aegir. In his fury at no being paid, Aegir made the water of the Roost boil, and Halfdan's ship sunk without trace. Not a single fighting man or slave aboard the ship survived, and not so much as a splinter of wood washed up to tell the tale."

Holmes nodded. "An interesting story indeed. Tell me if you would, Mr. Fullarton, where exactly did you see the selkie folk?"

"Down on the beaching at Carravoe. Near where McBane brought you in."

"Thank you, Mr. Fullarton. You have been most helpful. If you could point us in the direction of the Gibbs's holding, we would be much obliged."

Fullarton shook his head. "There's no need. Jock and Geordie will be here once they've got their cows in. Sit ye down and have some tea. Ye'll be staying with the Gibbs lads. My daughter Minnie and her husband, Tommy, dinnae have the room, but Jock and Geordie do."

With that, he ambled off into what appeared to be a kitchen annex and busied himself making a pot of tea.

It was perhaps an hour later that two large men knocked at the door. As they entered, Fullarton introduced them as Jock and Geordie Gibbs. They were younger than Fullarton, but probably older than Tommy McBane. Both of them were well on their way to being as weather-beaten as Fullarton.

The larger of the two introduced himself as Jock Gibbs. Both men refused tea and seemed impatient to leave. Taking the cue, we gathered our bags and followed them outside.

Few words were spoken as we walked towards the cottage that was home to the Gibbs men. Both men had informed us curtly, but politely, that they had had no dealings with the Grice Patersons, apart from greeting them when the came to their cottage to look around the land.

We left our luggage in the cottage and then the Gibbs brothers took us on a tour of the island. There wasn't much to see. Uffa was a bleak place with rugged rocks, a little grass, a few stunted bushes, and even less trees.

They showed us the beach where Fullarton had seen the selkie. It wasn't exactly where McBane's boat was moored, but a secluded bay just around from it.

Holmes insisted on going down onto the sand to investigate. The path down to the small beach was rocky and somewhat treacherous underfoot, with small pebbles rolling under the feet.

When we reached the beach, the first thing I noticed was a terrible smell which, at first, I thought was the seaweed. Then I recognized the sickly-sweet, cloying, stench of decaying flesh.

We hunted around until we found something that looked like a grave. Kerr sent one of the Gibbs brothers to fetch a spade.

He returned with two such implements, and, with some trepidation, we began to dig.

It only took a few spadefuls of sand to be removed before we found the source of the smell. Two skinned corpses.

Geordie Gibbs leaned forward. "Those are nay human," he observed.

"Quite right, Mr. Gibbs," Holmes said softly. "If I am not mistaken, these are the corpses of seals."

I was puzzled. "Why on earth would anyone bury perfectly good meat? I mean, I am sure that it doesn't compare with beef or lamb, but it would surely be a good source of food?"

"People around here don't eat seal meat, Dr. Watson," Inspector Kerr said.

"Why ever not?" I asked.

"Many people in the islands believe that they have selkie blood. It would be bad manners, to say the least, to eat something could be a relative."

I looked again at the carcasses. "Surely skinning a relative would be just as bad?"

Geordie Gibbs nodded. "Aye, Doctor, it is. I dinnae know why someone has done this, but they have done a bad thing. The selkie folk will be crabbit. They'll nae like this at all."

"Crabbit means angry," Kerr murmured.

Holmes stood frowning at the grave. He turned and looked out across the Roost towards Arran. Then he began turning on the spot, taking in the surroundings, before nodding to himself. "Come, gentlemen, let us get in and rest."

"Rest, Mr. Holmes?" Kerr asked.

"Yes, Inspector Kerr. A good rest for the three of us, for we shall be up late tonight."

"We will?" I asked. "Doing what, exactly?"

Holmes grinned mischievously. "We shall be catching ourselves a selkie."

Kerr and I exchanged bewildered looks, whilst the Gibbs brothers looked at Holmes as if he was insane. Which, by their reckoning, he probably was.

It was close to midnight before Holmes, Kerr, and I returned to the beach. Holmes had lit our way with his dark lantern. Inspector Kerr made to go down to the beach. Holmes grabbed his harm. "No, we'll watch from up here. If we try and go down there now, one of two things will happen."

"What are they?" I asked.

"We will be seen or, more likely, one of us will break his fool neck!"

We laid flat on the cliff top and looked down at the beach. There was nothing to see. The moon was close to full but didn't provide an enormous amount of light, due to low hanging clouds. There was enough light to see the vague shape of a fishing boat in the Roost, and the wavering reflections of the moon and such stars that were visible in the restless movement of the waves.

All was still and silent, except for the crash of the waves on the rocks, and the murmuring of the occasional seabird disturbed in its sleep. I found myself drifting towards sleep myself when Kerr grabbed my arm. "What is that?" he hissed.

Peering into the dark, I could see the vague shape of a man come out of the sea and on to the beach. At least I thought it was a man. Moonlight reflected off something that, though man-shaped, didn't truly resemble a man so much as a seal!

I swallowed reflexively. "Holmes!" I whispered, my voice sounding hoarse in my own ears. "What do we do?"

Holmes chuckled dryly under his breath. "We come back tomorrow and capture ourselves a selkie." He shuffled backwards from the clifftop before getting to his feet. "Come, gentlemen, it is time we got ourselves some sleep. We will be having a busy evening tomorrow."

Not one word would he say until we were back in the Gibbs' cottage.

"Did we really see a selkie?" I asked as we readied ourselves for bed.

Holmes paused, then shook his head. "No, we did not."

"You know what has happened?" I asked.

Holmes shook his head. "I have suspicions only."

I thought back to the beach. "The creature came out of the sea."

"He appeared to," Holmes corrected me. "Now, it is time to sleep. All will be explained tomorrow night." He paused. "Did you bring your gun?"

"Of course. I rarely travel without it."

"Good man. You'll need it tomorrow night. Well then, good night, Watson."

"Good night," I replied.

Just before sunset the next day we returned to the beach, this time accompanied by the Gibbs brothers. Holmes had assured them that we weren't dealing with a real selkie, but a case of human trickery.

We settled in behind a protrusion from the cliff face. Geordie Gibbs assured us that we wouldn't be seen from the beach. "We used tae hide doon here as wains," he said. He grinned widely. "Until our da's temper cooled."

"Children have always needed hiding places from angry parents," Holmes observed softly.

Beside him, Inspector Kerr sighed in agreement.

We spoke little, and quietly. There was an unspoken understanding that we need not attract attention.

Finally, no words were spoken at all as we watched the darkness begin to engulf Uffa.

Sitting down here there in the silence, broken only by the waves, I heard something that I hadn't heard the previous night on the cliffs: Somewhere out in the Roost, a boat was being rowed slowly towards the shore. I could hear the unmistakeable sound of oars gently grating in their rowlocks. There was a pause in the sound that was followed by a splash, as if something heavy had entered the water. Then the oars began their scratching chorus again. Beside me, Holmes gripped my arms tightly. "When I say go," he whispered harshly, "bring down the creature on the beach."

Splashing told us that whatever was in the water was approaching the shore. The splashing stopped, and a shadow passed over the rock.

"Go!" Holmes roared.

The five of us jumped out from our hiding place and raced towards the startled figure.

Seeing five men bearing down, the creature tried to turn and run, but Jock Gibbs was too quick, bringing his prey down in a tackle that would have made the heart of any rugby coach glow with pleasure.

Jock Gibbs began coughing. "Och! He smells!"

"I rather think he does," Holmes said dryly, "seeing as he is wearing uncured seal skins."

As we got closer, the rank smell of uncured – and most likely slowly rotting – animal pelts became more noticeable.

"Let us see what we have caught," Kerr said.

The Gibbs brothers hoisted the captive to his feet. Holmes shone his bullseye lantern on him.

It was clear that this was no selkie. The roughly made garment of seal skins was mostly tied onto the wearer, though, in places, it appeared to be pinned.

Kerr and I disinterred the occupant from his revolting fur suit.

A man in clad fisherman's garments was revealed beneath the skins. He was blonde with pale watery eyes. He looked at us with fear.

The Gibbs didn't know him. Holmes's tone was grim. "Where are the Grice Patersons?"

"I . . . I . . . ." The man's eyes flicked towards the sea.

Holmes stepped away and flashed the lantern towards the cliff top. A light answered it and then vanished.

"What in the world – ?" I asked.

"I asked Mr. Fullarton to keep watch at the top. If he saw my light flash, he is to signal Mr. McBane, who is currently sitting in his boat at its moorings."

"But why?"

"We need transport to where the Grice Patersons are being held."

"Where is that?" I asked, more than a little confused.

"Out there," Holmes said. "On that boat."

"But it's just a fishing boat," I protested.

"An odd fishing boat that doesn't move once in an entire day," Holmes retorted. "No, Watson, that is where our treasure hunters lurk."

"Treasure hunters?" Kerr asked. His face showed the confusion that I was feeling.

"All in good time, Inspector. For now, we must release the Grice Patersons from their durance vile."

Our prisoner was staring at Holmes with a shocked expression that was tinged with fear. "How do ye know all that?"

"I am Sherlock Holmes. It is my business to know what other people do not."

He looked at Inspector Kerr. "Are ye from Scotland Yard?"

Holmes chuckled drily. "I am afraid that Uffa is a little out of the Yard's jurisdiction. This is Inspector Kerr from Glasgow."

"Still, you're police?"

"I am," Kerr said gravely.

The man swore briefly, but sadly. "I knew Duncan's idea was daft."

"Duncan?" Kerr asked.

The man nodded towards the sea. "Duncan Stewart. He owns the boat. This was all his damn-fool idea."

"What was his idea?" I asked.

"Tae search for Halfdan Hardfist's Treasure."

"Why don't you tell us the entire story," Holmes said. "Starting with your name."

The man shrugged. "I'm Rabbie Cameron. The four of us – Duncan, Jamie Wright, Davie Buchanan, and me – all worked on fishing boats out o' Arran. None o' us are frae Arran. We all come from Glasgae."

I frowned. "You said that Duncan owns that boat out there?"

"Aye, he does. But he didnae own a boat when this whole kurfuffle started. We was workin' fer another when Duncan found a wee box in the nets."

"A box?" I asked.

"Aye – last month. It was covered with barnacles an' kelp, but Duncan scraped it clean an' found it were made of gold an' had a jewel on it. A big ruby. He didnae tell the owner. Finders' keepers an' all that. Duncan asked around, quiet like, and learned about the treasure of Halfdan Hardfist. He said if we could find the rest o' the treasure, we'd be set fer life. So first chance he gets, he's off tae Glasgae an' sells the box. I dinnae how much he got for it, but it were enough tae buy the boat. He came back an' we started searching." Rabbie Cameron fell silent.

64

"What happened next?" Kerr asked.

The prisoner sighed. "Duncan said we needed to keep people away from the beach, so they could nae see what we were doing. So he killed a couple o' seals for their skins, an' we takes turns walking up and down the beach tae scare people away."

"Did it work?" I asked.

Cameron sighed, as if he hadn't heard me. "Nothing has gone right since Duncan killed those seals," he mumbled. "The man an' his son came along, and they wouldnae go away, and Duncan said we had tae keep them from the treasure. I think he wanted to kill them, but the rest o' us baulked at that. I hate doing this. I always feel like someone's watching me and they ain't happy." He looked at us with tears in his eyes, "I just want this tae end."

I could hear the gentle sound of oars. I turned my head to see McBane approaching in a boat. It wasn't the boat we had come from Arran on, but a smaller one.

Kerr patted Rabbie Cameron on the shoulder. "Dinnae worry, Rabbie lad. It will all be over soon."

Inspector Kerr was as good as his word. We left Geordie to watch over Cameron, as the man was adamant about not being left alone on the beach.

McBane took us out to the fishing boat. It didn't appear to be the most-sound of vessels. It was old, creaky, and I suspected that it leaked. A rowing boat around the same size of McBane's was tied at its stern.

Inspector Kerr hailed the boat, identified himself, and loudly demanded to be let aboard. A man who identified himself as Duncan Stewart objected equally loudly, but there was a sound of a scuffle aboard, followed by a loud thud.

Another voice spoke up, "Ye can come aboard, Inspector. Pay no mind tae Duncan. He'll nae object now."

We clambered up the rope ladder that dangled over the rails.

Upon gaining the deck the first thing I noticed was a man with a sulky expression sitting on the deck, nursing a split lip.

"Duncan Stewart, I presume," Holmes said dryly.

The man looked at us, and then looked away.

Holmes examined the other two men standing near the wheelhouse. "First of all, let me tell you that we have no interest in whether or not you have found Halfdan Hardfist's Treasure. All we want is the return of Mr. Grice Paterson and his son. Their employer, the Duke of Hamilton, is anxious on their behalf."

One of the two men sighed and looked at Duncan Stewart. "I told ye it were a daft idea, Duncan, ye wee gowk."

65

While my family does have some Scottish roots, I was a little perplexed by the language.

Inspector Kerr saw my confusion. "'Gowk' means idiot."

I nodded my thanks.

The man turned back to look at us. "I'm Davie Buchanan." He gestured at the other man standing. "This is Jamie Wright. He'll show you where the men are being kept."

Inspector Kerr and Jock Gibbs remained on the deck, and Holmes and I followed Jamie Wright toward the hold. The trapdoor was fastened with a brand-new bolt and padlock, which Wright opened. It was damp inside, dark, and smelled strongly of old fish – very old fish. Wright gathered a rope ladder from one side and fastened one end to the trapdoor and dropped the other down the hold. Then he then leaned over and called, "Ye can come up now. Ye going free."

"Are we now?" came a cross sounding voice from below.

Shortly afterwards a man came up the ladder and clambered out, closely followed by a younger one.

The older one looked at us, his stance belligerent. "Who the devil are you?"

"Sherlock Holmes, at your service," Holmes replied with a slight smile. "The Duke of Hamilton employed me to find you and your son."

Gabriel Grice Paterson almost sagged with relief. "It is over?"

Holmes nodded. "It is, once we get back to Uffa. My friend, Doctor Watson, will make sure you are in good health, then we shall return to Arran and let the Duke, and your good wife, know that you are safe."

It took us until sunrise to get everything sorted. Once everyone was safely back on Uffa, discussions were had on what to do with Duncan Stewart and his cohorts.

"There's nowhere to hold them on Uffa until I can get more police here," Inspector Kerr said. "I would have to go across to Arran, and possibly even back to Glasgow. Arran has no telegraph."

"One of the Duke of Hamilton's men had to travel to Glasgow in order to send him a telegram," I said.

Gabriel Grice Paterson spoke up. "What crimes have been committed, other than the kidnapping of my son and me?"

Inspector Kerr scratched his head. "None that I can see."

"A case could be made for attempted theft," Holmes said softly, "seeing as the Roost lies between Arran and Uffa, and the Ducal seat is on Arran."

"I wouldn't like to argue that in court," Kerr said.

"Neither would I," Holmes replied. "It is a little too tenuous an idea."

"So, maybe we could just leave?" Rabbie Cameron asked hopefully.

66

Gabriel Grice Paterson spoke up. "I think that is the best idea. If this goes to court, then more people will learn of Halfdan Hardfist's Treasure, and the place will be overrun with adventurers. His Grace will not like that at all."

"But what do *you* want?" Holmes asked. "It is you and your son who have been most incommoded by the acts of these men."

"Did they find any treasure?" Grice Paterson asked.

All four men shook their heads. "Apart frae the gold box that I first found," Duncan Stewart replied, "we've found nowt."

Gabriel Grice Paterson looked thoughtful for a while, and then nodded once sharply. "This is what we will do: You men will leave here, never to return. Not even to work the boats on Arran. Take your boat and go elsewhere. I care not where."

The four men looked at him and then at us.

Inspector Kerr nodded. "If Mr. Grice Paterson doesn't want to press charges, then you are free to go. Mind though, I will have your names and descriptions circulated around Arran, so that if you ever decide to come back, I will know."

"We'll no come back, Inspector," Davie Buchanan hastened to assure us.

"None o' us liked the place," Rabbie Cameron agreed. "Someone allus watching ye."

"There's bin nay bugger watching ye, Rabbie." Duncan Stewart snorted. "It's all in yer mind, small as that thing is."

"There has been," Cameron insisted. "Every time I walked this beach dressed in those skins, I felt them watching."

"Daft is what you are," Stewart muttered.

The man turned back to us. "We'll be going now." He marshalled the other three men, and they got in their little boat to row back to the fishing boat.

We watched the men return to the vessel and board it. We could see their small figures scurrying around on deck. Finally, the small vessel weighed anchor and began to move.

It wasn't a particular pleasant morning. The rising sun had been accompanied by a climbing wind, which was beginning to stir the waves into a light froth. Sand was beginning to whip along the beach.

We turned back to head up the cliffs to the Fullarton cottage when Jock Gibbs let out a sharp cry.

We swung back to see what had caused the man to cry out.

In the few minutes that our attention had been away from the sea, the weather had worsened. The wind was now virtually howling, and the light froth had become a fierce surge. The water boiled and writhed in a manner that seemed almost supernatural.

"Aegir's Ketill at full boil," Kerr said, his voice filled with horror. "They will never survive it."

Looking again to the boat, I could see that was true. The vessel was now whirling around like a cork in a bathtub when the plug had been removed.

Faintly, over the wind, I thought I could hear shrieks and cries for help. And something else. It was, I was in no doubt at all, some freak of acoustics that caused the crashing of the waves to sound like a deep throated howl of fury.

Then, with a sharp crack, it was all over. The boat tilted on one end and was dragged down into maelstrom and was gone.

We stood watching silently as the storm continued to rage for a while before slowly dying.

"There's no point in going out tae look for the bodies," McBane said softly as he readied himself to return his little boat to its mooring.

"Aye," Geordie Gibbs agreed. "What Aegir takes, he does nae give back."

In a sombre mood we turned again to continue up the cliffs. A movement out to sea made me turn back. Not far from where the boat had disappeared beneath the waters of the Roost a sleek, dark, head rose from the foam.

The seal and I looked at each other for a moment before it bobbed its head and slid back beneath the water. I thought of the seal carcasses we had found, and I had the oddest feeling that the seal, if it was a seal, was saying thank you.

I shook myself to clear my head of that flight of fancy and followed the rest of our party up to the cliff top.

The year '87 furnished us with a long series of cases of greater or less interest, of which I retain the records. Among my headings under this one twelve months I find . . . the singular adventures of the Grice Patersons in the island of Uffa . . . .

– Dr. John H. Watson
"The Five Orange Pips"

The Mystery of the
Three Mendicants
by Paul D. Gilbert

During the course of a quiet and unusually warm early October evening, I had been pleasantly surprised by my good friend Sherlock Holmes's agreeable disposition.

His practise had been curiously quiet of late, a state of affairs that would have normally left him in a most impatient and irritable mood. On this occasion, however, the opposite had been the case, and once he had returned from a "leisurely and refreshing" walk around the neighbouring streets, I was astonished to observe that he had been positively beaming from ear to ear. However, Holmes's inexplicable behaviour did not end there.

"You know, Watson," Holmes smiled, "there is much to be said for your tried and trusted adage that I could use a good holiday. The constant barrage of cases with which we have been engulfed during these past few weeks have certainly taken their toll upon both my mental and physical faculties, and I find myself grateful for the respite with which we have been recently presented. For once, might I thank you for some sound medical advice."

I had been so astonished by my friend's admission that I hadn't even considered the notion of having been insulted by his final statement. His conclusion had been at such variance to his usual state of mind that I even pondered upon the notion that he was being sarcastic. After all, was his mind not dissimilar to a machine that might wreck itself for not being used to its full potential? Nevertheless, there was certainly no hint of sarcasm when he continued.

"As you know only too well, my mind is like a finely tuned violin, and I am now leaning towards the hypothesis that were I to turn the key by even the slightest degree tighter, one of the strings would undoubtedly snap."

Holmes moved towards the desk whereon I had accumulated the notes and files that pertained to our more recent cases. He began to pick them up randomly and toss them back down again in a most haphazard fashion, thereby creating a state of disarray that almost drove me to despair.

"Really, Holmes!" I protested. "Those notes didn't attain their chronological order by mere chance, you know!"

I rushed over and attempted to salvage at least some of the logical sequence that I had previously arranged, before too much further damage could be done. My friend, however, was oblivious to my efforts and remonstrations and, without even a single word of apology, he continued with his discourse.

"I see, from within yours note, a patchy account of our encounter with the devilish Count Dubois and his devious machinations, the affair of the candid architect, and of course the reclamation of Charlemagne's armour, an effort that nearly cost us both our lives.

"All of these matters reached a successful and triumphal conclusion, of course," Holmes proclaimed. "However, each one also assuredly took its toll upon your old friend. Therefore, Doctor, I have decided to embrace this vacation from work and reacquaint myself with my violin and a study of Neolithic tools and art."

"Well, I for one am awfully glad to hear you say that. I must admit to being consumed with more than a little sense of dread and trepidation at the thought of a long period of inactivity and its inevitable effects upon your nerves. Consequently, I will now devote my time to the recalibration of my notes."

Holmes laughed heartily at my thinly veiled complaint, and he was also not unaware of my suspicious and cursory glance towards the bureau drawer wherein lay his lamentable Moroccan leather case and its lethal device.

"Oh, Watson, you may be assured that I have come to my epiphany by virtue of my own fatigue and contemplations, unaided by the intake of any narcotics."

I muttered an apology under my breath and began to rummage amongst my papers without casting my friend another glance. While I worked, I noticed Holmes begin to rifle through a pile of musty old books, doubtless each one upon the subject of his latest field of interest. However, Neolithic artefacts didn't seem to hold his interest for very long and he began to discard each book in turn, all the while emitting loud grunts of disapproval as each tome fell to the floor.

It now fell upon his violin to aid his distraction. Each of Holmes's discordant scratchings caused me to grimace, and I soon realised that any hope that I might have had of finishing my work uninterrupted were slowly becoming dissipated by my friend's torturous musical efforts. Fortunately, Holmes abandoned his beleaguered instrument before I had been forced to remonstrate with him still further, and he took to his chair with his pipe.

70

Once he had exhausted his tobacco, Holmes began to strum his fingers impatiently upon the arms of his chair, and I now realised that his illuminating realisation was to be short-lived. Finally, when he began to pace the room and glance anxiously out of the window every so often, I knew that all hope was lost.

I began to gather up my papers and then took to my chair with the latest newspapers to hand.

"Would you like me to scan these for any noteworthy items of interest?" I asked with a pronounced air of resignation.

"Ha, you know me so well!" He exclaimed with a brief half-smile while encouraging me with an impatient wave of his hand.

There was no doubting my knowledge of his ways, and therefore it was no surprise to me, as a pile of rejected newspapers began to build up upon the floor at my feet, that Holmes's impatient finger-strumming began to increase both in speed and intensity.

"Really, Holmes," I protested. "This most-welcomed vacation of yours certainly appears to have been a very brief one, I must say!"

Holmes didn't even attempt a counter-argument and, as he turned sheepishly away and across to the Persian slipper for some more tobacco, I made my way over to one of our windows. It wasn't unreasonable to propose that the unseasonably mild weather had enticed more people out on to the streets than one might normally expect at this time of year. A few businessmen hurrying home from work for a late supper, the occasional romantic couple walking along slowly arm-in-arm, an assortment of exhausted vendors desperately trying to end their day with a late sale or two, and the sad sight of those bedraggled few who rely upon the charity and goodwill of others, but through no fault of their own.

I digested the view in as much detail as I could, for I knew that soon enough my friend would expect me to report on anything that appeared to be out of the ordinary.

"So, Doctor," Holmes asked sarcastically, "have your observations revealed anything of note?"

I was on the point of replying negatively when something distinctly untoward did suddenly catch my eye. My silence and quizzical attitude had been enough to rouse my friend from his smoke-shrouded chair, and he followed my gaze at the window.

"The beggar?" he asked.

"Yes, for there is something in his manner that distinguishes him from those other sorry souls. See there? He isn't quite so persistent as the others in his approach to the passers-by – almost as if he expects to be given what he needs as a matter of right. Although his archaic garments are decidedly threadbare, he certainly keeps himself and his clothes pristinely clean." I concluded my observations, left both thoughtful and uncertain as to the nature of this individual.

"Excellent work!" Holmes exclaimed jovially. "We shall make a detective of you yet." Then his manner changed completely upon seeing two large constables bearing down upon the poor fellow with an urgent and aggressive intent. "Quickly, Watson! We must go to this man's aid!"

Before I had even roused myself from my reverie, Holmes had pulled on his jacket and made his way down to the street below, with an inexplicable speed and urgency. I joined him just a moment later, but barely in time to hear his address to the vigorous constables.

"You there!" Holmes called out. "What business do you have with this gentleman?"

The policemen turned in surprise and laughed at my friend in a most derisory fashion.

"Gentleman, you say?" One of them smiled aggressively. "This man is a nuisance upon a public highway, and he's coming along with us."

"Do you know exactly who you are addressing in such a manner?" I asked, pronouncing, "This is Mister Sherlock Holmes!"

Obviously, the constables recognised the name immediately, but even though their manner altered noticeably, they persisted with their intent.

"What business could you possibly have with such a person?" one of them asked.

"This person, as you so courteously describe him," Holmes replied, "happens to be an associate of mine, returning *incognito* with some valuable information to impart. You would indeed be impairing the passage of justice if you impede him any further."

Fortunately, the beggar played along with Holmes's charade and, after a brief and whispered consultation, the officers decided not to interfere further in the affairs of Sherlock Holmes. We ushered the poor befuddled fellow upstairs and out of harm's way, while the policemen meekly melded back into the throng.

Without a word, Holmes ushered our confused guest into a chair by the fire and then supplied him with a liberal measure of port. He stood before the fellow and rubbed his hands together excitedly at the thought of having procured a new client, albeit in an unusual fashion.

"So, what brings you to our door, by such an unconventional means?" Holmes asked once the man had sipped from his glass.

"You already knew that my purpose in coming to Baker Street was to seek a consultation with you?" the man asked.

"It wasn't hard to deduce, for you fell in with my little subterfuge far too easily and without even a moment's hesitation. Besides which, your look of anticipation and excitement, upon hearing the mere mention of my name, told me of your intent. However, if I am to be of any use to you, perhaps you might first supply me with your name and the nature of the problem that brought you to my door. I can assure you that Doctor Watson can be relied upon to deal with your problem with as much discretion as you might expect of me." Holmes indicated that I should now bring out my notebook and pencil and he, in turn, closed his eyes in concentration with an unlit pipe clenched between his teeth. The man drained his glass before beginning.

"Very well, then, gentlemen, my name is Cuthbert Daws and, despite my appearance, I can assure you that I am no beggar, but rather a mendicant of long standing. I am not a religious mendicant, for I don't preach for alms, but in the time-honoured tradition of our order, I do goodly deeds – not for wealth or money, but merely for the means to survive and the benefit of others. Indeed, I am actually forbidden to accumulate wealth and will shun financial favours for the sake of food, shelter, and items of clothing. As you can doubtless see," Daws added with a wry smile, "in the latter department I have been somewhat less than successful in recent times."

"Other than your sartorial shortcomings, I presume there is another matter that you wish to bring to our attention." Holmes further demonstrated his increasing impatience by jumping up from his chair and finally putting a light to his pipe.

"Of course there is, Mr. Holmes, for I shouldn't presume upon your generosity, I assure you. It is the matter of one of my fellows that I wish to set before you – the duplicity of his behaviour and the institution known as the Paradol Chamber."

"Excuse me," I asked in some puzzlement with my pencil poised. "Did you say the *Paradol Chamber*?"

"Yes indeed, Doctor Watson, and it is no surprise to me that you are ignorant of its existence. Indeed, even amongst my fellows, there is little enough known of the place, and that which is known is viewed with abhorrence by all true Mendicants. As I mentioned, Mendicants, regardless of the order to which they belong, resolve to shun the acquisition of wealth or property of value of any sort. We beg as a means of sustaining ourselves, and to help us travel from town to town in the hope that we might persuade others to embrace their inner compassion and kindness.

"The Paradol Chamber is the antithesis of everything that a Mendicant believes in and stands for. The chamber is nothing less than a meeting place for an absurd institution known as The Amateur Mendicant Society, who gather in an obscenely luxurious club deep within the lower vaults of Caldecott's furniture warehouse."

73

"Good Lord!" I exclaimed. "A paradox indeed."

"Yet, despite the undoubtedly outlandish nature of this institution, I have yet to hear of a crime that may have been committed, nor of a puzzle for me to solve." Holmes's thin lips almost spat out his irritation with a grimace of exasperation.

"Indeed not, Mr. Holmes, for I am yet to make mention of it. However, when you consider that members of our order shy away from the accumulation of wealth, or anything that isn't a necessity of life, you might understand why my curiosity as to the nature of this chamber had been aroused. I found the luxury on display there absolutely abhorrent to my principles, and I couldn't help but wonder as to the true meaning behind the society.

"Rich silks adorned the furnishings. Every vessel, whether for food or drink, seemed to be made of precious metals, and the walls were covered with valuable works of art. Amongst these there stood out a medieval engraving, '*The Three Mendicants*', that has assumed an almost mythical quality amongst my fellow mendicants, for we weren't even certain of its existence. Clearly, the members of this society were unlike any Mendicants that I had ever heard of, and I could only assume that the former owners of these riches had been duped into believing that they had contributed their possessions to a worthwhile cause.

"I was determined to discover the instigator of so abhorrent an institution, and the reason behind an accumulation of such treasures. I was concerned that, should the existence of such a place become public knowledge, the very notion of Mendicants would lose credibility, leaving those worthy of alms going without, and all of us left tainted by the same soiled brush."

"Therefore," Holmes stated, "you have concluded that this society has no connection to your fellow mendicants other than its name."

"Exactly, Mr. Holmes. My inquiries of the members yielded nothing. Some appeared to have been embarrassed by their presence there, while others responded to my inquiries as if they were in fear of their lives. In any event, I learned very little from my visit, and decided to broaden my quest to the offices of Caldecott's themselves.

"I had assumed that a firm that would so charitably donate part of its premises for the use of a mendicant society would deal fairly with my inquiries also, but in this I was sadly mistaken. A single glance in my direction provoked a most hostile response from the uniformed porters at the building's reception, and I was soon shown to the door in a most roughshod fashion. I was thrown to the ground outside, and the warnings against my ever returning to the place were still ringing in my ears as I went upon my way."

"Mister Daws," Holmes noted, "you have still to explain by what means you became privy to the inner sanctum of such a society."

"I wish that I hadn't have been, but I fell into a chance conversation with an old friend of mine earlier that day, Michael Elliot, who admitted to being a member of the society. He proposed a visit, and I must admit that I was lured to the place, not just by virtue of my curiosity, but I found the prospect of some dry and warm surroundings to be rather appealing. However, little could I have suspected what I was going to find there."

"Quite understandably," I agreed, but Holmes dismissed me impatiently.

"You mentioned the duplicity of your friend Michael Elliot, but there is more, I am certain, for you seem to attach a significance to the engraving that probably far exceeds your appreciation of its artistic merits." Holmes proposed.

"I know nothing of art, Mr. Holmes, but I can assure you that one of the Mendicants in the engraving bears more than a just a striking resemblance to my friend, Michael Elliot."

"In all likelihood, a mere coincidence, I suspect, and still no indication of any wrongdoing." However, Holmes's manner had now evolved from that of impatience to one of intrigue as he doubtless sensed that we had finally arrived at the crux of the matter.

"When I told him of my intention to call upon the offices of Caldecott's, Elliot and I had parted ways at the chamber. From that moment to now, Elliot has neither been seen nor heard of."

"No doubt," Holmes suggested, "you returned to the chamber, in order to persuade him to leave that place with you?"

"Indeed I did, and yet there wasn't a single soul there who would even acknowledge his existence, much less reveal his current location. It wasn't as if he had simply disappeared, for as far as the other mendicants were concerned, he had never even been there."

Finally, Holmes's tired grey eyes exploded with the fire of excitement, and he strode over to the window, as if seeking some inspiration from the bright night sky.

"You have done well in bringing this matter before me, although I will not make you any promises as to your friend's well-being without my having accrued some further information. Presuming that, like yourself, Elliot was of no fixed abode, it might be useful to my inquiries if you can recall where you first came upon him earlier that day."

"Why, indeed I do, Mr. Holmes. At this time of year, and especially after a bumper harvest, many of us congregate around the vegetable market at Convent Garden, where we find the costermongers to be of a most generous disposition with their unseasonal green fruit."

"Then that is where I shall begin my search," Holmes declared. "Where might you be found, should I have any news to impart?"

Daws smiled ironically.

"Perhaps it might be for the best if I were to pass 'round in a few days – with your permission of course."

Holmes seemed oblivious to our guest's question, so I answered for him as I led the fellow to the door.

"By all means, and hopefully we might have some good news regarding the whereabouts of your friend."

I raced back up the stairs in anticipation of hearing Holmes's initial theory, but to my surprise, my friend was nowhere to be seen. The mystery was soon solved however, when a cacophony of chaotic and agitated sounds began to echo out from the other side of his bedroom door. A moment later, Holmes emerged once more, and he was sporting a most startling transformation.

"Good Heavens!" I exclaimed. "It's perfect." For standing there before me was as good a depiction of a modern-day mendicant as one could possibly imagine. From the tightly trimmed ochre-coloured beard to the gnarled old walking cane, Holmes was unrecognisable to anyone who knew him. He laughed out loud when he observed the look of wonderment upon my face.

"So, Watson, I presume that I shouldn't look too out of place amongst my fellow mendicants when I arrive at Convent Garden?" he asked rhetorically.

"Indeed not, for I can barely recognise you myself. However, I fear that in your absence, I am to be deemed redundant once again, awaiting anxiously for your safe return, and perhaps a new set of instructions." For that had been my fate on so many previous and similar occasions.

"Not at all old friend," Holmes pronounced, "for right now there is too much to be done and little enough time for such idleness. I need to learn as much as I can about the engraving of '*The Three Mendicants*'. With that in mind, when I strike out for the Garden in the morning, I charge you to pay a visit to the offices of Caldecott's, there to discover the true significance of that ancient depiction."

"Of course I shall," I agreed, and then I went upstairs to my room with a stir of excitement in my step.

"Watson!" Holmes called towards me as he departed. "The journey begins!"

Although disappointed, I wasn't entirely surprised the next morning when Holmes decided that our breakfast was an unnecessary impediment to an early departure. My friend's disguise was once again fully in place even before I arose, and it was all that I could do to persuade him to partake of some coffee and a slice of toast before we went our separate ways. While Holmes embarked on his clandestine journey to Convent Garden, I made my way to Shad Thames in Bermondsey to learn what I might.

It was rather convenient when I discovered that Caldecott's offices were barely a ten-minute walk from the warehouse itself, right there in the centre of London's docklands, and in the midst of countless other similar establishments. Even at that early hour, the streets and alleyways that crisscrossed their way towards the edge of the river were positively teeming, not only with dockhands and barrowmen, but also the merchants and traders in their dark suits and high, shiny hats.

The cacophony of sights and sounds that greeted the uninitiated had been almost overwhelming, and it was several minutes after I alighted from my cab before I put the purpose for my journey into motion. I could barely hear the directions that I had been given by a passing tradesman above the constant hubbub, and as I slowly made my way towards the banks of the Thames, the roads became ever narrower, and I found myself being harried and jostled at every turn.

Therefore, it was with some relief that I finally found myself outside the offices of *"Caldecott's, Purveyors of Fine and Distinctive Furniture"*. I dusted myself down and straightened my tie and jacket before climbing the steps towards the rather unremarkable, red-bricked office building. Once inside, I found that the early morning excitement of a new working day was somewhat fortunate for my purposes. After all, in the middle of such enterprise, who would notice someone entering the building so unobtrusively.

Once I began to feel more comfortable in my surroundings and assuming the identity of a dealer in ancient art, I made a few discreet inquiries as to the location of the Paradol Chamber, and the possibility of viewing the antique engraving. However, I was only met with blank looks and shaking heads, and before long I realised that I had been attracting the unwanted attention of the uniformed porters that Daws had previously described. I decided to beat a calm but hasty retreat and I turned to leave, feeling disappointed that I would have nothing positive to report upon my return to Baker Street. I had reached the door and was about to step outside when a voice rang out cheerily behind me.

"Watson? John Watson? Surely not, after all these years!" The voice wasn't familiar to me, nor did I expect to hear my name called out in an establishment that I had never before visited, nor expected to visit again any time in the future. Yet there it was, and I turned around slowly to see if I recognised its source.

Unexpectedly, the man waving towards me was indeed vaguely familiar to me. He was quite tall and lean of build, and his cheery countenance was topped with a thin and wispy clump of red hair that seemed to be fighting for its very survival. He appeared to be of a similar age to myself, and he was dressed in a gabardine business suit that had clearly been tailored well. He was undoubtedly beckoning for me to join him, and my natural curiosity, not to mention a desire to avoid behaving in any way suspiciously, overruled my previous efforts at maintaining anonymity.

I followed the fellow down a series of quiet and labyrinthine corridors before he finally opened the door to an impressive, wood-lined office, into which he invited me. He closed the door behind us, but not before he had dispatched a young lady for a tray of coffee and cakes, a gesture for which I was grateful indeed. He indicated a chair opposite to his own and he was smiling excitedly at the prospect of entertaining me.

"Now come along, Watson. You must recognise me by now, or has my appearance altered so horrendously that my identity still escapes you?" He asked mischievously, but fortunately our tray of tea and cakes arrived most promptly and I was saved from my embarrassment for a moment or two longer.

The refreshments were excellent and once the last morsel had been consumed, I lit a cigarette and studied my host with a greater intensity. Taking into account the size of the office and the man's aura of authority, his name should have been obvious to me from the outset. Then as I thought back to my time at St. Bartholomew's, my reasoning was confirmed.

"Forgive my feeble memory," I declared, with an excitement that was probably a little too exaggerated for the sake of politeness. "You are undoubtedly Thomas Caldecott from our time together at Barts." Fortunately, Caldecott had a sense of humour and laughed at my discomfort with not a hint of resentment.

"My goodness, Watson, it has been a long time, and much has transpired since then. Apart from the moustache, your appearance has altered not a jot, whereas even I sometimes fail to recognise myself in the mirror! Now please explain how you came to be an intimate associate of the celebrated Mr. Sherlock Holmes and involved in those intriguing adventures that I have heard so much about."

Feeling somewhat awkward at receiving these gushing compliments, I proceeded to explain the circumstances of my first meeting with Holmes and especially the role that Stamford, our former colleague at Barts, had played in bringing about our association. Naturally enough, the very mention of Stamford's name precipitated a lengthy period of reminiscing that consumed more time than either of us could have thought possible.

"As I recall," I said thoughtfully, "despite your undoubted talent, your heart was never really set upon a career in medicine. You always seemed to have been of a more spiritual bent than the rest of us."

"You remember correctly, and my chosen path was always a big disappointment to my family. Indeed, they even threatened to cut off my allowance and refused to sanction or subsidise my path to the cloth. Therefore, I decided to make my own way in the world and consequently I embarked upon the life of a Mendicant." He made this statement in a challenging manner that implied my ignorance of such things.

However, he became most intrigued and then enraged when I told him of our recent introduction to the affairs of The Amateur Mendicant Society and the apparent corruption of the Paradol Chamber.

Caldecott leapt up from his chair and brandished a large cigar in front of him before lighting it by the window.

"I was finally summoned from my life on the road with the news of the premature demise of my father. Despite the acrimonious nature of our last meeting and the resentment that I had been harbouring these many years, I decided to attend my father's funeral. It was at the subsequent wake that my elderly and infirm Uncle Timothy implored me to take up the reigns of the family business in my father's stead. He explained that should I not, the entire enterprise would have to fold, and he outlined in chilling detail the dire consequences to the remainder of the family, were I refuse to do so.

"It was with great reluctance that I accepted my uncle's commission, having felt obliged to protect the rest of my family from the effects of the company failing. Nevertheless, I refused to sever my links with my fellow mendicants entirely, and I donated a large vacant chamber, deep within the lower reaches of our warehouse, for their use and shelter during the harshest of times. To now discover that my generosity has been betrayed in such a manner saddens me greatly," he concluded glumly.

Caldecott finally lit his cigar and stared out through the window, evidently lost in deep thought. When he finally turned back towards me, he seemed to be suddenly resolved and determined.

"Watson, would you oblige me and come down to the chamber to see how matters really stand?" Caldecott implored me with an eagerness that I found hard to resist. "After all, we only really have the word of a random stranger to go by, and his interpretation of what he saw might be questionable at the very least."

Nevertheless, I also needed to consider the effect that my visit to the chamber might have upon Holmes's investigations. After all, although not the most illustrious client that we had ever had, that was indeed the status of Mr. Cuthbert Daws, and he had entrusted Holmes and me with his inquiries. Furthermore, I had not even gained any further knowledge as to the significance of the ancient engraving that seemed to be at the core of the mystery, so enwrapped had I been at the thought of visiting the chamber before Holmes.

"By all means old fellow!" I found myself replying, despite feeling as if I had suddenly betrayed both Holmes and Daws. This simply wouldn't stand with me.

"Before we depart, would you mind explaining to me the significance of the medieval engraving, entitled '*The Three Mendicants*' and how it came to be in your possession?" I asked.

Caldecott eyed me quizzically before breaking into a sarcastic laugh.

"My possession? Oh Watson, your years in association with Sherlock Holmes have certainly imbued you with a most vivid imagination! The engraving is so steeped in legend and fancy that even its very existence is held in doubt. Even were it to exist, I am quite certain that its value would place it way beyond my humble means. But look at the time. You must be famished! Will you now allow me to treat you to a late lunch before we visit the chamber? We pass an excellent fish restaurant on the way, if that is to your taste?"

I agreed at once, and after Caldecott had left a note for his secretary to explain his absence, we struck out. My companion's assessment of the restaurant had been accurate indeed and, after an excellent platter of halibut and vegetables, not to mention a glass or two of Chablis, we finally set off for the Paradol Chamber.

By now of course it had become quite dark, and a fine veil of mist had risen from the Thames which was slowly caressing the surrounding streets with its chill and murky embrace. The streets had suddenly emptied of traders, and the subsequent silence, together with the moisture on the ground, caused our footfall to create a resounding and self-conscious echo with every step. Mercifully, the Caldecott warehouse was but a short way from their offices, and it wasn't long before Caldecott was fumbling in his pockets for his keys.

The building itself was entirely unremarkable, although the pale shadowy gaslights dimly illuminated the outlines of vast stacks of furniture as we moved slowly through the upper floor. It was only when we began the descent to the lower floor that a thrill of excitement ran through me, at the thought of finally entering the mysterious Paradol Chamber. The dark stairway was unusually damp, and I found the steps to be steep and treacherous.

80

In contrast, my companion didn't hesitate even for a second, as if he was far more familiar with his surroundings than I had assumed, and he only paused long enough for me to be able to catch up with him. Once we had finally reached the lower level, Caldecott produced yet another key and he slowly opened the heavy oak door with little effort.

"Doctor Watson, may I proudly present to you the infamous Parodol Chamber!" Caldecott pronounced this with a sinister tone that I hadn't noticed previously and of which I wouldn't have thought him capable.

I began to regret having left my army revolver in the drawer at home and I felt exposed as if I was in mortal danger. Too late, I realised that Caldecott had been progressing through the building with more confidence than someone who barely knew of the chamber's existence, much less its security measures.

My instincts were soon validated and confirmed as two pairs of strong and unseen hands suddenly reached out from the dark and grasped my wrists as if they had been gripped in a vise! These hands certainly didn't belong to Caldecott, and two large shadows slowly emerged from the gloom as his trap was violently sprung.

I realised the true nature of the note that Caldecott had left behind upon his office desk and the reason behind our protracted late supper. I knew now that my host was determined to shroud the dark secrets contained within the chamber by any conceivable means, and I was certain that they didn't bode well for me. I was powerless to prevent my wrists from being bound together by some strong, coarse cord, and I was dragged across the room to a set of metal rings, set into a wall and to which the cord was then secured.

The gas was still low, which prevented me from seeing the various treasures contained within this vast room, but not so dim that I couldn't make out the features of the man standing immediately in front of me.

"You know, it is a great pity that you have allowed your association with Mr. Sherlock Holmes to cause you to interfere with my affairs. After all these years, it would have been nice to have had the chance for us to be really reacquainted. Instead of which, we will now have to bid each other a rather hasty and premature farewell. However, before we reach that tragic moment, I need to know exactly how much you have found out about the chamber and, more importantly, how much Mr. Holmes has ascertained!"

"If you retain even the scantest of memories of my nature and my sense of honour," I replied emphatically, "you should know that I would never betray my friend and his findings, even had I been privy to them, which I am not! Remember," I said defiantly, "I have fought in some of the fiercest battles of recent memory and witnessed death in its many and horrific forms, so any danger with which you might threaten me now pales into insignificance!"

"Bravo, Doctor," Caldecott replied with a malicious laugh, "although I'm certain that none of the dangers that you have previously faced were anticipated with the absolute certainty of that which will now befall you."

"You will learn nothing from me." As I spat out these last words of defiance, Caldecott's men moved menacingly closer, and I began to struggle vainly against my immovable constraints. I could feel the warmth of blood on my wrists as I tried to force my hands from their shackles.

I braced myself for the inevitable blows that these ruffians had intended for me, when Caldecott suddenly called these proceedings to an unexpected but welcome halt.

"I think that my interests would be best served if you were to spend a night of silent and uncomfortable contemplation," Caldecott sneered. "Maybe by the morning you will have realised the futility of any further resistance and then comply with my wishes without the need of any violence. I suppose I owe you that much consideration." He then had his men loosen my bonds slightly, so that I could at least seat myself during the long and arduous hours that undoubtedly lay ahead of me. Then, by way of a precursor of what might lay in store for me in the morning, Caldecott swung his left boot into my ribs without warning, and the resulting pain told me that at least one of them had been cracked. I uttered not a sound, despite the intense discomfort of the blow, and glared defiantly up at my captor as he began to take his leave.

"Have a good night, Watson, and should you by any chance manage a few minutes sleep, I am certain that my little warning will weigh heavily upon your dreams." His manic and high-pitched laughter echoed around the chamber while he closed the heavy door resoundingly behind him as he and his men left the room. The lights were turned down and I was left incarcerated within a whirlpool of complete and absolute darkness.

I waited for my eyes to adjust, but in vain, and I soon realised that, with my watch invisible and no celestial bodies to indicate the passage of time, the length of my incarceration would be indeterminable and desolate. In an effort to afford myself some degree of relative support and comfort, I flattened my back and neck against the wall behind me. In doing so, I fought against the metal restraints, which created further discomfort around my wrists.

I soon realised the futility of any further efforts at movement and then sank into a dark reverie from which there was no consolation. Gradually the chill of my mausoleum began to intensify and penetrate my muscles, and of course my broken ribs. The pain became hard to bear, and my only form of distraction was to speculate as to my fate on the following morning. Eventually, I suppose, the sheer weight of my exhaustion began to obliterate my discomfort and I sank into a form of unconsciousness that must have been my body's only way of helping me shut out the pain and the hopelessness of my situation.

In any event, the sound of the chamber door finally reopening roused me from my self-induced state of anaesthesia. Mercifully, the lights had only been dimly reignited, but even then, my eyes struggled to readjust. Slowly, however, I began to recognise the three familiar and menacing shapes standing over me from the night before. Caldecott's voice, which had been so friendly and welcoming at the outset, now sent a chill of repugnance through me and I braced myself for the worst. There was something almost demonic about his shrill and coarse peals of laughter.

"Good morning, Doctor Watson!" he cackled. "I trust that you have enjoyed my hospitality, and that you have spent a warm and comfortable night?"

I responded with a series of mumbled words of anger and discontent, and Caldecott's men loosened my bonds so that I could be dragged unceremoniously back up and on to my feet. Obviously, after having spent so many hours in the same position, my legs proved to be unresponsive, and my three captors were amused by the sight of me slowly folding back on to the floor. I rubbed and shook my legs repeatedly until I could finally make it to my feet under my own volition.

"I trust that those many hours of silent contemplation have caused you to reconsider your unenviable situation, and that you will now cooperate a little more willingly?" The smile and laughter had now vanished suddenly, and Caldecott now considered me with a confident and threatening glare.

"I am sorry to disappoint you," I said defiantly, "but you will have to do your worst."

"Oh, I will, Doctor! I certainly will!" At this, his men moved towards me with their enormous fists fully clenched.

However, at the very moment that the first blow was about to be struck, and to everyone's great surprise, the lights were suddenly turned up fully by an unseen hand and an urgent though familiar voice echoed around the room from the depths of its darkest shadows.

"Now, Lestrade!" the voice called out stridently, and in an instant, two of Scotland Yard's finest stepped smartly forward and snapped two sets of handcuffs upon the wrists of Caldecott's ruffians.

Simultaneously, Inspector Lestrade levelled his revolver to the head of my former colleague, and Sherlock Holmes rushed over to undo my bonds.

"Oh, my dear fellow!" Holmes said with a genuine and heart-warming concern in his voice. "I apologise profusely for allowing matters to have progressed to this sorry pass. I trust that there has been no real harm done?"

He suddenly noticed my blood-stained shirt cuffs, "Watson, you have sustained injury!"

"I am afraid that my ribs have felt better in their time as well. It would be advisable if you were to exclude me from any physical work for a while – although I am a speedy healer." I added positively.

"You must tell me how I might best aid your recovery." Holmes offered.

"Well, a full and detailed explanation for today's events wouldn't entirely go amiss."

"Of course, old friend," Holmes smiled, "but not until we have returned to the comfort of our rooms and furnished ourselves with a liberal glass of your favourite Cognac."

"If I might be so bold as to interrupt this touching scene." Caldecott sneered with disdain. "Undoubtedly this must be the celebrated Mr. Sherlock Holmes. You have worked the thing very well and, might I say, in a most timely fashion. Had you not, Heaven knows what your friend might have been subjected to, for the sake of his loyalty to you. I suppose you now expect me to come along quietly with you, but I trust not before you have informed me of the crime with which you intend to charge me?" Caldecott appeared to have accepted his plight with a surprising air of calm, as if he had no fear of his impending fate.

"I would have thought that your crime is fairly obvious." Lestrade responded with disdain as he pointed towards the instruments of my restraint upon the wall.

Caldecott laughed uproariously as his wrists were being secured with a set of cuffs.

"I think that Mr. Sherlock Holmes has other plans for me, do you not?"

My friend stared at the former mendicant for what seemed to be an age, as if he couldn't understand the cause of Caldecott's merriment. He smiled maliciously at my friend and Holmes's features contorted into a fit of rage, the like of which I had never before seen upon him.

"Inspector Lestrade, if you can entrust your men to safely deposit these three creatures in your most secure of cells, you are invited to join us at 221b, where I shall construct a case of murder for you that will make the courts ring!"

The smile suddenly drained from Caldecott's face.

"For whose murder am I to be accused?" Caldecott asked nervously.

"None other than the true custodian of the sacred engraving known as '*The Three Mendicants*' – namely Mister Michael Elliot!"

At these words, Lestrade nodded to his men that they take up and act upon Holmes's suggestion and as Caldecott and his men were being led from the building, Caldecott let up an incessant cry.

"Mister Holmes, you have committed the gravest error of your career! Farewell, Sherlock Holmes!"

Although Caldecott's rantings sent a shiver of apprehension through me, Holmes managed to ignore this display of hysteria, and he offered me his shoulder to lean upon as we made our long and, in my case, agonising climb back up to the street and a waiting cab.

By the time that we had returned to Baker Street, the sun was fully risen, and it bathed the street in the warm mellow glow of a mild autumn morning. Despite these conditions, however, my night of discomfort and deprivation had left me in a cold and depleted state, and I allowed myself the doting attentions of our landlady, Mrs. Hudson.

I steadfastly declined my bed, so intent was I of hearing every word of Holmes's explanation, but I did wholeheartedly accept a hot pot of tea, Holmes's glass of cognac, and the indulgence of a stoked-up fire. Thus, with a warm woollen blanket flung across my shoulders, I entrusted Lestrade's notebook and pen with the task of recording Holmes's every word, while I hung on to each one.

Lestrade and I stared at my friend intently and expectantly, even while he went about the task of cleaning, filling, and lighting his pipe. He then sat down, rather uncomfortably it seemed, upon the edge of the window-sill and gazed down upon his beloved Baker Street as he spoke.

"You see, Watson, I had the advantage of you from the very outset of this sordid business, and you Lestrade, although to a lesser extent, because of the various delicate tendrils that I have set to the task of bringing me any news from the back streets of our great city that might be of significance.

"Consequently, word of a dark and insidious felon who has inveigled his way into the highest echelons of society and goes by the moniker of 'The Collector' has been brought to my attention, by means of rumours and whispers."

Holmes paused long enough to take a slow and luxuriant pull upon his pipe.

"'The Collector'?" I queried during this brief interval. "In Heaven's name, what exactly does he collect?"

"Anything that is of value to him and the success of his grotesque schemes. *Objets d'art* – and people! Oh yes, he accumulates people in the same way that a philatelist might collect stamps. He will stop at nothing in the pursuit and acquisition of his treasure, including the vilest crime of all. Don't feel put out or excluded, for Lestrade has only been made aware of this villainy in the last twenty-four hours or so, and I can assure you that we would have been no closer to the apprehension of this 'Collector' and his cohorts had it not been for your timely, albeit unwitting and painful, intervention."

I fingered my damaged ribs and wrists tentatively before issuing my bitter response.

"Well, I'm glad to hear that my ordeal hasn't been entirely in vain."

"No, not at all. Your previous association with Thomas Caldecott has proved to be invaluable." Holmes appeared to have been oblivious to my heavy sarcasm and smiled at me through a plume of smoke.

He turned away from us again and resumed his surveillance of the street below. A thick grey veil of mist had drifted into view by now and Holmes's sharp profile became accentuated by the silhouette effect of the fog.

"Would you mind explaining to me the connection between Thomas Caldecott and 'The Collector'?"

"Is it not yet obvious to you?"

I didn't have to consider Holmes's question for long, and Lestrade's knowing demeanour confirmed my shocking conclusion.

"So, how did this awful character degradation occur?" I asked with an air of resignation and melancholy.

"The deeper roots of his depravity were probably always a part of his nature, although the trigger for its manifestation doubtless occurred during his time on the streets. Remember, his family had ostracised him, and the sights and sounds of the suffering that he had encountered, once he had left behind him the comforts of his family home, had left him a bitter man."

"Excuse me, Mr. Holmes," Lestrade observed, "but for the life of me, I don't understand how you have come to have such deep insights into the man's character."

Holmes smiled mischievously.

"Ah, but you see, Lestrade, I do not. As Watson here would undoubtedly attest, I have long propounded the maxim that there is no greater font of local knowledge than the patrons of a public house. Well, I can tell you now that I would undoubtedly extend that to those who frequent the markets of Convent Garden. My simple disguise soon ingratiated me with many of those worthies, and once I had mentioned the names of Caldecott and Michael Elliot, I began to receive more information than even I could possibly assimilate.

"Caldecott soon realised that the life of a true mendicant wasn't for him, and he began to build up a network of donors exclusively from the wealthiest of classes. Consequently, once he had discovered the parlous financial condition of the family business, it was to these select few that he turned for help. In exchange for their donations, Caldecott opened up the Paradol Chamber under the guise of The Amateur Mendicant Society, but in reality, it served as a private club for the use of those who had no other refuge in which to practise and indulge in their various depravities.

"To add to the chamber's allure, and in order to satisfy his own obsession with such things, Caldecott decorated the place with fine works of art and all manner of objects that enhanced the opulence and decadence of the place. He contracted the collector's disease in its most virulent form, and he would go to any length in appropriating an object that took his fancy.

"Tragically, his obsession extended to the sacred, medieval engraving known as '*The Three Mendicants*'."

"Why do you say 'tragically'?" Lestrade asked quietly.

"Our initial brief, if you recall, was to locate Mr. Michael Elliot on behalf of our client, Cuthbert Daws. Down the centuries, '*The Three Mendicants*' has assumed the status of being something of a sacred relic within the order of mendicants, and with each passing generation an individual who is thought worthy of such a responsibility has been entrusted with its care. In recent times, the task of being the custodian of this holy engraving fell upon the head of the unfortunate Michael Elliot.

"A harmless man of peace wasn't going to stand in the way of an obsessional collector like Caldecott, and I am afraid that Cuthbert Daws will see his friend no more." Clearly imparting this sad news had been no easy task for my friend, and we all sat in a melancholy silence while Holmes continued to smoke by the window.

Lestrade proved to be the first one of us to break this silence.

"Well, I must say, Mr. Holmes," the inspector exclaimed, "that you have constructed a very fine case, though unfortunately comprised of nothing more than hearsay and theories. After all, we don't even have a body!"

I couldn't disagree with the man from Scotland Yard, and I now realised why Caldecott had appeared to be so confident when he was being lad away, and I told Holmes so.

"Ah, but once again, you have committed the most craven sin of all – that of assumption." From his desk drawer, Holmes produced his tool kit of ill repute, by way of explaining how he had gained access to the warehouse building without an invitation.

"I found myself with a little time before Caldecott's return, and came across an interesting anomaly in the lower floor – namely that this room was somewhat warmer than the rest of the building. I thought it strange, that on so mild an October day, there should have been a small residue of smoke still escaping from the chimney. On closer examination, I discovered that the furnace had been put to recent use. Not so recent, however, that I couldn't examine its contents without discomfort. There was no mistaking every indication of charred human remains, but though these were obviously unidentifiable, I also found this neck chain." Holmes produced this unremarkable object from his jacket pocket with the flourish and aplomb of a magician who had concluded an impossible illusion.

Holmes passed the chain to Lestrade, and I in turn and there had been no mistaking the initials engraved there – namely: $M E$.

"Good Heavens!" I exclaimed superfluously. "Michael Elliot!"

"Exactly," Holmes smiled, "and no one, other than your old friend and his bag of tools, could have possibly gained access to the warehouse other than its owner with his set of keys. Inspector Lestrade, I think that you would now agree that you have your case?"

"Oh, indeed, Mr. Holmes, and I am mighty glad to have such a devil behind the bars that will hold him until his inevitable date with the gallows. Although I shouldn't approve of such things, I shall certainly turn a blind eye to your own bag of tools, Or at least on this occasion," the inspector added furtively.

Holmes locked his tools away securely before producing a small rectangular object wrapped in brown paper.

"Now, I am expecting another guest." Holmes smiled at the look of confusion upon our faces, just as we heard the sound of a gentle rap upon our door.

"Gentlemen, might I present to you the new custodian of '*The Three Mendicants*' – namely Mister Cuthbert Daws!"

The unassuming man was clearly overwhelmed by Holmes's hullabaloo as he shuffled over to receive his sacred charge.

The year '87 furnished us with a long series of cases of greater or less interest, of which I retain the records. Among my headings under this one twelve months, I find an account of the adventure of the Paradol Chamber, of the Amateur Mendicant Society, who held a luxurious club in the lower vault of a furniture warehouse . . . .

– Dr. John H. Watson
The Five Orange Pips

The Difficult Ordeal
of the Paradol Chamber
by Will Murray

Letters sometimes come to Sherlock Holmes at Baker Street at all hours of the day, the London postal system constituting a regular rotation in which the postman may drop off as many as six deliveries on a single date.

While I don't keep track of such things, I have found in my association with Holmes that the afternoon mail is the most productive of unusual cases. Perhaps this is because letters written in the morning and swiftly posted in and around London tend to arrive by mid-afternoon. Those who seek to consult with Holmes often sleep on the prospect and write their letters the following morning. Hence, the preponderance of appeals arriving in the afternoon. At least, that is my belief.

On this particular afternoon at three o'clock, Holmes returned from an errand to discover the postal pile that Mrs. Hudson had left on the great table in our shared sitting room. Holmes gathered up his lot, but didn't open anything until he was comfortably seated by the cold hearth, and was smoking his familiar black clay pipe. A letter opener made short work of various envelopes, and he shook out the contents, referring to them one by one.

I paid this activity no heed, knowing that if anything was of significant moment, he would share it with me. This he did with the contents of the final envelope.

"Watson, I have received the most intriguing appeal from the Coroner of the town of Bristol."

"From the coroner, you say?"

"His name is Haversham. He writes with the approval of his superiors, which include an Inspector Wallace. The Bristol police force is exceedingly puzzled by a corpse that was brought to their attention."

I took out a cigarette and brought it to flame. "Do they not know the identity of the corpse?"

"No, they do not. But that isn't what is uppermost in their minds. The body was found in a wood not far from the town brewery – and it appeared to have been soaked in ale. Inquiries made at the brewery have produced no positive results. The man wasn't an employee. Nor was he known to any of the people associated with the establishment."

"That is odd," I remarked.

"Quite odd," agreed Holmes. "Additionally, the coroner has noticed numerous contusions on the man's hands, as well as other wounds and problematic features. Taken all together, he can make nothing of them. Even the cause of death eludes him."

"Could the poor fellow have drowned in a vat of ale?"

"The coroner doesn't appear to have ruled this out, but according to this appeal, he hasn't arrived at any conclusions, other than the obvious fact that the unidentified man is deceased. Hence, he has asked me to come 'round and lend a hand. He's offering a tidy sum on behalf of the town if I will do so."

"I take it that you're going to accept this commission?"

"How can I do otherwise? My purse has grown slim, and I'm a trifle bored with London life. I suggest that you accompany me. Your medical insight will no doubt prove valuable."

"More valuable than that of the county coroner?" I scoffed. "I rather doubt it."

"Oh, but where he has his fund of experience, you have an altogether different one. You have been my companion in numerous investigations over several years now, and you've learned to think outside of the ordinary, even if your thinking is sometimes superficial. At least you aren't bound by the conventions of a man whose livelihood involves performing the ordinary autopsy."

"I'll shall take that as a compliment," I stated.

"I would be pleased if you did. I make no bones about the fact that you, like so many others, often don't correctly perceive the obvious. That is a limitation you share with perhaps ninety-five percent of Britons. I wouldn't call it a fault. To me, perhaps it is an advantage in that this is how the common humanity thinks, for if everyone applied my methods, there would be no need for my consultancy, would there?"

I laughed. "No, I suppose that there wouldn't. When do you intend to depart for Bristol?"

"As soon as you are prepared to do so," rejoined Holmes, "for I'm ready to leave on a moment's notice."

"Permit me to fetch my medical kit," said I, and then went off to do that exact thing.

Two hours later, we were on a train to Bristol. Holmes had brought the letter, and I read it during the journey. It was rather long, and I will spare the reader the dull details, for the greater portion was given over to the coroner's befuddlement.

Folding the note and handing it back to Holmes, I admitted, "I don't take very much from this, scant as it is. I cannot tell if the man drowned in

91

ale, or was merely soaked in it prior to or following his demise. The other details, the abrasions and contusions, don't suggest anything revealing to me."

Holmes nodded, pocketing the note. "I must reserve judgment as well, but on the face of it, and from the descriptive elements, I lean in the direction of the unfortunate man injuring himself attempting to escape confinement."

"This is plausible. I'll not attempt to trump it. But I don't understand how and why the body became soaked in ale."

"There," replied Holmes in a measured tone, "I'll not venture any suppositions until I have examined the corpse. I might mention that in order to avoid damaging any pertinent clues, I wrote Haversham and asked that no autopsy be performed until after I had conduced my own investigation."

That was the extent of our discussion. We smoked in silence, and ultimately our journey concluded in Bristol. Hiring a cab, we were conveyed to the local mortuary. Dr. Haversham was pleased to see us, Holmes having telegraphed his intentions from London. He was a surprisingly jolly sort whose round face was half-enveloped in muttonchop whiskers the color of rust.

"My dear Mr. Holmes!" he said excitedly. "I am quite delighted to meet you. Moreover, I hope your presence will lift a tremendous burden from my soul. I would like to surrender this man's body to his proper relatives for Christian burial, but I am at another loss, for I cannot release it until we determine that no foul play was involved."

"Foul play was almost assuredly involved," suggested Holmes. "As I understand the known circumstances, the man was found in a field. He is unlikely to have deposited himself there to die, especially soaked in ale. I would think the body was dumped there, and if that is the case, the circumstances warrant investigation. They cannot be innocuous."

"Oh, I quite agree. I simply haven't advanced beyond the obvious. Nor do I wish to jump to conclusions."

"Neither do I," allowed Holmes. "But certain things are inescapable. Bodies don't fall from the sky. Nor do they claw their way up from the cold clay. It's abundantly clear that this man didn't perish on the spot in which he was discovered. Some person or persons placed him there. This is inescapable. Now, if you would be so kind to conduct us to the deceased, we'll begin our examination, for I've brought Dr. Watson with me in order to provide his professional opinion."

"Very good," said Haversham.

As soon as we entered the coolness of the room, my nose told me that the corpse was indeed redolent of stale ale. In anticipation of our arrival, the body was laid out on a porcelain table, covered in a crisp white sheet. To begin with, Haversham removed the sheet from the head down to the dead man's waist. It was immediately evident that, in accordance with Sherlock Holmes's request, no autopsy had taken place.

Holmes and I gathered around and I could see that this was a man of lean proportions, conceivably weighing but seven stone in life. His hair atop his narrow skull was a discolored ash shade and lay plastered to his skull, still moist with ale, even now.

Holmes examined the features. First, they appeared to have been rubbed raw, though by which agency it was difficult to tell. The chest didn't appear injured in any way. Holmes went to the right hand, lifted it, and turned it by the wrist while we regarded the man's fingers and open palm. Various scrapings and abrasions came to light. I noted that his fingernails were cracked and broken, and the surrounding skin was raw.

"Watson, if you would be so good as to lift his left hand to the light."

Going to the other side of the autopsy table, I did so. Similar abrasions were revealed. Here, too, the dead man's fingernails were severely damaged. One was missing entirely.

Holmes said, "In his last hours, this man appears to have been confined. If I didn't think it unlikely, for there is no soot upon him, I would have assumed that he was a held prisoner in a fireplace chimney – but I think it improbable."

"What makes you say that, Mr. Holmes?" asked Haversham.

"These contusions suggest a hard surface that isn't smooth stone. It is more like brick. If a man were to be bricked up in a chimney, rather like the fellow from Poe's dreadful 'The Cask of Amontillado', he would naturally climb upward to escape. But I don't think that was the case here."

Dropping the arm, Holmes went to the head and bent down. His narrow nose sniffed at the man's hair and said immediately, "He didn't die in the local brewery."

"How could you possibly conclude that?" asked Haversham, echoing my own thoughts.

"Quite simple. I've imbibed the products of your Bristol brewery, and even though the ale in which this man's hair was immersed has spoiled, it hasn't lost its specific aroma. This isn't the smell of that product. I don't recognize it, but I haven't sampled every brand of beer in England." Holmes smiled. "Perhaps I should remedy that. Otherwise, I might have immediately identified the brewery from which this concoction was created."

"Remarkable!" said Haversham.

"I gathered from your note that no identification was found upon this fellow."

Haversham shook his rusty whiskers vigorously. "None whatsoever."

Holmes went next to the man's boots and studied their work-worn condition. Removing his pocket knife, he opened it and began to dig the point into the junction between the boot soles and the upper leather. He removed a small bits of grit and examined these under his magnifying glass. "Yes, masonry brick. In some way, this man's demise involved brickwork."

"That scarcely narrows it down," clucked Haversham.

"Not so," said Holmes. "This is brown brick. We can safely rule out many residences, which are inclined towards red brick in their construction."

"Marvelous!" exclaimed Haversham.

"Can you tell anything about this man's occupation?" I asked, knowing that my friend was adept at deducing what an individual did from trifles that would otherwise go unnoticed.

Holmes frowned. "Under other circumstances, it would be child's play. But here, I'm afraid that any clues that might have been discernible have been eradicated in the course of this man's ordeal and immersion. From his attire, I would take him to be a tradesman of some sort. Beyond that, I cannot say, but I believe he died a very hard and difficult death, conceivably as the prisoner of some fiend."

"My word!" I exclaimed.

"All external evidence suggests this man endeavored to escape his doom, suffering numerous minor injuries in his futile attempt."

"Do you think he was jailed?" asked Haversham.

"Unlikely. Hence, my use of the term 'fiend'." Turning to me, Holmes asked, "Watson, would you agree that, despite this man's condition, he wasn't drowned?"

"I see no signs of it."

"I have all but ruled it out," added Haversham.

"Nor did he suffocate, it appears," said Holmes.

I lifted the man's eyelids, and examined his eyes. I didn't see burst capillaries.

"I will not dispute that," said I.

Haversham shook his head in agreement.

"Unless something suggests otherwise," decided Holmes, "I posit that this poor soul died of heart failure, brought on by terror created by his predicament. He knew he was doomed, and could do nothing about it, except to struggle against the obdurate environment in which he was confined."

"I cannot imagine what that could be," remarked Dr. Haversham.

"For a man's body to be fully immersed in ale," mused Holmes, "I'm inclined towards the belief that a brewery is involved, but not the brewery near which he was found. The body was obviously deposited there to throw any investigation off the correct scent."

"I can see your thinking," said Haversham. "How do you propose to get onto the proper scent?

"I'll avail myself of more bottles of stout and ale than I've ever come into contact with until I detect an odor that matches the one in which this unknown man is soaked."

Dr. Haversham looked a little taken aback. I could see in his eyes that he was suffering an acute disappointment. No doubt knowing Sherlock Holmes's reputation, he expected a miracle worker. But the miracles that Holmes wrought were often the product of the methodical application of thought, and not the result of brilliant flashes of intuition.

"Haversham, Dr. Watson and I will repair to London and further investigate this intriguing history. We shall be in touch with you in due course."

"Yes, of course. Thank you for coming to Bristol. I feel great relief knowing that you are hot on the matter."

Haversham's words were correct enough, but his disappointment was not undetectable.

Before we departed Bristol, Holmes and I paid a call at two other local breweries, where he prevailed upon the brewmasters to permit him to sample their wares. At the end of it, Holmes announced, "Watson, I'm confident that the dead man was not immersed in any local brew."

"Is this a dead end, then?" I inquired.

"Not at all, for I recognized the cut of the poor fellow's trousers as the work of a London haberdashery. This suggests to me that the body was removed from the City. Therefore, it is a London brewery that calls to us."

By late evening, we were back in Baker Street. Holmes sat ruminating in his customary chair, his black clay pipe fuming.

"Watson," he said, after getting his pipe going, "I trust that this is the result of some vendetta on the part of a vicious perpetrator who feels he has been wronged. Otherwise, I fear some maniac is at work. And if so, that ale-soaked wretch may only be the first victim of several to come."

Hearing these words, I repressed a shudder of horror.

"I pray that the latter isn't the case," I said fervently.

It was too late to go out into the night and seek refreshments in a pub, and so Holmes and I retired for the evening.

The next morning after breakfast, Holmes announced that he was going to sample as much ale as London had to offer.

"Do you not fear that you might become too inebriated before you hit upon the correct brew?"

"I have no intention of drinking any more than is necessary," returned Holmes. "I only need sniff it to locate the one that will point me in a fruitful direction. It's only a question of how long this operation will take."

With that, he was off. I knew that I could be of no use to him.

It was late that evening when Holmes returned, and there was a glow in his eyes that told me he had struck success.

He didn't speak until he had his pipe going.

"Watson, the brewery is north of London, at Ponder's End. It isn't a rare ale, but neither is it particularly popular. I've never sampled it before. Hence, my ignorance as to its aroma."

"Now that you've located the brewery, what do you intend to do?"

"I intend," replied Holmes slowly, "to sleep on the matter, for it's a delicate one – but I see no course of action other than to brave the brewery. The only question is whether or not I should take direct assault, or avail myself of subterfuge."

The following morning, I breakfasted alone. I didn't see Holmes. It appeared that he had been up before me and had gone on his way. This was very much like the industrious fellow, especially when he was on a promising scent.

Later in the day, I was in the act of returning to Baker Street from a long walk along the Strand when I all but bumped into a man I didn't recognize who was leaving as I was entering.

"Pardon me," I said, moving aside so that he could step out onto the walkway.

"No, pardon me," he returned gruffly. Without another word, he was off and on his way.

I had long before become accustomed to strangers coming and going from our shared apartments. I assumed that this was a new client who had just consulted with Holmes.

To my surprise, when I reached the first floor and stepped in through the door, Holmes wasn't in his usual chair. Looking about the flat, I saw no sign of him. Consulting with Mrs. Hudson, I asked after the man.

"Has a tradesman been by?" I wondered.

"No. Not to my certain knowledge. Have you asked Mr. Holmes?"

"He isn't in. Yet someone just left the building."

"Perhaps he left a message for Mr. Holmes."

Holmes has sometimes accused me of being rather thick – not in so many words, but the inference is that I am at times slow of wit. In my own defense, I must say this is an opinion not shared by persons of my acquaintance, and certainly not by others in my profession. But by contrast with Holmes's magnificent brain, I confess that I sometimes felt confoundedly slow.

It was several hours before I drew what should have been an obvious conclusion: The man I had passed, who was attired like a tradesman, was none other than Sherlock Holmes himself. He had made himself to look like a workingman, and had gone off in pursuit of the answers to the question surrounding the body that had been found soaked in ale.

This came as a relief to me. Had I been gifted with second sight or some equivalent, I wouldn't have felt relief. Instead, I should have been seized by a strong feeling of dread, for two days passed before I saw Holmes again wearing his recognizable face.

A messenger boy came round and handed me a slip of paper. I accepted the envelope. After sending the boy on his way, I opened it and read the note with a distinct shock.

"*Watson,*" it read, "*I have been admitted to St. Mary's Hospital. Come at once.*"

I lost no time in reaching the hospital and finding Holmes's room.

The poor fellow was confined to bed and looked much the worse for wear. He was quite pale, and his hair matted and plastered to his skull, faintly reeking of stale ale.

"Good Heavens!" I exclaimed. "What has happened to you?"

"Alas, what happened is what I half-expected might happen. Despite the fact that I was forewarned, I nevertheless fell into the trap. Only my wits and my preparedness allowed me to escape the diabolical chamber alive."

"What chamber are you referring to?"

"I have named it the Paradol Chamber, after the brand of ale called *Paradol.* Pull up a chair, and while I have the strength to speak, I'll tell you the entire sordid story."

I wasted no time in seating myself and waited for Holmes to unburden himself.

"Kindly excuse any lapses in my account, friend Watson," began Holmes. "I fear that my nerves have been shredded by my ordeal. I know that you like to take some of my cases as the basis for your little sketches, and may have questions, but I ask that you interrupt me little as I tell my tale."

I nodded silently.

Holmes continued in a tone that displayed a roughness that I rarely heard in his confident voice.

"I took it upon myself to arrive at the Paradol Brewing Company, claiming that I was seeking work. I dressed accordingly for the interview, calling myself Frederick Tinsley. I wasn't entirely surprised to find that the sprawling brewery was built from brown brick.

"The owner of the establishment, a humorless and owl-eyed fellow named James Paradol, took me into his modest office and asked several questions. After I had answered them to his satisfaction, he informed me that I was hired and suggested that I commence my work on the spot. This I was only glad to do, for it enabled me to plunge into my investigation without undue delay.

"I don't imagine that you've visited very many breweries. They are remarkable engines for producing drink. Tubs of hops and barley awaiting mashing. Great copper vats constantly bubbling and boiling. The brewery was a booming concern, as the Americans like to say. It produces pale ale in various varieties of stout and porter. My immediate duties involved a push broom and a rag for polishing such brightwork as required cleaning. From time to time, I was obliged to wield a wet mop, for spillage was a constant issue.

"It took me some time to become accustomed to the stirring odors of brewing ale, but otherwise there was no great difficulty or discomfort to my duties. Initially, I was all but ignored by my fellow workers who didn't inquire as to my name. If something came up, the brewmaster would call for me, and simply point at the job to be done.

"I didn't think any of the other workers would be valuable sources of information, so this was to the good, I reasoned. My obligations took me from one end of the establishment to the other, which was a substantial building. I saw that the vats were all in good working order, and so I paid them little heed once I had established that to my satisfaction.

"I looked about for anything unusual, but I descried nothing of the sort. I won't bore you with the details of the process of brewing beer. I imagine to some degree you have a passing familiarity with it – the milling and mashing, followed by the lautering, and then recirculation, sparging, and finally lagering.

"Pretending to be fascinated by this elaborate process, I was able to observe every square inch of the brewery, but I found nothing that would make me suspect that any of the equipment had been configured for the committing of murder."

Thinking of the body found in the Bristol wood, I shuddered inwardly.

Holmes took no note of my reaction. He continued speaking in his sometimes-halting manner. Occasionally, he gestured with one lean hand, which I saw to be abraded in a manner than brought to mind the roughened fingers and palms of the Bristol victim, and his nails were frightfully cracked.

"The first day, I worked until late in the evening, and when my duties were done, and the wagon had hauled away the last casks of ale, I was released. I loitered around the neighborhood, and then, impatient to get on with it, I stole back into the brewery through a window that I forced open with my pocket knife.

"Finding a lantern, I lit it and made a more thorough examination of the floor. I didn't expect to discover anything that night, but I thought it prudent to make this examination when I could do so without interruption or arousing suspicion.

"Alas, I fear I was too impetuous. I paid particular attention to one corner of the establishment, examining a depressed area where I had seen spoilt brew poured out. This was a large drain of sorts, a steel grating that presumably led down into the earth. The great square grate was fixed to the floor in such a way that it was unmovable.

"I was deep into my reconnoiter when I heard the main door being unlocked. Extinguishing the lantern, I slipped behind a great vat and made myself as still as the fox when he smells the hounds. For several minutes, I scarcely breathed. All my attention was on the figure moving through the darkness. I considered it peculiar that he didn't light the lantern. Soon enough, I realized why this was so.

"While my entire attention was concentrated on the figure moving amidst the shadows, a second figure that I didn't suspect stole up behind me, striking me down with an instrument whose nature I can only guess at. I don't think that I was driven unconscious, only hurled to the floor. Dazed and momentarily paralyzed, I was dragged to a far corner of the great floor. Before I could gather my wits about me, I was precipitated into what I could only imagine in the darkness to be a pit. A hitherto-unsuspected trap door fell heavily into place, and the darkness became unrelieved by any chink of light."

"Good Heavens!" I exclaimed. "Were you injured by the fall?"

Holmes shook his head heavily. "By the fall, not in the slightest. But due to the blow to the head, I was rendered *hors de combat*. I lay there for a considerable period of time while I gathered my strength.

"When at last I felt that my vitality had returned, I took stock of my limbs. Feeling for breaks or sprains, I found none. Listening carefully, I heard no sounds from above. At length, I decided that the brewery had been once again deserted.

"Reaching into my coat, I pulled out my briar along with a Lucifer, and, after inserting a plug of tobacco into the bowl, ignited the latter by striking it against a rough wall, which I found to be composed of carefully laid brown bricks. This naturally brought to mind the bits of brown brick detritus I had discovered in the boot soles of the corpse that I now understood to have been soaked in Paradol ale.

"The glow of the bowl showed that I had been dropped into a brick-walled chamber that was at least twelve feet deep. Fortunately, the floor was of dirt. Had it been of brick or stone, I wouldn't have been in a position to here telling my tale. Taking a few puffs from my pipe revived me after a fashion, but it was the light from the burning tobacco that gave me the greatest solace. I could see that I had been consigned to a square well that was nothing less than an *oubliette*. I'm sure I don't have to translate the word for you."

I understood perfectly what my friend meant. In medieval days, unfortunate prisoners were consigned to such windowless cells, where they were left to die of starvation and despair.

"Smoking away, I stood there contemplating my predicament and saw that approximately two feet above the top of my head ran a row of bricks that appeared to be loose, the crumbling mortar being insufficient to hold them properly in place.

"I had the foresight to take along my folding knife, as well as my revolver. The latter didn't seem to be useful at that point, so I took out the knife and I began to dig at the mortar. Initially, my thought was to remove and stack sufficient bricks to permit me to stand taller than my natural height. I imagined that I could contrive to push the trap door upwards. It seemed unlikely, but it was the only solution that I could conjure at that juncture.

"My excavation, however, opened up a different avenue of escape. When I got four bricks out and carefully set upon the earthen floor, I was able to stand on them, and by straining up on the tips of my toes, peer through the hole thus excavated. I could perceive that there was a void in the wall. It was difficult to maneuver my burning pipe bowl so that I could see it clearly, but I decided that I would attempt to enlarge the opening I had created sufficiently to squeeze through, and possibly worm my way into the adjoining space, for I imagined that I was trapped in a walled-off section of the cellar proper.

"As you might imagine, it took a considerable time to do this, and I had to rest often. Naturally, my pipe went out in due course. At length, I created a platform of brick. Stepping atop this enabled me to reach up and into the void, and thus pull myself rather painfully through the rough orifice. Regrettably, my precarious position did not permit me to light a

Lucifer as an aid, for I could not peer downward until my head and shoulders had breeched the opening, and I could hardly hold a lighted Lucifer between my teeth under the appalling circumstances.

"Deprived of illumination, I was at an extreme disadvantage. It was all I could do to work my way through the rectangular slot and trust that I would land on something not terribly injurious, for I could make out nothing without light. To soften the fall, I had first removed my coat and sent it ahead of me.

"It was fortunate that I did so, for the floor was coated with a thick accumulation of tacky matter. It rather reminded me of moss. As it happened, I suffered only such abrasions to my clothing and person as might be expected from tumbling down a short flight of stairs.

"Producing another Lucifer, its welcome but wavering flame showed where I had landed. Not in a spacious cellar as expected, but instead in a brick-bound chamber similar to the one I had escaped, albeit one perhaps half its dimensions and therefore suffocatingly narrow. My disappointment was profound, for I had simply exchanged prisons. I was no better off than before. Conceivably, I was in a worse position.

"The floor beneath me was ugly with what I believed to be a deposit of dried ale that had built up and thickened until it had become the consistency of blood pudding. Sitting down in it was out of the question. My coat was ruined, but that was the least of my worries. Once again resorting to my briar, I smoked silently as I considered my fortunes.

"Studying the ceiling above my head, I recognized the bottom of the great steel drain that stood in one corner of the working floor above. That possibility of escape didn't exist, even if I could have reached it. I had previously determined that it was fixed in place. No illumination filtered down from the holes in this ponderous place.

"I noticed that at one end of the chamber floor was a narrow stone slot that hadn't become encrusted with dried beer residue. I quickly understood its intended purpose: This was a drain, but it was useless to me, being no wider than the edge of my palm. I further understood that once the daily work of the brewery recommenced, I would, at best, be doused in spoilt brew.

"I don't know how much time passed. I considered returning to my original prison, but unfortunately, I didn't have loose bricks on the side with which to elevate myself. I felt that my physical condition was insufficient to pull myself up by main strength, but I didn't entirely discount the possibility, if conditions grew more extreme. I realized that I had but limited time to accomplish anything. I was without water and food. Sitting or sleeping would be uncomfortable in the extreme, and undesirable if I wished to survive. The longer I temporized, the more sapped would be my vitality.

"By checking my pocket watch, I measured the passage of time. An entire day had transpired. The day was now Sunday, so the brewery wouldn't be in operation. Shouting for help would do no good. This suggested to me that my demise was steadily creeping towards me – and at this point, I didn't fully suspect the truth of the chamber in which I found myself. I thought that I had been fortunate in finding escape from the first cell of confinement, but late that night, I heard sounds above my head, and these included footsteps, and what I took to be the rolling of beer casks about.

"When I heard the latter, I began to suspect certain things: One of which was that I stood in the very space where the unknown victim of Bristol met his ignominious end. I haven't mentioned before the odor of the chamber, but it smelt of stale ale. This wasn't remarkable by itself, of course, but when the beer casks began rolling over my head, I steeled myself for a dreadful dousing. I couldn't imagine that I was in mortal peril, for the floor drain would surely ingest the torrent faster than it could be poured.

"I could not know who it was who were moving about above me, so I raised my voice in the hope that they were friendly.

"'Halloa!' I called up. 'I am in need of assistance!'"

"The reply was dreadful. A voice I recognized as belonging to James Paradol commenced laughing nastily. A moment later a second one joined in, cackling like an idiot. Neither man spoke, and I recognized the supreme difficulty of my position.

"Paradol brew commenced spilling down into the chamber, to accumulate at my feet. I fully expected the foamy stuff to disappear down through the drain. To my horror, it didn't. Kneeling on the unpleasant floor, I examined the stone floor slot by the steady light of my briar. I found that a steel baffle had sealed it. I imagined that the drain had been blocked by a mechanism operated by lever from the floor above my head. I began to realize something of the fate that had overcome the previous victim."

Despite my horror, I forbore not to comment, for obviously, my friend Holmes hadn't drowned. But I was eager to learn how he managed to avoid such a terrible fate.

"I stood erect as the liquid swallowed my shoes and crept up my calves, to engulf my knees, eventually rising to my waist. There was nothing I could do otherwise. I could hardly sit down for I would swiftly drown. As the Paradol ale flowed freely, I realized that my industrious

102

antagonists were determined to quench my life before the resumption of operations on the Monday morning that was but hours away.

"While my fate appeared to be sealed, a strange calm came over me. In that calmness came a providential clarity. I realized that, as additional barrels of beer were poured into the brick chamber, if I kept my composure, I would eventually become buoyant. This would put me in a position to return to my original prison without undue exertion.

"Although it was an arduous wait, this soon came to pass. Upwards I floated, and so made my way back through the narrow aperture in the bricks by squeezing through. Regrettably, I landed on the very bricks I had stacked on the floor, and there lay incapacitated for some time. In the meanwhile, the rising tide of tepid ale continued to mount. In due course, it began to dribble and leak through the opening high up in the connecting brick wall. This rather surprised me, for I assumed that my silent tormentors would open the drain in some mechanical fashion. But no, they continued to introduce Paradol product into the second chamber, and now the first chamber was beginning to fill.

"Lying on the cold floor, I resigned myself to this inevitability. I confess that I slept for some time. When I awoke, the floor was entirely the consistency of mud. But that was of little consequence. I was already soaked in beer. As I lay there, I reflected on the condition of the unfortunate prior victim's body. Many of the conditions I had observed on it, I now suffered. Cuts, abrasions, contusions, and painful sprains. I wondered how he had managed to extricate himself from the first chamber in order to meet his doom in the second.

"It was then that it dawned upon me that the loose bricks I discovered weren't present by happenstance, but instead were a deliberate lure to get me to contrive a way into the second chamber, so that I would face the torrent of Paradol brew. This produced in me a gruesome understanding. This diabolical trap had been created by a very purposeful intellect, one that took delight in inflicting mental and physical tortures on anyone who fell into his foul clutches. As much dread as this produced in my brain, I firmly resolved not to become a victim of this fiendish contrivance, whose purpose I was only beginning to glean.

"As I mentioned before, I had a pistol in my pocket, but alas, it had become immersed. I strongly doubted the cartridges in its cylinder. Nevertheless, I removed it, and fired a shot into the ceiling. Nothing resulted from pulling the trigger – not that I expected to accomplish anything of worth. But I needed to ascertain the condition of its ammunition. There seemed to be no hope.

"As the foamy substance rose up my legs, I cast my mind back to my university days and my studies of volumes, liquids, and fluid mechanics in the hope that something of a utilitarian nature would occur to me. There seemed to be no way out, and for a time I believed this to be true – but when I attempted to envision poor Bristol man's ultimate fate, I realized that the slot at one end of the other chamber was wholly insufficient for proper drainage once the chamber was filled. Yet it must carry off any discarded brew eventually. Otherwise, the beer that had immersed him would still be present. Since drainage existed, I reasoned that it must debauch into a horizontal pipe – perhaps a pipe large enough for a man, if he isn't too stout.

"But how to get to that pipe? The adjoining chamber was nearly full. It occurred to me that the chamber I occupied was only beginning to fill, and it would be some time to before I was fully immersed. That interval couldn't be accurately measured, but I believed it to be approximately one hour. Bending into the beer and gathering up the bricks once more, I stood on them, and I used my jackknife and the butt of my useless revolver to work at the bricks surrounding the aperture.

"Some of these gave way easily. Others were more difficult, but I worked diligently and purposefully, for I knew that my time was short. Very carefully, I excavated a vertical notch in the brickwork, and through this, Paradol ale began to pour down with increasing force, partially emptying the adjoining chamber. It was no great effort now to pull myself back into the second chamber as it emptied.

"Finding my feet, I attacked the coating on the floor with my clasp knife. It wasn't only desperation that drove my frantic actions. It was reason, perhaps leavened by a species of intuition, for I hoped that no builder would construct such a drainage arrangement as this without ensuring redundancy. I had begun to suspect a larger drain – one that had, over time, become blocked and obscured by residue. And I soon found it. Necessity forced me to plunge into the swirling brew and employ my bare hands until I could make out its outlines by groping. It proved to be a perforated metal shield, held in place by great steel screws. But how to get at them?

"As I mentioned before, Watson, I had a pistol in my pocket, but alas, it had become immersed. I strongly doubted the cartridges in its cylinder. However, knowing that the first victim had been found soaked in ale, I had the foresight to carry spare ammunition in the same oilskin pouch in which I had placed my briar and supply of Lucifers.

"I broke the cylinder, shook out the wet ammunition, and reloaded. Going to the end of the chamber where the slot stood, I aimed downward into the sudsy Paradol brew beneath which I knew the drain to be. I emptied my weapon. As I hoped, my bullets dislodged the baffle, and the liquid began to swirl and subside.

"Above my head, I could hear voices raised in consternation, but there was nothing they could do about my actions. Nevertheless, they hurriedly moved another cask into position, opened the stopper, and another flavorful downpour was visited upon my head. In his instance, I thrust my face into the torrent, drinking liberally. This had a revivifying effect, and provided renewed strength.

"After the new flow had ceased and drained away, I took out my briar and methodically got it charged and flaming. Keeping the stem between my teeth, I positioned the glowing bowl so that it showed me the floor without spilling the helpful fiery tobacco. I waited for the cold brew to drain away, and then I knelt down on my soaked coat and attacked the round drain cover with alacrity, for although my immediate peril had been forestalled, I didn't know what my captors might do to prevent my escape. I glanced upward once, and could see the gleam of wicked human eyes regarding me through the perforations over my head.

"This operation presented its difficulties. The screws were held fast in place, but eventually, I worked the first one loose. There were six in all, and I was able to loosen each one in its turn, although I broke the tip of my blade in doing so. This proved to be in actuality a boon. The flat end proved more useful than the pointed tip. Once I had accomplished this task, I wrenched the cover from the drain and saw that it was of sufficient size to accommodate me. There was no baffle barring my way. The drain had been blocked by years of accumulation in the drain holes, sealing them.

"It was at this point that another ponderous cask was upended over my head, with the inevitable result. In this instance, I couldn't protect my pipe and the bowl was doused, plunging me back into inglorious darkness. Needless to say, the last remnants of the swirling malodorous brew swiftly drained down this exposed pipe. I stood aside while this action completed itself.

"It is a difficult decision, whether to plunge into a pipe whose terminus was unknowable. It might have led to a river, such as the Thames, or to some less savory destination, but I resolved to dare it. In the bedraggled state in which I found myself, it was an unpleasant undertaking. I was forced to go head first and crawl blindly along. I went some distance, and then paused, where I attempted to ignite a Lucifer, but it wouldn't fire. This forced me to continue on without illumination.

"On and on, I crawled. Eventually, I discerned a faint light. When I reached the terminus of the outfall pipe, I found the way blocked by yet another confounded steel grate. Beyond it lay wood, and a stagnant pond into which the pipe ultimately drained. Here, I feared that I was defeated,

105

for I lacked the muscular strength to exert pressure on the barrier. But all wasn't lost.

"Lifting my voice, I called for assistance. Fortunately, aid wasn't long in coming. Of all people, a constable heard my outcries and investigated. Once I explained that I was Sherlock Holmes and that I was trapped behind the grate, the man assured me that succor wouldn't be long in coming. Nor was it. Workmen soon removed the blocking grate, and I was hauled out, a frightfully sodden and fatigued figure. From there, I was conveyed to this hospital, as you can plainly see."

I spoke up at last. "That was a remarkable escape. I'm exceedingly grateful that you persevered to the end." It was all I could say, for I was all but breathless from listening to the harrowing account.

Holmes nodded. "Undoubtedly, it was the most remarkable escape of my life. I'm fortunate to be still counted among the living."

"What of the blackguards who did this to you?"

"I've spoken to Lestrade, and he has agreed with me that the owner of the brewery, Mr. James Paradol, should be taken into custody. I imagine he is being questioned quite closely even now. What Lestrade will learn, I can only guess, but it wouldn't surprise me if we find that the owner is a fiend who derives pleasure from tormenting innocent victims who fall into his hands."

Several days passed before Holmes was well enough to be discharged from the hospital. Once again seated before the familiar hearth, to which he crowded more closely than normal, Holmes puffed on his pipe as he recuperated in mind and spirit, as well as in body.

During this period, a letter was received from Bristol. Mr. Haversham had written to inform us of the results of his autopsy.

"It seems that the poor fellow found in Bristol had perished of heart failure," stated Holmes as he folded the letter.

"Brought on, no doubt, by the horrific ordeal to which he was subjected," I suggested.

"No doubt," mused Holmes wearily, laying the letter aside.

Inspector Lestrade turned up in due course. He gave such explanations as were possible under the extenuating circumstances.

"This fellow Paradol is mad – a lunatic. There is nothing more to it than that. He built the double chamber for the purposes of casting the unwary and undeserving soul into a personal perdition."

"Had he no other motive?" I asked.

Holmes replied to my question. "It's obvious that he had none, because in his unbalanced mental state, he needed none, for madness responds to prevailing and ever-shifting mental winds a sane man can never comprehend."

"True," agreed Lestrade. "James Paradol simply took delight in torment. My men found him at his home. He hadn't thought to flee, perhaps believing that you had perished during your flight through the great outfall pipe. I imagine he will be consigned to a madhouse rather than hanged. His brain isn't normal. He had a confederate who was a simpleton – one who did what he was told and lacked conscience in the same way that Mr. Paradol did."

I was aghast at these words. "Is that all there is to it?"

"I fear so." replied Lestrade. "The insane have no motives in the normal sense of the term. He confessed to the destruction of Mr. Wilfred Noyes, who was the first victim. He had been a worker in the brewery whom Paradol selected as his initial subject. To cover for his crime, he and his accomplice conveyed the corpse to Bristol, depositing it near a brewery in order to throw all investigation wildly off the scent, as it were. It's fortunate that Mr. Holmes undertook his investigation when he did. Otherwise, there would have been a second fatality, if not a third and fourth and so on."

And there the matter lay. The demon was eventually tried, and sentenced to be consigned to the Bethlem Asylum for the duration of his sorry existence. His confederate, however, was consigned to Wormwood Scrubs prison. In due course, he was hanged.

The newspapers did not mention it, for Scotland Yard chose to keep the matter as quiet as possible.

I will admit that all these years later, this particular investigation stands out in my mind as one of the most unpleasant in Sherlock Holmes's long and celebrated career. I wish I could forget it, however, for it haunts me, especially on sleepless nights. For many months, it put me off stout.

The year '87 furnished us with a long series of cases of greater or less interest, of which I retain the records. Among my headings under this one twelve months I find an account of the adventure of the Paradol Chamber . . . .

– Dr. John H. Watson
"The Five Orange Pips"

The Amateur Mendicant Society
by David MacGregor

Readers who have been kind enough to cast an occasional eye over these short tales related to the activities of my friend, Sherlock Holmes, may recall that in "The Five Orange Pips", I made passing reference to a few of the cases that had come to his attention in 1887. Among them were the adventure of the Paradol Chamber, the sinking of the British barque *Sophy Anderson*, and the bizarre series of events concerning the Grice Patersons on the island of Uffa. Some of Holmes's more ardent admirers have upbraided me over the years by noting that there is no "island of Uffa" in existence, which is quite correct. Indeed, I have an entire file brimming with letters from various cranks who seem to take special pride in attempting to correct my supposed errors and mistakes, apparently unaware that I regularly used alternative names for places and people in an effort to shield the privacy of individuals whose only crime was to be the victim of a crime.

With the passage of time, I feel more comfortable in revealing that "Uffa" was my pseudonym for the Isle of Arran, which can be found in the Firth of Clyde on Scotland's west coast. With that mystery solved, let me address the unwritten case which, aside from "The Giant Rat of Sumatra", has caused the most comment among the followers of Mr. Sherlock Holmes – namely, "The Adventure of the Amateur Mendicant Society". This too occurred in 1887, and part of my reluctance in telling this tale is due to the fact that Holmes and I were both present when the crime occurred, and to this day it remains one of the most horrific scenes I have ever witnessed in my life.

If I cast my mind back to the early months of 1887, I recall thinking that it was destined to be one of the most cursed years in the annals of British history. In January, the British ship *Kapunda* had collided with the barque *Ada Melmoure* off the coast of Brazil and had sunk so rapidly that no lifeboats could be launched, with over three-hundred poor souls perishing in the waters of the Atlantic. In February, an underground explosion had killed thirty coal miners in Wales, and in March, *The Times* had disgraced itself by publishing a series of letters intended to ruin the reputation of Charles Stewart Parnell, with the letters subsequently proven to be outright forgeries.

Then, as the sun progressively rose in the sky to announce the coming of spring, I was pleased that the news, like the weather, became better and better. In May, I had greatly enjoyed the opening of Buffalo Bill's Wild West Show, where I was positively astonished at the displays of bronco riding, calf roping, and the appearance of several members of the Ogala Lakota tribe, not to mention the magnetic personality of William Cody himself. This exhibition, it will be recalled, was part of the Golden Jubilee of Queen Victoria, and a command performance was given for the Queen herself in June. That same month, Holmes was discreetly consulted regarding what came to be known as the Jubilee Plot, which was ostensibly a plan by radical Irish nationalists to assassinate the Queen and blow up Westminster Abbey. However, as Holmes quickly determined, it was a rather disgraceful attempt by the British government itself to stir the Fenians up in an effort to justify further violence against them. Aside from this and a few other minor blemishes, all of the Golden Jubilee ceremonies and activities proved to be an unqualified triumph for Her Majesty.

And so, time trundled on, as it is wont to do, and before I knew it the days had shortened, the temperature had fallen, and upon glancing at the calendar on this particular morning, I had been mildly discomfited to discover that Christmas Day was almost upon us. When I had ventured out for a morning newspaper, I found Baker Street more crowded than usual, with countless carriages and pedestrians scurrying to-and-fro on what I suspected were various shopping expeditions and other excursions related to the upcoming holiday.

Now settled in front of the fire with my paper, I was dimly aware that Holmes's tall, lean figure had been staring out into the slanting morning light for some time, when a sharp intake of his breath made me look up. He turned, nodding to himself, then looked at me.

"Why not?"

"Excellent question, Holmes," I responded. "Why not, indeed?"

Holmes offered a thin smile by way of answer. "As much as I appreciate your agreeable nature, Watson, you haven't the faintest idea to what I am referring."

"On the contrary," I returned. "It's obviously a question of whether you take the case or not. Don't imagine you're the only person in these rooms capable of the occasional deductive insight."

"Interesting." Holmes took the seat across from me and fixed me with a steady stare. "If you would care to explain your reasoning process, I would be most grateful. How did the two words '*Why not*' reveal to you the innermost workings of my mind?"

"It's quite elementary," I began, working mightily to keep the smile off my face. "Those words coming from almost anyone else would convey a universe of possibilities: *Why not go for a walk? Why not make the acquaintance of a particular individual? Why not purchase a periodical or have roast mutton for dinner?* With Sherlock Holmes, however, his interests are confined to a much narrower spectrum than most other people – specifically: *Cases.* To take them or not to take them. That is the entirety of his universe. So then, quite a commonplace deduction."

I returned my attention to my newspaper and was gratified to hear a small laugh coming from Holmes. "Well, well, well. Clearly, I sit before you with every nook and cranny of my private thoughts on full display. It would be useless to deny it, so would you care to accompany me to the Bank of England for a private conference with two gentlemen regarding the Amateur Mendicant Society?"

"The what?" I answered, setting down my paper.

"Oh dear," said Holmes. "You don't say that the Amateur Mendicant Society has somehow eluded the net of your omniscience? Get your coat and I shall endeavour to explain as we make our way to the City."

It was only a few minutes later that Holmes and I found ourselves rattling along in a hansom cab in the direction of Threadneedle Street. Holmes gazed around at the kaleidoscope of passing London as he spoke.

"The fact of the matter is," he began, "very few people have any awareness of the Amateur Mendicant Society. I hasten to add that this isn't due to any nefarious activities on their part. London is positively awash in various clubs and societies, largely because of men looking for any excuse to escape the watchful eyes of their wives and mothers. If a man has access to this or that club and frequents it on a regular basis, it serves as an excellent excuse to avoid the more unpleasant areas of a domesticated life."

"Come now," I chided. "There are many men who look forward to time with their wives and children and quiet evenings at home."

Was that an involuntary shudder I saw pass through Holmes? "If you say so," he answered. "But now to the activities of the Amateur Mendicant Society. What do you suppose they do with themselves? Why does the society exist?"

"Well, they're beggars of some type, yes? That's what a mendicant is – a kind of religious beggar, I believe."

"In theory," returned Holmes, "but would you expect to have a conference with two religious beggars at the Bank of England?"

"I suppose not."

"Precisely. No, Watson, their name is an attempt at somewhat ironic humour. These particular mendicants are all very well-to-do. Some of it is inherited money, some of it is due to industrious enterprise, and some of it is due to successfully navigating their way to the public trough through various bribes and connections. Nevertheless, the putative goal of these mendicants is to solicit money from the public, but to keep none of it for

110

themselves. Rather, it is then distributed to the more unfortunate members of the community. They are a charitable organisation *ne plus ultra*."

"Excellent!" I enthused. "It's always gratifying to hear of people trying to make the world a better place. Why have they contacted you?"

"I'm not entirely clear on that," answered Holmes. "Their missive was brief and to the point, but apparently a shadow of some concern has recently fallen across the Society. We are meeting the two chief officers of the Society at the Bank of England because that is where they are both employed. But here, all of our questions will soon be answered."

As we turned a corner, the Bank came into full view in all its splendour. The remarkable design of architect John Soane had created a veritable island of solid stone to convey the absolute permanence and trustworthiness of this venerable institution, and moments later Holmes and I were striding between two massive pillars into the interior of the building. Upon communicating the nature of our visit, we were swiftly conducted to the office of the Deputy Governor. He rose from his desk at our entrance and strode towards us with a smile on his face and his hand outstretched.

"Mr. Holmes and Dr. Watson," he began. "This is, indeed, a pleasure. I am Trevor Granville."

As we shook hands, I took stock of Mr. Granville and his office. Both were large and inviting, and I feared for the links in the gold watch chain that was stretched taut across his considerable bulk. His blue eyes glistened with friendliness as he directed Holmes and me to chairs near his desk. Bookshelves crowded with leather-bound volumes lined the walls, and perched upon various pedestals and shelves were what I took to be either replicas or originals of ancient Greek pottery. On the wall behind his desk was a rather remarkable oil painting of a man wearing a crown and surrounded by gold coins, facing a rather pained-looking gentleman being held by what I took to be two courtiers.

"My colleague, Mr. Hurst, will join us shortly," said Granville as he settled himself into a well-padded armchair.

As was his custom, Holmes's eyes had scanned the room, taking in every detail, before finally landing on the painting. "King Croesus, I presume?"

"Yes, indeed!" Granville nodded enthusiastically. "The old boy being put in his place by Solon the Athenian. Are you familiar with the story?"

"I'm afraid not," I answered.

"Well, Croesus, as you know," began Granville, "is generally regarded as the wealthiest man who ever lived. When he granted an audience to Solon the Athenian, he was most anxious to ask him who was the happiest man in the world, fully expecting that Solon would say King

111

Croesus himself, due to his inestimable riches. However, Solon proceeded to confound Croesus' expectations by listing men who had led selfless and exemplary lives dedicated to helping other people, which infuriated Croesus. It's my little reminder to myself that money isn't everything – although in all candor, it is most things. Ah, but here is Mr. Hurst!"

True enough, a slim, mournful-looking man had slipped into the room, wearing a black dress coat and white cravat. Introductions were made, and as Granville pulled another chair near to his desk, he expanded on the duties of his comrade.

"Mr. Hurst is the Librarian of the Bank, but not to be confused with the sort of librarian with which you may be more familiar. His duties have nothing to do with books whatsoever."

"Indeed." My curiosity was most definitely piqued. "Then if I might be so bold as to enquire, Mr. Hurst, what are the duties of a librarian with no books?"

"It's really quite simple," Hurst replied as he favoured me with a glance that revealed penetrating green eyes. "I am responsible for notes that have been paid in at the bank. Once they come to me, they are completely devoid of value, but we must keep track of them and preserve them should a claim of forgery or theft arise. After a suitable period of time they are burned, which is an absolute necessity, as fresh bundles and parcels of notes arrive every day and reach almost to the ceiling."

"Most interesting," observed Holmes. "Now then, down to business. Tell us more about this Amateur Mendicant Society and your concerns."

Before either gentleman could say a word, the door to the office opened and a clerk brought in a tray with four small glasses filled with an amber-coloured liquid.

"Ah, excellent!" said Granville. "A touch of sherry makes everything a bit more civilised."

In turn, the clerk offered each of us a glass, then retreated as silently as he had come. Granville raised his glass and we all followed suit.

"To your very good health, gentlemen!"

Sipping my sherry and savouring the warm, nutty taste as I once more gazed around the room, it was easy to feel in that moment that I was at the very centre of civilisation. Granville looked at his glass with appreciation, then set it down and turned his attention to the matter at hand.

"Might I enquire if either of you gentlemen are familiar with the origin of the Mendicants within the Catholic Church?"

"I have a passing knowledge," answered Holmes. "I believe it was the Second Council of Lyon in 1274 that established the four main orders: The Franciscans, the Carmelites, the Dominicans, and the Augustinians."

"Quite right, Mr. Holmes," Granville nodded his approval. "Up until that point, the various religious orders had focused on staying in one place, often perfecting a particular trade, and gradually accumulating land, buildings, and considerable wealth. The Mendicants, in contrast, had no property or possessions beyond that which they carried with them, and travelled from place to place as itinerant preachers. Theirs was a lifestyle of poverty and sacrifice, dedicated entirely to spreading the Word of God to all the world."

Mr. Hurst had followed this disquisition closely, and as he put his sherry glass down, he proceeded to enlighten us further. "Human nature being what it is, tensions soon arose between the so-called 'begging friars' and their religious brethren who preferred a more, shall we say, comfortable lifestyle. In my experience, there are chiefly two branches of humanity, those who seek to do everything they can to benefit themselves and those who seek to do everything they can to benefit others. The humble and ascetic lifestyle of the mendicants was a repudiation of the wealth and splendour of the Vatican. Thus the mendicants came to be seen as a threat by the powers that be, with the result that the more rigorous mendicant orders found themselves suppressed by various popes down through the years, and many went extinct."

"Which brings us to our own little society, the Amateur Mendicants," declared Granville. "We are dedicated to the principles of the original mendicants, but with no religious associations whatsoever. Whatever funds or goods we are able to gather go entirely to the poor and needy. Our name is simply a little joke, nothing more. However, it would appear that our mission and sense of humour isn't entirely appreciated by everyone."

With that, Granville withdrew a small slip of paper from his pocket, and Hurst did the same. As they set both pieces of paper on the desk, Holmes and I could see that they were almost identical, and bore the same words:

The Amateur Mendicant Society must be disbanded immediately. Ignore this warning at your peril.

Holmes picked up one of the notes, then the other, holding them both up to the light, smelling them, then comparing them next to one another.

"Both the paper and ink are unexceptional," Holmes announced, "and they would appear to be written by the same hand, but the individual letters themselves were slowly and laboriously composed, indicating the writer was attempting to disguise any identifying features of his own handwriting. How did you come by these?"

113

"They were delivered by post four days ago," answered Granville, setting a torn envelope on the desk, with Hurst doing the same.

After a cursory glance at both envelopes, Holmes leaned back in his chair. "Anything else?"

Granville and Hurst flickered a glance at one another, and it was Granville who spoke first.

"After receiving the warning, as you might expect, I was alert to any other possible threats, and came to feel that I was being followed on my way to and from the bank. Normally, my mind is on business, and I take very little note of passersby or other people in my vicinity, but by stopping abruptly and turning on numerous occasions, I began to feel quite certain that I was being pursued by two priests."

"Priests?" I asked in surprise.

"I wish I could be more specific," continued Granville, "but they never approached closely enough for a more accurate description. I may, of course, be fabricating this out of my own imagination. You know how it is. You pay no mind to chimney sweeps for most of your life, but then you see or read something about chimney sweeps and suddenly you find the streets are positively swimming with them."

"Mr. Hurst?" Holmes turned to the bank's librarian. "Did you notice anything similar?"

Hurst nodded. "Once Trevor mentioned that he was being followed, I began to be more mindful of my surroundings, and yes, I feel quite certain that I am being watched."

"By priests?" asked Holmes.

"Possibly," answered Hurst warily. "Or at least gentlemen wearing priestly garb. It's most unsettling. I am used to living my life and conducting my affairs on an almost completely anonymous basis. I have never sought out attention and I never shall. It isn't in my nature. I am a private man. To suddenly find myself the object of unwanted attention is distressing in the extreme."

"My colleague's distress is my own," said Granville, "and so I wrote to you, Mr. Holmes, in the hope that you might be able to shed some light on the situation. To disband the Amateur Mendicant Society based on nothing more than a threatening note doesn't sit well with me, and yet having the proverbial Sword of Damocles hanging over our heads is most definitely worrisome."

"Especially considering this evening," added Hurst.

Holmes looked quizzically from Hurst to Granville, who folded his hands in front of him and gazed at Holmes and me in turn.

"Tonight is the occasion of our annual dinner," began Granville. "The Amateur Mendicants gather together in very humble surroundings to enjoy

114

the most lavish feast imaginable. It's our little gift to ourselves, you might say, and encourages continued participation within the Society."

"Given that," Hurst picked up the story, "in discussing the matter, it seems obvious that if someone were looking to inflict some kind of harm or mischief upon us, this would be the ideal opportunity, as it is the only time of the year when we are all gathered in one place."

Holmes took all this in, his mind instantly assembling together the pieces of this remarkable story to come to a logical conclusion. "You have made your position quite clear. Dr. Watson and I would be happy to attend your dinner this evening."

Granville and Hurst looked at one another in surprise.

"Well, yes," said Granville. "That is precisely what we were about to propose."

"Of course, we wouldn't introduce you by name," continued Hurst. "We would simply note that you were prospective new members. Should any unpleasantness arise, it would no doubt be to our advantage to have you and Dr. Watson on the premises."

Holmes rose from his seat and began making a tour of the room, stopping before a particularly magnificent urn featuring Hercules doing battle against the Hydra as one of his Twelve Labours.

"I take it," said Holmes, "that you are concerned not only about threats from without, but also from within."

With his back to us, Holmes couldn't see the furtive glance exchanged between Hurst and Granville.

"A slim possibility," acknowledged Granville, "but one that we must bear in mind. Ours is a Society of quite exceptional gentlemen, each used to having his way and manipulating circumstances to his own benefit. It would be fatuous to declare otherwise."

"But surely," I expostulated, "if any of these gentlemen should disapprove of some aspect of the Society, they could simply resign their membership, so to speak."

"Which would raise uncomfortable questions," answered Hurst. "The slightest ripple in this particular pond is a cause for alarm, because it indicates more powerful currents running beneath the surface."

"To the public eye," Holmes had rejoined us, "there is nothing to connect seemingly disparate industries, noble families, and departments of the government. However, they are all part of one web, and a tremor in this part of the web can result in cataclysmic consequences elsewhere."

"Well put," agreed Granville. "You have a nice understanding of things, Mr. Holmes, and I feel certain we can rely on your abilities and discretion to put this current unpleasantness behind us."

"Is there anything else I should know?" asked Holmes.

115

"Yes," answered Granville. "In a further effort to bring everything out into the open, we have invited two members of the Diocese of Westminster to join us this evening."

"The Professional Mendicant Society, as it were," added Hurst with a wry smile. "Our fundraising activities pale in comparison to theirs."

"But if the threats against us are simply their way of demanding money," concluded Granville, "we will simply buy them off with a superb dinner and a donation to their coffers."

Our conference with these two gentlemen concluded shortly thereafter, and Holmes eschewed a cab in favour of walking back to Baker Street. We proceeded in silence for some time, and it was only as we passed Chancery Lane that Holmes emerged from his musings to cast a glance at the leaden sky above us.

"What is it that's troubling you?" I asked.

"Everything," he answered. "Typically, powerful men and powerful institutions make it their business to tilt the game to their advantage and to wreak havoc on the classes below them. For the most part, there is an unspoken agreement that certain activities and territories are inviolate, and it is in this way that the Church, the government, and our captains of industry can blame our various social ills on whomever they please: Immigrants, Socialists, the Jews, the Irish, and so on. However, if two of these forces should come into direct conflict – for example, the Church and the Bank of England – there is no telling the amount of damage they could do to the country."

"Good Heavens" I said. "Does the situation really appear that dire?"

"Difficult to say. Human nature being what it is, it may resolve itself down to nothing more than a personal grudge. Still, I think we would both do well to arm ourselves for this evening's adventure. It is a wise man who anticipates and a foolish man who reacts."

I will admit that I passed the rest of the day in a bit of a haze, wandering from this book to that periodical, but all the while with my mind racing ahead to what events might unfold that evening. Holmes was unusually quiet, smoking pipe after pipe, with only occasional forays into this or that volume of his Index to verify some point of information. Darkness had fallen by the time that he abruptly announced, "I do believe our presence is requested."

A moment later I heard a knock on our door and we proceeded down the stairs to the carriage that had been prearranged for us. Upon entering the carriage, I immediately noted that smoked windows prevented us from looking out, just as they prevented anyone else from looking in. About to voice an objection, a terse shake of Holmes's head silenced the words in my throat, and I sat across from him with my heart rate already accelerating. The ensuing journey took over half-an-hour, although I couldn't determine just how far we had actually travelled. For all I knew, we had done nothing more than move in an enormous circle, so that we may very well have ended up several miles away or merely a street away from Baker Street.

As the horses slowed, I could see Holmes's eyes darting back and forth, listening to anything that might give us a clue as to our location. When the carriage door was opened, Holmes and I descended into an alleyway outside a rather unremarkable warehouse which loomed forebodingly above us in the dim gaslight. As our carriage clattered off into the distance, I heard a low, mournful ship horn sounding on the Thames, and pulled my coat tighter.

"This can't be right," I began. "Devilish sort of place for a dinner party."

Holmes nodded. "Then let us see what form of devilry awaits us within."

As we approached the building, a door swung upon, anticipating our arrival, and a doorman appeared and beckoned us towards him. A moment later we were inside the warehouse and descending one flight of stairs after another, my unease increasing with every step. Feeling my trusty Webley by my side was the only thing that calmed my nerves as we reached the basement of the building and proceeded down a bleak, cheerless corridor. A door at the end of it was opened, and upon stepping through it was as if Holmes and I had entered a different universe. A large, capacious room was filled with golden light, a string quartet was encamped in one of the corners providing music, and a roaring fire welcomed all weary and cold travellers. I quickly ascertained that the long dining table in the centre of the room was positively groaning with all manner of culinary delights, and estimated that approximately twenty gentlemen were already sitting at the table, at the far end of which sat both Granville and Hurst, flanked by two men wearing simple clerical vestments.

Granville rose from his place at our appearance. "Welcome, gentlemen, welcome! We're so glad that you're able to join us. Please, take your seats, and let the yearly dinner of the Amateur Mendicant Society commence!"

Holmes and I had no sooner settled into our places than a dozen servers appeared out of nowhere and began filling our plates with anything that we desired. There was glazed ham, roasted goose, lamb with cold mint sauce, broiled brook trout, *au gratin* potatoes, all manner of delectably prepared root vegetables, fruit of every description, sweetmeats, and so forth. A palate cleanser of chartreuse sherbet appeared halfway through this feast, then the table was liberally festooned with camembert and

Roquefort cheeses, as well as crystallised ginger, Tunis dates, and table figs. As much as I tried to keep my wits about me, the siren song of this sumptuous banquet had lulled me into a kind of daze, when I was suddenly brought back to reality by Granville tapping insistently on the side of his glass with a spoon.

"Gentlemen! If I might have your attention please, a delicious Italian amaretto from Saronno has been procured for your delectation and will now be served. The lights will then be extinguished for our final and most spectacular course of the evening. Following that, I shall announce the various bequests of the Amateur Mendicant Society for the upcoming Year of our Lord, 1888."

In short order, every glass was filled with amaretto, and then the room was pitched into complete darkness before I observed two glowing blue balls of fire approaching. It was an eerie, exhilarating sight, as what I immediately recognised as two Christmas puddings doused with brandy and then lit on fire apparently levitated on their own through the room. By the time they were set on the table, the brandy had almost burned off, the lights came on again, and we all spontaneously applauded this remarkable and memorable demonstration.

Granville rose from his chair, raised his glass, and addressed the gathering.

"A toast, gentlemen, to the Amateur Mendicant Society, to our members, to our deeds, and to this quite delectable dinner. Cheers!"

As one, we raised our glasses and drank. When Granville flamboyantly tossed his glass into the fire, we all followed suit with a rousing cheer. Granville then proceeded to produce a paper from his pocket, unfolded it, and put on a pair of spectacles to read what I supposed were the newest recipients of the largesse of the Amateur Mendicant Society. However, instead of reading, his face took on a shocked expression and he began to wheeze audibly, struggling for breath. To his side, Hurst was already clawing at his own throat, his eyes bulging from their sockets as his entire body twisted in agony. Mere seconds later, both men had collapsed to the floor and in the ensuing panic the room was soon cleared of all of its inhabitants – save for Holmes and myself.

Even as I knelt by Hurst, a terrible death rattle emerged from him as he took his last breath and fell still, while Granville writhed on the floor, froth streaming from his lips. I attempted to force open his jaw, with the intent of thrusting my fingers down his throat to induce vomiting, but he struggled and convulsed so violently that I was unable to do so. Endeavouring to control his thrashing to the best of my ability, I saw that Holmes was bending over the still form of Hurst, sniffing at the dead man's lips.

"What is it?" I asked.

Holmes turned to me. "A distinct odour of bitter almonds, which one would expect from a man who just consumed a glass of amaretto, but also consistent with the odour of prussic acid, otherwise known as hydrogen cyanide."

Granville's contortions had slowed, and a low moan escaped him. I saw his eyes open and a flicker of humanity behind them. He was still alive, at any rate, and Holmes sent me off to fetch the police and medical help as he stayed behind to monitor Granville's health and to more closely investigate the location of the crime. In due course, the police arrived and Holmes related everything that had transpired to Inspector Lestrade of Scotland Yard, as Granville was taken away to Barts Hospital, and the covered form of the late Mr. Hurst was conveyed to the mortuary. It was close to three hours later that Holmes and I dragged ourselves back to Baker Street and I immediately fell into bed and a deep sleep.

When I awoke, it took me a moment or two to orient myself. At first, I imagined that the events of the previous night had simply been a nightmare, but then, as a greater sense of consciousness asserted itself, the whole hideous sequence of events played itself out in my memory with disturbing clarity. Dragging myself to my feet, I made my way to our sitting room, where I encountered what I can only describe as a veritable London pea-souper. The room was utterly suffused in smoke, with Holmes at the centre of it, still puffing on his pipe. Despite the frigid temperature outside, I opened a window, gulped in several lungfuls of brisk December air, then turned back inside.

"What the devil, Holmes?" I enquired. "Have you been sitting here smoking since we came back from the Amateur Mendicant Society?"

"What do you make of it?" answered Holmes, ignoring my question. "I would value your opinion of last night's tragic events."

"It seems perfectly obvious to me," I replied. "The priests sitting next to Granville and Hurst poisoned both of them!"

"A bold claim," returned Holmes, "and one devoid of any meaningful details. Can you be more specific?"

"Holmes, you saw everything as well as I did. The amaretto was poured into each man's empty glass. The lights were then extinguished so that we might better focus on the arrival of the flaming Christmas puddings. It was in that moment of darkness that one or both of the priests took the opportunity to introduce prussic acid into the glasses of both Granville and Hurst. Once they drained their glasses, it took a moment or two for the poison to take effect, following which Hurst passed away almost immediately, and Granville barely survived."

119

"Indeed," Holmes rose from his chair to walk to the window. "Does it strike you as odd that Hurst died so quickly and yet Granville is still alive?"

"Not particularly," I replied. "For one thing, Granville weighs at least twice as much as Hurst, so the poison would affect Hurst all the more rapidly. Or perhaps there was a larger dose of the prussic acid in his glass."

"Perfectly logical," Holmes nodded. "And yet, while we were both encouraged to see an elaborate conspiracy unfolding before our eyes, I suspect that a much more simple crime took place."

"How so?"

"If I might put it in somewhat poetic terms, I would call it the curious case of the absence of grace."

"Pardon?"

"I would expect any dinner with two priests in attendance as special guests to include the saying of grace before the meal. Failing that, I would expect the two priests to say a quiet grace between themselves. Neither of those events occurred."

"What are you suggesting?" I asked.

"Let us forge the logical chain that might proceed from this observation," began Holmes. "The two priests neglected to say grace. Therefore we must consider the possibility that they weren't actually priests, but merely actors playing the role of clergymen. But why? To what end? Well, Granville had planted the seed in our minds that the Amateur Mendicant Society was being threatened by the Church. He claimed that he was being followed by clergymen."

"And Hurst said the very same thing!" I added.

"So he did. I would suspect by the same actors who arrived at the dinner."

"But why all this subterfuge?"

"Quite simple," answered Holmes. "Because Mr. Granville wished to murder Mr. Hurst and to have the blame placed elsewhere – specifically, on two mysterious figures who would disappear as quickly as they had appeared. The police would be on the hunt for two clergymen who never existed."

"Holmes!" I cried. "Are you forgetting that Granville very nearly lost his own life?"

Holmes arched his eyebrows in response. "Did he?"

"You saw him yourself! He was in spasms of agony!"

"Was he?"

My mind was in a whirl. Was Holmes simply having a bit of fun at my expense? But surely this was too horrible a situation to treat so lightly.

"Holmes," I began, "please explain yourself."

Knocking a dottle of tobacco from his pipe, Holmes proceeded to sit in his armchair and steepled his fingers together.

"I suspect something along the following lines: Mr. Granville likes money. He is surrounded by the world of high finance. His not-inconsiderable collection of Greek pottery would require sizable amounts of capital to amass, because the Panathenaic amphorae that I inspected all appear to be authentic originals. He quite literally has a painting of King Croesus above his desk, and you may take it from me, a wealthy man who declares that money isn't everything is lying through his teeth.

"Any salary from the Bank of England would scarcely meet his requirements, so he began to augment his income in a variety of not entirely ethical or legal ways. When this still proved insufficient, he conjured up the concept of the Amateur Mendicant Society out of thin air and enlisted the aid of his colleague, Mr. Hurst, to give the whole enterprise a patina of greater respectability. I don't doubt that some of the funds gathered by the Society made their way to the poor and needy, but I suspect that a considerable portion of that money made its way into Mr. Granville's pockets.

"All it would take is a bit of accounting legerdemain to obscure his nefarious activities, but here we must bear in mind the expertise of Mr. Hurst, who specialises in keeping track of financial affairs. Something regarding the accounts of the Amateur Mendicant Society aroused his suspicions to the extent that he expressed his concerns to Mr. Granville. This, of course, would never do, especially should Mr. Hurst's suspicions lead him to other enquiries at the Bank of England. And so the plot was hatched in Mr. Granville's brain.

"Threatening notes were produced. Actors to portray priests were hired. You and I were brought in as witnesses of impeccable reputation. Amaretto was served instead of port to provide the odour of almonds so that the smell of his own breath and that of Mr. Hurst would be virtually identical. The lights were doused, Mr. Granville surreptitiously introduced prussic acid into Mr. Hurst's glass, and then the amaretto was consumed. Mr. Granville grandly tossed his glass into the fireplace to obscure the fact that there was never any prussic acid in it, with the rest of us following suit. He then had to merely feign violent illness, while his colleague died a horrible death not ten feet away."

I sat down heavily, still taking in everything Holmes had said. "Well, if what you're saying is correct, what can we do?" I began. "Should we try and get the books of the Amateur Mendicant Society?"

"I suspect they are nonexistent," answered Holmes. "Mr. Granville would have seen to that prior to last night's dinner."

"Then the Bank of England," I suggested. "Perhaps more concrete proof can be found there."

"Perhaps," agreed Holmes. "But then we are in the world of larceny or embezzlement, not murder, and a respected gentleman like Mr. Granville would most likely be let off with a gentle tap on the wrist so as not to draw attention to his crimes, which would alarm the general public and undermine the reputation of the Bank."

"Then he gets away with it?" I asked. "Committing cold-blooded murder under our very noses? Surely we can do something?"

"That is what I have been mulling over these past few hours – considering what tactics we might take in this quite remarkable case."

"And?"

"I suggest the following very speculative plan," said Holmes. "Let me contact Lestrade at Scotland Yard and ask him to meet us at Barts. We'll arrange a private conference with Mr. Granville and see what sort of condition he is in. I suspect he'll be feigning some kind of after-effects of the poison, so we'll consult with a doctor as to his prognosis. I would simply ask you, Watson, to be alert to any direction the conversation may take. Whatever I say, no matter how outlandish it might sound, please agree with me immediately. If Mr. Granville can concoct a charade for our benefit, it's only fair that we should return the favour."

It was three hours later that Holmes and I were walking down a corridor in Barts, accompanied by a young, nervous doctor, who couldn't have been more than a year or two out of university. As we approached Granville's room, I saw Lestrade lurking in the hallway, where Holmes had clearly told him to wait for us. Approaching Lestrade, Holmes spoke in low tones.

"Notebook out, Lestrade," directed Holmes. "Not a word once we step into this room. Watch, listen, and you may hear something to your advantage."

As a group, we all filed into Granville's room, where the patient was sitting up in bed, looking somewhat apprehensive, but none the worse for wear.

"My dear Granville," began Holmes solicitously, even going so far as to take the man's hand in his own. "How are you feeling?"

"A little shaken, Mr. Holmes," answered Granville. "It has been quite the ordeal. Poor Hurst!"

"Indeed," Holmes nodded. "And how is your stomach? It isn't every man that can take a dose of prussic acid and survive."

"Unsettled, to be sure."

"I can imagine. Ingesting prussic acid can result in violent cramping for up to two days after the event. Were you able to sleep, at all? Are the spasms tolerable?"

Granville's mouth twisted in a slight grimace, "I don't like to complain, Mr. Holmes."

"Have they offered you anything for the pain?"

As Granville shook his head, Holmes whirled on the doctor standing behind him. "What's the meaning of this? Do you have any idea of the agony this poor man must be in? I once witnessed a man clawing the flesh off the back of his own hands due to a mild dose of prussic acid. My colleague, Dr. Watson, treated countless men on the battlefields of Afghanistan. Let me ask you, Watson, was it typically your habit to let soldiers suffer the tortures of the damned when they had been wounded?"

"Good God, no!" I retorted. "That's what morphine is for. My job was to alleviate suffering, not prolong it."

Holmes turned to the doctor, his eyes blazing. "I demand an explanation!"

The poor doctor was so overwhelmed by Holmes's imperious manner and my comments regarding my wartime experience that he immediately fled the room. Lestrade was frantically jotting something down in his notebook as Holmes paced briefly, and then a moment later the doctor was back with a syringe of morphine. As it was injected into a vein in Granville's arm, he immediately settled back onto his pillows with a serene and glazed expression.

"Excellent!" Holmes looked at Granville approvingly. "That's better, isn't it?"

Granville managed a nod and even a small smile as the sedating effects of the morphine coursed through his system.

"Then we won't trouble you any further, Mr. Granville," continued Holmes, "but I would be grateful if you could answer one question. Why did you wish to kill Mr. Hurst?"

"What's that?" mumbled Granville, an expression of shock slowly spreading over his features.

"I watched you do it," answered Holmes. "The lights were doused, the room went dark, and you poured prussic acid into Mr. Hurst's glass."

"No . . . ." Granville faltered, fighting through the fog in his brain. "The lights were doused . . . there was no light to see . . . no light . . . ."

"Ah, I should explain," continued Holmes affably. "I am afflicted with a rather rare condition in which my eyes do not require the usual length of time to adjust to the dark. It has proved invaluable in at least two of our cases, hasn't it, Watson?"

"I should say so," I replied, mindful of Holmes's instruction that I should agree with everything he said. "'*Retinal homeostasis*', as it's known. Quite rare indeed."

"Which allowed me to watch you pour the prussic acid into Mr. Hurst's glass as clearly as I see you now, Mr. Granville. I can only assume, therefore, that he must have threatened you in some way."

It would be impossible to describe with any accuracy the emotions that swept across Granville's features as Holmes's words penetrated his opiate-addled brain. Holmes had said everything with such certainty and conviction, that the idea of contradicting him in any way must have seemed impossible. All recollection that he was supposed to be suffering from prussic acid poisoning himself had been utterly effaced from his memory.

"He . . . ." Granville tried to wrench his thoughts into place. ". . . It was the damned bookkeeping . . . poking his nose where it didn't belong. Numbers . . . I knew he was poking his nose . . . the Mendicants . . . questions at the bank. We're talking ruin, Mr. Holmes . . . it would be absolute ruin . . . I couldn't bear it . . . only a matter of time unless . . . it's a bad business to be sure . . . but it couldn't be helped . . . couldn't be helped . . . ."

Granville lapsed into a groggy silence, and as I glanced at Lestrade I observed his mouth quite literally hanging open.

"And with that," said Holmes, "I leave the case in your capable hands, Lestrade."

Holmes was out the door in an instant, his long strides taking him down the corridor as both the doctor and Lestrade ran after him. It was the doctor who caught up to Holmes first.

"Mr. Holmes! I must object! To drug a patient and then induce a confession out of him is most irregular."

"The ends justify the means," replied Holmes tersely, "and it was you who administered the morphine, not I. Besides, the man was still in some emotional distress following the excitement of last night, and a little morphine can have an agreeably settling influence. I speak from personal experience."

"The doctor is quite right." Lestrade had finally caught up with Holmes. "You can't drug a suspect to interrogate them."

"Perhaps your position precludes such a tactic," answered Holmes, "but you will recall that I am not a member of the police force, nor am I a physician. I merely made the point that morphine is used to alleviate suffering. What followed was entirely out of my hands, and I hope you took accurate notes of Mr. Granville's statement. I might add that an audit of the Bank of England's books might prove edifying and, to the best of my knowledge, prussic acid isn't in the inventory of most shopkeepers, so where did he procure it? Good day, gentlemen!"

As Holmes and I rode in our hansom back to Baker Street, a light snow had begun to fall and with a jolt of recognition I remembered that tomorrow was Christmas Day. I had fully intended to present Holmes with a new cherry-wood pipe in the morning, but recent events had prevented my intended visit to a tobacconist's. Happily enough, I spotted just such a shop just ahead of us and inspiration struck.

"I say," I began, "perhaps I'll just get out and walk back to Baker Street. I fancy stretching my legs a bit."

Holmes turned to me with a quizzical expression, but one that quickly turned to bemusement as his gaze turned to the street and he spotted the tobacconist's shop.

"Very thoughtful, Watson, but you have already given me the finest Christmas present possible."

"I have?"

"'*Retinal homeostasis*'," replied Holmes with a low chuckle. "Quite wonderful. I knew I could count on you and your powers of invention."

"Thank you, Holmes," I answered, a feeling of warmth and pride welling up in me.

"Thank you, old friend. Now then, I must confess that I found my appetite keenly whetted last night before events took a dark turn. Given that, it is absolutely imperative that we embark on our next mystery immediately: Where to find a Christmas pudding?"

The year '87 furnished us with a long series of cases of greater or less interest, of which I retain the records. Among my headings under this one twelve months I find an account of the adventure . . . of the Amateur Mendicant Society, who held a luxurious club in the lower vault of a furniture warehouse . . . .

– Dr. John Watson
"The Five Orange Pips"

125

The Amnesiac's Peril
by Barry Clay

Those who are familiar with my attempts to edit the manuscripts of Dr. John H. Watson (that I found quite by chance), know that I also attempt to understand why the manuscripts went unpublished. Sometimes, the reason seems obvious, as when publishing during his lifetime would mean the embarrassment of someone still-living whom the doctor respected. Though the reason is less obvious for this case, "The Amnesiac's Peril", I wonder if the date of the case doesn't give us a clue. The larger adventure of The Sign of the Four *must have followed some months this narrative. As the longer and more elaborate of the two cases, perhaps the Good Doctor – or even his publishers – decided concentrate on the latter, and with the fame of Sherlock Holmes ever growing, this affair was lost among the increasing number of investigations for which he was engaged. But that is sheer speculation. What is clear is that this record remained unpublished during the doctor's lifetime. I submit it now to the reading public in the hopes that they will find it as satisfying as those that were released contemporaneously over a hundred years ago. – B.C.*

My friend, Sherlock Holmes, created the position of "consulting detective" several years before I met him. He committed his considerable talents to that profession to the exclusion of more mundane pursuits, and he reached the pinnacle of success due to his uncanny ability to deduce from seeming inconsequential observations facts that had gone unnoticed by others. To my knowledge, he had been consulted by royalty, the wealthy, and most surprisingly, by Scotland Yard. When the latter required his services, it was almost always due to the commission of some kind of crime that had left them baffled. Holmes proved his worth to them, and for this reason they returned, time and again, when faced with a case that, to them, appeared inexplicable or insolvable. There are many men (and some women) who served time in gaol or even ascended the gallows when they would otherwise have eluded the arm of the law and might perhaps even have gone unsuspected, save for Holmes's efforts to bring them to justice.

As the reader might imagine, this profession was not without its dangers. The criminal elements rarely abandoned their pursuits willingly, and there were times when my friend was in danger from scoundrels, those of low repute, and other villains who hoped to avoid the law by adding murderous violence to their crimes, assuming they had not already previously broken the Biblical Sixth Commandment by killing another.

126

Some cases announced their danger from the outset. Others, like a viper hidden in the grass alongside the road, were initially less obvious. Such was the visit of "John Doe" to our lodgings in Baker Street. No hint of danger suggested itself at that time. It was only later that the peril materialized.

It was early spring in 1888, and Holmes and I were occupied with our individual pursuits in our lodgings. Holmes was organizing his clippings. I was reading *She, A History of Adventure* by H. Rider Haggard, a mixture of improbable romance and hazard, but no less gripping for all that. So engrossed was I in the book that I lost track of time until Holmes's voice interrupted my reading. "I do hope that you don't intend to employ such lurid prose as I perceive this book uses when you recount further cases that you and I share together."

His remark surprised me, and I considered it unfair. "You are judging the book by its cover," I pointed out, for indeed, there was the drawing on its front of a voluptuous woman surrounded by shrouded menace.

"Not at all. I am judging the book by your reactions while you read it. You have held your breath several times in the course of an hour."

"It *is* very exciting," I admitted. "I am quite taken with it."

"And thus my request that, should you publish another account of an adventure you share with me, you maintain a more measured, steady tone than the one to which you first resorted." Holmes was referring to our first case together. When I realized that Scotland Yard intended to take the credit for Holmes's work on their behalf, I had written an account of the case and had shared it with him. I thought it a travesty of justice that he receive no credit, and I wanted to see my friend obtain the praise that was his due. To my delight, it was published by *Beeton's Christmas Annual*, and then later in book form by Ward, Lock & Co. At my behest, and only at my behest, he had read the account, which I christened *A Study in Scarlet*. To my disappointment, he had pronounced it sensational and melodramatic. "Even the title!" he'd commented.

And yet, I felt I had not strayed far from the facts, if at all, for the facts themselves held no little drama and sensation. And for all his implied censure, I was not certain that he was truly displeased at my efforts, for he never actually forbade me to write another. Since that first case, I had accompanied him on many other adventures and made notes of them, but I had not so far decided to write them down, as I was working toward establishing my own practice as a general practitioner and lacked the leisure time to do so.

It was at that point that Mrs. Hudson, our landlady, brought visitors to our door. One was known to me: Inspector Lestrade of Scotland Yard, who Holmes declared one of the more intelligent Yard inspectors, though cursed by a face that made one think of a weasel. He was a thin, energetic man, not very tall – almost short – and at that time of night, his face was showing the growth of his beard. He was holding his hat in one hand, the same one in which he was carrying a bag. Mrs. Hudson announced him, referred to his companion as Mr. John Doe, and withdrew with the tact for which I had always known her to employ when bringing visitors to our flat.

The man who was with Lestrade was older, perhaps in his late fifties or possibly his early sixties, but with a full head of white hair and a face only partially wrinkled with age. His blue eyes were bright and intelligent, but it was clear that he had been subjected to some kind of accident. His head was bandaged, and I could see bruising from under it. His step was firm.

"Please, come in," invited Holmes. "Lestrade, you can take your usual chair. Mr. Doe, you may take that one. I'm sorry to observe that you've had an encounter with the less-savory elements of our city."

The older man started. He spoke in tones unaffected by age. His voice was resonant, almost musical. "What do you mean?"

"You have evidently been ruthlessly set upon by the criminal element."

"I might have only had an accident," the gentleman protested.

"Unlikely, seeing how you are accompanied by an inspector from Scotland Yard. If the Yard is showing an interest in your case, I would be very surprised to find you came by your injuries due to simple misfortune. Why did you wait so long to bring him, Lestrade?"

Lestrade was used to Holmes's deductions, as was I. This was one time I followed them, though I would not have recognized its meaning without Holmes's words. Bruising with the colouring such as was evident on Does' face only followed an injury after several days. The inspector explained, "Didn't think we'd need you, Mr. Holmes."

"What changed your mind, Inspector?"

He shrugged. "We can't get any farther, and I thought you might be able to provide us some help."

"I will do my best. I assume Mr. Doe has been awarded his name because you don't know who he is, and I further assume that neither does he."

"That's correct, Mr. Holmes."

"Let's have the particulars."

"Mr. Doe was found three nights ago in Pimlico by a beat constable. He was insensible, and lying in a depression in the lawn alongside the walkway. He had a severe head injury. I understand his face was covered with blood. The constable was able to rouse him, only to discover that he had no memory of who he was or how he came to be there."

"And hence, the name of John Doe."

"We had to call him something."

Holmes turned to me. "Watson, this is in your purview more than mine." He explained for our guest, "Dr. Watson is a physician of great skill, and he has often helped me in my cases.

I was rather embarrassed by my friend's praise. I said, "It is known that a head injury of sufficient severity can cause temporary amnesia."

Our visitor spoke up, hope evident in his voice. "Temporary, you say? Then I may indeed recover my memory?"

"In all likelihood, though I could not tell you when, nor, truth to tell, give you complete assurances that you will. The workings of the human mind are still a mystery to my profession."

I could see that my qualification deflated his hopes more than I would have wished, but it would have been unpardonable and unkind to provide him with false assurances that were not within my power to give. Rather dejectedly, he said, "Oh. So I may never know who I am?"

Lestrade spoke before I could answer. "This is why we have come to Mr. Holmes. Even if you never recover your memories, he might be able to help discover who you are." He turned to Holmes. "You asked me why I didn't come earlier. That is easy to explain: I thought someone would come forward to report a missing person."

"And no one has," concluded Holmes.

"Right you are. The local constabulary brought him to the Yard, hoping our greater resources would be able to help discover his identity."

"I infer he had no identification."

"He had no wallet or money with him. Our assumption was that he was beset upon and robbed."

"A reasonable assumption. Here is another: He must live a solitary life or he would have been missed by now. He either has no employer to miss him, or he is on holiday. May I see his clothes in which he was found? It is obvious he is wearing borrowed clothing. They show no indications of having recently been in a ditch, and they don't quite fit."

"I have them right here, along with what little else was in his pockets," Lestrade said. He handed the bag he'd been carrying to Holmes. "When it became clear no one would come forward after the first day, we couldn't let him go without a change of clothes. A local vicar provided what he had by way of donations to his church for the poor."

"Splendid," Holmes said, withdrawing the soiled clothing from the bag. "I was afraid you would have had them cleaned."

"I know your methods," Lestrade pointed out.

129

My friend said nothing, but I could infer his opinion from his impassive face and my experience as his companion. He would never trust the police to leave clues undisturbed. Even Scotland Yard, Lestrade amoung them, had disappointed him too many times in the past by accidentally obliterating clues during their investigations.

He stood and walked to our dining table, where he laid out a charcoal grey three-piece suit, off-white shirt, maroon cravat and matching pocket handkerchief, grey hat the precise colour of the suit, black shoes, and other clothing, which he then proceeded to examine with a magnifying glass. At one point, he lifted a tie pin and examined it closely. The three of us watched his methodical examination quietly. Doe looked questioningly at Lestrade, who shook his head and made a motion to indicate that he had expected this, and his companion should be patient. Holmes turned the clothing over and used the same care he had exercised on their fronts. He then turned the clothing inside out, making a sound rather like a grunt of surprise or discovery. Lastly, he examined the underclothes, socks – which were also a matching grey – a small set of keys, and spent a significant amount of time examining the shoes, particularly the sides and soles. After a good quarter-of-an-hour, he returned the items to the bag from which he had withdrawn them and rejoined us.

"May I see your hands?" Holmes asked our guest.

Doe held them out, and Holmes made his examination before releasing them and returning to his seat. During the procedure, I noticed a ring on Doe's right hand.

"One can learn much from a man's hands," Holmes said by way of explanation.

"What did you learn from mine?"

"You have performed manual labor in the past, for your hands are calloused and roughed, but you have not done so recently. I saw no indication that would suggest you are familiar with tools that would be used in practice of the trades – no scratches, no abrasions. Likewise, you do not work in an office. At least you do not work as a clerk, for there is no mark on either of your hands as I would expect from frequent long toil wielding a pen. There are no indications of dirt or stains that one would expect from factory work. There are few forms of work that would leave your hands as they are: Perhaps work on a dock or a transport, but that was your past. You have left that work recently – not so recently that there are no signs remaining of it, but long enough that your hands are softening. I would estimate no more than two months ago. Perhaps you have come recently into money, and have decided to live a life of leisure, which would explain why no employer has missed you."

130

But I could tell Holmes was not satisfied with that explanation. "In all likelihood, you have received a promotion that no longer requires you to engage in manual labor, perhaps as a manager or supervisor. You may be on holiday. That is not only speculation. Some of the keys on the ring obviously fit a home, but the others are newly minted, and they suggest you have the confidence of your employer. They are not the sort of keys that would admit an owner to his private residence. They would more likely fit larger locks, such as padlocks or security locks."

"Did you learn something from my clothing?"

"There is not much to learn from the clothing, I'm afraid, except the obvious. The suit is of good material, but not overly expensive, The cut is a trifle out of date. From this, we can deduce that you are a man of modest means, but of means nonetheless. If you have come into money from an inheritance, it is one that you are husbanding frugally. If it is a promotion, the increase in income is limited."

"It seems to me that you have learned a lot," said our guest, with surprise, and perhaps growing respect.

"Perhaps, but there are inconsistencies. The cravat and matching pocket handkerchief are of fine silk – surprisingly fine, in fact – and of a luxury that I would expect only in the upper class. And yet, your diction, while educated, is not of the London social set. The shirt is stiff, but there is no launderer's mark on it that would proclaim it newly starched, suggesting that it is new. The off-white colour is unusual. But the suit, as I alluded to earlier, is not of a recent cut. And then, there are the stains."

"What do you mean?" said our client.

"I am puzzled by the lack of blood stains on the clothing. A severe head wound, such as I assume you sustained from seeing the bandaging you now wear, should have bled copiously and stained your clothing."

"I wondered about that myself," said Lestrade.

I suggested, "If he was struck and fell directly, the blood may have run off his face onto the ground, rather than onto his clothing."

"There is always that possibility," agreed Holmes. "But then there is the soiling of the clothes."

Doe asked, "The soiling?"

Instead of answering him directly, Holmes turned to Lestrade. "Did the constable who found Mr. Doe see anyone near him?"

"It would have been in his report if he had done so," responded the inspector, shaking his head.

"Then I am at a loss to account for the condition of his clothing. It is obvious from way the clothing is stained that the depression in which Mr. Doe was lying was wet, with some standing water, and that he lay in mud. If the ground had been dry, the stains would not be so thick. They would be more soiled than smeared. The mud has dried to a cake. It is clear that he was indeed in mud, as opposed to what one would expect if he had come in contact only with soil. The water should have been muddy, and it was, but the muddy water did not have time to seep through his outer garments. There are no stains on his under clothing, nor even indications that the muddy water made its way completely through his suit. His shirt is nearly unstained, except, perhaps from being in the same bag as his outer clothing." I detected a note of censure in Holmes's voice at this remark, but he continued. "True, the material of the suit is thick, and this alone might account for it. That being said, he could not have lain there very long. And yet, you say the constable reported seeing no one."

"I can confirm that if you think it important."

"Please do. It would account for much if he saw Mr. Doe's attacker and neglected to include that in his report. Mr. Doe would have been only a short time in the water, and that would explain the condition of his clothing."

"I will do that, Mr. Holmes." The inspector sighed. "I'm afraid this doesn't get us very far."

"Perhaps not, but I don't think we're quite done. You said Mr. Doe was found in Pimlico?"

"I did."

"And I assume the area was canvassed around where he was found?"

"Of course. That's standard procedure."

"And the majority of the time, that procedure would suffice. Even the mud that is now dried on his shoes would confirm that course of action, for it is common to that area. However, there is soil on the shoes incompatible with Pimlico, and I should have expected it to be found in Battersea."

"Battersea?"

"It is only a short half-an-hour walk from Pimlico. I would suggest that, as Pimlico has been unfruitful, that you try Battersea. Mr. Doe might come from there and have only been on a long walk. It is certainly within the realm of possibility. Watson and I take longer strolls on occasion."

Lestrade asked Doe, "Does Battersea mean anything to you?"

He shook his head. "I'm afraid not."

"And there is one other clue," said Holmes, turning to our guest and holding out his hand. "Could you give me your ring?"

With a questioning look at my friend, Doe removed it.

Holmes turned it over in his hand. "From its weight, we can deduce that this ring is majority gold, and yet, our thief, who relieved Mr. Doe of his wallet, money, and identification, left this ring."

"Perhaps the thief didn't have time," suggested Lestrade. "Or perhaps he was frightened away."

"Possibly," agreed Holmes perfunctorily, without conviction. Wordlessly, obviously distracted, he rose and went to the bookshelves, where he opened and consulted a volume, comparing something he found in it to the ring. Seemingly having found that for which he was searching, we watched him read for several minutes before he closed the book and returned the ring to our guest. "Lestrade, if all else fails, you might take Mr. Doe to Freemason's Hall here in London and see if he is recognized."

"How's that?" asked the inspector.

Holmes pointed. "The ring has a Masonic symbol on it. Wearing such a ring indicates he should be a member."

"What do you mean?" I asked.

Holmes explained. "I was refreshing my memory just now. I thought I recognized the engraving on the ring as one of the Masonic symbols, and I was correct. It is. Freemasonry is a fraternity which is thought to have begun in the Middle Ages, perhaps among a guild of masons, which later expanded their membership to include any man deemed worthy of admittance and sponsored by another Mason. In this day and age, I suspect few members of this fraternity have actually laid stones. They have a reputation – whether it is deserved or not I could not say – for secrecy." He turned to Doe. "If you're wearing that ring because you are a Mason – and I don't know why else you would have one – inquiry among Masonic lodges will eventually uncover your identity."

I could see that my friend's statement heartened our visitor.

"Fancy that," said Lestrade. "I never noticed it had a symbol."

And that, in a nutshell, was why my friend was successful. He noticed *minutiae* that others did not, and noticing them, made deductions from them. Soon, Lestrade and Doe were on their way. As they left Holmes said, "I would appreciate it, Lestrade, if you would let us know how this turns out."

"Of course," agreed the inspector.

After they left, Holmes didn't return to his clippings. Instead, he stuffed his pipe from the tobacco he habitually kept in a slipper and began to smoke. Past cases and taught me my friend's habits, and I didn't need his observational powers or his deductive skills to see that something was bothering him about our visitor.

"What disturbs you?" I asked.

"The inconsistencies."

"Of the clothing, you mean?"

"That, and the fact that his ring was left when he was robbed. The pin for his cravat, while not of the same quality as the ring, wasn't something

133

I would expect a thief to leave behind – not when it might fetch a few shillings at one of the less-reputable pawnbrokers."

"Why do you dismiss Lestrade's explanation that the thief had no time?"

"I do not dismiss it. But we understand from what Lestrade related to us that the constable saw no one. Or, at least, omitted that fact from his report, an omission I consider unlikely. The local constabulary and Scotland Yard may lack imagination and find more difficult crimes beyond their capabilities, but they can be depended on to perform their duties thoroughly and dependably. No. I expect that Lestrade, upon interviewing the constable, will find that he mentioned no one in the report because he saw no one."

"Perhaps the miscreant had difficulty removing the ring," I suggested.

"You saw Doe just now, Watson. Did you perceive he had any difficulty in removing it?"

"No," I admitted, "but I still do not see what this disturbs you."

"Let me put it like this: Let us suppose you are a robber."

"I am supposing this," I confirmed.

"Of course, this is quite out of your normal occupation," Holmes responded with a twinkle in his eye. "But you have helped me on a number of cases, and you are not unfamiliar with the habits of the criminal classes. Now let us suppose you have in your possession a cosh and the lack of morals to use it. You find an older gentleman strolling alone in the dark. You look both ways. There is no one about. You approach him stealthily, strike him on the head, and he falls off the walk into a depression, a ditch perhaps, partially filled with water. He has fallen, not on his face, which would certainly have stained his white shirt, but on his back. What do you do next?"

"Why, I relieve him of his wallet?"

"Is that what you would do next? Are you certain?"

I was surprised at his insistence. "But of course," I responded.

"But his wallet is certainly in one of his pockets. You cannot know precisely where it is, and you must move Doe's insensate body to find it. Certainly, before you turn him over searching for his wallet, you relieve him of his tie pin and ring. After all, they're right there in front of you. Only after you have stuffed them in your pocket do you turn over the body searching for the wallet."

"I can see that," I admitted, for Holmes's reasoning, as always, was sound. "But are you not assuming that his assailant was thinking reasonably? Might Lestrade not be correct? The man attacked Doe, and then panicked?"

"It is of course possible, but our assailant had the presence of mind to rob Doe of his wallet, a far more elaborate process than taking the pin and ring. If our assailant did panic, would it not be more likely that the wallet be left and the ring and pin taken?"

"I see what you mean. Very well, what does that mean to you?"

"That the ring and pin were not abandoned due to lack of time."

"Then why were they not taken?"

"That," said Holmes, "is the question whose answer eludes me, and that I find that disturbing."

Several days later, I had just arrived home during the late afternoon after attending my last patient of the day when Mrs. Hudson announced Inspector Lestrade. After we exchanged greetings, he sat and said to Holmes, "I must hand it to you. Almost everything you said turned out to be true."

"Only 'almost everything'?" Holmes returned, with a raised eyebrow.

"Now, none of that," admonished Lestrade. "You yourself said you weren't certain about some things."

"But he was a Mason?"

"He was. We had to go to Battersea, the New Wandsworth Lodge to be precise, to find someone who knew him, but know him they did. His name is Orlo Wilkerson. They said he had been a member for six months."

"That long?"

"Yes," answered Lestrade, but the inspector had caught the same note of surprise in Holmes's voice that I had heard. "Why? Did you expected he would have been a Mason longer?"

"No. I expected he would be a new member."

"Well, he is. Six months isn't all that long a time to belong to a club."

"No, but it is longer than I expected."

"Well," said Lestrade with a grin, "you can't be right all the time."

"I don't see why not," responded Holmes. He seemed to consider. "Would you know who stood him for membership, by chance?"

"As a matter of fact, I do. The clerk at the temple was quite proud to tell us that he was sponsored by a man none other than Henry Staunton." Lestrade shrugged. "I had never heard of him, but I gathered he's a big name in Battersea."

"Staunton," repeated Holmes slowly.

"That was the name," Lestrade said, then looked at my friend keenly. "You seem rather upset about it."

Holmes came to himself. "I am marveling at the coincidence. Do you remember the New London Bankers embezzlement case?"

Lestrade nodded.

135

"Not I," I admitted.

"It was rather before your time, Watson," explained Holmes. "It was at the beginning of my career. The bank manager of the New London Bankers engaged me on the recommendation of an acquaintance of his for whom I had provided a small service. He had first applied to the London constabulary to investigate a very clever scheme of embezzlement, but they had been unable to make headway. He suspected his personal secretary, Morgan Bowditch, of a breach of his trust, but investigation uncovered a pair of carelessly abandoned deposit boxes and some torn bank notes which pointed to a junior clerk, Laurence Staunton, as the mastermind behind the scheme, using accounts he had established in Bowditch's name to implicate him. I testified in the trial, and he was sent to gaol."

"Where he belonged," stated Lestrade.

"Indeed," agreed Holmes.

"Well, *Staunton* is not an uncommon name."

Lestrade was unimpressed. "You think it's the same man?"

"I couldn't say for certain without seeing him," replied Holmes.

"Well, I don't see that it matters if it is."

I tended to agree with the inspector. Just two months earlier, I had been pleased to encounter an Army man on whom I had operated in the field when in Afghanistan. I had never thought to see him again. He lived in Berwickshire and it was only by chance that he recognized me when passing through London. Coincidences simply happen. And yet, I could tell that Holmes wasn't satisfied.

After a moment of silence, Holmes decided to abandon his preoccupation. "Is there more?"

"Yes, there is. "Wilkerson used to work on the docks there, but was recently promoted to supervisor of the men. A clever piece of deduction there, I don't mind admitting, though it was the ring, of course, that identified him, and we'd have gotten on to that eventually."

I rather doubted the assertion, but I said nothing.

"Has he come into money?"

"Not so anyone said, though he has quite a nice little home there in Battersea, certainly more than I could afford on an inspector's salary. They must pay their dock foremen well, or, as you suggested, he has come into money. If he did, he doesn't remember it, and no one else knows."

"And he lives alone."

"That he does. He looked around the home as if quite lost. 'Are you sure this is mine?' he asked me. 'As sure as I can be," I told him, and I pointed out that the house key on his ring opened the door." Lestrade smiled at the memory.

"Was there anything unusual or remarkable in the house?"

"Not that I could see. It was a bachelor's residence. No pictures. No lithographs. It was bare of decoration. Some rooms were entirely empty of furniture."

"Odd that he would have purchased such a large house and left it unfurnished."

"He must not have gotten around to it," observed Lestrade.

"Were there framed awards? Flower vases? Were there books or periodicals?"

"None that I noticed," admitted Lestrade. Privately, I wondered if Lestrade would have noticed such things.

"Rather odd, that," Holmes remarked. "Even Watson and I, confirmed bachelors, have mementos from our cases. You can see some of them from where you sit. You will notice *The Times,* folded from being read, on the table. I know that Watson has a lithograph of his parents in his chamber."

"Mr. Holmes," said Lestrade, "People are different. If you were to deduce from the number of pictures in my home, you would be forced to conclude that I had no parents!" He laughed at his sally, rather a barking, almost-growling laugh that had a trace of mockery in it.

"Quite," returned Holmes coldly. "But the home you describe seems unusually devoid of memorabilia, even of furniture."

"I suppose it was."

"And yet, if I had not asked you directly about it, I doubt you would have thought it important enough to mention."

"Of course not, because it isn't important." Lestrade had spoken with a trace of annoyance in his voice. He calmed himself. "You listen to me, Mr. Holmes. You seem to have a bee in your bonnet about this case. It's over and done with, and you've given us good help. I'll have your normal fee sent to you. Let it rest. Goodness knows we have enough to do solving real crimes than worrying about this. All's well that ends well, I always say."

"Did you speak to the constable?"

Lestrade lost his newly-found calm. He was visibly irritated. "Yes. I knew you'd ask me about it. He is quite adamant that he saw no one about. In fact, he admitted that he might have missed Wilkerson if it hadn't been for his shirt."

"So, Wilkerson was lying on his back in the ditch."

The observation surprised Lestrade. "Why, I suppose he was. I can't see why that matters."

Remembering my earlier conversation with Holmes about the pin and ring, and his remarks about the cleanliness of the shirt, I could see why

Holmes found this worthy of confirmation. My friend nodded, but said nothing else.

Lestrade recovered his good humour. He had known Holmes longer than I had, and he was no doubt accustomed to having his feathers ruffled by my friend. "The only thing the constable remembered that might be considered out of the ordinary was hearing the call of an owl while turning the corner. He thought it odd, as he had never heard an owl in that patch before. Well, I must be off. Criminals never rest, and I've spent enough time here as it is." He turned to me. "Keep an eye on him, Doctor. He doesn't seem able to leave this alone. He may need your professional services if he keeps it up."

I considered that last remark entirely inappropriate. I gave the inspector his hat without a word and opened the door for him.

But he had one last parting shot, "Oh, Mr. Holmes, there's one thing you missed in all your examination of his clothes and hands."

Holmes raised an eyebrow. "Indeed. What is it you think I missed?"

"I don't think it – I *know* it! Wilkerson is colour-blind. Can't tell one colour from another."

Holmes made a quick intake of breath. "How do you know this?"

"I told you I took him to a church to get him some clothes."

"You did," Holmes responded.

"It was there. While waiting for the vicar, I pointed out the stain glass windows and how beautiful they were. Here, he couldn't make them out! All the colours were the same to him!" Lestrade barked his laugh again.

"I do not see how you could expect me to have known that." Holmes's tone was icy.

"Well, perhaps not. But after the way you go on about observing and deducing, I couldn't resist getting your goat, and I think I've done quite a good job of it. What do you think, Doctor?"

I was pleased to be able to shut the door behind him. There were times when Lestrade could be insufferable. When I turned back to Holmes, I could see he was deep in thought, and troubled thought at that. I thought I perhaps his pride had been wounded by the inspector's inconsiderate words.

"Holmes," I said, "I think he behaved quite abominably just now. You couldn't possibly have known that Wilkerson was colour blind."

Holmes met my eyes. "Indeed not, particularly since his suit, hat, cravat, and pocket handkerchief matched so well."

Holmes's statement took me by surprise, but as soon as he said it, I could only agree with it. We take matching a suit, hat, and other clothing for granted. I recalled that there was nothing jarring about Wilkerson's ensemble. In fact, I remember thinking how well the maroon tie and handkerchief contrasted with the gray of the suit, and how even the socks and hat were exactly the same grey.

At the same time, I couldn't see any import in the observation. I was on the verge of saying so, but restrained myself. To my eyes, Holmes seemed uneasy. He asked me, "What do you know of colour blindness?"

"Only what most of us know. A percentage of men and women, but mostly men, suffer from the benign affliction. In most, it is mild – an inability to discern red from blue, or green from yellow. I understand some do not even know they have it!"

"But to be unable to see any colour at all, like Wilkerson?"

"That is far rarer, but known to happen. Again, it is mostly men who have it." I considered. "I suppose they see the world in shades of grey."

"And yet, our visitor from several nights ago seemed to have no difficulty matching the clothing in which he was found."

"Perhaps he had help," I suggested.

Holmes looked at me keenly. "He most certainly had help, but who helped him? Lestrade tells us he lives alone. There are no pictures that would indicate he has a family. He has no wife, not even a manservant to report him missing. Who then, helped him match his clothing? Certainly not his employer."

"I couldn't say."

"Neither can I." He considered. "In the course of your practice, how many patients have you had who were colour blind?"

"I couldn't say. As I said, many who have it don't know that they do. They just perceive colour differently. In fact, you might think the cover of that books is red, and I agree, but who knows if we are really perceiving the same colour? The colour you call 'red' might be quite different than the colour I see, but we have both merely learned to call what we see 'red'."

The corner of Holmes's mouth turned up, mischievously I thought. "You appear to becoming quite the philosopher in your old age."

"Not at all."

"So, you have never met someone whose color blindness was so severe that they couldn't appreciate stained glass windows?"

"I can't say I have."

"I have. They called him 'Grey Boy.' Norman Willers was his given name."

"How do you know him?"

"Knew him. He went to the gallows for killing a man after a bar fight. He had lost the fight, but he waited outside the pub and ambushed him. When the man's lady friend tried to intervene, he used his knife on her face. He was a rough sort, and known for violence. The woman was quite

139

disfigured. But he left a trail of clues behind him even a blind man could follow."

"And you helped convict him?"

"I did."

"And he was colour blind?"

"Completely. It was why they called him 'Grey Boy'."

"What an odd coincidence."

"Perhaps. In my opinion, they are coming quite fast and furiously. Do I recall correctly that colour blindness runs in families?"

"I believe so. I can check my medical journals, if you want."

"Please do so." He walked by me and took his coat from rack.

"Where are you going?"

"Out." His face was grim. "I have some investigative work that needs done, I think." He added, "It may be nothing." And then added again, "But I doubt it. Don't wait up for me."

And he was gone.

Holmes never came back that day. At the expected hour, Mrs. Hudson served an exquisitely seasoned cut of beef, roasted with onions, potatoes, and carrots, accompanied with seared Brussels sprouts and followed by a pudding for dessert. Sadly, she wasn't unaccustomed to Holmes missing meals and forgetting to warn her he would be out.

She only commented, "Mr. Holmes is on one of his cases then?"

"Yes, Mrs. Hudson. He'll be sorry he missed this feast."

"That may be, but I sometimes wonder if Mr. Holmes notices what he eats."

"Well, *I* do, and I find your meals as good as any I have had."

"Bless you, Doctor, you are always the gentleman."

I stayed up later than my habit, hoping Holmes would return, but eventually I was forced to turn in when I awoke in my chair, my book overturned on my lap, a crick in my neck, and saw that it was past midnight.

The next morning, I discovered Holmes still hadn't returned, for the door to his room was still open. I was not alarmed by this. He had done it many times before. I made my toilet, breakfasted on eggs and rashers of bacon, and then went to see my patients. Later in the day, I had the opportunity to confirm, by way of research in various medical journals. that colour blindness was known to run in families, and was thought to be inherited. When I returned to our lodgings, Holmes still had not. I warned Mrs. Hudson that I thought our friend would miss still another meal, and I was proven right.

The next day was much the same, except that when my day was done and I had returned to Baker Street and found our flat empty, I was beginning to worry about Holmes's prolonged absence. I was relieved when Mrs. Hudson announced a visitor who, she said, "has information about Mr. Holmes."

The visitor was a grey-bearded, bow-legged man dressed as a sailor and who listed to the right. His face was visibly weathered by years at sea. He had neglected to remove his hat, but suddenly realizing the solecism, he did so. Mrs. Hudson withdrew, and I said, "I am told you have news of Mr. Holmes."

"That I do, that I do," he agreed, with a wizened voice cracked with age. "How much is it worth to ye?"

I was flabbergasted, and not a little indignant. "Do I understand that you are here to sell me information?"

"That I am! That I am!" His tone was almost cheerful. I began to expect I would hear him echo anything he had to say. "I am only a poor sailor. A poor sailor hoping to make an honest bob."

"It is hardly an honest bob to ask for money to deliver information I suspect Holmes has asked you to convey."

"That is most unfair! Most unfair! I agreed to come."

"Then you should conduct your business honestly!"

His voice became whining. "Mr. Holmes said you would pay. He said you would pay. Only a bob for a poor sailor? Only a bob?"

I had half-a-mind to call a constable, or simply turn him out, but I decided the price was worth it to relieve my mind. I turned to get some change. As I did so, I heard Holmes's voice. "Well, perhaps two-bob would be in order, given the import of the information."

I turned, and the sailor had straightened and was removing his beard. "Holmes!" I said, recognizing him.

"Do forgive me. I wanted to be assured that my disguise would fool even you, as it was important for my investigations that I not be identified."

"I am content to see you back. Where have you been?"

"Battersea, introducing myself as a retired sailor looking for work ashore. I'm pleased to announce that Mr. Wilkerson has recovered his memory. His home in Battersea has become quite a popular place."

"You spoke to him, then?"

"No, but I observed him. As I said, his home in Battersea has become quite popular. And Lestrade was correct. It is quite a nice home, though it is a rented one. It is only leased through the month."

"Is that important?"

"It is certainly suggestive."

141

"Of what?"

"Of impermanence – and *that* is important."

Holmes said nothing more about his disappearance. Again, this was not uncommon. When I asked him about it, which I did several times in the next couple of days, he would only say, "It will become clear – sooner rather than later, I think."

Indeed, two days later, when I returned to Baker Street from my rounds, Holmes handed me a letter from the post. "Wilkerson has invited the two of us to his home in Battersea for a meal this weekend to thank us for our efforts in uncovering his identity. Saturday. He informs us that his memory has now returned, and he is very grateful for what we did on his behalf."

"That is very considerate of him." And not unusual in my experience for Holmes's clients to express their gratitude above paying his fee, and in this case, there had been no fee from our client, only from the Yard.

"Very considerate indeed, though he seems to have neglected to invite Lestrade, and I would have thought the inspector, who brought him to us, did at least as much as we did."

"As much as *you* did," I corrected Holmes. "I did nothing."

"You gave him hope, Watson, and honesty. In my experience, both are a rare commodity in this world."

"Will you go?"

"I intend to. I would be obliged if you would accompany me. He did invite us both, after all."

"It would give me great pleasure, though I do not expect a meal at a bachelor's home to be the equal of Mrs. Hudson's."

"I wouldn't worry about that. I'm sure he will have something extraordinary prepared for our visit." He considered the invitation. "I think I will apprise Lestrade."

"Of the invitation?" I asked, surprised.

"Yes. No doubt, neglecting to invite him was an oversight."

I hesitated before speaking, but I found I had no choice but to point out, "Holmes, you cannot invite someone else to another man's home!"

He suppressed a smile, but there was a glint in his eyes that hinted that he found my objection humorous. "Oh, I will not be as *gauche* as all that. Trust me, Watson, inviting the inspector will make his day."

I had rounds for a half-day on Saturday, which thankfully had few patients and routine problems. I returned to our lodgings, spent a few hours relaxing, then dressed for dinner. Holmes joined me shortly after that, changing quickly after his arrival. To my surprise, he asked if I was carrying my service revolver.

"Of course not!"

"I should do so."

"But why?"

As he withdrew his own revolver from the desk drawer in which he kept it and checked to ensure it was loaded, he said, "Because we will have need of it before the evening is out, or I miss my guess."

Mystified, and not more than a little disquieted, I returned to my room, retrieved my revolver, which I kept loaded out of habit, and put it in my pocket. When I returned, he examined me. "Too obvious, Watson. Too obvious. Let me." He removed the gun from my pocket, lifted my coat jacket, and wedged it in my pants and shirt on the left side, butt facing front, letting the coat fall over it.

"This is deuced uncomfortable!"

He raised his own coat jacket, showing me that he had done the same. "But it is less obvious, and we do not want to alarm our host." He was correct that his jacket hid the fact that he was carrying a gun.

"But why are we doing this?"

"I told you: I expect we will have need of it. There is no little danger. Can I count on you?"

"Of course," I affirmed. "I just don't understand the need."

"Trust me, Watson, it will soon be clear. If I hide the information from you, I do it for your safety. You are far too honest. I do not want you to accidentally alert those who mean harm to the fact that we are on to them." I didn't know what to make of that statement. He then said, "Do me the favour of reaching for your gun." I did so, a little clumsily, I thought. I wasn't used to this arrangement. As I'm right-handed, I had to reach across my body, but when I did, I discovered that the gun, which as I said was positioned butt-first, could be withdrawn easily. "Splendid. Please return the gun and withdraw it three more times." I obeyed, finding the motion easier each time. Holmes nodded his approval. "I think that will do."

We left our lodgings, hailed a cab, and Holmes gave Wilkerson's address in Battersea. When we were both seated, I again asked Holmes what we were doing.

"We are going to foil a most heinous attempt at murder," he informed me.

I recalled that Wilkerson had been robbed and injured. Could it be, I reflected, that he was in more danger than what had already occurred to him? I had assumed that his assault had been the work of a robber, and that he had been identified at random, but what if it were more? What if his injuries had really been the result of an attempt to murder him? I remembered Holmes's concerns about the disparities in Wilkerson's clothing, its condition, and the fact that the constable who found him had seen no one. And that the wallet was taken, but the ring and tie pin left. And then there were the coincidences of the name Henry Staunton, and Wilkerson's colour blindness, and that of the ruffian nicknamed "Grey Boy". These were all related in some manner, I concluded, though how I could not fathom.

It was a short ride to Battersea. Upon reaching the address, I could see why Lestrade had been so impressed by the home. It was a square domicile, but with dormers peeking out from the roof and suggesting a first storey. The home was of some size, painted white, with decorative trim that was painted red with yellow highlights. The effect was striking. Even the garden was impressive, though it wasn't the best time for a garden. I surmised that, in summer with the flowers at their peak, it would be striking. The house was surrounded by a picket fence and gate, which Holmes and I opened so we could walk to the front door.

We had been expected, for the door was opened by a butler before Holmes could twist the bell. I don't know which surprised me more: The fact that Wilkerson had a butler, for I had understood he lived alone, or the utter hideousness of the man. The butler's square face was badly shaven. His eyes were sunken, giving him a porcine appearance, and several scars adorned his face. His hands, I could not help but notice, were overly large, and also scarred. Although dressed as a butler, he looked as if he would be more at home as a pugilist, and more likely to steal the silver than to polish it. In short, I had never in my life seen a butler whose appearance was so at odds with his position.

"You must be Mr. Holmes and Dr. Watson. Please come in. You're expected."

Even his voice was rough. His diction was appalling, and that despite the fact that I could tell he was attempting to be as polite as possible, almost as if he was playing a part, and playing it very badly.

Holmes was unaffected. "Thank you, my good man."

The butler shut the door behind us. "This here way," he said. What butler ever said *This here way*? I glanced at Holmes, but my friend seemed more amused than disconcerted. We followed the butler, who opened double doors for us and permitted us to precede him into a large room, evidently for dining. Four men were standing at various positions around the room. One was Wilkerson. He was holding a glass of wine. Another could have been the brother of the butler, for his low brow and shifty air made him look more like a criminal than a house guest. The other two were more prepossessing. Both were older and well-dressed, one in particular. The number of men surprised me, for the invitation had mentioned no other guests. While not saying so explicitly, it had led me to believe that Holmes and I were the only ones to attend. After all, not even Lestrade had not been invited.

Behind us, to my surprise, the butler entered the room instead of withdrawing when he closed the double doors, and I was astonished to hear the turn of a key in the lock.

"Ah, Mr. Staunton, I thought you would be here."

The best dressed of the men smiled, and not kindly. "Did you, Mr. Holmes? I think not."

And, to my surprise one of the men extracted a gun from his pocket. I turned, only to see that the butler was also pointing a gun at my friend and me. "Holmes!" I said, by way of warning. "We're trapped!"

The man Holmes identified as Staunton said, "And quite neatly, I think." He affected a note of pity. "The poor, conceited consulting detective walks quite willingly and unsuspectingly into danger, bringing his faithful companion with him to share his doom. Sad. Very sad. Did you enjoy the clues I left for you? I see you followed them as if I had been leading you by the nose."

I did not understand what he was saying, but one thing I knew: Holmes had expected this, and that was why he and I were both armed. What good this did us, I could not say. We were indeed armed, and the men around us did not seem to know this, but we dared not reach for our revolvers without running the risk of being shot.

"Who are you?" I asked Staunton.

He responded, "I'm sure your friend could tell you."

Holmes said, "Watson, let me introduce you to Henry Staunton. You will remember that I sent his son, Laurence, to gaol for embezzlement."

"Where he died!" declared Staunton savagely. "He died there at the hands of men not worthy to tie his shoes! Your Mr. Holmes made sure he served his time because of his oh-so-clever deductions and his butter-wouldn't-melt-in-his-mouth testimony on the stand. What had my boy done, other borrow a little money from a bank?"

Drily, Holmes said, "And attempt to frame another man for his crime."

"He would have repaid it! He didn't deserve what happened to him!"

Holmes, after a moment, said, "He certainly did not deserve to die for that crime. He was not sent to the gallows."

"But die he did! Suddenly! Viciously! You killed him as assuredly as if you had beaten him to death yourself!" His words were wild with fury. He was almost screaming. There was an edge of madness to his voice. The men around him looked at him uneasily. He seemed to take notice of this, and he calmed himself. "You will pay for that, Mr. Holmes."

The glint in his eyes was expectant with pleasure. I attempted to deflect him from Holmes by asking, "Who are these other men?"

Holmes answered instead of Staunton. "If you will allow me?" Staunton smiled cruelly and nodded. Holmes began explaining. "Mr. Wilkerson is, in reality, Hobson Willers, the father of Norman Willers, who was called Grey Boy, and who ascended the gallows for the murder of a man and the disfigurement of a woman."

"He was a good boy!" the man I knew as Wilkerson said. "It was an accident the man died."

Holmes was unmoved. "It was no accident. He laid in wait for him. Your son was a violent miscreant whose sentence was a mercy to those who came into contact with him, and a favour to those who would have come into contact with him had he lived."

"It killed his mother to have him die like that. That's your fault, Mr. Holmes."

"I would say rather it was your son's fault." Holmes turned to another man. "Giles Brewer's son Hubert killed his lady friend – or I should say *former* lady friend – when she decided that his character was less handsome than his appearance and broke off their engagement. I had a hand in bringing him to justice, for until my entry in the case, an itinerant vagabond had been suspected of the crime." He nodded at the last man. "Logan Pettitt, who I helped incarcerate for larceny." He addressed the man who was holding a gun on us. "I am surprised you have already been released."

Pettitt, the low browed man, said, "Glad I could be here for this."

"And, last, our butler: Carson Murphy, who served three years for assault and theft, and who left the prints of his distinctive shoes behind one too many times."

"I found them all," said Staunton, coming around the table and approaching us. "Willers was the first and quite by accident. He told me his story, so like mine, at a low pub such as I have begun visiting after my son's death. He, like me, wished there was justice for his son. Because of you there was no forgiveness for their mistakes. No leniency for their crimes. After that, I had my lawyers search for those you had wronged. I knew there had to be more. It was only a matter of time and money to find them, and I had plenty of each."

Holmes said, "But Watson had nothing to do with any of these cases. They were all before I knew him. You have me. Leave him go."

I had a surge of hope. If I were released, I could draw my service revolver and rescue Holmes. My hope was short lived.

"Wouldn't you like that, Mr. Holmes, so your friend could run for help." He smiled, not quite sanely. "It will be justice that your innocent friend suffers for your crimes."

The men began to move closer to us. Pettitt said, "Let me shoot him now."

"No, we must make him suffer," said Staunton. "I am paying you well enough."

"Only in the leg," Pettitt bargained.

But before Staunton could answer, the shrill sound of a police whistle shrieked in the room. We were all taken by surprise, except for Holmes, who suddenly darted to the man closest to him, Giles Brewer, and used him as a shield. The butler, Carson Murphy, made the mistake of pointing his gun at Holmes and firing, hitting Brewer. No longer having a gun pointing at me, I drew my revolver and fired at the butler. I was close enough that I could aim at the shoulder of his gun arm and be assured of hitting him. He dropped his weapon, cried out, and stumbled to his knees. Staunton drew his own gun, but the room exploded with policemen, and the shooting was soon over. Murphy and Brewer were injured, and the constables restrained the other men, relieving them of their weapons.

Lestrade strode in behind them. "Well, Mr. Holmes, you throw a fine party. I will enjoy putting these men where they belong."

"When did you first know?" I asked my friend later. "More importantly, *how* did you know?"

We were back in 221b Baker Street. Lestrade and his men had rounded up the five would-be murderers and even tended their wounds. "Don't know why," Lestrade had remarked, "since it will likely be the gallows for them all. The Crown takes a dim view of attempted murder."

"I would think that my reasoning is obvious now," Holmes told me, enjoying a pipe while I indulged in a cigar. "From the first, there were inconsistencies, as you know. Our 'John Doe' had very fine, silk cravat and matching pocket handkerchief, and yet the suit he wore was older and of medium cost. His clothes matched, even though he was blind to colour and its shades. It was as if more than one person was dressing him, which was indeed the case, and yet, he was supposedly a solitary man with no one to even report him missing. And why should a robber leave the ring and tie pin and take only the wallet? Even then, it occurred to me that the reason was to ensure that we did not know his identity, and yet leave sufficient clues behind that we could determine it."

"Is that what Staunton meant – that he was leaving clues for you to follow?"

147

"Indeed. Staunton, having meet Hobson Willers, decided to stand him for Freemasonry membership. He knew the membership ring would lead anyone with an eye for detail and moderate deductive abilities to find Willers' identity as Wilkerson."

"Why did he change his name?"

"Staunton had Willers changed his name so I wouldn't recognize it. He did so only for the Masonic temple – all part of the attempt to create a believable character with an extensive background. Elsewhere, he was still known as Hobson Willers. It was Staunton who provided his confederate his own rented lodgings – lodgings which were far beyond his means – for the simple expedient of having a place where they could be undisturbed when they murdered the two of us. It was why the house was so bare. Willers only lived there when he was pretending to be Wilkerson."

"Why didn't his workplace report him missing?"

"As we knew was possible, I confirmed when investigating that he had taken holiday, but for a more nefarious purpose than idle relaxation."

"So, Staunton purposefully planted clues that would permit you to uncover Willers's false identity?"

"Precisely. There were enough discrepancies, he felt, to raise my interest, and he was correct. From his point of view, he can be thankful no one at the Yard noticed the Masonic symbol on the ring, or the case may never have arrived at our door. I'll wager that if we ask the local constabulary and then Lestrade, we would learn that Mr. Wilkerson himself had asked if there was anyone who could help the authorities learn his identity."

"So, he had never lost his memory?"

"No more than you or I."

"But the injury?"

"Intentionally inflicted on him. As you well know, head wounds bleed copiously. I'm sure it looked worse than it was."

"But to injure him just for this ploy!"

"It was that or abandon their plans, and Staunton, in particular, was unwilling to do so. They dared not fake an injury. It might have been noticed. They had to have a plausible reason for the loss of his memory. But he was injured before donning the clothes in which he was found, which was why they were free of blood stains. You heard Staunton. He was paying them for their parts in the conspiracy. I would be interested to know just how much that head injury cost him."

"Why not simply lay in wait for you? Or just invite you to the house?"

"He couldn't be assured that chance would give him the opportunity he craved. Remember, he didn't simply want to kill me. He wanted me to suffer. He wanted to ensure that I knew *why* I was to die. Lying in wait for

148

me wouldn't achieve that end. Nor could he simply invite me to his home. I'm certain he feared a bald invite would raise my suspicions, and he would have been correct. No, he determined to lure me to my death by using against me the very attributes that have caused me to be successful and which have effectively brought so many to justice: My observational and deductive skills."

I pondered this. "But you were suspicious?"

"I was. You will recall my observations about the mud on the clothes. Why were the underclothes unstained? It was a puzzle, but we now know the answer. Wilkerson, alerted by one of the others – no doubt the call of an owl heard by the constable – knew that the constable was coming and then put himself into the depression. This was why the constable saw no assailant. There was none to see. It was why the water hadn't soaked through the suit. He hadn't lain long in the mud.

"I became more suspicious when the dual coincidences came to light of Wilkerson's colour blindness and the name of Henry Staunton, both connected with past cases of mine. It was at this point that I decided a more thorough investigation was in order. From the two days I was investigating in disguise, I learned Wilkerson's real name, and I observed three other men I recognized and who I knew did not wish me well. At that point, it was obvious that I had become the target of a conspiracy."

"You knew you were walking into a trap."

"I did."

"Why didn't you tell me?"

"And have your face give the game away before I sprang the trap of my own making? You have many excellent qualities, but dissembling isn't one of them."

"But why go through the danger? Why not tell Lestrade what you knew and have them arrested?"

"On what charge? Attempted murder? They had, so far, attempted nothing of the sort. Of wasting the time of the police and Scotland Yard? Would a magistrate care? Of hiding one's identity? Could we prove Wilkerson had *not* lost his memory? And if he had not, hiding one's identity is hardly a crime. Renting a house under a false name? Not illegal as far as I know. If I had asked the Yard to intervene too early, the five criminals would have become alerted to the fact that I had uncovered their plot. I couldn't let that happen, or they might develop another, and they might concoct a better one than they had so far done and succeed on their second attempt. No, I needed to provide Staunton and his accomplices an opportunity to reveal themselves and their homicidal intentions before witnesses, including an incomparably honest witness such as yourself. And *that* they did. In addition to yourself, four constables and an inspector

149

with the Yard heard them. Nor can they say they didn't really intend to murder me. In attempting to shoot at me, one of their number was struck. Their game is up. No jury will be convinced that these are anything but dangerous men, and if they do not go to the gallows, I will be very much surprised."

"We can hope so," I agreed. I mused aloud. "So, Staunton planted the clues that led you to him."

"But it was the clues he did *not* plant that did him in. With those who wish us harm behind bars, what do you say if we obey the injunction to 'Eat, drink, and be merry'? We have missed our evening meal, and we are owed one, I think."

And that was what we did, ending a case in which the peril was at first hidden, but in the end, ultimately avoided.

". . . and there was Henry Staunton, whom I helped to hang . . . .
– Sherlock Holmes
"The Missing Three-Quarter"

The Mystery of the Unstolen Document
by Mike Chinn

It was a clear, warm evening, summer declaring it was far from done with us. I watched from our Baker Street window as the setting sun cast a roseate glow across the city, faded to a smoky pink by distance. Even those out enjoying the last of the warm rays seemed to be extra cheered by them. The ruddy face of a child split by a grin was mirrored in the more corpulent features of a fellow who strode with a precise tempo, his jauntily swung stick marking time to a private rhythm. Laughter and gaiety were abroad in that time.

All of this was of course lost on my friend Sherlock Holmes, absorbed as he was at the moment in contemplating a specific form of immortality.

"I submit to you, Watson," said he, "that the more adventurous criminal mind will be remembered by the public long after the reputations of the great and good are as much dust as they."

I turned away from the window and removed my pipe from my lips. "Are you suggesting that a creature such as Moriarty – or his notoriety, at least – will live on longer than your own fame?"

"Ha! All that posterity will know of me is already published in your lamentably romanticized volume based on last year's Lauriston Gardens case – a prospect which fills me with a certain degree of horror." Holmes permitted himself the briefest quirk of a smile. He leaned back and puffed solemnly upon his own noxious pipe for a moment. "But you go some way towards supporting my hypothesis. The public is more interested in the crime, and the dramatic way in which you have me arrive at my conclusions, than the cold facts. If Moriarty was not, by necessity, such an occluded figure, he might already be the hero – if that is the correct term – of a series of weekly penny instalments. Another Spring-Heeled Jack, his nature transmogrified by the pen of a Charlton Lea or some other pseudonymous hack."

"I was unaware you were so well acquainted with such publications," I smiled.

Holmes stared back, a poorly concealed glint in his eyes. "My point, Watson, is that the public appetite for sensationalism will always prevail. The rogue has a twisted appeal that no man of charity or good works can match. Saints have statues raised to them in quiet corners. Devils have libraries written about them, conflating fact and fiction until it becomes a trial to determine one from the other."

"I think," I said after I had allowed a reflective moment to pass, "that you are starved of work and your brain begins to feed on its morbid fancies."

Holmes nodded. "It is true that the criminal world has been exceptionally quiet of late. Perhaps it is the clement weather. Whatever the reason, it is quite tedious."

At that precise moment, there was a familiar knock upon the door, and Mrs. Hudson entered the room. "There is a Mr. Chillingford downstairs," she said to Holmes. "He begs to speak to you. He is most insistent."

My friend barked a laugh and sprang to his feet, his disreputable dressing gown crumpling to the floor as he shrugged it off. "The universe listens, Watson! Show him up, Mrs. Hudson! Show him up!"

By the time our new visitor was ushered through the door, Holmes had slipped on a coat and knocked out his pipe into the hearth. I stayed by the window, observing the newcomer as my friend gestured for him to sit. After a certain degree of hesitation, the man took a seat, while Holmes flung himself down onto the sofa and regarded the fellow with keen eyes.

"Very well, I am Sherlock Holmes, and this is my friend, Doctor Watson. Now, Mr. Chillingford, what is so urgent that you need to see me at such short notice?"

The newcomer glanced briefly in my direction, giving me a terse nod of acknowledgement, before turning his face once more in Holmes's general direction. He didn't look at my friend directly, I noted, but rather his skittish gaze danced around the fireplace and the various objects stacked along the mantelpiece, never resting for more than a heartbeat or two.

Chillingford was dressed in a well-cut suit that spoke of the more-expensive tailors. His waistcoat and tie were fastened with precision, but his shirt collar needed starching. His boots were new and polished. Yet for all that, there was an air of untidiness about him: His dark hair was unbrushed, he was in need of a shave, and his long sallow face was coated by a sheen which inspired in me some concern for his general well-being. He was not, I thought, a healthy man.

He swallowed fitfully and spoke, his voice high and querulous. "My name is Sheraton Chillingford. I am the victim of blackmail – "

Holmes cut him short with an impatient hand. "Blackmail is not my concern, Mr. Chillingford. I suggest you consult with the police."

The other shook his mournful face and looked at Holmes directly for the first time. "No, no, Mr. Holmes, you misunderstand. It isn't for that

152

reason that I am here. I have sinned, and blackmail is my penance. I am reconciled to that, even though acceding to the blackmailer's demands will certainly cost me my job, if not my reputation . . . ."

Holmes sighed loudly and Chillingford nodded, his gaze once again affixed to the fireplace. "Perhaps I had better tell you everything."

"That is usually an admirable start."

"Very well." Chillingford straightened himself in his chair, obviously composing himself for a distasteful confession. "I work for a firm of solicitors, Coleborn and Edwards of Holborn, in a role that you might equate to a solicitor's clerk – although I flatter myself my job is somewhat more elevated than that."

"Is this a firm of criminal lawyers?"

"No, sir. Our main business is concerned with the sale and purchase of property. Land, conveyancing, and such . . . ."

"Indeed. And you have a well-salaried position, Mr. Chillingford. So much is evident in your attire. As is the fact you have recently become quite careless in your dress and work habits. There is ink upon your coat's right cuff, and under the nails of your left hand. Clearly you aren't in the habit of removing your coat at your workplace, which implies a degree of formality. You are normally much more careful, for it wouldn't do to have such an expensive item of wardrobe stained in such a way. Also, I observe you are unmarried."

"No, but – "

"No wife would tolerate her husband presenting himself to the world unshaved and with an unlaundered collar. You are also overdue a visit to a barber. You aren't betrothed in any way?"

"No."

"Do you have parents? Siblings?"

"My parents passed away several years ago. I had a younger sister, but she died in childhood."

"Well, then." Holmes relaxed, closed his eyes, and placed templed fingers against his lips. "Whatever sin you feel requires expurgating isn't one which may be used as a threat against loved ones. An exposed affair may be uncomfortable – even shaming – but it is clearly nothing so mundane. Whatever fall from grace has left you vulnerable to the blackmailer must therefore be a threat to your position and character."

"Indeed." Chillingford's eyes lowered themselves until he was staring at the floor. "I – collect books . . . ."

Behind his slim fingers, Holmes's lips tightened into a thin smile.

"There is a part of London with which you may not be familiar, Mr. Holmes – "

"Forgive me, Mr. Chillingford, but I doubt there is an inch of this city with which I am unfamiliar, either by reputation or personal experience."

"No. Quite." Chillingford composed himself once again. "Then you will know of Holywell Street, close by to Fleet Street and the Strand."

For a moment Holmes said nothing, but I doubt it was through ignorance of the thoroughfare of which Chillingford spoke. Once described by *The Times* as *"the most vile street in the civilized world"*, even I knew of the street's repugnant character.

"A narrow road of crooked, timber-framed buildings," spoke Holmes at length. "The site of what is claimed to be the oldest shop sign in London, on the corner of Half Moon Passage. Originally the terrain of radical pamphleteers and printmakers – until a government crackdown on subversive publications in the early years of the century forced the printers to seek other markets. From that moment, the second-hand bookshops punctuating the ancient street changed from selling radical politics to volumes catering to mankind's baser appetites. Despite the sale of such books being illegal since eighteen-fifty-seven, a lucrative trade continues. Ironically, this sink of depravity is almost overlooked by the Royal Courts of Justice." Holmes opened his eyes and gave Chillingford a level stare. "A building with which you are equally familiar, I think."

The other nodded slowly. "I am, on occasion, required to courier documents both to and from offices within that edifice. Major disputes over property ownership and the like are dealt with by the Chancery Courts . . . ."

"*Jarndyce versus Jarndyce*, as Dickens so ably catalogued it." Holmes sat upright, his eyes alight. "We get to the meat of it at last. Well, Mr. Chillingford, allow me to expound upon your difficulties, since you are – understandably – reluctant to do so yourself. During your occasional visits to Chancery you have taken the opportunity to visit the unspeakable Holywell Street, where you sought out certain volumes to sate your particular vice, and this has brought you to the notice of one who was eager to exploit your weakness. He or she was aware of your position?"

Chillingford nodded again. "On our first acquaintance, it was clear he already knew who I was and what business I had at the legal offices."

"Then we are dealing with a cool, scheming brain. You will not know him by name, of course?"

Chillingford shook his head. "They were heavily bearded. A disguise, I am sure."

"Intriguing. What form did this blackmail take? Not money, I imagine?"

"There was a certain document, one detailing a recent dispute over probate, to which he required access"

"You were to leave it somewhere accessible so that he might remove it?"

"The office was to be left unlocked." Chillingford's voice grew fainter with every word as he made his confession.

"Which you did."

"Three nights ago, Mr. Holmes." The man's voice was barely above a whisper. "But that isn't the whole of it. To my shame, I did exactly as I was told, and yet – "

"The document in question was untouched."

Chillingford's eyes widened in shock, his voice finding new strength. "Precisely, sir! I left it in a drawer, partly hidden so that a casual eye wouldn't spot it, but one knowing of its presence would find it easily enough. Yet in the morning, it was still where I had placed it."

"Exactly? It hadn't been moved at all? You are certain?"

"Positive. Two sheets of paper had been lain across it at an angle, just so, enough to obscure its content. They hadn't been moved. I would swear to it."

Holmes's brow drew down. "And the blackmailer?"

"A day later I received a note thanking me for my assistance and a hope I would feel free to visit Holywell Street again." Chillingford's hands were twisting in knots of anxiety. "I am on the hook, Mr. Holmes, am I not? This was a test, to see how I would act to protect my name. How low I would descend."

"To the contrary, I think you have been set free, Mr. Chillingford. You have performed exactly as your blackmailer wished and, unusually, he wants nothing more from you. As to the depths to which you allow yourself to sink – that is entirely a matter between you and your conscience."

"But what does it mean, Mr. Holmes? What have I done? Indeed, have I done anything?" Chillingford's voice grew ever more plaintive, although I confess, I couldn't feel sorry for him. He had broken the law, after all. If he required his conscience to be cleared, he would have to approach the police and make a full confession to them, not my friend.

"I will have to investigate further," said Holmes, "if only to put flesh on the bones of my suppositions. It is an intriguing case, but not complex. I'll be in touch once I have all of the answers I require, and my assurance this blackmailer will not trouble you again."

Chillingford sprang to his feet, hands reaching as though to grasp Holmes's in gratitude. Seeing my friend's reluctance to reciprocate, the man's arms dropped to his side and he deflated visibly. "Thank you, Mr. Holmes," he said quietly. "I imagine I am not worthy of your consideration, but I thank you anyway, humbly." He bowed in my direction. "Doctor. I will await you word, then."

After he had left I said to Holmes, "Are you really going to investigate this sordid affair? Are you so desperate for stimulation?"

He laughed. "The wretched Chillingford and his tawdry vices hold no interest for me, Watson, but the document that was requested yet never taken . . . ." He clapped his hands together. "What does that suggest?"

I thought for a moment. "It was a test, just as Chillingford said. The blackmailer will return, demanding he commit something worse."

"Possibly. Once such a creature has claws to its quarry, it is often reluctant to grant the victim any release. But no – when something is specifically demanded, yet apparently ignored, there is another, quite obvious reason." Holmes placed his pipe between his lips and lit a match. "Something else was taken in its stead," he said between puffs. "The blackmailer's true objective."

Holmes returned to Baker Street in the early hours of the morning. I awaited his return, fortified by Mrs. Hudson's coffee, and searching through the newspapers for any detail on recent and pending courtroom proceedings. It wasn't a difficult task, for as with my friend's recent experiences, the courts of London – if not the entire country – seemed to be unusually quiet: Nothing but the most petty cases, many requiring nothing beyond a magistrate's attention or the sitting of a local assize.

When my friend came through the door, he was still masked by the disguise he had adopted soon after the wretched Chillingham's departure, and a mischievous gleam lit his eyes as he removed a slightly worn top hat. An ill-fitting overcoat was draped over a tailcoat and white tie – despite the night's warmth – and mud-flecked spats topped his boots. Much of his face was buried under a luxuriant set of brown side-whiskers and moustache, so much so that his mouth was all but hidden. His aquiline nose was padded out into a ruddy toper's potato, and what could be seen of his cheeks was flecked with spidery veins. He had also thickened his lean frame so that an impressive girth poked through the unbuttoned topcoat.

From under his long, outer garment he produced a clutch of small books, glancing at them with distaste before tossing them carelessly into the open hearth.

"If nothing else they will provide kindling," he said, shrugging off both coats and reaching for his dressing gown. "It was necessary for me to buy something to avoid suspicion, and they were the cheapest of such items I could find."

"What else did you discover?" I asked, passing him a cup of hot coffee. He took it gratefully and lowered himself into a chair.

"Rather it was I who hoped to be discovered. I visited several of the establishments to be found along Holywell Street, browsing and enquiring somewhat imprudently about the availability of certain notorious volumes which are too rare to be found even in that avenue of depravity. Naturally, all of the proprietors were unable to help, but one assured me that he knew of someone – a gentleman of taste such as myself – " Holmes barked a laugh even as he peeled off his facial adornments. " – who would certainly be able to guide me to another specialist vendor – " He laughed again. " – if not in a position to offer me at least one of the books himself." Holmes finished removing his whiskers and dropped them carelessly to the floor. "I, of course, excited at the prospect of attaining something of what I desired, handed him my card – A very unwise thing to do under the circumstances, do you not think? – and left his shop. I now await word, which I anticipate will not be long in arriving."

"Your card?"

He took a sip of coffee. "My apologies, Watson, I spoke imprecisely – an unforgiveable slip. What I handed to that unsavoury bookseller was the card of one Sir Edwin Thornton Styles: A major landowner who lays claim to many estates and properties across the country. Magistrate, master of the hunt, and general *bon viveur*." He drained his coffee and patted his straining girth. "A man who comes down to London on a regular basis, taking rooms at the Clarence Hotel – he is staying there tonight, after arriving earlier this evening – although he usually has little reason to bother the hotel staff."

"You created an alias?"

"I have several, in fact. Ready to be drawn on and inhabited as necessary if the situation demands it. All have easily traced lives – should anyone find it necessary to check their various provenances. I'm ashamed to admit I am quite proud of them."

I confess to being astounded. Not that Holmes had created pseudonyms for himself – I had known him as a master of disguise many times, although rarely for a day or two – but that he had a repertory company of aliases, created with cunning and foresight, ready to be slipped into like a suit of clothes. More, that he could maintain the deceit to the point where these avatars had a life, of sorts, entirely independent of him.

"And how do you believe you will receive word?"

"Through the hotel staff." Holmes began to remove his false nose. Some of the drawn-on cheek veins smudged as he peeled off the theatrical putty. "A message for Sir Edwin will of course be left at the reception, awaiting his appearance. It will be intercepted, copied, and its contents relayed to these rooms in due haste. Meanwhile, did your examination of the papers yield anything?"

"Very little. I found nothing in the court records of any obvious importance."

"Then we must broaden our search." Holmes flung the now-mangled false nose aside and stood, making his way towards the pile of newsprint. He began to scan through each broadsheet. "If the answer doesn't lie with a recent or pending case, then it may be elsewhere, and consequently harder to recognise. But it will be here. I am certain . . . ."

"May I be of further assistance?"

He paused, looking round at me. "I thank you for the offer, Watson, but you look tired. A night's rest is best for you, I think. I will see you in the morning, when more will be clear, I trust." With that, he returned his attention to the newspapers, and I was dismissed.

"Well then, goodnight," I said, although I'm certain he didn't hear me, submerged as he was in his trawling for the least snippet. I retired to bed.

In the morning, after a decent period of sleep, I arose and left my bedroom to find Holmes gone. The newspapers were scattered around the room, dismembered and chaotic. That Holmes was missing I took as a sign that he had found something amidst the mess of newsprint. All I could do was await his return.

I filled in the time tidying up the room and reassembling the newspapers into something like their original form before Mrs. Hudson delivered breakfast and saw the mess Holmes had left behind him.

He returned shortly after I had finished my task, and moments before Mrs. Hudson entered with a breakfast of kippers and scrambled eggs. Holmes poured himself coffee but ignored everything else, except for a slice of toast.

"Well?" I asked when it became obvious he wasn't about to volunteer any information. "Did word come? Have you been to see the blackmailer?"

"Not at all, friend Watson. I have been on a small errand. There are some tasks which are best conducted during the hours of darkness, when honest souls are abed." He poured himself a second cup and sat by the empty fireplace.

"Then you found something? In the newspapers?"

"I did. They are as ever filled with titbits and *minutiae*, but little worth a farthing. There is, however, nothing about whatever was actually taken from the solicitors' office."

"Then was anything taken?"

158

"Be assured it was. Yet so far, its absence hasn't been noted – or if it has, its absence is being kept quiet. That it was of some importance is obvious. They couldn't allow Chillingham to place it ready for removal, lest he speak of it. They dare not test if their hold over the wretched man was strong enough. Leaving the office door unlocked was sufficient."

I recognised the barely suppressed energy vibrating through Holmes's frame. "What did you uncover?" I asked.

He took a scrap of torn newsprint from a pocket and handed it to me. I smoothed it flat and read aloud:

> *The Duke of Foynes wishes it to be known that his estate in the South Riding is to be put up for auction. All sealed bids must be received by his London agent C and E by September the first.*

I glanced at the calendar. "That was four days ago."

"Exactly. You see the connection? *'C and E'*? *Coleborn and Edwards*? The very firm for which Chillingford works. The blackmailer cared nothing for some minor probate dispute, but a folder of sealed bids for an extensive estate in Yorkshire . . . ."

I saw the reasoning. "But to what end?"

"For that, I need to consult with the blackmailer himself. I have a hypothesis, but it must be tested, and for that I will need both our perpetrator and the assistance of Sir Edwin Thornton Styles once more."

I sat down to eat, but I couldn't persuade Holmes to take more than he already had. I recognised the symptoms: He was too excited by the case. All of his faculties were focused on the outcome, his mind sifting through what data he had, probing for weaknesses in his reasoning. He wouldn't eat until all was resolved.

After a while Mrs. Hudson returned – not to remove the breakfast things as I assumed, but with a note.

Holmes leapt to his feet and all but tore it from the poor woman's hand. He scanned it for a second.

"A response, Watson! Our man rises to the bait quickly. Clearly the lure of Sir Edwin Styles was too much of a temptation."

"Perhaps too quickly," I commented. "Could he be suspicious?"

"It is a possibility – but we know he is audacious. And he wishes to meet this evening, at ten-minutes-past-five. A very precise time. It would seem he is a creature of exactitude, and not afraid to expose himself during daylight hours."

"He was disguised when he met with Chillingford," I said. "I don't like it. It would be too easy for him to spring a trap."

159

"Ever the voice of caution, Watson. Perhaps, but he has elected to meet on the Serpentine Bridge. There will be more than sufficient people enjoying the park to make any type of spectacle unlikely. I'll wager he has chosen it for that very purpose: He has no reason to trust Sir Edwin will follow his request to be alone, after all."

"And will you?"

Holmes's lips twitched into a brief smile. "The request is for Sir Edwin to come alone, not Sherlock Holmes. I trust you will be there, friend Watson, maintaining an as unobtrusive watch as possible. And," he added, "with your trusty service revolver as a precaution."

We shared a cab to the park, Holmes once again be-whiskered and padded, his corpulent frame draped by an opera cloak, and a top hat sitting squarely on his head. My revolver was a comforting weight inside my coat as I silently fretted over the risks my friend could be taking.

I alighted on the North Carriage Drive and began to make my way on foot towards the Serpentine and the bridge across it, cutting across the park while Holmes's cab turned south onto the West Carriage Drive. I reached the lake and found a bench overlooking the water that was within easy sight of the Serpentine Bridge. Sitting back, I looked about me as though enjoying the late afternoon sun. As Holmes had predicted, the pathways around the lake and across the bridge were busy with couples out taking the warm air, nannies with perambulators, cyclists, and groups of children running wildly along the water's edge and through the clumps of undergrowth. It seemed inconceivable that blackmailers might be abroad, but Holmes often remarked that crime paid no attention to the weather, and little heed of the hour. As I sat on that bench, surreptitiously watching the bridge – and the rotund figure standing upon it, occasionally pacing, occasionally looking down at the swans and ducks – I amused myself by wondering how many of the strolling couples might include a potential murderer, how many nannies stole from their employers, how many of the solitary gentlemen – even as they smiled and tipped their hats – had souls of the darkest hue.

Such thoughts cast a pall over the warm sunlight, and I endeavoured to dismiss them, instead concentrating on the wildlife – when I wasn't watching Holmes's disguised figure waiting on the bridge. I thought I detected a tension in his frame. An impatience. He was eager for the game to begin and our man to show himself.

I took out my watch. It was nine minutes past the hour. If our quarry was as exact as his timing of the rendezvous indicated, he would appear shortly.

Although I resisted the temptation to consult my watch again – I was fearful such an action might arouse the suspicion of anyone the blackmailer had engaged to stand guard, much as I was doing – I counted down the seconds in my head. Almost to the moment as I timed them, a tall, distinguished looking figure approached Holmes and raised his tall hat in greeting. I couldn't distinguish any features, even though the sun was, in general, shining full on him. He seemed relaxed, gesturing with his cane, as though discussing a recently planted herbaceous border with the man he believed to be Sir Edwin Thornton Styles.

Holmes appeared less sanguine: Twitchy, annoyed, irritated by this stranger who had demanded an audience. Yet also subdued, as the reason for the interview might already be guessed and weighing on his conscience. It was a masterly performance.

They talked for over five minutes as I reckoned it – although it struck me that the other man did most of the talking while Holmes listened. As each minute passed, Holmes's corpulent figure deflated further, sagging under the realisation of where his particular taste in literature had brought him. By the time the second figure bowed in farewell, tapping his hat brim with the cane in insolent salute, "Sir Edwin" was clinging onto the bridge's stone parapet, quite overcome by the enormity of his situation.

Holmes stayed in that position for several more minutes, giving the blackmailer adequate time to satisfy himself that he wasn't being followed and leave the park. Then his figure straightened, allowing the parapet to take his weight, and, turning to face me directly – for of course he had spotted me earlier – gave a nod that was just enough for me to perceive at that distance. He turned and walked north along the Carriage Drive, back to the cab he would have awaiting him, still a soul wracked by guilt and whatever the blackmailer had demanded. Once I had lost sight of him behind the bushes which grew parallel to the lakeside, behind my bench, I also came to my feet and headed back towards the Bayswater Road and Hyde Park Place.

I made my way unhurriedly, not wishing to be seen rushing by any stalker placed there by the blackmailer – for I couldn't shake off the belief there was at least one. As I neared Hyde Park's magnificent John Nash Arch, I saw the cab. A head appeared, and despite the heavy makeup I recognised that keen gaze as Holmes raked the landscape behind me, searching for any indication I was being followed. He gestured tersely, indicating I should come ahead and I made my way closer, climbing up beside him.

Holmes rapped with his cane, indicating to the cabby. We pulled into the city's chaos, and I allowed myself to relax. Our carriage began its deliberately indirect return to Baker Street.

161

My friend was already divesting himself of his disguise. Whiskers and false nose were pushed unceremoniously into a small bag at his feet. He was in a state of high excitement.

"Did you see him, Watson? Did you recognise him?"

I shook my head in apology. "Too distant, I'm afraid. Who was he?"

Holmes pursed his lips. "He was disguised, as you thought, but it was a poor effort. I am sure I know him, but until I have access to a likeness and can be positive, I dare not say." He continued to clean off his face and said no more.

Once our circuitous route was completed and we were back at our rooms, Holmes sorted impatiently through his collection of almanacs and reference works. He flicked through the pages of one until, with a cry of satisfaction, he jabbed a slender finger at a small photograph, reproduced within a column of print. "It is he! Good Lord, Watson, but this case takes on a devilish turn!"

I leaned in closer, the better to see the image at which he pointed. It was of a fine-boned face, with a neat moustache upon aristocratic features. Even though the photograph wasn't a particularly sharp one, I could still detect traces of arrogance in the dark eyes and tilt of the lips. It was all too easy to imagine the owner of that face to be the one I had seen on the Serpentine Bridge, saluting cockily with his stick.

"But his is Lord Jabez Pulborough!" I said.

"Exactly, my friend." Holmes stood back, his heavy brows drawn down. He found a thick pencil and quickly sketched muttonchop whiskers onto the lean-faced image. Once he was done he grunted in sombre satisfaction. "The same – a philanthropist who has spent nearly a quarter-of-a-million upon the London poor. A man whose good works has provided him with the aura of a modern-day saint."

"Yet a blackmailer . . . ?"

"And most likely the publisher of some of the most repellent books to be found in London, the distribution of which enable him to select his victims. These are deep, dark waters, Watson. The least unsubstantiated accusation of such a man, the smallest hint without proof, and we are finished, our reputations irrevocably destroyed."

"That much is clear." I calmed my racing thoughts. "What did he demand of you – or rather, of Sir Edwin?"

My friend permitted himself a cold smile. "I have already said that my avatar owns estates across Britain – or apparently so. There is one, a large estate in the north of England, in which Lord Pulborough is particularly interested. He suggested – in a manner that could never be proven to mean I was buying his silence – that I sign over that particular property to him."

"But there is no estate – ?"

"Yes, but do you not grasp the significance?" Once again. he produced the square of paper torn from a newspaper. "The Duke of Foynes' lands are in Yorkshire, but a short distance from Sir Edwin Styles' fictitious estate." He shook his head. "I had thought our blackmailer to be merely a man who took advantage of those with a weak character – and no doubt in the main he is – but there is also method here. A calculated, premeditated method."

He crossed to the mantlepiece and began to fill his pipe. "The wretched Chillingford was blackmailed into leaving his offices unlocked so that Pulborough might take the sealed bids for the Duke of Foynes' South Riding properties – or so we believe. A substitution will have taken place – else the partners of that firm would surely had noticed. The folder containing the sealed bids was replaced with an identical one containing a single bid."

"Lord Pulborough's – "

"No doubt several, in many envelopes, all the better to imitate the genuine folder. How Pulborough must have rejoiced when Sir Edwin Styles fell into his snare – a man with property adjacent to that he was sure to be buying." Holmes laughed heartily.

"But why?"

Holmes took a deep drag on his pipe and exhaled a large noxious cloud. "That, my dear Watson, is something I hope to prove in the days to come. Lord Pulborough required that the requisite documents pertaining to Sir Edwin's estates be forwarded to him *post haste* – "

"There are no such documents . . . ."

"There are, but their legitimacy is questionable. Last night, after discovering the Duke of Foynes' advertisement in the newspaper, I took it upon myself to have a complete set of property deeds drawn up."

That at least explained his late return before breakfast. "You had them forged."

Holmes's lips quirked. "I try to be thorough. I fancy Sir Edwin Styles will be receiving quite an angry note from Pulborough in the near future, after His Lordship has attempted to utilise those false documents to his advantage . . . ."

In fact, it was over a fortnight before Lord Pulborough demanded the presence of "Sir Edwin". During this time the weather took a distinctly autumnal turn and a cold breeze seemed to blow constantly. Holmes took on three minor cases, as well as contacting the firm of Coleborn and Edwards to predict that the folder containing the sealed bids for the Duke of Foynes' South Riding properties would be from only one person, and

163

sending a brief telegram to Inspector Lestrade. The solicitors answered by return of post, amazed and alarmed that Holmes knew as much as he did, and agreeing to postpone the auction *pro tempore*. Lestrade didn't respond, perhaps awaiting a fuller explanation from my friend before he would act.

Word came through an agitated young man in a sombre suit – although he had no overcoat, despite the chill – who was shown up by Mrs. Hudson. Holmes seemed to know him, so I assumed he was one of the network of informers and observers with which my friend had seeded the city streets. The young man gasped out between gulping breaths that Lord Pulborough was even now at the Clarence Hotel, demanding Sir Edwin Styles meet him in the foyer, instantly.

"Is he in good temper?" enquired Holmes, idly scratching at his brow with the long stem of a pipe.

"No, sir," said the youth. "He is severely vexed and red of face."

"Would you say it is straightforward anger? Or furious bluster to cover – " He circled the pipestem in the air. " – something more damning?"

The other thought a moment, his ragged breath gradually calming. "I would say there is much bluster there, sir. Like a gentleman who is caught out trying to underpay his bill and then falls back on anger when bluff doesn't work."

"Capital!" Holmes sprang to his feet. "Come, Watson, we have a rendezvous!"

I stood. "Not Sir Edwin?"

"That venerable gentleman has done his work and must perforce be retired. I shall miss him. Did you come in a growler?" This to the young man.

He nodded. "It awaits me outside."

"Excellent!" Holmes grabbed his coat, hat, and stick and swept from the room. The young man fell in behind, and I followed, donning my own overcoat and scarf.

It was a short drive to the Clarence Hotel, through streets that were noticeably less busy than the day when this whole business had begun. Those who did brave the chill were muffled against the weather and much less cheerful. I was compelled to feel grateful it hadn't been so inclement on the day I sat beside the Serpentine.

Our cab drew up outside the hotel, the young man vanishing through a side door the moment we stepped down from the cab. The Clarence was a small, elegant place which had clearly seen better days. Its paintwork was sad and fading. The fittings on the double doors inside the portico were in urgent need of a good buffing. Indoors was a similar story, the underlying scent of polish belying the obvious fact that the woodwork was dusty, and the chairs and sofas arranged throughout the dim foyer as faded as the exterior paintwork. It was the ideal place for the Sir Edwins of this world to hide themselves while pursuing their questionable hobbies.

It was, however, an unlikely place for the figure lounging in a high-backed chair just within the doorway: The backs of the chairs were turned to the outside world so that those seated might observe all those entering and leaving the foyer while themselves remaining half-hidden. Dressed in an exquisitely tailored suit, his brushed topper perched on the handle of an ebony cane, Lord Pulborough would have been more at ease in an exclusive club. His dark hair was smooth against his skull due to an excessive application of Macassar oil, while the expression on his well-proportioned, handsome face was even more arrogant than I recalled from his photograph. High cheekbones lent an extra cruelty to his sharp eyes, while his mouth, with the full lips of a sensualist, seemed to be set in a self-regarding sneer. His eyes flickered towards Holmes and me as we approached, momentary curiosity within them, before we were dismissed as inconsequential.

"I have the pleasure of addressing Lord Jabez Pulborough," said Holmes, pulling a chair across that he might sit and face the other.

The curiosity returned to Pulborough's expression, leavened with a degree of irritation. "I am sorry, sir, but I am expecting – "

"Sir Edwin Thornton Styles," said Holmes. "I am sorry, Lord Pulborough, but I must extend Sir Edwin's apologies. He cannot attend."

Pulborough's eyes snapped back and forth between us as his mind tried to make sense of what my friend had said. After a moment he made to rise.

"Very well, if that is his decision, woe betide – "

"Please sit, Lord Pulborough!" Holmes's voice cracked like a whip, and the other fell back into his chair. "Your childish threats mean nothing, your spiteful tantrums even less. I am here to explain your situation, my Lord, and to ensure your full understanding. If not your cooperation."

Pulborough glared at us both, rage fulminating in his eyes, yet he made no further attempt to stand. "Who are you, sir?" he demanded.

"My name is Sherlock Holmes, and this is my friend, Doctor Watson. You will, of course, have heard of us."

Pulborough's eyes narrowed. "Indeed. And what have you to do with me, Mr. Holmes?"

My friend's thin lips quirked in a momentary smile. "Blackmail. Theft. The publication of obscene literature. And of course, the small matter of trying to obtain property by the use of forged documentation."

Some of Pulborough's poise deserted him, although he attempted to mask it with a brazen grin. "I'm afraid you have the advantage of me, sir."

165

"You have been playing a clever game, my Lord. The volumes you publish are stocked at certain bookshops in Holywell Street. The proprietors of these shops advise you whenever any, shall we say, more *exotic* books are bought or requested, and you assess if these purchasers or enquirers are likely marks for blackmail. Both of these activities have provided you with an excellent lifestyle."

"That is slanderous, Mr. Holmes." Lord Pulborough took a silver case from his coat and selected from it a long cigarette. Lighting it, he blew out a large, fragrant cloud. "Prove it, if you can. Where is your witness? My reputation as a philanthropist – "

"You will shortly have no reputation – save one that no man covets. Certainly I will find it difficult to prove what I have said, but not impossible. You aren't invulnerable, my Lord, although I appreciate how a man of your standing often has a certain . . . immunity. However, once your edifice of respectability beings to crumble, I warrant there will be more than one soul willing to step forward and help bring you down. Your peers will certainly not wish to associate themselves with you."

Pulborough remained silent, smiling with forced self-confidence around his cigarette.

"I imagine you considered yourself blessed when Chillingford felt into your grasp. The merest amount of research and you knew for whom he worked, and the importance of Coleborn and Edwards. Did you already have designs upon the Duke of Foyne's Yorkshire estates, or did you seize upon the opportunity, immediately seeing your advantage?"

The disgraced nobleman continued to hold his tongue.

Holmes shrugged. "No matter. You hatched your plan, forced Chillingford to leave the offices of Coleborn and Edwards unlocked under pain of exposure, and sneaked in under cover of darkness to replace the many sealed bids with one of your own. That was devious, but clumsy. Did it not occur to you that once the bids were opened, it would cause suspicion, risking the auction being declared void?"

Pulborough tapped ash from his cigarette to the jaded carpet. "Am I not the great philanthropist, Mr. Holmes? The solicitors couldn't prove if the bids I replaced were from any other person or persons. You know yourself that suspicion isn't proof. I might desperately want the land for another of my many philanthropic schemes."

"You desire the land because there is coal under it," said Holmes. "A detail which is easy enough to discover. Reserves which the Duke once declared too costly to mine."

"Only because the geriatric fool is actually too impoverished to exploit it." Pulborough crushed out his cigarette. "He needs money, and that is why he is selling up."

166

"Indeed. And when Sir Edwin Styles also came into your orbit, and admitted that he had a claim to land adjacent to the Duke's, I imagine you thought yourself doubly blessed."

The other's face darkened. "So I did – until I discovered I had been played for a fool. Sir Edwin had no such claim – as the fake deeds with which he tried to buy my silence proved! The man for whom you are acting as an agent is a rogue!"

Holmes smiled. "Not at all, and you make two false assumptions. I don't act for Sir Edwin, for he is no more real than the many estates listed against his entry in *Who's Who*. A small detail you would have uncovered, had your caution been equal to your greed."

Now Pulborough's face paled and the last vestiges of his bravado faded.

"You understand, I see," said Holmes, not without satisfaction, I thought. "You may have kept yourself at a far enough remove from your other activities to escape the law, but you will easily be found guilty of fraud on two accounts: Attempting the procurement of property with forged documents, and doing so under a clumsy alias."

"That isn't so – " His Lordship blustered.

"Is it not?" Holmes leaned back in his chair. "I have already informed friends at Scotland Yard of the existence of the forged property deeds. That you came here – demanding to see the fictious Sir Edwin, and failing to disguise yourself – is evidence enough that you have already tried to pass off the documents as your own and been rebuffed. *There* is my witness, Lord Pulborough. They will testify to your attempted fraud. The evidence is more than compelling."

Pulborough fell back against his chair, deflated. "Then I am ruined."

Holmes shrugged. "At the very least." He took out his own cigarettes, offering one to me but not Pulborough. "Do you still have the original sealed bids?"

His Lordship nodded.

"Return them forthwith to Chillingford at the offices of Coleborn and Edwards. I will grant you time enough for that."

"And then?"

"And then it is up to the law. I cannot restrain the bloodhounds of Scotland Yard, now they have the scent. They will come for you soon enough, and I doubt all of your carefully orchestrated façade will withstand full public scrutiny. Your philanthropic persona will not save you."

Pulborough watched us both for a moment longer. Then he stood, with as much dignity as he had left to muster, smoothed his coat, removed his hat from its perch on the cane, and walked from the foyer into the chilly air.

"You were lenient with him," I said after a pause.

"Perhaps. Lestrade will have to be quick with that one, for I feel he will not await the knock on the door."

"He will flee, you think?"

Holmes nodded sombrely. "He may or may not return the purloined bids. If he does, it may partially help Chillingford, for it's true he has some way to go before clearing his own name." Holmes drew on his cigarette. "Even if he does, it's certain the auction will still be declared void, and the Duke of Foynes will have to wait a while longer to sell his property. Meanwhile, a part of Yorkshire will obtain a temporary reprieve from its inevitable despoilation." He crushed out his cigarette and came to his feet. "Pulborough will most likely attempt flight, rather than face the inevitable disgrace."

"But where will he go?" I also stood, enjoying a last puff of tobacco. "His face is not unknown."

"The United States, perhaps. Australia. I fancy wherever he goes will never be far enough. The past, and our deeds, have a way of catching up with us eventually, no matter how fast we run. That is the fear upon which blackmailers most depend."

I thought a moment. "What are the chances that one day someone will recognise Pulborough – someone as despicable as he – and attempt to make him buy their silence."

"Ha! That would be an irony, Watson. A delicious and deserving one."

Together we walked from the Clarence Hotel and went in search of a cab.

". . . the most repellant man of my acquaintance is a philanthropist who has spent nearly a quarter of a million upon the London poor."

– Sherlock Holmes
The Sign of the Four

The Adventure of the Infernal Philanthropist
by Tim Newton Anderson

"There are secret currents that flow through the life of London, touching us all, Watson," said my friend Holmes as he sat thumbing through the pile of newspapers lying on a table by his chair.

I had cleared a space on the dining table to write another of my chronicles of Holmes's more interesting cases, following my successful first publication the previous year. There were many cases to choose from as Holmes had been particularly busy and successful. The Ealing cat burglar and his one-armed assistant, the unusual affair of the Minster Compact and the cottage garden, the disappearance of the Nottingham mail car, and many more. I looked up from my writing to see what had prompted Holmes's remark.

"Are you detecting more actions by Moriarty?" I asked. My friend had become somewhat obsessed by the man he called "the Napoleon of crime" since he had first identified his hand behind a large swathe of the criminal activity in the capital.

"In this case, it is one of his allies," he said. He had laid the copy of the day's *Times* back down on the table and reached for his pipe, which he filled with tobacco from the Persian slipper he insisted on using for its storage. "There's a story quoting the so-called philanthropist Sir Randolph Clement, who believes donating a quarter-of-a-million pounds to help the destitutes of the East End could prevent murders like that of the unfortunate prostitute Polly Nicholls yesterday."

Holmes had once pointed out Sir Randolph Clement to me when he sat in a box opposite us at the Opera. He was a short stocky man with wide side-whiskers, dressed in a brown tweed Norfolk suit. Even without Holmes's prompting, he would have stood out amongst the dinner jackets and bow ties considered *de rigueur* at such occasions. The society pages politely mocked him for his country accent and the turkey farms which were supposed to be the source of his wealth. I sympathised with him as, despite Holmes's skills having helped the great and good of Britain on many occasions, I always felt the landed gentry saw us as "trade" to be employed, but not of the same social standing.

"Surely he is correct in stating that the appalling conditions of the London poor are at the root of many crimes," I said. "Not every misdeed has the complexity of some of your cases. As a doctor, I've seen the effects of poor conditions and nutrition on too many of our population, and the desperate lengths to which they will go to alleviate their misery."

Holmes rose from his chair and lit his pipe with a spill he'd thrust into the fire. Although it was the first day of September, the streets were already touched with the first fog of autumn, and its chill could be felt radiating from our windows overlooking Baker Street.

"What is it you have against Sir Randolph?" I asked. "If he is a confederate of Moriarty, one would expect him to be stealing money, rather than giving it away. Just last week, he opened a soup kitchen in Limehouse, and there are several orphanages which owe their existence to his generosity."

"What better recruiting grounds for Moriarty's criminal organisation?" asked Holmes. "Simply identify those with cunning and ambition, and train them to use those traits for the Professor's benefit. At the same time, Clement gains a reputation for benevolence amongst the powerful and moves in circles which Moriarty cannot. I have no doubt his ambition is to gain a peerage or a safe constituency which will give him a greater platform to further legislation benefitting him and his associates. A common criminal may ruin the lives a few dozen people, but a politician can ruin those of millions."

"What evidence do you glean from your perusal of the newspapers?" I asked.

Holmes picked up *The Times* and handed it to me. Several articles had been circled in pencil.

"You will note a burglary at the home of Lord and Lady Wilmot in Surrey, where Clement was a guest last week." he said. "The Member of Parliament for Oakhampton is giving up his seat, doubtless due to rumours about his private life emanating from Sir Randolph's mouth. While he claims to help the poor of the East End, he is busy building sub-standard homes in Stepney to house them at inflated rents. A company whose board Clement sits upon is buying land in the India Docks for new wharves, which I believe will provide an opportunity for the illegal importation of gin and opium destined for the public houses in which he also has an interest, and the movement out of the country of jewellery stolen by Moriarty's men which will pay for them. I've been examining the comings and goings of vessels bound for likely destinations. The money Clement donates to 'good causes' is a mere fraction of the cash he invests in seemingly legitimate enterprises which transform the fruits of Moriarty's illegal activities into clean money. The organisation is operating on too vast a scale to rely on traditional fences to convert their loot."

170

"Why have you circled the article on the proposed further improvements to the sewage system?" I asked.

"I must confess, I haven't yet ascertained how that fits in to their schemes," he said. "However, Sir Randolph is lobbying hard in favour of the proposals, so there must be some link to Moriarty's plans. Nothing any of his lieutenants do is without a reason."

"I sometimes wonder if you ascribe too much to this Moriarty," I said. "You have mentioned his name in connection with everything from the failed assassination of our beloved Queen to the Bloody Sunday riots last year in Trafalgar Square. Yet when Scotland Yard follow them up, they cannot find any proof of your assertions."

"Moriarty and his associates play a very deep and wide game," Holmes said, "with criminality hidden behind respectability. But mark my word, there will be a reckoning between us."

Our conversation was interrupted by noise from the street below. I left my chair to see what the commotion was, and observed a dozen poorly dressed boys arguing with Mrs. Hudson.

I knew immediately they were Holmes young protégés, and that our landlady was trying to ensure only their leader – Wiggins – was admitted as per Holmes instructions. After a minute or so, the lad managed to get his gang to calm down and he was allowed to enter.

I believe that Holmes had insisted on restricting the members of his "Baker Street Irregulars" attendance because he preferred to get his intelligence from a single source rather than half-a-dozen excitable urchins talking at once. It could not have been because of their appearance, as he cared little for such things. In a lounge littered with papers, scientific equipment, and grisly mementos of previous cases, it was our clients who looked more out of place than Wiggins and company.

Holmes had adopted them to help out in cases where even his skill with disguises could not gain him entry. The poor are often invisible and can go anywhere as long as they don't constitute a "nuisance". People might suspect them of picking their pockets, but not that they are monitoring their movements and conversations. Holmes paid them a retainer for their work and had arranged lessons in literacy and numeracy which he hoped would avoid them falling into the hands of gangs such as those he ascribed to Moriarty. Even without their recruitment into the underworld, the uncertainty of life on the streets could easily have led them into a life of crime.

"We needs your help, Mr. Holmes," said Wiggins as he pushed his way into the room past Mrs. Hudson, who had opened the door. "It's young William. He's gone missing, he has. No one's seen hide nor hair for days, and that isn't like him. Regular as clockwork in his habits, he is."

"If, as I understand, you are trying to commission my professional skills, then you should take a seat like my other clients," said Holmes, smiling sympathetically. "Although I am surprised that you haven't been able to locate him yourself, given your skills and contacts."

Wiggins looked at the basket chair by the fire which Holmes and indicated and settled into it. As soon as he sat down, his body slumped in relief. I noticed that his clothes, although obviously second-hand, were better made than those I had first seen him wearing years earlier. He had been aged about ten at that time, and had grown into his role as protector of the other Irregulars. I wondered if Holmes had plans to find him more regular employment once Wiggins had trained up a replacement. The skills he had acquired, and his tall frame, would be an asset to the Metropolitan Police Force, and Holmes's contacts there would surely provide an easy passage.

"I can't say as we can pay you very much, Mr. Holmes, but we would do anything you asked if you can find him," Wiggins said. "We looks out for each other, see, and if something happens to one of us, we have to do something about it."

Holmes sat down in his usual seat. Mrs. Hudson had been hovering by the door in case Wiggins misbehaved, and Holmes gently requested she bring us all tea and some of her fruit cake.

"Now, young Wiggins," he said, "I think you had better tell us what has happened. Tell me everything you know, leaving out no details, however insignificant."

Holmes sat back in his chair, closed his eyes and steepled his fingers, listening intently.

"I hope I can rely on you to be discreet-like, Mr. Holmes," he said. "Some of this isn't exactly legal."

I noticed a momentary raising of my friend's eyebrows, but he also nodded to put Wiggins at his ease.

"William works sometimes as a tosher," Wiggins said. "Him and Old Gregg sneak into the sewers at low tide to rummage around and see what they can find. It's been harder since all the new sewers have been built. Old Gregg says it used to be a good living back in the day, although it's also a lot safer now. Loads of his mates died from disease or gas flares, or tunnel cave-ins. But he found lots of stuff: Money, jewellery, even false teeth – clean 'em up and you can get a few coppers for 'em. Most of the stuff gets flushed through the big new sewers now though, and goes straight into the river where even the mudlarks can't find it. Straight down to the bottom.

"William never goes down alone – he isn't stupid. There's rats the size of cats down there, and you don't want to get caught unawares. You always want at least two of you, and the rule is share and share alike with whatever anyone finds."

"Why is it more difficult," I asked, "if the sewers are safer?"

"They've clamped down, haven't they?" said Wiggins. "Doors or bars on the entrances. Laws to stop you going in. More police about so you can't open up a manhole late at night without being nabbed. Used to be in the old days that we were doing people a favour, like the night soil men, but since the work gangs started going down to keep the sewers decent, they don't want anyone else around."

"And you think that's where William has gone," Holmes said.

"He was talking to Tootles about a tosheroon that was supposed to be down there – a big ball of coins all stuck together that would make his fortune. Him and Old Gregg have been finding more and more money, even sovereigns, not just coppers. They were supposed to go back and follow the trail to the source, so to speak, but Gregg fell over and broke his leg. William must have decided to go it alone."

Before he could continue with his tale, Mrs. Hudson entered with the tea tray. I reflected again how long-suffering she was as a landlady, with clients coming and going at all hours, apart from Holmes's own eccentricities as a tenant. I suspected she had a soft spot for young Wiggins, however, as she had provided more slices of cake than she would normally serve to a client.

"Where is this sewer?" asked Holmes.

"It's near Mile End Road," said Wiggins. "The coppers don't bother policing as carefully there – not as many posh people to worry about, so you can still lift a manhole."

Holmes leaned forward. There was an expression on his face I had seen many times during an investigation. The game was afoot, and he knew his quarry.

"I think I need to have a conversation with your Old Gregg," he said. "There is a dangerous game here, of which I'm afraid young William may have fallen foul."

"No problem, Mr. Holmes," said Wiggins. "I can bring him here if you like. His leg is on the mend."

"I think I need to meet him in his own environment," said Holmes. "Watson and I will accompany you to his dwelling. And perhaps he can show us where this tosheroon may be located."

Holmes indicated I should wear my galoshes and oilcloth coat. "No need to dress too warmly, Watson. I'm assured the temperature in the sewers is quite balmy."

"Are you suggesting we are to descend into this underworld?" I asked.

"In both senses of the word," he said. "I'm sure we'll find some human rats in the sewers, as well as the animal kind. You had better bring your revolver and bulls-eye lantern."

We engaged a hansom cab to Old Gregg's hovel in Whitechapel – a first for Wiggins, I believe. He insisted on sitting next to the driver and waving to passers-by as we entered his familiar territory of the East End.

"There is the alley where poor Polly Nicholls met her grisly end," said Holmes as we passed the former stables in Bucks Row. There were a couple of uniformed police standing by the entrance looking bored with the assignment. Murders of prostitutes were all too common in the area. "I believe the case is one in which I may have to take an interest at some point.

I always felt saddened when I entered the East End. When working in a hospital mortuary, I had seen hundreds of bodies ravaged by drink, poverty, and illness, as well as the effects of work in the tanneries and lead foundries, and the backs broken in the docks. The narrow brick lanes and courtyards were full of sub-standard dwellings with families crowded eight or nine to a room, and the new buildings further East were hardly an improvement. There seemed to be a gin shop or public house on every corner. Successive waves of migrants hoping for a better life were marooned there until they could fight their way up the social ladder, and it was hardly a surprise that many resorted to illegal activity to do so.

Old Gregg's house could only be distinguished from those of his neighbours by a front door that had been more recently painted and clean curtains at the windows. Although dangerous, toshing was obviously more remunerative than the employment of others in the tenement.

Holmes indicated to Wiggins that he should be the one to knock on the door, while Holmes and I kept a discreet distance. After a few moments, the door was opened by a man who looked in his sixties, but was probably two decades younger than that. He was wire thin with a few days growth of pepper-and-salt beard and thinning white hair. He leaned on a stick, and his right leg was still bound in the bandages and splint that had been used to set his broken tibia. Despite his apparent emaciation and injury and the forty-five-degree angle of his back – no doubt caused by constant bending in sewers – he appeared sprightly, and smiled as he invited us inside.

Although there were signs of damp on the walls and ceiling of his parlour, the whitewash on the walls looked recent, and most surfaces were covered in small ornaments which he had presumably liberated from the sewers. Each had been meticulously scrubbed clean of the detritus in which it had been found and polished with care. An ancient oak table stood

174

by the window with yet more finds on it in the process of cleaning, and four mismatched wooden chairs were gathered in a semi-circle in front of the fireplace. A blaze danced in the grate, and I spotted a chair leg amongst its fuel.

"When did you last see William?" asked Holmes. We had taken our places on the chairs and our host had provided us each with a strong cup of tea. He had offered to top them off with a tot of whisky, but we had declined.

"He came 'round to see me the day-before-yesterday," the tosher said. "He's a good lad, looking out for me and seeing I was recovering. Changed my bandages and everything. Couldn't ask for a better partner."

"I gather you had some success together?" Holmes said.

Old Gregg looked suspiciously at Holmes, but Wiggins said, "Don't worry, chum. William would want you to tell Mr. Holmes everything. He's just trying to find him."

"All right," Gregg said. "I suppose as how it won't do much harm and could help the lad. We've been finding more and more valuable stuff. Jewellery, coins – all gold. Never known such fortune. I thought William was my lucky charm. I don't mind telling you, times has been hard since the new sewerage system was built. Less dangerous I suppose, but the pickings ain't been as good. Used to be dozens of us working down there and earning a decent living, but there's only a few left. Not many mudlarks sifting stuff down at the river either. It's progress of sorts, and I can't say as how I miss the old stinks we used to get from the river or the explosions and collapses in the tunnels, but it's sad to see the old ways go. I used to have mates who earned their crust taking away night soil, but now everyone has these indoor water closets instead of the old privies, and lots of the boys have started scraping up the pure from the streets after the horses so there's too much competition. Then there's the Peelers. We used to be left alone – useful we were. Now if you're as much as seen near a manhole, they'll run you in."

"Tell them about the tosheroon, Gregg," said Wiggins.

There was that sly look again before he continued.

"That's a bit of a legend," he said. "Like the wild boars that's supposed to roam underground, or the Queen Rats that can turn into humans to trap unwary gents looking for a bit of fun. Never gave it much reckoning myself. But when we started to find all of this gold, I wondered if there wasn't some truth in it. Most of the stuff we find is things what has fallen into the toilet or down a grating, or been dropped down there deliberate, because they don't want it anymore and the rubbish collectors can't find a use for it. But this was different. I reckoned someone may have hidden some stuff down the drain planning to collect it later, but mebbe

175

they died before they could get it back. Mebbe it was in a sack that's rotted, or a storm or the stronger current of these new sewers has washed it loose. Anyways, it was worth going upstream to find it."

"Why would anyone hide their money in a sewer?" I asked.

"I can see as how you don't know much about how people live 'round here," Gregg said. "The kind of thieves you get in these parts ain't the society burglars you read about in the papers. If they was to be seen casing a place in the West End, they would be taken off the streets. It's a sad truth that more often than not, they steal from their own. There ain't many jewelled tiaras to lift in the East End, but there ain't no big locks on the doors or butlers checking on things either. You don't want people to now you've got anything worth stealing, see, or leave it where it could be lifted, so you hide it away until you've got enough together to move somewhere smarter. And banks ain't too friendly to the likes of us, neither."

"Can you show us the entrance to this source of treasure?" said Holmes. "You can come with us, and I promise we will not steal it away."

Old Gregg was still suspicious, but Wiggins said he would come too. He was obviously trusted by the tosher, who reluctantly agreed.

"I'm not sure as I'll be able to come with you, but I drew this map," he pulled a piece of paper from the back pocket of his trousers. "I've marked all of the tunnels William and I explored, so we could do it methodical-like. The biggest rat's nests are on there too. If there's an *X*, it means there's pockets of fire damp, or the roof's caved in. The bricks are like butter in the older tunnels after all these years, so you have to go careful."

We followed Gregg through the alleys until he found the grating he'd been using and waited until Wiggins had used the crowbar Gregg had handed him to lever it up. A metal ladder led down into the depths.

"I'll wait here 'til you get back," Gregg said, "but I ain't coming in after you if you come a cropper. Try and send someone back and I'll see if I can get some of the boys to come down and help."

Holmes insisted on entering the Stygian depths first, followed by myself, with Wiggins taking the rear. Although my war wound had bothered me less and less, my leg still felt stiff as I climbed carefully down the ladder. I must admit, my cautious descent wasn't purely occasioned by the rusted and unsafe nature of the ladder. I have little fear of darkness, but have always been wary of rats. In Afghanistan, I saw several wounded comrades whose wounds from bullets proved less dangerous to their health than the gnawings of the rats which were attracted to the battlefield by the dead and dying. It was the rat that brought the plague to our fair city, and could well again if a ship were to enter the river from some diseased nation. I dismissed Gregg's fanciful tales of Queen Rats and the Rat Kings

As I climbed behind Holmes, I felt glad to be out of the gloom of the sewer. Whatever was at the top of the ladder, it would at least be out of the claustrophobia I had been suffering for the last hour. Holmes paused as he reached the trapdoor at the tunnel's summit and slowly eased it open to peer around. Then he pushed it back and quickly climbed out. I followed and found myself in a wine cellar lit by several kerosene lanterns. There was no one to greet us, and I let go of a breath I hadn't realised I had been holding. Holmes held a finger to his lips to indicate silence and we walked quietly towards a set of steps at the far end of the cellar. I couldn't help glancing at the bottles as we walked, noticing several good vintages. This belonged to someone of some wealth.

There were some barrels near the entrance. Holmes shifted one in its mount. Instead of the *glug* of liquid I expected, there was a rattling noise. It was obviously being used to store some of the gang's loot, hidden amongst genuine wine barrels for transportation. Next to the steps was a bound person.

Holmes again gave the sign for silence as he leaned over and removed the gag from the person's mouth.

"Hello, William," he said quietly. "I hope you aren't injured."

The young lad nodded. Holmes removed the knots from the ropes binding his hands and feet and helped him stand upright. William was unsteady from being so long in his cramped position, but I massaged his legs to restore the circulation.

"Wiggins is waiting at the bottom of the ladder you'll find through that trapdoor," Holmes whispered. "Join him and wait for our signal. I hope our business won't take long."

Holmes had extinguished his lantern and placed it on the floor so that he had both hands free, and I followed suit before stepping up the stairs. He paused at their summit to listen at the closed door, and then slowly opened it and stepped through into a large kitchen.

"I believe the person we're looking for will be found in the study," he said in hushed tones. "He obviously isn't expecting anyone, or we would have been greeted by members of his gang."

I followed Holmes out of the kitchen and into a corridor. He seemed to be familiar with the layout of the house, and I wondered if he had already examined the plans of the building. The place was decorated with good taste, and at some expense. I noticed a Ming Dynasty vase on a marble plinth, and the paintings on the walls were good examples of the Dutch Landscape school. There was an expensive rug on the floor which muffled our footsteps as we approached a door at the corridor's end. Grasping his pistol firmly in his right hand, Holmes opened the door with

179

his left and strode through. I followed and saw a man at a desk hurriedly opening a drawer and scrabbling inside.

"I wouldn't pull out your gun if I were you," said Holmes. "Both Watson and I are excellent marksmen, and couldn't fail to hit you at this range."

I recognised the man from our visit to the opera: Sir Randolph Clement. He wasn't the suave figure we had seen then, as his face was flushed with fear and anger.

"What is the meaning of this?" he grunted. "Has the famous Sherlock Holmes stooped to breaking and entering?"

"I fancy that is more your line of business than mine," said Holmes. "Or one which you direct your men to do, once you've surveyed the premises as a guest of the owners."

"I have no idea what you are talking about," he blustered. "This is a foul slander."

"I'm sure the contents of the barrels in your cellar will provide all the proof the constabulary need," said Holmes, drawing the necklace from his pocket. "Like this bauble which one of your minions carelessly dropped in the tunnel below your home while transporting it to the docks. It's unfortunate for you that we arrived before you were able to open your new houses in Mile End, and the new tunnels beneath which you have been lobbying for to provide less-incriminating base for your enterprise."

Sir Randolph had been darting his head from side to side, looking out of the windows, as Holmes spoke. There was the sound of the front door opening.

"If you're hoping that is your men returning, I'm afraid you'll be disappointed," said Holmes. "I had suggested to Inspector Gregson he keep an eye on the building and arrest any unsavoury characters who tried to enter. That is probably his men coming to take you in for questioning."

Sir Randolph's hand was still hovering over the desk drawer, and before Holmes or I could prevent it, he pulled out a revolver. I was about to shoot him when he lifted it quickly to his mouth and pulled the trigger. His head snapped back as the bullet entered his skull.

Holmes had started to leap across to the desk, but fell against it, even as two burly constables entered the room at a run.

"Blast!" he cried. "I had hoped to take him in alive to expose Moriarty. That spider makes sure that only those at the top of each strand of his criminal web know who sits at the centre."

By instinct, I stepped over to examine Sir Randolph's body, but I knew the bullet had extinguished his life. I came back round the desk and placed my hand on Holmes's shoulder.

"You have saved the life of an innocent young man, and broken a criminal gang," I said. "Moriarty must wait until another day."

Several hours later, Holmes and I were back in our Baker Street sitting room. We had been joined by Wiggins, William, and Old Gregg, who had each been given a glass of brandy.

"I hope you will give up your perilous profession," Holmes said to Gregg and William. "Several of those burgled had offered rewards for the return of their possessions, and you can have it to remove the need to return to the sewers."

"Most kind, I'm sure," said Gregg, "but I can't help but admit I'll miss the old trade. Certain it was dangerous, but the thrill of finding a lost treasure was sommat I loved."

"There are treasures to be found everywhere," said Holmes. "You have an eye for the valuable, and would make an excellent antique dealer. If you wish to support young William, employ him as your spotter to attend house clearances. The danger of kidnapping will be much less."

"What happened to the rest of the gang?" asked Wiggins.

"Gregson tells me he was able to round up those on Sir Randolph's ship and at his warehouse at the docks as well as those outside of his home," said Holmes. "More loot from the burglaries was recovered there as well – quantities of smuggled goods, including opium and other drugs destined for Moriarty's network of vice dens. However, as I suspected, none of them knew of any part of the organisation apart from Sir Randolph. The network of blind cells worked too well. But mark my words, Moriarty and I will have a reckoning."

He lifted his glass in a toast, and we each did the same.

". . . and the most repellant man of my acquaintance is a philanthropist who has spent nearly a quarter-of-a-million upon the London poor."
– Sherlock Holmes
The Sign of the Four

The Adventure of the
Murdered Mistress
by Ember Pepper

"Do you think Mrs. Hudson would allow me to tinker with the bath pipes?"

I sipped at my tea, my attention on the notes in front of me. "What do you mean by 'tinker'?" I scratched out a name – my list of possible invitees to my upcoming nuptials was painfully short and shrinking as I realized most of the men I used to know were my comrades in the military, and many had not retired to civilian life in or around London. I doubted they would want to make the long travel for an old army friend to whom they had not spoken in years.

Holmes, for his part, was sprawled out in his chair, dressed but unkempt. Since the Agra case, he hadn't left the flat, opting instead to indulge in that seven-percent solution at an alarming rate. Even distracted as I was by my wedding plans, I had been looking in vain for something to distract him before the drug finally made irreparable damage to that brilliant mind of his.

He shifted his stockinged feet closer to the crackling hearth. The firelight drew attention to the numerous puncture marks and bruises dotting his forearms. His sleeves were rolled up, displaying the evidence of his dismaying activity in the most brazen manner.

"There has been some success in the installation of showering mechanisms in modernized bathrooms," he answered, "and I'm of like mind with many experts that the overhead shower provides a more effective cleaning than a bath."

I set my cup down, giving him an amused look. "You intend to install a shower in Mrs. Hudson's bath?"

He shrugged. The motion was meant to appear idle, but it seemed a forced gesture. "It shouldn't be too difficult."

I turned back to my list. "I didn't realize you were an expert in indoor plumbing."

"As I said, it shouldn't be too difficult." I could feel his darkened gaze on me. I felt a surge of regret.

I tempered my tone. "Perhaps you could draw up some plans," I humoured. "Or find a new case."

He waved a dismissive hand. "Boring. Banal."

"Beneficial," I finished cheerfully. Then, taking a sip of my tea, I muttered under my breath, "Can't be any more tedious than this."

He heard me. I could feel his glare. "What can compare to a treasure, a wooden-legged men, and poisonous darts, Watson?"

"Lower your standards," I answered tightly.

"Not advice I'm generally willing to heed, in any area of life," Holmes said, bitterly, and then stood, his face suddenly clouded with abstract concentration. "Perhaps I could sketch out an idea. The existing pipes are new . . . ."

He settled at his writing desk and fell into the quiet work of jotting quick notes on a piece of scrap paper laying nearby. I took a moment to observe him privately, noting the disarray of his hair and the looseness of his undone collar, and silently prayed for a client with a diverting problem to harken our doorstep. Holmes had taken the news of my engagement with neutral grace and had given no indication that it weighed on his mind, but I couldn't help feel a pang of worry that I was abandoning him to his own often-unhealthy devices. My friend, for all his solitary intellectualism, didn't seem to do well on his own.

"I believe you were completing your guest list, Watson," he interrupted dryly without turning. The man must have had eyes on the back of his head. I returned my attention to my task, flushing with embarrassment.

An instant before the doorbell rang, he raised his chin and cocked his head like a cocker spaniel hearing the dinner bell. I cast a silent thank you to the Heavens as I heard Mrs. Hudson open the door, leading our unexpected visitor up the stairs after a moment of discussion.

Our long-suffering landlady entered, bearing a card. "A Mrs. Oswald to see you, Mr. Holmes."

To my absolute dismay, he waved his hand irritably. "Tell her I am unavailable."

"No," I stood abruptly. "Send her in," I overrode, doing my best to ignore the look of indignant irritation my companion was levelling at me.

Mrs. Hudson, of the same mind as me as to the recent state of her tenant, obeyed my directive and politely showed in a middle-aged woman of graceful carriage and sensitive face. She tugged at her lace gloves, her pretty green eyes shifting from me to my companion as if attempting to decide which of us she was seeking.

Holmes spoke before she was able to introduce herself, "I'm sorry for the confusion, but my schedule is full at the moment." Rudely, he hadn't even bothered to turn to look at her.

183

"No, it is not," I said firmly. I gestured her towards the wicker chair. "Have a seat. And my friend will sit here," I said pointedly, patting his chair by the fire, "and listen to your problem."

Holmes's look of disbelief quirked into a wry amusement. He dropped his pen dramatically and padded over the chair and fell into it, stifling a sigh.

I sat, clearing my throat in what I hoped was a subtle warning. In the early days of our arrangement, I may have demurred to Holmes's every mood, but after all these years, I wasn't above kicking him if he deserved it. I trusted he knew this.

He cleared his own throat, straightening in his chair. "Apologies, Madam. Would you like a cup of coffee or tea? I see you've loitered about outside in the cold for some time."

She turned down the offer with a wave of her hand but didn't ask him to clarify his observations. I could easily see the dampness of her shoulders spoke of one who had spent some time in the London drizzle after alighting from her cab and before ringing the bell.

"I don't wish to intrude any more upon your valuable time than I need to, Mr. Holmes," she stated politely. If Holmes detected the slight sliver of irony in her tone, he made no indication of it.

"You're here out of concern for a loved one, though this concern has an element of selfishness to it." He paused, considering. "A husband, then."

She nodded. "The matter does concern my husband, who isn't aware I have come to see you." She pulled a few folded notes from her small handbag. "My name is Constance Oswald. I married Percival Oswald twenty years ago. We've resided in relative peace with one another in Mayfair. My husband is a complex man. In some ways, he is very vibrant, unrestrained, but in other cases he is extremely reserved." She paused as if expecting a response. Holmes pressed a finger to the bridge of his nose, and I nodded hastily to urge her on, hoping she would quickly come to the point before Holmes's very short patience ebbed entirely.

"My husband is a man of independent wealth. I know nothing of his finances – besides some indication that he invests – and much of his private thoughts are kept from me. He does, however, hold a not-so-minor position in the government as the Assistant Secretary to Indian Affairs."

"I know of him," Holmes interjected. He gave her a quick, insincere smile. "My brother occupies a very minor role in government, so I have some familiarity."

She nodded, looking flustered at this before continuing. "He believes wholeheartedly in the theory that women mustn't be burdened with masculine matters." A flutter of exasperation crossed her elegant brow.

184

"Nay, he believes women cannot understand masculine matters." Finally seeing the look of impatience clouding my friend's expression, she hurried on, "This often forces me to – excuse my frankness – snoop if I wish to know anything that happens under my own roof. It was in the course of this snooping that I found these."

She held out her folded notes. Holmes didn't accept them, so I took them from her, shuffling through them.

"What do they contain?" he asked instead, languidly.

"I believe my husband is being blackmailed. The notes speak of his 'secret', and make numerous requests for money to be left at different areas in town." She looked expectantly at me. I obediently skimmed one correspondence and hummed.

"Yes," I corroborated. "Do you know if your husband has entertained any of these demands?"

"I'm afraid I don't. I can hardly ask him."

Holmes stood suddenly, taking the notes from me and passing them back to our guest. His movements weren't rude or abrupt, but he was decidedly brusque.

"I'm sorry. I cannot help you with your problem. I advise you to simply ask your husband and accept his answer."

"Sir – " she started as my companion turned away.

"Holmes – " I began, but he cut me off with a sharp glance.

"I cannot help you with your problem," he stated firmly in a voice that brooked no argument, even from me, "I apologize as I see you are greatly distraught, but this isn't a matter in which I specialize."

She glanced at me for aid, but seeing my own hopeless look, she stood and inclined her chin frostily. "I am sorry for bothering you, sir." She separated one letter from the rest and handed it to me. "In case your busy schedule clears, perhaps you could be bothered to take a cursory glance over it," she explained, and then left in a rustle of skirts.

"Holmes!" I exclaimed once the door had closed behind her. "How absurdly discourteous of you!"

He picked up his violin and forestalled my remonstration with a loud screech of the bow against the strings. He tucked the thing under his chin and rolled his eyes at me.

"No amount of boredom will induce me to get involved in the trite romantic affairs of this city's denizens. Clearly, the letters were written by a former mistress demanding money from Mr. Oswald in exchange for her silence. I am honestly shocked the clearly intelligent Mrs. Oswald hasn't already figured this out. I would think it would be a woman's first thought." He played a few low, melancholic notes. "I do not chase down missing love letters or spy on philandering men."

185

"He does work for the government. It would not be out of the realm of possibility that this is a matter of political – "

"No, the letters ask for money. There is no political inclinations reflected there. In my experience, the most common behavior gentlemen regularly engage in while desperately pretending they do not is adultery."

"You could have very well taken a moment to tell her that," I reprimanded firmly, sitting back down at the dining table. "Without payment, you would have been doing a kindness, not work."

"Would that have been a kindness?" he answered.

I couldn't think of a sufficient response, so I dug back into my now-cold tea and crossed a few more names from my list, resolved to put the whole encounter from my mind.

Holmes fiddled on his violin, all thoughts of indoor showers apparently forgotten. He droned upon the thing for half-an-hour, but upon striking a bad note more than once, he flung the treasured instrument down and paced in front of the fire.

I ignored him the best I could, keeping track of his movements from the corner of my eye. For quite some time, I had meant to ask him to serve as best man at my wedding, but in his current state, I couldn't risk spoiling the moment. I was also worried he would decline my request, and I'm not sure how our friendship would proceed in the face of such a rejection.

He stopped and idly picked up the letter Mrs. Oswald had left, unfolding it and reading it quickly.

He stood, looking at the letter for a long while, a chagrined expression slowly transforming his face. "Well, Watson," he said at last, "mark this day and time for I am about to say something I rarely say, much to your everlasting frustration."

I set my teacup down. "And what is that?"

"I believe I was wrong."

My eyebrows shot up into my hairline. I scrabbled for the small notepad in my jacket pocket and made a show of jotting down the time.

Holmes let out an irritated grunt and took the three steps that brought him close enough to wiggle the paper in my face.

"This isn't a woman's hand, Doctor," he explained and waited for me to get my humour under control. I took the paper from him and peered closely at it.

"Notice the surety of the T's and I's."

"Mmm," I agreed despite my complete ignorance as to what I was meant to notice.

He snatched the thing from me, the first spark of excited interest lighting up his grey eyes. He went back to the fire and examined the thing minutely in the glow of the flames, smelling the paper and running his fingers over the corners and edges. He knelt down and tilted it towards the fire until I could nearly see through the material before letting it hang listlessly from his fingertips and gazing into the flames, his thoughts turned inwards.

I knew that Holmes had made an exhaustive study of any and everything that could be used to trace someone: Clay, tobacco, shoes, clothing, ink, stamps, and, yes, stationery. I could imagine that strange mind of his rifling through his brain attic of carefully collected information for what he sought.

After a moment, he stood and slid the letter into his waistcoat pocket and disappeared into his room, reemerging minutes later looking pristinely put together in a dark-blue frock coat, his collar straightened, and his hair neatly brushed back.

Snatching his coat and hat from the rack, he left without a backward glance or even an acknowledgment of my existence, leaving me alone with my pitiful, short list of friends and a question dying on my lips.

When he returned, his expression lacked that bright gleam of excitement that so often accompanied a fascinating problem, but he looked satisfied.

I had already eaten dinner and had settled into my chair with the evening *Times*. "You look like a man who found what he was looking for," I commented, folding my paper away.

He packed his pipe and sat in the chair opposite me. "Indeed. While this was certainly not the thorniest case I've ever encountered, it was a pleasant, albeit brief, distraction. I was able to track the stationery to a printer near Evesham. From there, I was led to a small barristers' office. They were accommodating enough to speak to me and informed me that one of their colleagues hadn't been to work in the last two days. It was simple work to compare the typeface of the letter to his typewriter. Our blackmailer is Michael Everett. Thirty years old, unmarried, and, by all accounts, usually reliable."

"Did you acquire an address?"

"I did, but I was informed that there have been unsuccessful efforts to reach him there. It may be a simple matter to station myself nearby and watch his house to see if he comes or goes, but the very pleasant and talkative secretary described Mr. Everett to me as a dashing tall man with blonde hair, and as the most devoted Catholic who can be found every Sunday at St. Andrews for confession, come Hell or high water – a fitting idiom, in this case – so it seems this would be the most efficient avenue to pursue."

"You mean to waylay a man at church?"

"I said nothing of waylaying him," he protested, but there was a mischievous gleam in his eye. "But knowing when and where a man will be makes it an easy thing to arrange a meeting."

Sunday morning, I awoke to find Holmes already gone, a brief note commanding I wait for him outside of St. Andrews at noon left on the mantel.

I had no other pressing engagements until I was to meet Mary for dinner at six, so I dressed and hurried to make the appointment.

St. Andrews was a small church near Soho and blessedly quiet, even on a Sunday. I mounted the steps and entered the sanctuary. Statues of the crucified Messiah bore down on me ominously. A small empty pulpit and a priest's double-curtained confessional stood at the front of the pews. The only other occupant of the darkened room was the priest. I could hear the shuffle of his shoes in his designated booth. He didn't come out to meet me, and I sat gently on the front pew bench and looked up at the beautiful stained glass window filtering the grey sunlight into the room in muted, pleasing colors.

I wasn't Catholic. Indeed, I was a Protestant only by name. My time in Afghanistan had caused some definite disillusionment about our place in the world. I often wondered if there was truly any higher power out there, and if so, how could such horrors as I had seen on the battlefield of Maiwand be permitted?

My upcoming nuptials with Mary had certainly renewed some of my faith in the innate goodness of the world, but I couldn't think of that without an accompanying pang of regret about leaving my flat-mate to his own devices.

The rustle of movement in the centre compartment reminded me that I wasn't alone. Feeling a bit awkward, I rose and stepped over to the confessional, wondering if I wasn't committing some sin by stepping in when I did not practice this faith.

I was not going to kneel, so I sat, barely able to make out the form of the priest through the lattice barrier.

I said nothing at first, feeling suddenly lost as to what I was doing. On the other side of the booth, the priest shifted and then, appearing to realize I was not going to start, murmured kindly, "May God, who has enlightened every heart, help you to know your sins and trust in His mercy. Do you have a confession to make?"

"As unorthodox as it is, Father, I am not Catholic. Are we allowed to speak?"

"Of course, son. Is there something you need to confide?"

188

I sighed, leaning back, feeling a bit more comfortable at how kind the man sounded. "I'm not sure. I have done nothing sinful, but there are some things I feel guilty about."

"Mmm?"

"I will be married early next year."

There was a heavy pause. The priest's voice was benevolent but sure when he spoke again. "Is this a wedding of necessity?"

"No, no." I clarified quickly. "You see, I live with a good friend of mine, and I'm afraid I'm leaving him quite abruptly."

The priest took a deep breath, giving my words serious contemplation. "Surely," he started, "this is the way of the world. Your friend must understand."

"He does. He claims he does. But his behavior is becoming more worrisome."

"What behavior?"

I had no desire to speak in detail of the detective's personal habits, even in the safety of a confessional booth. Instead, I answered obliquely, "I don't think he does well on his own."

"Perhaps you could help find him his own wife to be his companion?"

I stuttered. "I don't think that's a feasible avenue – "

"Why not? Is your friend terribly hideous?"

"No, indeed not – " I stammered, flustered at the odd direction this conversation had taken. Then I felt an angry flush flare up my face, and I banged out of the confessional loudly, forgetting for a moment that we were in a house of worship.

I swung open the door to the priest's compartment. Holmes, dressed in a full priest cassock, smirked up at me, unrestrained glee dancing in his light eyes.

I pressed my fingers to the bridge of my nose.

"You forgot to say 'Forgive me, Father, for I have sinned'," he said with mock solemnity. "Don't you know your rite of confession?"

"Holmes, I will strike you!"

He gave me a look of exaggerated shock. "We're in a church, Watson!" He laughed and stood, sidling by me with no appearance of trepidation in the face of my anger.

"Why do you even have a cassock?" I demanded. "You aren't allowed to pretend to be a priest."

He waved his hand like he was swatting away a fly. "There is no law against impersonating a priest or cleric of any church. At least, as long as I'm not attempting to marry someone."

"There may be no man-made laws, but the sacrilege!"

"You aren't even Catholic, Watson!" he laughed.

189

"You did that on purpose!" I accused. "Strictly to embarrass me."

"I did nothing of the sort," he protested, failing to restrain his delight. "I had no idea you'd enter confessional – especially since I had clearly told you to wait outside. Especially since, as we have both already pointed out, you aren't Catholic."

"What if another priest had been in here?"

"We're between services. Everett didn't attend this morning, evidently trying to lay low for some reason. I hope he will slide in during this period of inactivity."

As if on cue, the main door began to creak open. Holmes pushed me suddenly towards the curtained wall near the confessional. "Quick, man – *Hide!*"

I floundered but allowed myself to be ungracefully deposited in the hiding place. I heard Holmes reenter the confession box. Through a small gap in the curtain, I could see the figure entering the church.

He was a tall man, slightly taller than me but not as tall as Holmes. He had a robust, sportsman's figure, and sandy hair. He was quite handsome, of the sort that many women would pay attention to.

Belying these natural gifts, he walked with timid, nearly hunched steps, stopping for a moment in the aisle as if expecting a full church before seeming to shake himself and making his way to the confessional. As he drew close, I steadied my breathing, frightened of being caught out. I heard him kneel on his knees.

I felt a flush of shame. Here I had scolded Holmes for the sacrilege of impersonating a priest, and yet I was now hiding, fully intent to eavesdrop on a man's private confession. I could hardly step out now, however. For not the first or last time in my long relationship with Holmes, I inwardly cursed the detective and my apparent inability to disobey him. Knowing that it was Holmes there and not an authentic priest caused me to send up my own prayer, hoping we could be forgiven this transgression.

From my vantage point, I could hear their conversation clearly.

Unlike me, Everett began, "In the name of the Father, and of the Son, and of the Holy Spirit. Amen."

Holmes clear voice, gentle and nearly fatherly came through. "May God, who has enlightened every heart, help you to know your sins and trust in His mercy," he repeated, and I wondered where he had learned this script.

"Bless me, Father, for I have sinned. It has been a week since my last confession. These are my sins . . . ." Instead of enumerating them, he fell silent. Holmes shifted. Because I knew him, I understood it was impatience. He was obviously hoping this man would confess to attempted

190

blackmail, and the silence that hung was creating no shortage of anticipation.

Finally, my friend prompted, his voice restrained, "What sins have you to confess, son?"

"The woman I love died, and I caused it."

I startled. Even through the walls of the booth, I could sense Holmes too hadn't been expecting this declaration.

When he spoke again, there was an edge of restlessness to his voice. "Are you confessing to taking someone's life?" he asked carefully.

"Not directly, Father. But my actions caused events that I believe led to Jeanette's murder – " The man broke off, stifling a sob.

Holmes cleared his throat. I suspected he hadn't prepared for this and was struggling to know what a real priest would say in such a situation. A misstep could mean his game was up, and dealing with the consequences of his little pantomime may prove humiliating.

"What actions may that be, son?"

"I threatened someone, and I suspect that he thought the threat came from her."

"What was the nature of this threat?"

"It doesn't matter," he said hurriedly. "I am sorry for these and all of my sins. My God, I am sorry for my sins with all my heart," he recited. "In choosing to do wrong and failing to do good, I have sinned against you whom I should love above all things. I firmly intend, with your help, to do penance, to sin no more, and to avoid whatever leads me to sin. My God, have mercy." He stopped, and the silence that followed was awkward, expectant.

At last, Holmes seemed to realize he could push no more without drawing attention to himself. He ran through the absolution quickly, but our heartbroken and guilt-ridden confessor didn't seem to notice.

The man nearly ran from the confessional once he was dismissed, and I waited until his footsteps receded before quietly removing myself from my hiding place.

Holmes opened the confessional door and came out looking sober and unsettled.

"Holmes," I murmured with a sort of horrified awe, "you just absolved a man of his sins."

"Not the worst act I've ever committed," he replied absently. He rubbed his chin. "These are deeper waters than I suspected. Yet another rare event – something occurring that I didn't at all anticipate."

"It's easy enough to put together," I commented. "Everett penned those letters threatening to expose some aspect of Oswald's past in

191

connection to this Jeanette, and he believes Oswald assumed the notes originated from her and killed her."

Holmes arched an eyebrow but didn't argue with me. "Deeper waters, indeed. Possibly, Jeannette was a former mistress."

"Should we take this to Lestrade?"

Holmes nodded but appeared distracted. "At least he may be able to give us some information about this unfortunate woman. Our speculation is all well and good, but I'd prefer some evidence as well."

He stripped off his cassock and folded it carelessly on a pew, reaching under the seat and pulling out his own frock coat and tie.

At my questioning look, he clarified. "This isn't my garb, Watson. I've yet to add priest to my wardrobe of costumes."

"You stole a priest's cassock?"

"Borrowed. Now it will be found, and all is well. Come – to Lestrade."

The inspector wasn't happy to see us. The Metropolitan Police were feeling the after-effects of the Ripper killings, and the shake-ups happening at the higher levels of office were trickling down to the inspectors and the men on the beat. Our colleague and occasional friend looked haggard and harried, and the sight of us in his office doorway seemed to aggravate rather than alleviate his stress.

He rolled his eyes heavenwards. "For the love of all that is holy, please, not now, Mr. Holmes. I haven't called for you. I have no need of you. I have no time for you."

Holmes entered his office and swept into a chair without being invited. "I have need of you, Lestrade."

"Well, if Mr. Sherlock Holmes has need of something, we must tend to it immediately," he said dryly, dropping his pen and leaning back wearily in his chair.

Holmes observed him, taking in everything in that quick way of his. "Cheer up, Lestrade," he said cheerfully, "I may be able to assist you, actually, in what I suspect is an unsolved murder."

Lestrade gestured irritably to a large stack of files on his desk. "I have plenty of those, Mr. Holmes."

I could tell it took great forbearance for Holmes to restrain himself from making a jesting, derogatory comment. When he was very young, he would have lacked the wisdom of silence when faced with a clear opportunity to make a dig at the inspector. Age, and I believe very real affection for Lestrade, had taught him to occasionally hold his tongue.

"Well, we are interested in a particular one. A woman who goes by 'Jeanette'. We have no last name."

192

Lestrade thought for a moment before sighing and digging through the pile. "We do have a case with a woman of that name: *Jeanette White*." He rifled through the file pages after he freed it from the mess. "Performer who lived in a neat but cheap row of flats near Convent Garden. Twenty-five years of age, unmarried. She was strangled. It seems clear the intruder entered and exited her rooms through a window with a lock that had been broken."

"Motive?"

"None that we can find. No one had any complaint against the girl. We suspect someone passing by saw her, took a fancy, perhaps meant to cause her some mischief. Things went awry, she fought back, and lost her life for her troubles." He tossed down the file. "Other than that, we have no leads."

Holmes cast a nonchalant glance around at the whirlwind of papers. "Your office is a bit closed in, Inspector. Fancy some fresh air?"

Lestrade leaned back. "If I say no, you'll simply break into her flat, won't you?"

"Yes."

He frowned. "Why does this interest you, Mr. Holmes? There is nothing unique about this case at all." His face cleared with recognition. "Or is there? What do you know?"

"Speculation, only," Holmes demurred and stood, clearly expecting us to follow. As usual, we did. Lestrade shook on his coat with no shortage of overt exasperation.

"You better make this worth my time," he warned, but it lacked any real heat.

"Always, Lestrade. Always," Holmes declared, already striding down the hall.

Lestrade let us into the tiny, one-story flat. The front room faced the street, affording its previous occupant with a nice little view of the people coming and going to the small shops that lined the main thoroughfare. Her little bedroom tucked up against the alley, and a half-kitchen completed the amenities. It was not the worst of living spaces, but it was clear that whomever had resided here wasn't well-off. Indeed, a young single woman on her own, without the benefits of family wealth, could unfortunately not expect much more.

Holmes stood examining the front door for quite some time. "You say you believe the killer came through the window. Was the door locked when you arrived?"

Lestrade nodded. "Yes, and, at least to me, it appeared that it hadn't been picked."

193

Holmes leaned down and took some time examining this for himself. When he stood, he nodded as if satisfied.

"May I see the report?" He held out a hand, and Lestrade passed him the papers from his coat.

He read through them carefully, glancing up now and then as if searching for some item referenced. When he handed them back to Lestrade, he looked annoyed.

"There is no mention of the removal of shoes, or the fact that the killer turned off the stove."

"I beg your pardon?"

Holmes pointed at the scratched wood near the doorway. "Our intruder removed his shoes – I say 'his' because they are clearly a man's dress shoes – and proceeded into the house on stockinged feet." He strode into the kitchen, where the remains of a half-cooked dinner still remained, drawing the attention of flies. "Did it not also strike you as odd that she was evidently murdered while cooking, yet the stove was off and the food didn't catch fire?"

Lestrade looked a bit flustered. "I didn't pay it much mind, Mr. Holmes. She could have turned off the stove when she heard a noise."

Holmes shook his head dismissively but said no more, going to the bedroom and bending down to look closely at the window's broken lock. He opened the window and then closed it, clearly listening for what sound it made. It was loud, scraping in its old metal railing.

Satisfied with that, he stepped back and took in the small table sat next to it, knocked slightly askew, its little vase of now dead flowers tipped to the side.

He narrowed his eyes and then opened the window again, pushing his head out into the alley.

"Someone stood here."

Lestrade and I leaned over. Outside were some pallets and a few discarded sheets of work canvas. A clear circle had been cleared right beneath the window. Lestrade nodded. "I can see that. But that aligns with our report, Mr. Holmes. The intruder obviously entered through the unlocked window. There is no other way to enter the flat."

"How did this intruder get to the front door to remove his shoes while leaving no trace of footprints or dirt anywhere in his wake?"

"Maybe he was careful."

"If he were careful, he would have removed his shoes here, and not traipsed through two rooms to do so."

"We only have your speculation that he removed his shoes at all."

Holmes hummed but let the comment pass as if unworthy of his attention. "This lock has been broken for months, but no one entered or

194

exited here." He bent down and looked closely at the sill with his magnifying glass. "No scrapes that would indicate shoes. Though there is an odd scratch here." He dug around in it with a pair of tweezers. "Looks like metal chipped off in the ridge, as if a heavy metal object was slid over the wood. Unfortunately, there isn't enough here for any further analysis."

"How do you know that he didn't exit by the window?" Lestrade asked, irritated.

"The table could very well have been knocked askew at any time. The key is not that it is askew, but that it is not askew enough to allow an adult to lift themselves over the window sill without knocking it completely over."

"Now – "

"Attempt it. Go on – try to lift your leg over the windowsill without hitting the table."

Lestrade didn't attempt it. He gave Holmes a witheringly dark glare and tapped his stubbed pencil against his small notepad. After a strained silence, Holmes slid his hands into his pockets and spun around to cross towards the unmade bed. Lestrade made an annoyed clucking sound with his tongue and continued. "Well, then. I guess, therefore, the murderer entered through the front door after all. Unless, of course, you mean to reveal that he dug an underground mine beneath the flat and came up under her bed in some elaborate plot."

"You do know I adore an elaborate plot, but alas – " The detective dropped down and peered under the bed in a sprightly move meant entirely to chafe at the inspector. "No, there is no mine here." He stood and spun on his heel, pretending not to notice – or relish – Lestrade's exasperation.

"However," he continued, "if our man entered through the front door, which was locked, then he is either a master lock pick, which I doubt – there is literally no sign of tampering – or he knew Miss Jeanette White. That would mean this wasn't a random act of opportunity, but premeditated murder by someone who knew her. But I suspect you already suspect that, do you not, Lestrade?"

The inspector tapped his pencil again. "I may have wondered the same thing myself, but I have little evidence to support my theories. You may feel free to speculate, Mr. Holmes, but need I remind you that I work in an official capacity and must therefore base my theories on concrete facts?"

Holmes hummed again and wandered into the kitchen. I followed him into the main room and glanced around. It always felt odd to be in someone's home after his or her death, surrounded by items that spoke of that person's life.

195

Miss White was clearly a curious girl. Her rooms were a bit untidy but overall clean, containing items that spoke of her interests. A small bookshelf filled with fiction, a table with an old but clearly well-maintained Edison phonograph and scattered music sheets. Above her small fireplace was a pretty watercolor painting that I knew at a glance was worth very little. On the mantel itself were various figurines and dried flowers. On the end was a strange little alarm clock – a posing skeleton leaning on two bells. I imagined when it rang, it made the skeleton dance. A smile pulled at my lips. What an interesting girl she must have been. I felt a pang of regret that I would never get to meet her.

Holmes interrupted my thoughts, addressing Lestrade. "Your report said that because of the delay in discovering the body, *rigor mortis* could only provide a wide range of possible times of death. But in your report, you also mention that she must have died after eight o'clock at night, but before ten."

"The next-door neighbor heard her singing at approximately eight."

"Singing?"

"She was an actress, and apparently favored musical theater. The woman next door said she could often hear her in here, singing to herself. That narrowed it down a bit. The coroner is certain she was killed before ten o'clock."

"Therefore, we have a two-hour window," Holmes said under his breath. "You've been enormously helpful, Lestrade," he announced, starting for the door.

"Mr. Holmes," the inspector said tiredly, "at least tell me that you will pass along your conclusions at some point."

Holmes looked affronted. "Of course, and grant you full credit, Inspector, as I so often do." For the first time in our relationship with Lestrade, I noticed a sliver of actual hurt in my friend's tone. I was certain Lestrade wasn't perceptive enough to sense it, but his tone softened, and I quickly rethought my assumption.

"And I'm forever grateful for that, Mr. Holmes. But while the way you flutter about, keeping everything so close to the vest, may be exciting for you, it has caused me no shortage of grey hairs."

"Vibrant description, but at least in this case, I'm only keeping mum because I don't have all the facts. You would never let me hear the end of it if I was caught in a mistake." He laughed, tipped his hat in farewell, and we were out of the door.

"Where are we going?" I asked as we regained the kerb.

"The Oswalds."

"You're going to confront him?"

"I haven't made up my mind. I wasn't lying to Lestrade. I wish to have all the facts before I go off at half-cock accusing others of murder."

The Oswalds lived in a very nice three-story townhouse in Mayfair. We passed the butler our card and were promptly escorted into the drawing room.

It was a cluttered but large room. Mrs. Oswald had clearly been at some knitting, there was a pile of it on her chair. On the comfortable divan was a plump calico that stared at us with wide, black eyes, sniffing us out for danger. A roaring fire was in the hearth, and next to the large French doors looking out to the manicured back garden was a birdcage with a pretty blue-and-green parrot bobbing happily on its perch. The delicate nameplate on the front of the cage said *"Bella"*.

Mrs. Oswald took our hands warmly, clasping my friend's for a bit longer in lieu of effusive thanks for reconsidering her plight.

"Gentlemen," she welcomed, "while I'm pleased you've taken in interest in my concern, I wasn't expecting you." She looked a little worried, and I wondered if Holmes hadn't made an uncharacteristic misstep by coming here where her husband might see us.

Holmes glanced around the room, taking in all the details, and then cutting to the heart of the matter in that brusque-but-at times refreshing way of his, "Is your husband home at the moment?"

She nodded a bit nervously. "He is. I thought it was clear that I wished this matter to stay between us."

"I thought he was normally at his club at this time?" Holmes asked, frowning.

Mrs. Oswald and I startled, surprised that Holmes's interest had evidently extended that far. I wondered when he had taken the time to look into the man's usual schedule.

"He was feeling a bit under the weather," she explained.

"We'll be quick then. I hope you'll pardon us for asking, but where was your husband last Thursday night between roughly eight and ten in the evening?"

She peered intently at him, as if trying to discern the reasoning behind such an inquiry. "We were at the opera. It started at seven, and then we went to dinner afterwards. We weren't home until well after midnight."

"You're certain?"

"I'm quite certain, Mr. Holmes." She gave me an amused, questioning glance.

"And there is no way you could be mistaken about the time?" he pressed.

197

She glanced at me again, as if worried she was failing some sort of test. "I remember where I was, Mr. Holmes. It's hardly a thing to get confused about."

"Of course," Holmes reassured, his smile tight. "It's just that this information complicates some things." He and I shared a meaningful look, which our quick hostess noticed. Before she could ask about it, she seemed to hear something in the hall and straightened up perceptibly as the drawing room door opened, revealing a short stout man with a wide, expressive face.

He smiled broadly at us, a pleasant and playful light dancing in his eyes. "Constance, you must tell me we have guests! I could have barreled in here and embarrassed myself!"

Mrs. Oswald laughed, though it rang a bit forced.

"Forgive me, Percy. I wasn't expecting guests, actually. This is Sherlock Holmes and Doctor John Watson."

"Mr. Sherlock Holmes? The consulting detective?" he exclaimed excitedly, shaking our hands firmly. "I read about your adventure in *Beeton's*. You are mentioned often in the newspapers, as well. To what do we owe the great honor of your presence?" He put a companionable arm around his wife. "I hope we haven't been connected to some vile plot."

"No, not any serious business, sir. We are sorry for intruding," Holmes said pleasantly, clearly looking for an excuse to take his leave.

"I don't imagine Sherlock Holmes finds himself engaged very often in trivial matters," our host pressed, squeezing his wife's shoulders.

Mrs. Oswald broke in deftly. "I left my gloves at the opera house and, as unlikely as it seems, these two famous gentleman happened to find them. They very kindly returned them to me. Tell me, Doctor, how did you like *Manon*?"

I had no idea what *Manon* was and wondered what would have led the woman to think, between the two of us, why I would be the one to help plaster over her lie and not Holmes.

Holmes interjected smoothly, saving me, "Charming, though I see why it was banned for some time."

"I did not care for it," Oswald complained happily. "It seems an easy thing to put a woman in her place, and yet I had to endure nearly two hours of lovesick men being run around by a woman infatuated with glitter and gold."

"Of course," my friend said with false agreeableness. "I prefer Massanet's *Werther*. We are very sorry to have come unannounced. Good day, Madam."

"Thank you again, gentlemen. Have a lovely night," Mrs. Oswald said as she shrugged off her husband's embrace and showed us to the door.

198

She made brief, but meaningful eye contact with Holmes as he tipped his hat to her, and we stopped at the front door while Holmes passed the butler a hastily scribbled note.

"Would you please give this to your mistress? With discretion."

The butler seemed to understand our intent and, with that practiced neutrality of one of his station, he nodded and slipped the thing into his pocket.

"'Complicates' seems an understatement, Holmes," I commented when we were well away from the doorstep. "The man couldn't have killed Miss White if he was sitting comfortably at the opera when she died."

Holmes pressed his fingers together under his chin, looking contemplative. "Indeed. You see now why I refrained from telling Lestrade our theory."

"Could he have hired someone to do the dark deed?"

Holmes sighed, shaking his head. "It's possible, but I can't imagine a man so averse to being blackmailed involving another party in his crimes."

"But we are sure it was him?" I asked tentatively.

Holmes nodded but, in truth, seemed slightly unsure.

As we strode down the darkened street, Holmes glanced at his pocket watch, arching an eyebrow. "You are late."

"I beg your pardon?"

"Aren't you meant to meet Mary at six? It's five past."

"Oh, good Lord!" I exclaimed, panicked.

Holmes stepped into the street and masterfully fetched a cab for me. He urged me in. "Go on. Hurry! Give Mary my love and sincere apologies in holding you captive."

In the morning, at half-past-nine, Holmes received a telegram from Mrs. Oswald. After an obligatory tap on his door, I entered, jostling his shoulder and waking him. He looked sleepily up at me until I passed him the missive.

He sat up, eager, reading it quickly.

"What is it?" I asked as he swung his covers off and rose.

"We are to meet Mrs. Oswald at her home between eleven and one tomorrow."

"I am to assume that is when her husband will be out?"

"Capital observation, Watson. Indeed. In the interim, I wish to speak to Lestrade's witnesses to see if some clue was overlooked. That window interests me. Specifically, whatever was passed through it."

We found ourselves picking our way back into the flat. Holmes spent more time at said window. This time, he left and came around the alley, standing in the cleared circle and reaching inwards, as if testing his reach

199

towards the little round table nearby. Seemingly satisfied, he came back around and joined me in poor Miss White's old bedroom, giving the table a more thorough examination but, from the frown creasing his brow, I could tell he had found nothing new.

He did a quick survey of the main room. He fiddled with the peculiar little alarm clock that had caught my eye but led me back into the hall, carefully relocking the door behind him.

We slid down the hall to the next flat, tapping loudly on the green door. After a moment, it creaked open and an older woman peered out. I guessed her age to be a little over sixty. She squinted at us. I could see from the faint indents on the bridge of her nose that she was missing her usual spectacles.

"Aye?" she asked, a bit distrustfully.

"Good day, Madam," Holmes said gallantly. "My name is Sherlock Holmes, and this is my good friend, Doctor Watson. We're making inquiries about your former neighbor."

She opened the door wider. "Sherlock Holmes? The detective? Are you here to finally find who hurt poor Jeannie?"

Holmes clasped his gloved hands together and nodded solemnly. "I am. Were you close to Miss White?"

"She was such a sweet girl," she lamented softly. "I believe she was meant to be married soon. She made some coy remarks to me about it, and I met her young man a few times."

"Before that young man, did she have any other suitors?"

"Not that I know of. I've only been living here for five months, in any case."

Holmes nodded in understanding. "Of course. You told the constables that you heard her singing at eight o'clock the night she died, Is that correct?"

"Yes. The walls between our flats are a bit thin," she explained.

"Was she in the habit of singing?"

"Oh, all the time. She had some success in minor musicals, but she had aspirations of becoming an opera singer. Her voice was delightful."

"Did you notice anything odd about her singing that night?"

"Odd? Not particularly. She didn't sing for very long – perhaps only a few seconds."

"Did you hear anything else around that time?" I interjected.

"I don't believe so. I wasn't paying rapt attention, however."

"Did you see her or anyone else enter or exit the flat?" my friend asked.

"I did not, but I wasn't looking. The only other thing I remember is that she was cooking at about five o'clock. I could smell the spices she liked to use in her food."

"Five o'clock?" Holmes looked sharply at her. "That may help, ma'am."

"Oh, I don't see how it does, but I sincerely hope so. She didn't deserve what happened to her. Wait here a minute, dear." She walked back into her small flat, leaving the door cracked open, and returned a second later with a small palm-sized cabinet photograph. She handed it to Holmes. "This is Jeanette," she told us. "See how sweet she was?"

Holmes angled the photograph towards me. A very pretty girl with black curly hair smiled back at me. I felt a pang at how young and happy she looked.

Holmes fiddled with the thing for a few moments. He gave no outside indication of it, but I could sense he was slightly uncomfortable. He passed it back solemnly. "She was a very lovely woman," he commented.

She nodded sadly. "I hope you discover whoever did this to her."

We asked a few other flats, but most denied any knowledge of Miss White's comings and goings and saw and heard nothing unusual. One young man, however, who told us he was working from seven o'clock in the evening to one o'clock in the morning, informed us he saw a man turn into the alley as he approached the building's steps on his way home from work. He estimated the time to be close to two o'clock.

"Was he coming from inside the flats?" Holmes asked.

"I couldn't be sure, sir. I really only noticed him because he was dressed nicely. I wondered why someone like that would be skulking down the alley at that time at night. Or morning, rather."

"Did you notice his face?"

"No. He had a scarf pulled up over his mouth and nose. He was a bit on the short side, but that's all I can tell you. I was tired from my work at the factory and was simply eager to get into my bed."

Holmes fell into deep thought for a moment. The young man, looking drained and confused, glanced questioningly at me.

Finally, my friend spoke, "Was he carrying a heavy object?"

"No, nothing."

Holmes, nearly vibrating with excitement, pressed a grateful hand to the man's shoulder. "You have helped me immensely."

He would say no more, settling back in the carriage and closing his eyes. I knew he wasn't resting, but shifting and organizing the details in his mind until the sequence of events came into relief.

When we reentered our rooms, I was surprised to see Everett of the infamous confessional booth debacle waiting for us with a warm cup of tea by the hearth. I flushed, embarrassed.

Holmes didn't seem surprised and, to my everlasting relief, our guest did not seem to recognize my friend as his counterfeit priest.

He rose and shook the detective's hand. "I must admit I was a bit startled by your summons, sir. I imagine, however, I know what this is all about."

Holmes gestured for him to retake his seat and stretched out in his own. "I would think so," he commended, "I take it your life must have been relatively mundane until recently . . . My condolences on your loss."

Everett seemed just barely able to hold back his emotions. He merely nodded, clearing his throat. "I guess I should ask how I came to your attention?"

"It was a simple thing once I was in possession of one of your letters."

"Yes. Quite a foolish thing I did there." He paused and then continued curiously, "Who showed you the letters?" Then, with more outraged anger in his tone, he demanded, "Did the blackguard actually come to you for help?"

Holmes remained impassive. "I assume you mean Mr. Oswald, and, no, he isn't my client. His wife found your blackmail material and brought it to me. Why did you target Mr. Oswald?"

The man put his teacup down on the table between the armchairs, sighing. "Simple. Jeannie told me about her . . . past . . . with Mr. Oswald. He had tricked her – she hadn't known he was married, and she believed he loved her. When she found out she was being used, she broke things off. She claimed to hold no real ill-feelings for him and wished to put the entire thing behind her."

"But you did not?"

A blush of shame spread up his face. "I'm not a rich man," he admitted. "I wanted to provide for her. At least, give her the wedding she deserved. I knew he was a wealthy man and a man whose reputation was important to him because of his connection to the government."

"And you thought blackmailing Mr. Oswald was an easy way to gather some coin."

"I did. I never thought it would result in her death."

Holmes lit a cigarette and tilted his chin at our heartbroken visitor. "So you believe her killer is Mr. Oswald?"

"I do." The answer was firm, steely with rage. "But there is no way for me to prove it. I can produce some letters, but that may not be sufficient, and all it would do is ruin me as well."

Holmes leaned back, pulling contentedly on his smoke and observing the man through narrowed eyes. At last, he knocked the ash out into the fireplace and began, his voice carefully measured. "As a general rule, I am not fond of blackmailers. You take a person's moments of weakness and dig into them, twisting, until your victim is bled dry. However, with the full picture in front of me, I see that your crime is the lesser of evils. I will try my best not to expose you. But I make no guarantee."

Everett swung his hand sharply through the air with barely restrained excitement. "Oh, as long as you bring that man to the gallows, Mr. Holmes, I don't care what becomes of me."

"Splendid!" Holmes declared cheerily. "Now, I'm close to cornering our villain. I will send word to you as soon as I can." He stood, a clear sign that our meeting was over. Everett understood, standing as well and letting himself be bustled out of the door.

"I'll do anything to help," he assured as he swung on his coat.

Holmes clapped him on the back, using the gesture to gently guide him over the threshold. "I'm glad to hear it. Good day."

He spun around once the door was closed, his eyes twinkling.

"Holmes," I admonished, "that was a bit rude."

He waved his hand dismissively, "He'll be all right. But you see how it has all come together?"

I did not. "I understand who our killer is, but I confess I am still confused as to how exactly he enacted the plan. There is still the matter of his alibi."

Holmes eyed me for a disconcertingly long moment, the twinkle dimming a bit. He shrugged. "Well, if one of us knows, that is sufficient," he stated.

He jotted down a missive and sent Billy off to Scotland Yard. "Tomorrow," he declared, "all will be clear, and our Mr. Oswald will be uncomfortable in a cell where he belongs."

In the light of day, Mrs. Oswald's drawing room looked larger, the air drifting in from the tall French windows. That same calico cat lay upon the divan, stretched out on her back as if she didn't have a care in the world. She was deep asleep.

Mrs. Oswald was already standing and, once again, she took both our hands in turn, pressing gently and welcoming us to sit.

She fixed the folds of her skirt as she took her seat. "I haven't been able to rest since your last visit, Mr. Holmes. Why were you asking about my husband's whereabouts?"

Holmes leaned forward from where he sat next to the entirely unbothered cat. He clasped his hands together. "I'm afraid that by bringing me your husband's private letters – and you must be aware of this – you have necessitated an investigation into what secret a blackmailer might be able to hold over your husband's head?"

She fiddled nervously with the button of her waist-shirt. "I was aware of that, yes."

"And you are aware that this information may be dire?" He stared carefully into her face, as if trying to impress upon her the seriousness of her actions.

She inhaled deeply, steadying herself. "I've long suspected my husband may be tempted to act in self-interest instead of the best interest of his country.I likely will not be shocked by any facts that come to light. As to what effect they may have upon my own situation, I suppose I will have to deal with that as it unfolds."

Holmes looked disconcerted with this declaration. He gazed intently and, to my surprise, sadly at her. "That is an admirable attitude. I'm sure it will help as you find yourself faced with sudden, unexpected changes."

She paled a bit at his ominous warning and nodded mutely, gazing intently back at him.

Holmes broke the contact and stood, taking a circle around the room and petting the calico gently as he passed.

"This may be an odd question," he asked, "but does your husband have an unusual clock? One that is likely recently purchased?"

She looked caught off-kilter by the bewildering question. "As a matter of fact, he brought home a strange looking thing that he found somewhere. We don't use it, though. It's more a bric-a-brac type oddity that caught his fancy."

"Could I trouble you to fetch it for me?"

She came back in with an exact copy of the strange skeleton alarm clock I had seen in Miss White's flat. Holmes looked simultaneously pleased and dismayed to see it. He took it from her gently.

"When did he purchase this?"

"A little over a week ago."

Holmes took a deep breath and set it on the mantelpiece, fiddling with the knobs.

"What does this have to do with my husband's letters, sir?" Mrs. Oswald questioned, her voice curious.

"That may be proven in a moment." He stepped back, and we waited for whatever he expected to happen. He had evidently set the alarm for only a few seconds. The little bell went off, sending the skeleton into a jittery little happy dance.

A woman's clear voice rang out, operatic, startling me and Mrs. Oswald. The woman spun around, hand to her chest, searching for someone hiding in the room. My hand had tightened around my walking stick, as well.

"There is no one else here," Holmes assured softly. He went to the bird cage and shifted the cover off. "Little Bella is serenading us." The bird fell quiet, bobbing happily up and down. Holmes put a lithe finger through the bars, and the creature put its foot there.

"I'm confused," Mrs. Oswald confessed haltingly after a long period of prolonged silence.

"Understandably," Holmes reassured. "Tell me, is this cage always in this room?"

Still looking perplexed, our hostess shook her head. "At times, my husband brings her into his chamber. She also visits a specialized veterinarian on a regular basis."

"Of course," Holmes murmured, "so you wouldn't miss her if she were gone for a little while." I could sense that familiar excitement in his voice when he stumbled upon the key to a puzzle, tempered only by his consideration for Mrs. Oswald's feelings. Even being as slow-witted as I was, the chain of events were clear to me, and I realized what was to come to light would upheave this woman's life.

"I will do you the courtesy of warning you that Inspector Lestrade from Scotland Yard will be paying your husband a visit this afternoon. He will place your husband under arrest."

He would tell her no more, reassuring her that the police would likely prefer to speak to her. He pressed a soothing hand to her arm when she seemed inclined to press him for an explanation.

"You have proven yourself an admirably practical woman. This quality will serve you well through what is to come."

Lestrade was happy to see us, eager to hear Holmes relay the events that had led to the man's arrest. Oswald was currently locked in a holding cell.

"Well, I can't say I'm surprised, Mr. Holmes. You prance in here, seemingly pick an unsolved murder at random, and supply me with a culprit all neat and tidy wrapped in a nice little bow in just a few days. And with a prominent figure at the centre as well." There was grudging respect in the inspector's tone, tinged with not an inconsiderable amount of resentment.

"People usually appreciate gifts wrapped in nice little bows, Lestrade," Holmes countered good-naturedly. "And to be fair, I had the benefit of Mrs. Oswald visiting me and setting me on the leads that cleared the matter up."

"Unusually gracious of you. Now, can you please explain to me what is going on?"

"Simple. Watson?"

"Umm," I stuttered, put on the spot. "Well, it seems to me that the parrot is the key to it." I glanced at Holmes, who nodded encouragingly. I continued, "The next door neighbor heard Miss White singing, but what she heard was the parrot. Mr. Oswald, as Miss White's former paramour, had a key to her flat. He entered while she was cooking dinner around five, strangled her, and then – " Here I looked to Holmes once more, unsure. " – to avoid anyone seeing, went to the alley and slid the birdcage into the room through the broken window."

Holmes nodded and picked up the story, "This provided him with the perfect alibi because he, after turning off the stove to avoid a fire, went to dinner and the opera with his wife. He returned in the early hours of the morning, slunk into the alley, and removed the cage."

Lestrade looked befuddled. "But how would he have guessed the bird would sing when he needed it to?"

"Easy. He trained her. Parrots are highly intelligent birds. It doesn't take long to teach them new mimicry."

"The clock," I explained patiently at Lestrade's annoyed look. "Mr. Oswald has the exact same clock in his room, and we tested it as a cue on the bird earlier today."

Lestrade let out an amazed chuckle. "It's no wonder, Mr. Holmes, that you often appear to one-up me. The sheer ridiculousness and audacity of some of these criminals!"

"Very creative," Holmes agreed, skimming over the insult.

"This all might be a bit hard to prove."

Holmes shrugged. "You have the bird, the clock, a key to Miss White's flat that I suspect is somewhere amongst the man's effects, and a witness by the name of Michael Everett who can supply you with the connection between Miss White and Mr. Oswald, as well as the catalyst for this crime."

We were interrupted by a knock on the door. A young constable poked his head in.

"Mrs. Oswald is here, Inspector. She is adamant about speaking to you."

We met her and Inspector Gregson in the hall. She had changed into an immaculate walking dress and hat. She looked at us with clear, steady eyes.

She waved away Lestrade's invitation to enter his office. "Inspector Gregson has already given me a general sketch of events. May I see my husband for a moment?"

206

Lestrade looked annoyed at Gregson and unsure about the request. He cast a glance at Holmes as if for guidance. "That is quite unorthodox, ma'am," he hedged.

"I only wish to ask him a question or two. I need the truth from his own mouth. One cannot function in an ethical or moral way without truth."

Holmes looked at her appreciatively. "On the whole, I'm of the same mind."

"Perhaps I should have wed you."

Lestrade and I felt the understandable sharp awkwardness of such a bold statement, but Holmes chuckled softly, unbothered.

She grew sober and tugged gently on the fingertips of her lace gloves. "Well, Inspector? May I have just a minute of time with my husband alone?"

"A minute, but not alone."

We escorted her into the dingy holding cell. She looked entirely out of place there, bedecked in her immaculate sage-green dress and expensive hat.

Oswald looked surprised to see his wife. The surprise melted into a flush of shame as she placidly circled the old wooden table and stood at his side.

"The inspectors here tell me that you are responsible for the death of that young opera singer," she stated dully.

"It was a misunder – "

He didn't get through his sentence. Pure rage flashed across the woman's face and, quicker than could be seen, she pulled her hat pin from her hair and flung herself at him, aiming for his neck.

The glint of the sharp item froze me, but Holmes reacted with lightning quick reflexes, nearly vaulting over the table and scattering the chairs in his effort to reach her before she could deal a killing blow. He tackled her bodily, landing in a heap of struggling limbs. She continued to fight, spitting invectives at her husband and giving Holmes plenty of trouble keeping her under control.

"You murdered that girl!" she cried, her voice cracking, "You strangled her and sat next to me at the opera as if she were nothing!"

Oswald, from behind the shield of Lestrade's body, unwisely kept speaking. "I couldn't lose you!"

That didn't help. His wife screamed again, lurching from Holmes's grasp for a moment. She made it to the table before he secured her once again. Far beyond being gentlemanly, he picked her up and swung her out of the room, manhandling her all the way back to Lestrade's office.

The commotion had brought a crowd of officers in the hallway, but the inspector barked at them at all to mind their own business and secured the cell door before following us.

Holmes was leaning over the woman as she sat, breathing heavily in the inspector's chair. She was still flushed with rage and defiantly refused to meet his gaze, but she was sitting obediently, and I could see his softly whispered words were having a calming effect.

"You mustn't let your anger ruin your future," he urged, "You are an innocent in this, but murder, no matter how you may justify it, will not allow you to walk away from this without consequence." He took her by the shoulders firmly, forcing her to look at him. "He isn't worth it."

"That girl – " she began, voice trembling with emotion.

"Was as innocent as you are. We know. But the gallows wait for him. Don't rush justice only to your own harm."

She pressed her fingers to her eyes for a long time before glancing up at Lestrade. "Forgive me, gentlemen, for my unforgivable behavior. If you must arrest me, sir, could I please ask that you do so discreetly?"

Holmes rose. "Arrest you for what?" he asked with feigned confusion. He glanced at Lestrade. "I saw nothing occur worthy of arrest, did you?"

Lestrade glared but shook his head. "I suppose I didn't see anything. I had turned around to close the cell, you see," he lied.

Glancing at me for confirmation, which I gave without hesitation, Holmes gestured to the office door. "Seeing as no crime has been committed, you are free to go."

She looked startled but quickly obeyed, apologizing once again in a low murmur before leaving. We followed her out, watching her depart.

Holmes let out a small chuckle. "An admirable woman, indeed."

I frowned curiously at him. "Strange. I would have thought her emotional outburst would have diminished her in your estimation."

He laughed again. "Not at all. Had I been in her place, I cannot say I would have acted any differently. At times, emotional outbursts are the most expected – even logical – course of action."

He bid Lestrade *adieu*, and we settled into the relative warmth of the hansom cab. The sun was just beginning its descent, and our time spent at Scotland Yard would result in us missing a very important caller who would grace us with an ordinary walking stick and a fantastic story.

Holmes leaned back, still chuckling. "One small silver lining: Mrs. Oswald is now a free woman."

"Are you seriously considering her suggestion?" I teased. "Serving as her second husband?"

He laughed. "Marrying a younger, smarter man who doesn't chase skirts behind her back would be a definite improvement," he said, the arrogance of the statement negated by the sparkle of mischief in his eyes. "But alas, you know my domestic preferences, and marriage doesn't align with my need for solitude." While Holmes was indeed not a man easily swayed by feminine qualities, he did seem to have an admirable view of Mrs. Oswald, or even a protective view, going so far as to send me to Baskerville Hall without him in order to testify in Oswald's trial and do what he could to spare the wife a scandal larger than that which was already inevitable – one of the most revered names in England, indeed!

"Speaking of marriage," I started, realizing he was in a good mood and had been free from his chemical distractions for at least three days, "There is a small matter I've been meaning to broach with you."

"Indeed?"

"You may feel free to refuse. You have no obligation to spare my feelings," I blustered on, feeling suddenly nervous as he stared impassively at me across the way. "But I was wondering if you would mind serving as best man at my wedding? There is very little required of you: A passing of the rings, and the ceremony will be short – "

"Watson," he cut me off curtly. Then he smiled. "I was beginning to think you'd never ask."

"At the present instant one of the most revered names in England is being besmirched by a blackmailer, and only I can stop a disastrous scandal."
– Sherlock Holmes
"A Scandal in Bohemia"

The Rouen Scandal
by Martin Daley

Chapter I

In the years following the publication of my first account of an adventure involving Sherlock Holmes, his notoriety quickly grew, not only nationally but internationally. This was often to his annoyance and – I must confess – to my own embarrassment. Whenever I am now introduced to someone new by a friend or acquaintance, I'm invariably asked to choose just one case among the thousands my friend has undertaken during his career. I always find it an impossible choice to make. Over the years, I have often struggled to choose which investigations to put forward for publication and which to leave out. After all, Holmes has been involved in uncovering almost every crime imaginable. There have been some investigations where our own lives have been put at risk, and even some others that have baffled those peculiar analytical qualities unique to my friend.

Although I usually bluster my way through some response before changing the subject, whenever I'm asked the question, it invariably leads me to reflect on our friendship and some of the incredible things I have witnessed through my association with that remarkable man. If it was a case of the ridiculous, then surely the matter of the hapless Cumberland cartographers would be near the top of the list. If there was a light-hearted tale to be told, then the amusing denouement involving Mrs. May's egg-timer must surely merit mention. But if I were asked to concentrate my thoughts on the cruelty of mankind, then it would unquestionably be characters such as Baron Gruner or Jonas Oldacre, who would no doubt be at the forefront.

That all notwithstanding, there does remain another case that I still find the most sickening of all whenever I recall it, for it was not only the slandering of an innocent woman that I found repellent, but the fact that members of my own profession could enter into such an evil conspiracy was astonishing, as was the scale on which such despicable actions were perpetrated.

The case began as a seemingly trivial matter that gradually developed into something beyond imagining. I had left Holmes earlier on the morning in question and went out for a walk. Upon my return, I heard voices as I climbed the familiar stairs to our sitting room – clearly Holmes had a client. Upon knocking and entering, I found my friend in his usual chair by the fire, talking to a man opposite.

"Ah, Watson, the very man!" cried my friend. "Do come in as you may be of invaluable assistance. I don't believe you have previously met Inspector Merivale of the Yard?"

Holmes's guest stood and offered a hand. "Good morning, Doctor, Mr. Holmes has told me a lot about you."

"Pleased to meet you, Inspector. Holmes has also mentioned your name in the past."

"Merivale has been telling me about an unusual little problem in Camberwell. I think it may be worthy of our interest."

Merivale responded to Holmes's gesture, indicating that he should repeat his story for my benefit.

"We had . . . not so much a complaint . . . more of an observation passed our way yesterday from a Mrs. Baxter of Grove Lane. She reported that she had seen her neighbour recently with a baby."

"What's so unusual about that?" I commented with a smile. "Hardly a crime, I would have thought."

"Well, no, not really, but the thing is, Mrs. Baxter said there was no sign of this neighbour ever being pregnant. She is around thirty years of age, unmarried, and lives alone. Doesn't seem to have any gentleman callers. Yet suddenly, she is seen walking out with an infant in a pram."

"It sounds more like a busybody neighbour to me. The woman could be looking after the child – a nephew or a niece perhaps?"

"That is what I thought initially, but it was brought to my attention by my desk sergeant, Hendricks. What prompted him to do so is that he remembered two other similar reports over the past twelve months. He didn't think any differently to you at first, Doctor, but each case followed the same pattern – young, unmarried woman suddenly being seen with a baby. In each case, the person reporting the matter has commented on how reluctant the 'mother' was to speak to them about the newborn when asked. Working on the principle that once is happenstance, twice is coincidence, and third is suspicious, Hendricks brought it to my attention. As we are a little short-handed at the moment, what with Gregson on holiday and Jones laid up with a nasty bout of influenza. I wondered if Mr. Holmes would be interested in looking into the matter."

"Not within our usual purview eh, Watson?" interjected Holmes. "But anything to break the stagnation and monotony of the last few weeks."

He took the details of the three separate accounts from Merivale and informed him he would report any significant findings within a week.

211

"Probably nothing, gentlemen," said the policeman, as he made to leave, "but we appreciate your help as always."

The three reports Merivale referred to were at locations in Battersea and Brixton, as well as the case in Camberwell.

"Where should we start?" I asked.

"We shall start," announced Holmes, "with a note. Billy!" he cried.

Within seconds, the page came scampering up the stairs.

"Yes, sir?"

Holmes was scribbling a message as Billy entered. "I want you to deliver this note to a Miss Sally Potts of 3 Mortimer Street, Lambeth."

"Right away, sir," said the lad, darting away on his latest mission.

"Who is Miss Sally Potts?" I asked.

"Another vital member of my underworld network. It would be inaccurate to say we are embarking on women's work, but the assistance of the fairer sex in such delicate matters won't go amiss."

Three hours later, a young woman was announced by our landlady. "A Miss Sally Potts to see you, Mr. Holmes."

"Thank you, Mrs. Hudson," replied Holmes, rising from his chair.

In the doorway stood a woman of about thirty. She wore her auburn hair under a blue bonnet – attractive but with a bearing that suggested that she was not unfamiliar with the hardship of the working classes.

"Good afternoon, Sally," said Holmes, welcoming our guest. "This is my friend and colleague, Doctor Watson, before whom we can speak freely."

"I came as quick as I could after I got your message Mr. Holmes. What can I do for you?"

Holmes informed our guest of the meeting we had that morning with Inspector Merivale. He gave her the three addresses passed to him by the Scotland Yard man.

"I would like you to find out what you can about these women and their babies," he concluded.

"Certainly, Mr. Holmes. Give me a few days and I'll let you know." With that, she left.

"How on earth did you know that young woman?" I asked.

"Sally and her mother both worked in the service of a Duchess in Chelsea," said Holmes, as he re-lit his pipe with a glowing cinder, which he held between the tongs. "They were both wrongly accused of stealing from their employer some years ago. It was before your time, I think, but Sally was so grateful, she said she would be willing to help with my work if there was ever need for a woman's touch. On occasion since then – when the use of the irregulars or my rather heavy-handed informants have been

212

inappropriate – she has demonstrated herself to be extremely useful. I'm sure she will prove to be the perfect ally in this case."

"You never cease to amaze me," I said, shaking my head as I picked up my newspaper once more.

Unsurprisingly, Holmes's confidence in Miss Potts' abilities proved to be well founded. She returned to Baker Street three days later with a summary of her findings.

"I've heard of middle-class women who, unable to have children, seek out people who can help them. From what you told me, Mr. Holmes, it sounded to me as though this was the case here, and so it proved to be. I spoke to all three of them – gaining their trust and making as if I was wanting a baby myself. Rather than shoo me away and risk me going to the police, each of them took me in and told me their stories. And in each case, the same name came up. They referred to an 'Agnes Jakes' and gave me an address in Kensington. She was the one who supplied the kiddies to these women, although they don't know where she got them from. As they were so desperate for a child, they didn't ask. They just paid her the money and took their new baby. I thought you would want to follow her up, so I took the liberty of going round there myself with the same story."

Holmes smiled at Miss Potts' initiative, but offered a mild rebuke. "I don't want to put you in any danger, Sally. In future, make sure you check with me first before taking on any extra task."

"Yes, sir," said the young woman with a slightly embarrassed smile. "Anyway, as soon as I told this Mrs. Jakes what my business was, she hurried me into her house and took me into a room at the back. I told her that I couldn't have children and I had been given her details by a friend. She accepted what I said and told me she could arrange something for me. It would take a month to organise and would cost one-hundred pounds."

Holmes whistled. "What did this woman look like?"

"She would be a bit older than me – in her forties? Attractive woman, black hair, green eyes. Spoke in a funny way. I couldn't quite put my finger on it, but it sounded strange."

"Strange? What – like an accent?"

"Yes, it could be but it was difficult to say. If she is foreign, she is a very good speaker of English."

"Anything else?"

"I noticed there was a cross with Jesus on the wall."

"A crucifix?"

"Yes, that's the word I was looking for – a crucifix."

"Thank you, Sally. That's excellent work." Holmes handed the woman an envelope.

213

"Oh, thank you, sir! You needn't have bothered with this after all you did for us."

"Please pass my regards on to your mother," said my friend, drawing the meeting to a close. And then, once Miss Potts had left, "I have a strange feeling this case might be much bigger than it first appears."

"Are we now to visit this Agnes Jakes?" I asked.

"No, not yet." He opened the door to our sitting room once more. "Billy!"

After he had sent the page to the telegraph office again, he explained that he was contacting the British Embassies in Madrid, Paris, and Rome.

"Why?" I asked.

"Sally's observations may prove significant in this matter. She referred to the woman possibly having a foreign accent and referenced a crucifix. If this is true, then the likelihood is that the woman hails from a country heavily steeped in the Roman Catholic faith."

"Surely someone with any type of faith couldn't be involved in something as cruel as this?"

Holmes looked at me kindly. "The complexities and hypocrisies of humanity know no bounds, my friend. Some can go to any lengths to justify their actions to themselves and sadly, even the most pious are seldom exempt from cruelty and wrongdoing." He paused before adding, "As the three most likely countries to follow that faith are Spain, France, and Italy, I contacted the Embassies there to enquire with the respective police headquarters as to whether there is any record of such a woman involved in child abduction."

Much to his frustration, there were no replies to the telegrams for three days. Then all at once, they arrived together. It was Mrs. Hudson who brought them up, and Holmes practically snatched them from her tray in his haste. Our landlady – well-used as she was to such unintentional rudeness – rolled her eyes and left him to it.

He ripped open the telegrams and snorted his contempt at the first two, tossing them behind him into the fire without a second glance. The third, however, obviously gave him the answer he was looking for.

"Ha! Into our coats, Watson!" he cried, as he hastened to his room to change from his dressing gown.

I reached for my hat and coat and met him on the landing as he made to hurry downstairs. We almost bundled over Mrs. Hudson, who had only just reached the hallway from visiting our sitting room.

"Billy!" shouted Holmes once more, almost frightening the life out of the poor woman in the process. As ever, the lad appeared momentarily. "Go to Scotland Yard immediately and ask for Inspector Merivale. Tell him to meet me at this address urgently. He'll know what it is about." He scribbled down the address in Kensington.

"What if he's busy?" asked Billy, not unreasonably.

Holmes looked startled at the lad's question. "Tell him to come anyway!"

"Right away, sir," said the page with a salute.

We followed Billy outside and, while he dashed off down Baker Street, we hailed a hansom. Once inside, I asked Holmes to explain the contents of the telegram.

"I asked if there were any unsolved cases involving child abduction or smuggling. The responses from Madrid and Rome were negative, but the third message from Paris informed me that there is a continuing investigation into a suspicious number of infant deaths in a clinic in the northern city of Rouen. While one of the suspects has been arrested for murder, the other one absconded three years ago. Her name is *Agnès Jacques*."

"*Agnes Jacks!*" I exclaimed in wonderment.

"Quite possibly. That is what we're going to find out."

Under Holmes's instruction, our cab pulled up a little further along the road from the address given to us by Sally Potts. Significantly, there was another hansom waiting outside No. 32, the address in question.

"We'll walk the rest of the way," said Holmes, descending onto the pavement. I paid our fare and hurried after him. "It seems we're just in time," he said over his shoulder as we climbed the steps to the front door that was ajar. He rang the bell.

"Yes, I'm coming!" shouted a woman's voice from inside.

The door swung open and the woman visibly stepped back in surprise at the sight of two strangers.

"*Bonjour*, Madame Jacques. *Je m'appelle* Sherlock Holmes, *et voici mon ami, le Docteur* Watson."

Before the woman could respond to Holmes's flawless French, my friend had eased passed her into the entrance hall. I followed and observed two suitcases, waiting to be collected.

"What is the meaning of this?" cried the woman, trying to regain some composure.

"Ah, English it is, then," said Holmes casually. "I see you appear to be planning a little trip?"

"Who are you? What are you doing here? Do you have a warrant to enter my home?"

"We do not, but officials from Scotland Yard do and they will be here shortly."

The words appeared to deflate the woman, who gave the appearance of someone facing defeat. Holmes continued.

"You are Agnès Jacques, wanted in you home country for infanticide."

"That is an outrageous accusation!" cried the suspect. "I have never murdered a child in my life!"

"In that case, you are either party to such atrocities, or you are guilty of another crime – kidnapping. Or smuggling perhaps?"

Significantly, the woman never responded. Just then, the police wagon drew up outside and Inspector Merivale and two constables appeared at the door.

"I received your message, Mr. Holmes," said Merivale. "What's all this about then?"

"I think you need to take this woman away, Inspector, and inform the *Sûreté* of her arrest. I wouldn't be surprised if one of your colleagues from across the Channel may wish to come and help you with your questioning. If my suspicions are correct, then this woman's crimes run far deeper than her involvement in providing babies to wealthy middle-class childless mothers in London."

"Very good, Mr. Holmes. Thank you as always for your help."

"If you need any further assistance, Merivale, don't hesitate to ask. Oh, and by the way: I would draw your attention to the telegram she has carelessly left on the little bureau in the hall. This, coupled with her apparent imminent departure, suggests she had been alerted to your interest."

Merivale picked up the telegram. "It's in French!"

"Yes. It has been sent from Rouen, in Northern France, and is alerting Madame Jacques here to the exposure of their operation."

Jacques kept her head down as Holmes concluded his theory. The two constables led the woman away and we took advantage of the waiting cab outside to return to our lodgings.

Chapter II

It wasn't long before Merivale availed himself of Holmes's offer of further assistance. Within twenty-four hours, my friend received a note from the Scotland Yard man inviting him to attend the matter, as Inspector Francois Le Villard from the *Sûreté* was travelling from Paris and had asked that Holmes continue his involvement in the case.

"Le Villard!" Holmes announced. "This must be a bigger case than first imagined. Since my last encounter with him, I had heard that the authorities were now using him all around the country. Now abroad!"

I had never met the French detective myself, but had heard Holmes speak favourably about him in the past. I agreed with my friend that it must be a serious issue if the French authorities were sending over one of their best men to oversee the matter. It was with a sense of eagerness and anticipation that I accompanied Holmes the following morning to meet Le Villard and find out more about this mysterious Madame Jacques.

The Frenchman greeted my friend warmly, as is their custom, much to Holmes's discomfort and the amusement of Merivale and myself. Holmes introduced me and I thrust out a firm hand in greeting, having looked forward to meeting the man for some time.

"*Bonjour*, Doctor. I am pleased to meet you."

He spoke only broken English, but as Holmes was fluent in French, communication was of little problem. Le Villard explained that Agnès Jacques had fled France three years earlier, upon the death of her brother, Claude Carere. The two had been running refuges across Normandy for impoverished women and unmarried mothers, telling them they could find homes for their babies with wealthy couples in exchange for money. In reality, far from being philanthropic, the establishments they were running became known as "baby farms", where any monies received found their way into the coffers of Carere and his sister. When the atrocity was uncovered, Carere had a sudden heart attack and died, while his sister fled.

"We finally now know where to," concluded Le Villard.

"It seems that this woman has commenced the same despicable practice here in London," I stated.

"Not so, Doctor," Le Villard replied before his English failed him. Holmes translated. "It would appear that at least one of these refuges still exist, as we now believe the babies that have appeared in London originate from France."

"How do you know this?" asked Merivale.

"We had information passed to us from an anonymous source claiming that there is a clinic in Rouen that has seen several suspicious baby deaths. I have men there as we speak."

I noted the reference to Rouen, the city from where the telegram received by Madame Jacques was sent.

"If the brother is dead," said the Scotland Yard man, "then who do you suspect of coordinating the wicked scheme."

"Based on the information we have, we suspect his widow, Madame Marguerite Montpensier. If the structure of the villainous practice were in place during her husband's lifetime – and she was party to it – it would not be impossible to continue it in his absence."

The three of us looked at the Frenchman for further explanation.

217

"Madame Montpensier married Carere six years ago. When he died, the Republic seized most of his assets. Therefore, his widow inherited very little of his estate. Potentially, she therefore has the knowledge and the motive. She re-married two years ago, and our information is that she has been running an even more sinister operation since – an operation that has seen babies being kidnapped from the clinic of St. Marie in Rouen. Certificates of death are forged and the infants are then be whisked abroad to be sold for money."

I was dumbfounded by the narrative. How anyone could be so cruel was quite beyond me.

It was Holmes that broke the silence. "I assume that Madame Montpensier has been arrested. The note I received said someone had been charged with murder?"

"Yes, but not for the murder of the children," replied Le Villard. "Those individual cases are still being investigated. It is on the suspicion of murdering her stepdaughter, Mademoiselle Lucille Carere."

"Her stepdaughter!" I repeated, involuntarily.

"What does she have to do with it?" asked Merivale.

"That is what we are trying to establish, Inspector. We have yet to find the body."

"Then how do you know she has been murdered?" asked Holmes.

"When we were alerted to the suspected practice, a separate source came forward and suggested that the stepdaughter had found out about Madame Montpensier's wrongdoing and was about to go to the police. As there appears to be some substance to the Rouen clinic, we have taken the woman in for questioning about both matters."

"And this second source was also anonymous, I assume?" Holmes's question garnered a nod from the policeman. "And what was her response to the charges?"

"She naturally denies all knowledge of both the child kidnappings and the disappearance of her stepdaughter. I didn't have an opportunity to fully question her myself when I received the message from London about Agnès Jacques."

"Yes, this woman is interesting," said Holmes, turning to Merivale. "What is her response since her arrest?"

"She has been evasive and non-cooperative. It'll be interesting to see her reaction when our French friend here walks in. Would you like to accompany us, Mr. Holmes?"

"No, I'll follow my own line of investigation, gentlemen. But before I do, Merivale, could I trouble your man Hendricks once more for the actual dates of the suspicious child sightings you told us about?"

218

"Certainly." The inspector returned a few minutes later and handed Holmes a piece of paper.

"Thank you. Perhaps we could all meet later tonight in Baker Street to share our findings?"

"Yes, certainly," agreed Merivale, a little confused.

"Excellent. We shall see you both at seven."

"Where are we going?" I asked as we left the two policemen to their questioning.

"To the offices of the Southwestern Railway Company."

"Are we to book tickets for the Continent?"

"Not yet, but I think a trip to France may prove to be of interest in this case. For the moment, however, we're interested in trying to identify Madame Jacques' confederates. I believe this case involves more individuals than the one we encountered in Kensington.

"You will recall that we intercepted her during the act of her departure? The telegram on her bureau confirmed that she had been alerted to the authorities' pursuit of her. It was probably sent by the person – or more likely – *persons* who transported the infants from France."

"You think there will be more than one?"

"A woman on her own travelling with a child would be a slightly unusual sight and would attract a little attention. For a man to travel alone with an infant and remain inconspicuous would be impossible, but no one would ever suspect any wrongdoing involving a young couple travelling with their new baby. As we now have at least three dates when young children appeared in their new homes – and working on the hypothesis that Madame Jacques was recently expecting another visit – it will be interesting to examine the passenger lists of the Channel crossings run by the company to see if we can identify any repeat travellers who were making the journey at the corresponding times."

As Holmes concluded his line of reasoning, our cabbie pulled up at our destination. We entered the offices of the Southwestern Railway Company and approached the official on the front desk. He had all the appearance of a railway devotee and therefore someone who loved working for one of the top companies in that industry. His bald dome protruded above a visor that shielded his eyes, while his slightly faded black waistcoat and matching over-sleeves gave some indication of his length of service in the role. Sadly, his manner didn't match his appearance of enthusiastic professionalism. His expression was one of being inconvenienced as we approached.

Naturally, Holmes wasn't put off by his demeanour. "Good morning. We would like to inspect the passenger lists for the Channel crossings from the Normandy ports over the past two years."

The man reluctantly removed the *pince-nez* that teetered on the end of his nose. "For what purpose? Such records are not easily obtained."

"My name is Sherlock Holmes, and I'm assisting Scotland Yard and the French *Sûreté* in a matter of extreme importance."

The demeanour of the man changed instantly. He clearly recognised Holmes's name, and this, combined with the mention of Scotland Yard, made him leap from his seat.

"Certainly Mr. Holmes, I'll get those records for you right away!" He hurried off and returned within five minutes. "Here you are, Mr. Holmes. We have records here from the crossings from Caen, Cherbourg, and Dieppe dating back the last two years. You can study them over here at this desk if you like. Just let me know if you require any other records. They're all readily available."

I smiled to myself, as the man couldn't be more helpful. Holmes paid little attention to the change in his conduct, concentrating instead on the ledgers with which he had been provided. He gave one to me and – armed as we were with the relevant dates – we sat down to study the list of names that travelled to and from the Continent around the times in question.

We had been examining the lists for about an hour when Holmes asked, "What have you found?"

"I think I have something," I replied with some enthusiasm. "On or around the dates in question, there is a Mr. and Mrs. Fox '*with child*' – as it states – arriving at the various British ports from Normandy."

"Each journey being a one-way ticket." It was more of a statement than a question.

"Yes, now you mention it, they are."

Holmes gave me one of the ledgers he'd been studying. "Now examine the departures listed for the days following our dates and tell me if there is another pattern."

I followed Holmes's instruction and after about ten minutes announced, "Yes, there does appear to be regular entries for a French couple making repeated journeys in the opposite direction. A Monsieur and Madame – "

"Renard," interrupted Holmes.

"Yes," I said, looking up. "How did you know?"

"Because I had observed the exact same entries. Again, taking one-way journeys."

"Yes."

"And with no indication of a child?"

"No."

"I think we have our confederates."

"How can you be so sure?"

"Because, my dear fellow, the French for the *fox* is *renard*. Let us do a little more digging of our own and see what addresses are associated with these two couples."

The official who had provided us the ledgers earlier was only too pleased to help further and hurried off following Holmes's request. Upon his return some minutes later, Holmes immediately scoured the pages, placing markers in each one of interest. Finally, he announced his discoveries.

"As I suspected, the address attributed to '*Mr. and Mrs. Fox*' is the same as Agnès Jacques in Kensington, while the address of '*Monsieur and Madame Renard*' is a house in Rouen. These people are the next link in this chain of misery."

"That's remarkable. I must congratulate you."

"It is true we have advanced, but there is still a long way to go. We'll meet with our Anglo-French friends tonight and decide on the next steps."

When the two police inspectors did meet with us in Baker Street at the appointed hour, they were both equally as fulsome in their praise of my friend's remarkable deductive powers.

"*C'est magnifique!*" cried La Villard.

"Even I understood that," said Merivale, "and I couldn't agree more."

"Let's not get ahead of ourselves, gentlemen," said Holmes, characteristically dismissing the praise. "There is still much work to be done. We may have a plausible hypothesis regarding the process for moving the infants across the Channel, but we are no nearer to establishing the actual identity of those involved. What's more, it is highly unlikely that these people are the only ones involved in such heinous activity."

"I am aware of that," said the French detective in his broken English. "We must try to identify these people."

"And for us to do that," replied Holmes, "we must go to France."

"That's a little beyond my jurisdiction, Mr. Holmes," said the Scotland Yard man. "I'm afraid I'll have to leave you to it."

Holmes addressed the French detective. "You will no doubt be taking Madame Jacques back to France with you?"

"Yes."

"Then we shall come with you – " He turned to me almost as an afterthought. " – if you are receptive to such a suggestion?"

"Why yes, of course," I said, excited by the prospect of a trip to the Continent, even if it was in such distasteful circumstances.

221

As it was one less matter for Merivale to trouble himself with, I had the impression that he was content enough to see a satisfactory conclusion to the London end of the nefarious operation. *"Bon voyage*, then!" he said in the worst French accent imaginable as he rose to leave.

We agreed to meet Le Villard at Scotland Yard the following day, where we would accompany him and his prisoner, along with a matron, to Newhaven, before crossing to Dieppe and then on to Rouen.

Chapter III

The Channel crossing was bleak and uncomfortable. We sat in a communal area with the other passengers while the wind howled and screamed outside. The visibility was virtually non-existent as oversized raindrops assaulted the windows of the boat like bullets. The vessel bucked and swayed violently, much to the distress of some of the passengers, but throughout Madame Jacques remained silent, refusing offers of food and staring directly ahead.

Although the subsequent two-hour rail journey to Rouen could hardly be described as comfortable, I was thankful to be on dry land again, knowing that we were on the final leg of our trip.

The Rouen police headquarters was a modest, rundown building in what seemed to be a quiet backwater town. From the villains' point of view, it was an ideal location from which to run such a despicable operation. Far from Paris, Lyon, and Marseilles – not to mention its close proximity to the northern ports – its geography combined with its anonymity provided the perfect setting.

Once again, I relied on Holmes to act as translator when speaking with and being party to conversations with the local officials.

I had the impression that the Rouen officers thought that such horrible activities as those they were investigating had ended with the demise of Carere some years earlier. Perhaps a little complacency had set in during the subsequent duration, but the presence of Inspector Le Villard from the capital was certainly now renewing a sense of urgency among them.

We were shown into an office that was stark and cramped. I could only guess at the last time it had been painted. I was surprised therefore when the Parisienne detective commented to Holmes how tidier the station was and how smarter the uniformed officers were since his last visit a few days earlier.

The sergeant on the front desk took Madame Jacques into custody and showed her to a cell at the rear of the station. Le Villard informed us that Madame Montpensier was already held in one of the other cells.

"I have arranged for us to lodge at l'Hotel de Ville. I suggest we go there now, have something to eat, and get some rest. We will then question the two women in the morning."

I sensed Holmes's frustration at the suggestion, but he knew that after a full day of travelling, the proposal was a logical one. For my own part, I was delighted, as it had escaped my memory that I had eaten nothing meaningful since breakfast."

Suitably refreshed after a good night's sleep, we returned to the station to interview the two woman at the heart of the case. Madame Montpensier was first and, although I couldn't understand her first-hand, she struck me as being quite sincere in her protestations. Holmes apprised me of what was being said.

"Madame, you know the charges against you," stated Le Villard, "and you must surely be aware that these are considered capital crimes. Not only your liberty, but your life is at stake here."

"I am well aware of that, Inspector. If I knew anything of significance, I assure you I would have told you when I was first arrested."

"Let us go back to the beginning. When did you first meet Monsieur Carere, your late husband?"

"It would be about seven years ago. We were introduced by a mutual friend. He was a charming man – a widower – and the two of us became close from there."

Le Villard referred to his notes. "And you married the following year?"

"That's correct. We were married for two years when he was arrested and passed away."

"What did Carere tell you about his business?"

"Very little. I believed he was a philanthropist who helped people. I was astounded and ashamed of my own naïveté when I found out the truth."

"You didn't inherit his estate?"

"I did not want it, gained as it was. It was seized by the Republic and they were welcome to it. I was questioned at the time about my involvement, and the Sûreté were satisfied that I had nothing to do with the matter."

"It could be viewed that you were bitter about losing an estate worth tens of thousands of francs, so you were motivated to keep the practice going."

"That is a despicable thought, Inspector. You can think what you like, but I would never consider getting involved in anything so horrible as that. I met my current husband, Monsieur Montpensier, two years ago. We run

223

a little *boulangerie* together in Bois-Guillaume. This is hardly the lifestyle of people who are making fortunes from illegal activity."

The suspect was making a compelling case regarding her innocence. Le Villard clearly had little evidence to associate her with the removal and abduction of children from the clinic in the centre of the town. He therefore moved on to the matter of Carere's daughter, Montpensier's stepdaughter.

"When was the last time you saw Lucille Carere?"

The woman laughed. "This was put to me when I was brought in earlier this week and accused of her murder. It's ridiculous! I haven't seen Lucille since her father died. We were never close, and I think it suited both of us to start a new life apart."

"You say you were never close. How old was she when you married her father?"

Madame Montpensier thought for a while. "She would be in her early twenties – about twenty-two, I think. I believe she had not long returned from studying at university in America. Her father used to boast that she was amongst the first female students admitted to one of their so-called 'Ivy League' universities."

"And what did she do upon her return?"

"Not very much, from what I could see. She was close to her father, who seemed to find her work at the hospitals from time to time."

At this point, Le Villard broke off from his questioning and glanced at Holmes, who gave the merest shake of the head, indicating there was nothing further to be gained by pursuing the questioning. Almost as imperceptibly, the French detective nodded his agreement.

"I think that will be all for now, Madame. You are free to go. I would ask that you remain at home, however, as we may need to speak with you further regarding both the abductions from St. Marie's and the disappearance of Lucille Carere. I will arrange to have you taken home."

The detective called for assistance and a uniformed officer entered, escorting the dignified woman from the room.

"What do you make of it, Mr. Holmes?" Le Villard asked after they had left.

"There is little or no evidence to associate her with either crime. It would appear on the face of it that Madame Jacques and her confederates have steered you towards the woman to divert attention away from themselves. I assume others from St. Marie's have been detained?"

"Of course. A registrar, two midwives, and a Catholic priest have all been arrested in connection with the practice."

"No doctors?"

"No. There are only two resident consultants at the clinic – " Le Villard referred to his notes. " – Dr. Villeneuve from Brittany, and a Dr.

Róka from Hungary. Villeneuve has been on a leave of absence for two months as his wife is suffering with cancer, and Róka had to leave urgently for Budapest, as his mother has apparently been taken ill."

"How long has he been away?"

"Just a matter of days apparently. I have contacted the Budapest authorities to try and locate him, but I haven't heard anything from them as yet. I also have a man speaking with Villeneuve. I will receive an update from him later today."

"How is the clinic being covered in their absence?" I asked.

"*Locum* consultants are covering the duties, Doctor. We have checked on them all, and do not suspect any complicity."

"No doubt you are now going to speak with Madame Jacques?" mentioned Holmes.

"That was my intention."

"Then with your permission, we will go to the clinic of St. Marie and see what we can find out."

"Certainly, Mr. Holmes. Your help is most welcome."

"Until later, then."

Holmes and I made our way to the clinic. It appeared a soulless, dirty building from the outside, but perhaps my assessment was influenced by the knowledge of what had happened at this place. Upon entering, I was surprised at the cleanliness and seemingly professional environment. What came as no surprise, however, was the gloomy atmosphere that pervaded the interior. It was though a heavy cloud was following the staff that remained around the building as they tried to continue their duties, no doubt full in the knowledge that their place of work – and their association with it – would be tarnished forever.

Two uniformed officers were present in the entrance area and Holmes introduced us, explaining that we were helping Inspector Le Villard with his investigation. One of the two men saluted and turned to one of the hospital staff who appeared to be performing reception duties. Clearly the policemen were there to oversee the various activities within the facility, given the recent revelations.

Again, Holmes translated for me the officer's instruction to the staff member. He informed the man that we should be treated with the same respect as if we were policemen. Holmes thanked him for his assistance and asked the man behind the desk if he could see Dr. Róka's file. Within a few minutes, the man returned and handed him the buff-coloured folder.

"Been here for almost five years," Holmes mumbled into the folder. "First position as a qualified consultant . . . excellent qualifications . . . ." He suddenly looked up from the page and stared into the middle distance with the merest hint of a smile.

"Tell me," he said, addressing the man once more, "do you have a telephone in the clinic?"

"Of course, sir. Please come with me."

We followed him into an office at the end of the main corridor and the receptionist indicated the telephone on the desk before leaving us to resume his duties. Holmes picked up the receiver, spoke to the operator, and asked to be connected to the Hungarian Embassy. I was amazed when he put the phone down a few minutes later after asking only one question. He spoke to the person on the other end in French but I recognised him mentioning the name of the Hungarian consultant, Róka.

"Very clever," he said with a laugh.

"What was the purpose of that?"

"All in good time, my dear fellow," was his infuriating reply. "We are not quite there yet."

"Well, where to now then?" I asked, more than a little chagrined.

He ignored my question and picked up the receiver again to speak with the operator. I heard him mention Cherbourg. Again, there was a delay as he waited to be connected. Once a voice was heard on the other end, Holmes launched into his native-like fluency in his effort to solve another strand of the mystery. I couldn't possibly understand everything that was being said but I distinctly heard him mention, "Monsieur *et* Madame Róka." Although I could neither understand of even hear exactly what the man on the other end was saying, his excited jabbering was clearly audible. I took this to be an objection to Holmes's request but as soon as my friend mentioned the name of Inspector Le Villard of the *Sûreté*, the man stopped immediately. When Holmes replaced the receiver, he said the man would be ringing him back shortly.

"Who were you speaking to then?" I asked in response.

"In a moment," he said as he rose to leave. "Perhaps you could man the telephone while I clarify something with our friend at the reception desk."

He didn't wait for me to reply and I was left sitting there, staring in terror at the telephone in case it rang. Fortunately, Holmes returned within a few minutes.

"I have asked our friend if he could arrange some refreshment for us. Perhaps you could go and collect it from him while I wait for our telephone call?"

I did as I was asked, relieved that I didn't have to answer the telephone, which – with my ignorance of the language – could only have resulted in me infuriating the man on the other end still further. I collected two cups of what could barely be described as "tea" from the man and returned to the office in which Holmes sat impatiently, drumming his fingers on the desk.

Finally, after around fifteen minutes, the telephone rang and Holmes snatched at the receiver. There was a momentary delay as the operator connected the two parties. I knew that Holmes had had his theory confirmed as he gave a clipped smile following the information conveyed by the Cherbourg man.

"Dare I ask what is next?" I asked, as he hurriedly replaced the receiver.

"Quickly – to the telegraph office! We are at the mercy of the winds of the North Atlantic!"

"The Atlantic?" I exclaimed, as I scurried after him.

"I am hoping that Mr. Leverton, of Pinkerton's American Agency, may be able to assist us."

The comment left me even more confused but, knowing that I was unlikely to get any further information out of Holmes, I simply followed him out of the clinic and down the street, at the end of which was the telegraph office. He did share with me that he had asked the man on reception where the nearest office was, when he left me to guard the telephone. I waited outside as Holmes dealt with the postmaster. When he reappeared, he must have sensed my frustration at being kept in the dark.

"I'm sorry, Watson. I fear I have used you unfairly."

"It would be nice to be a little more informed," I said, rather sulkily. "It's difficult enough being in a foreign country, unable to communicate, without my friend adding to my frustration."

"Quite right, my dear fellow. I must apologise. If you will just show a little more patience, all will be revealed when we return to Le Villard."

Within fifteen minutes we were back in the company of the French detective, who looked as frustrated as I felt.

"My dear Le Villard," said Holmes, "how was your interview with Madame Jacques?"

"Unsuccessful!" was the young man's reply. "She continues to say nothing."

"Then perhaps I will be able to help. I have just sent a telegram to an associate in New York who may be of some assistance. I gave him the address of this police station and asked him to reply urgently. In the meantime, perhaps we can visit your prisoner again and see if I can have a little more success."

Le Villard looked up with a confused expression but acquiesced without hesitation. We followed him into the room where Madame Jacques was being held.

"I will not waste my time asking you any questions," said Holmes as we entered. "I will simply inform you and my colleagues of what I know. It will be then your decision as to whether you co-operate or not.

"You are Agnès Jacques, sister of Claude Carere. You, your brother, and your respective late spouses made your despicable living by selling babies delivered at your illegal – " Holmes searched for an appropriate word. " – *establishments*. When Carere's wife died, he remarried the unfortunate and perfectly innocent Marguerite – now Montpensier – someone who you have recently had no hesitation in falsely implicating to save your own skin. When the authorities uncovered your activities, your brother died while you fled to London.

"Madame Montpensier may not have been involved in the dreadful operation during her marriage to Carere, but what the authorities overlooked was the fact that her stepdaughter – your niece Lucille Carere – certainly was.

"She studied at the Cornell University in the state of New York where she met István Róka, a medical student from Budapest. They returned to France together following their studies, and your late brother employed Róka at the facility here in Rouen. Once you had established yourself in London, following your brother's death, you reignighted your foul practice, this time with your niece who had access to the clinic through her husband."

"Her husband!" cried Le Villard.

"Yes, her husband," repeated Holmes, turning back to Madame Jacques. "István Róka. He would steal the children from the clinic, informing the mother that her child had died. He and his midwife associate would then whisk the child away to Mademoiselle Carere, the name she still used, lest she attract attention to herself and her husband. The two would then travel together to London, under the name of Reynard, where they would hand the child over to you. You, in turn, would have your desperate client waiting.

"When your wretched scheme was discovered, your niece alerted you, and you promptly fled. You then sought to confuse and distract the police by anonymously informing them that the perfectly innocent and unaware Madame Montpensier had murdered her stepdaughter. Dr. Róka then slipped away, informing everyone that he was visiting his sick mother in Hungary, when in fact he was meeting his wife at Cherbourg from where they boarded the S.S. *St. Paul*, bound for New York five days ago."

During Holmes's narrative, Madame Jacques' expression gradually changed from one of stoic resistance to one of complete incredulity at what she was hearing. It was clear that Holmes had struck home and uncovered the whole unbelievable truth. There was silence for quite some considerable time before Inspector Le Villard addressed his prisoner.

"What is your answer to Mr. Holmes's summary?"

It occurred to me how little I had heard the woman speak in the few days I had been in her company. I was almost surprised therefore when she responded to Le Villard.

"You cannot prove any of this," was her rather weak response.

"There are simply too many unanswered questions, Madame," said Holmes. "Where were you going in such a hurry when we stopped you? What evidence is there that Madame Montpensier murdered her stepdaughter? If she did, how could a baker's wife commit such a crime and dispose of a body without being seen or somehow alerting the authorities? How is it that Dr. Róka disappeared at exactly the same time as your niece, just as St. Marie's was being raided by the police? Dr. Róka cannot be traced in Hungary – not to mention the fact that a Mr. and Mrs. Róka are listed as being on board a vessel bound for New York, a place where both Róka and your niece studied together. How can you explain his whereabouts?

"No, no. It simply will not do, Madame."

"How do you know that the passengers on board the ship are the people you say?"

"On the balance of probability," was Holmes's assured reply. "Although your confederates were wicked in their actions, thankfully, they were not very imaginative in covering their movements. The couple who delivered the children to your house travelled under the name of *Fox* in England, and *Renard* in France. As you know, *renard* is French for *fox*. In Hungarian, *róka* is the name of the same creature. They simply translated their name as and when required, as an expedient to avoid suspicion."

Just then there was a knock at the door and a young officer entered.

"I'm sorry to disturb you, sir, but you asked for news from America."

He handed Holmes the telegram reply he had been eagerly awaiting. He passed me the note but the expression on his face already informed me of the disappointing news.

S.S. St. Paul *docked early this morning before I received your telegram. STOP. All passengers disembarked before I could attend. STOP. Roka whereabouts unknown. END*

Leverton

The prisoner understood the wordless exchange and gave a slight smirk.

229

"The message may be disappointing," said Holmes, but your expression confirms your guilt and my theory concerning your allies."

Le Villard also addressed the prisoner. "I will speak with the Prosecutor, as I believe we have enough to charge you with the crimes with which you are accused. You should be aware that these are capital offences."

Madame Jacques' expression changed immediately, but before she could respond, Le Villard indicated that the interview was over by rising and leaving the room. Holmes and I followed. I would be the last time we would see the woman.

Le Villard was levering himself into his coat outside when he announced that we were to visit the Prosecutor. I was impressed with how the detective was taking charge of the situation, and it was clear to me that Holmes felt the same way. It was a short distance to the Prosecutor's office, which was situated immediately beside the city's courts. Le Villard announced our arrival and we were shown straight in to see Monsieur Clément, a large, impressive man who projected an air of authority commensurate with his position. Fortunately for myself, he also spoke fluent English.

"Mr. Holmes!" he cried, thrusting out a hand of greeting, upon Le Villard's introduction. "It is an honour to meet you, sir. Since your detection of that treacherous Brossard and his accomplices, your name is revered throughout France."

Holmes was politely dismissive of Clément's comments. "Thank you, Monsieur, but we have a more urgent matter to deal with."

Holmes introduced me and invited Le Villard to share with the senior official what we had discovered.

Clément sat quietly for a while, shaking his head. "I have been in this line of work all of my adult life, and I am still amazed at the evil some people have in their hearts." He snapped out of his reverie. "What about the two in New York?"

It was Holmes that answered. "I have a good understanding with an excellent detective with the Pinkerton Agency. I will ask him to continue the search for Monsieur and Madame Róka and report his findings to Inspector Le Villard."

"Excellent! Thank you, Mr. Holmes. We can ask no more."

"There is one last thing," added my friend. "It occurs to me that no one defended Madame Montpensier from the accusations against her during her detainment. I might suggest that the poor woman deserves an apology."

"Quite right," agreed the Prosecutor. He turned to the policeman, "We will question the staff we have under arrest and charge Jacques.

230

Perhaps you could then arrange to have Madame Montpensier brought here and I will speak to her personally."

"Certainly, sir," replied Le Villard, and we all took our leave.

We later learned that, of the people arrested in connection with the scandal, one of the midwives was released without charge. It transpired that the other one was the anonymous source who alerted the police to the wrongdoing in the first place. Apparently, she had got into a dispute with Róka over how much she was owed for her part in the deception. His refusal to pay her what she felt she was owed proved to be the starting point for the whole extraordinary chain of events. Because of her co-operation with the authorities, her capital sentence was commuted to one of hard labour and she became one of the first female prisoners to be sent to the French penal colony on Devil's Island. She was joined by the registrar who had faked the death certificates and the ex-communicated Catholic priest who aided and abetted the criminals.

It was six months following our return from France when we heard from Leverton, who succeeded in finally tracking down and arresting the stepdaughter of Madame Montpensier, along with her husband-doctor in New York. The Pinkerton man had alerted hospitals throughout the state to the rogue consultant, anticipating that sooner or later, Róka would apply for a position. His working hypothesis proved well-founded when the Hungarian submitted a résumé to a maternity hospital in New York. Had he been successful with his application, his horrifying long-term intentions could only be guessed at. He and his wife were arrested and transported back across the Atlantic. I should finally record that my conscience is perfectly clear when I state that I was delighted to hear that they both followed Agnès Jacques to the guillotine.

Since the tragic upshot of our visit to Devonshire he had been engaged in two affairs of the utmost importance, in the first of which he had exposed the atrocious conduct of Colonel Upwood in connection with the famous card scandal of the Nonpareil Club, while in the second he had defended the unfortunate Mme Montpensier from the charge of murder, which hung over her in connection with the death of her step-daughter, Mlle Carère, the young lady who, as it will be remembered, was found six months later alive and married in New York.

– Dr. John H. Watson
The Hound of the Baskervilles

The Adventure of the Cheerful Prisoner
by Arthur Hall

The exact function of Sherlock Holmes's elder brother among the procedures of Whitehall was always a mystery to me and, I suspect to a lesser extent, to Holmes himself. It was always apparent that he commanded great respect and had great power within his circle of colleagues, and even my friend usually treated him with some reverence. Until my meeting with him during the affair involving Mister Kratides, which I have related elsewhere, I was completely ignorant of his existence, but since that time his hand or his presence has featured often in our enquiries and investigations.

"I take it," I said as our plates were cleared away one early spring morning, "that you expect no clients today, since you ate your breakfast in such a leisurely fashion."

This was an easy observation, since his usual behaviour of immediately leaping from the table on the completion of our meal to hurriedly retrieve our hats and coats while displaying extreme eagerness to embark upon an enquiry was noticeably altered. Today he had slowly consumed both the last of his toast and his final cup of coffee while staring absently and silently into space, not moving from his chair.

On hearing my words, he seemed to come to himself. "You are quite correct. I dispatched a telegram to Gregson yesterday, with sufficient evidence to put Ambrill in the dock. I have nothing else on hand at the moment."

"Then I prescribe a short holiday for both of us, since we have shown symptoms of excessive weariness lately. What do you say to a change – sea air or open spaces?"

I saw that my suggestion didn't sit well. Holmes's expression showed no enthusiasm for adopting a different scene and a slower pace, even for a short while. I remembered his response to similar proposals on previous occasions, and reflected that I should have felt no surprise.

"If you need to travel, Watson, then pray do so. As for me, I feel no desire to leave the capital. Who knows what new problems might present themselves and remain without attention if I am absent?"

"Holmes!" I exclaimed. "You really must keep in mind that there is

232

more in life than work. I understand that this is your consuming interest and that it is your means of survival but, need I remind you that over-exertion has brought close to nervous exhaustion before."

"I have explained to you before, my need for almost constant mental stimulation. Without it, my existence is colourless and stagnant. If you wish to leave Baker Street for a holiday then do what you must, but do not include me in your plans. I have no doubt that you will encounter others who will become your temporary companions, for you are a far more sociable fellow than I."

It was thus clear to me that, if I were to undertake such a journey, it would be alone.

Nevertheless, I decided on one more attempt to cause him to change his mind.

"Do you not recall the other occasions when we have returned here refreshed and like new men? I merely wished to – " I was interrupted by the peal of the doorbell, and Holmes brightened instantly.

"Our immediate future may have been decided for us," he speculated. "Or mine, at least."

We listened in silence as we waited for our good landlady to answer the door. The cries of barrow-boys and the sounds of passing hansoms drifted up to us through the half-open window as we heard the door close after a few moments. I believe that we had both concluded, because of the light tread upon the stairs which we recognised as Mrs. Hudson's alone, that our visitor was not a new client. Instead, she had arrived with a message.

At the sound of a knock on our door, Holmes called for Mrs. Hudson to enter. She presented him with a telegram upon a polished tray, which he accepted with thanks. He had torn open the yellow envelope before the door closed behind her, and I leaned forward in my chair expectantly.

"From Mycroft," he informed me, holding the message up to the light. "He asks that we visit him in Whitehall, at ten. Apparently, it is an urgent matter."

I rose. "I'll get our hats and coats."

"But what of your holiday?"

"He specified both of us, according to your narration. I didn't say I intended to depart this morning."

Not long after, a hansom pulled by a sprightly young colt deposited us near the office of Holmes's elder brother with a few minutes to spare.

As on previous occasions, a uniformed aide awaited us. He led us through a maze of corridors, marching stiffly and saying nothing since his formal greeting. At last we entered a short passageway, with but three anonymous doors before us. Our companion knocked upon the second of

233

these, and I heard a muffled response from within. He opened the door and stood aside to admit us, announcing us in a toneless voice.

Mycroft Holmes looked up from his desk as the door was closed behind us. I saw at once that he had changed little. He struggled to raise his bulk from his chair.

"Sherlock, Doctor Watson! How good to see you. Do come and sit down. I think you will find the chairs comfortable. Would you care for tea?"

"I think not, thank you, Mycroft." My friend answered for both of us. "I would be grateful if you would tell us why we've been summoned with such urgency."

Our host lowered himself back into his chair. The leather creaked as he adjusted his position.

"A problem has arisen, involving a colleague who has worked closely with me for some time. I would rather someone outside my department look into it, since this individual would be previously unknown to him and his judgement therefore, wouldn't be coloured by any familiarity."

"To whom are you referring?" Holmes asked.

"His name is Mr. Matthew Faber. He has acted as my liaison with many of our people in Germany and elsewhere for a good while now, and it was something of a shock to discover that his loyalty appears to be in question."

"I haven't heard of the man. But then, that is as it should be."

"Quite. Another of my people, Thomas Ollshaw, who knows Faber well, holds a similar position here, and it was he who informed me that news of a succession of incidents that we shall refer to as 'The Biesdorf Affair' had filtered back to him from one of his informants in Berlin."

"This, I presume, was a matter with details thought to be known only to Faber and yourself,"

"You are perceptive as always, Sherlock. That is indeed the case. Any knowledge of the Biesdorf business that exists in Germany must have originated from Faber. I confess to being confounded by both the man's actions and his reasons for them. I summoned both he and Ollshaw at once, but Faber would say nothing."

"Is he married?" I enquired, as a possibility occurred to me.

"Yes, Doctor. He and his wife live in Highgate." Mycroft's tone told me that he considered my question to be irrelevant, and I abandoned the thought.

"Where is he now?" Holmes asked. He would, I knew, have already formed some sort of supposition.

"At Ollshaw's suggestion, I had Faber placed under guard and later transported to Dartmoor Prison. We agreed that it was better he should leave the capital for a place where any of his German contacts, if indeed he has any, would have great difficulty in obtaining more information from him."

"You have doubts about his guilt, then?"

"Ah, Sherlock, you concluded that because I said 'if indeed he has any'."

"Precisely. I saw at once that you find it difficult to believe that you could have misjudged Faber so, after a considerable time of working with him closely."

Mycroft nodded. "There is something here that strikes a false note. I am involved at present in negotiations concerning the Trieste Agreement, so I haven't the time to go into this further. I thought you might be prepared to assist me . . . ."

The question was left hanging in the air.

"Very well," Holmes answered after a few seconds had passed.

Mycroft's expression altered slightly. I took this to be a sign of relief.

"Excellent. I have prepared the answers to any questions you might have as to details, addresses, and so forth." He slid a folded paper across the desk and my friend accepted it. "Where will you begin?"

Holmes gave his brother a look that told me he felt mildly insulted.

"Why, at Princetown of course. I believe it to be the site of Dartmoor Prison?"

"You wish to interview Faber at the outset. I would have been surprised had you suggested otherwise. The temporary prison governor, I understand, is Mr. William Crout, who occupies the position because of the illness of his superior. I will see that he is notified to expect you. Naturally, you will be departing for Devonshire this morning?"

"Watson and I will be departing for Devonshire by either the midday or afternoon train," Holmes corrected. "We have some minor affairs to settle and our bags to pack."

"Of course," Mycroft scowled impatiently. "I look forward to your report."

Holmes said not a word until we were settled in a hansom and well on our way back to Baker Street. I could sense his anger.

"Were you planning to spend the day otherwise?" I asked him as our conveyance turned sharply to avoid an urchin who scuttled across the road. "Clearly, the interview with your brother has perturbed you."

"Not at all," he answered in a restrained voice. "It is Mycroft's assumption that infuriates me – that he can treat me as one of his lackeys. He presumes on our brotherly relationship too much. 'I look forward to your report,' indeed. He has done this before now, despite my protestations."

I saw that it would be as well to shift the conversation.

"I wonder if this man Faber could be innocent," I said.

"There must be reason to suppose so, or my brother wouldn't concern himself with the man's fate. Hopefully our investigation will indicate the truth."

We arrived at our lodgings shortly afterwards, and to my astonishment I discovered that it was already almost time for luncheon. Mrs. Hudson served a satisfying meal of roast pork followed by apple pie, but Holmes ate little.

When our plates had been cleared and the coffee pot emptied, we hurriedly packed our travelling cases.

"It's hardly worth the trouble for one night," Holmes remarked. "Normally I would have taken no more than a clean collar and a toothbrush, but I feel an uncertainty about this. If events take an unexpected turn, then our stay may be extended."

Having made our preparations, we summoned a passing cab for the short journey to Paddington. I waited on the platform while Holmes procured our tickets, and the early afternoon train departed on time.

With the next five or six hours before us, I seized the opportunity to persuade my friend to relate one of his past cases, having recognised his mood as one most likely to allow this. After a reluctant few minutes he agreed, and as the grimy suburbs of London passed us by I was privileged to hear the tale of Miss Barbara Forsythe and the African tinker – one of his cases from his time in Montague Street.

Presently his revelation came to a close, and he lapsed into a morose state and then into silence. I was eventually lulled into sleep by the motion of the train and awoke, astonished at the length of my unintended slumber, to see him staring unseeingly in my direction, yet far away amidst his own thoughts.

A glance at the passing scenery was enough to tell me that we were now in Devonshire. The soil was now of a deeper, ruddy colour and the grass and trees were luxuriant. Fields of cattle and sheep, interrupted by stone cottages, were plentiful among the rolling hills. After a while the land took on a more level but wilder appearance, and I knew from of old that we were nearing the moor.

We left the train at Okehampton Station, and soon enlisted the services of an elderly man who had used his cart to deliver several cages of racing pigeons to await a later train.

When Holmes informed him of our intended destination, he gave us a sharp look, but bid us board his conveyance nevertheless. He spoke little during the journey, except to point out the way to various villages and warn

236

us of the danger of our surroundings.

This, I felt, was quite unnecessary. At the moment when we reached the point where the outskirts of the village gave way to that sinister and deserted waste, all that I had felt during our previous adventure of the previous year ago came flooding back to me. As the cart bumped over a winding track that must have seen centuries of wheeled traffic, I recalled the mysterious and remote atmosphere that hung heavily over the place, the eerie sounds and strange movements among the ferns and bracken that had been known to terrify superstitious folk, and the noisy streams that flowed beneath small stony bridges.

I dwelt on such thoughts for some little time while Holmes rode in silence, perhaps also reminiscing.

I had resolved to put past impressions out of my mind and to concentrate on our present purpose when he suddenly pointed ahead.

"There, Watson: A structure as unprepossessing as that can be nothing else but a prison."

Our driver confirmed that this was indeed the place we sought, a large and dull structure that already seemed to me to be surrounded by gloom. We alighted, paid the man, and watched the cart out of sight before Holmes struck the great doors with his fist and shouted to announce our arrival.

We were admitted at once and, on stating our names and purpose, were led along a cheerless stone-flagged corridor to be shown into an office containing a battered desk and several badly worn chairs. Pictures of our Queen and stern-looking men who I presumed were past governors adorned the walls, and the place had the chill of the grave about it.

The middle-aged man behind the desk was apparently unaffected. He rose and greeted us.

"Good evening, gentlemen. I trust your journey was pleasant. I am William Crout, governor here until my superior regains his health."

We introduced ourselves, and his face brightened.

"We have heard of you here of course, Mr. Holmes, but I was surprised to receive a telegram from Whitehall, especially in connection with the prisoner, Matthew Faber."

"Is he then in some way different?"

Crout pulled at his moustache, as if momentarily at a loss for words.

"Well, you see, it's like this, sirs: To begin with, we haven't been told what the man has done, nor any details of his trial. The instructions we received were simply to confine him while waiting for further orders. That's odd in itself, but the behaviour of the man has me baffled."

"He has tried to escape?" I ventured.

"No, Doctor, the very opposite. We're used to prisoners trying to get out from time to time, using various schemes they've invented, though few

237

of them get very far. But this man, in my experience at least, is like no other. Ever since he was brought here, he has shown every sign of contentment and happiness. He sings to himself in his cell, jokes with the guards who take him his food, and laughs a lot." The temporary governor scratched his head. "I really cannot make any sense of it."

"Intriguing," said Holmes. "We were asked to interview him regarding his behaviour in Whitehall, in the course of his employment."

I noticed that my friend spoke in vague terms, mentioning nothing that Crout couldn't easily have deduced for himself.

"Perhaps then, you will more fortunate than myself and others. It may be that you can get him to confide why he is in such remarkably good spirits in a place where it is usual to experience extreme melancholia." He raised his stocky form from his chair. "Come, gentlemen, we will see him now."

He led us from the room, and a guard joined us in a walk along empty corridors. We entered several where our passage was accompanied by shouts from behind the barred doors, together with appeals and oaths. Often, implements were rattled against the bars. The guard retaliated with harsh warnings, and the noise ceased quickly.

Our little procession came to an abrupt halt before a door that was identical with its neighbours. The guard produced keys and selected one which opened the cell.

We looked in to see a smiling young man look up from a tattered book.

"I take it you would prefer to interview the prisoner alone?" Crout enquired.

"If you would be so kind," Holmes replied.

"Then I will return to my office. Martland here will station himself nearby so that you can call when you wish to leave. I will see you presently, gentlemen, and I wish you success."

With that, both prison officials turned and left before the cell door was closed behind us.

Matthew Faber put down his book and got to his feet. He approached Holmes and shook his hand vigorously.

"Did Mr. Mycroft Holmes send you?" he asked expectantly.

"Indeed he did."

"What is his message for me. Tell me quickly."

Holmes appeared faintly puzzled. "We are to discuss the circumstances surrounding your imprisonment."

"But he instructed me to . . . ." His pleasant manner vanished, and his expression became furtive. "Wait! This is a test. I have nothing to say to you gentlemen. You may tell Mr. Holmes that."

238

"He suspects that the circumstances may have been incorrectly understood. We merely wish you to explain your actions, if indeed they were yours, that brought about the accusation."

"I repeat, I can tell you nothing."

"I am a doctor," I explained. "I would like to know if you have been injured, or if your health is suffering since your incarceration."

"There is no need to concern yourself, sir. No misfortune has befallen me, and I haven't been brutalised. Nothing here has disagreed with me. I have endured worse before now."

He then fell silent, and no amount of questioning or encouragement would dissuade him from his course. Holmes regarded him thoughtfully as I made further attempts to learn something without success.

"Very well." Holmes approached the door and I followed. He turned to the prisoner. "Have you anything that you wish me to tell Mycroft?"

Faber shook his head but then relented, changing his demeanour and saying quickly, "If I might beg a favour: Could I prevail upon you to visit my wife – my Iris? Please inform her that I am well and in no danger. When this is over, I will be home."

All joviality was gone, replaced by concern.

"It will be attended to," Holmes answered, before calling for the guard.

Martland escorted us back to Crout's office. The temporary governor now looked tired.

"Well, gentlemen, were you able to learn anything?" he enquired hopefully.

"Nothing," Holmes admitted, "except that he seems to be convinced that his release is imminent. That, I would think, explains his unusual pleasantness. He believes that whatever he is accused of will be found to be false and the charge dropped. I regret that I can enlighten you no further."

"That at least explains his unusual response to incarceration." Crout consulted his pocket watch. "But how will you gentlemen return to the capital? By now it will be dark outside, and it is as well not to be abroad hereabouts. As you must have seen, Princetown is a small community, but we do have a respectable inn that will be able to put you up for the night. If you turn right as you leave, into the main street and past the church, you will come to The Flag and Anchor, a public house of local repute." He struggled to his feet as before and shook both our hands. "Goodbye, gentlemen. I wish you a safe journey tomorrow."

We left that grim place to discover that a light mist had appeared. As we walked the short distance through the darkness, our previous encounters on the moor again came back to me. I dismissed them from my

239

mind as we approached the ill-lit main street and, having passed a few darkened shops, the Post Office, and the church, soon found the inn. We hadn't eaten since luncheon and hunger pangs were making themselves felt. Holmes, of course, showed no signs of discomfort. Nevertheless, we enjoyed a fine meal of roast chicken and spent the evening with pints of the landlord's best beer. A few local people gave us queer looks, but no one approached or spoke to us. Holmes commented that such distrust was common in rural or isolated communities, and we retired to our rooms early. I lay listening to the faint conversation and occasional laughter from below, which ceased before long. I heard the landlord slamming home the bolts on the front door, after which I fell asleep in absolute silence.

After a breakfast of local ham and eggs, Holmes asked the landlord about transportation to the station. A man with a cart appeared soon after, and earned himself a generous tip as, carrying our meagre luggage, we left him near Okehampton Station.

Holmes and I had spoken little about our visit to Matthew Faber. As we began the journey back to London he was silent for a while, and I was about to make a remark when he ended his reverie abruptly.

"There is something more here, Watson," he said suddenly.

"You mean regarding Faber?"

"I do. Two things stand out: The first is that he expected some message from Mycroft, yet resisted further conversation upon learning that we were there to discover more about his predicament. He seemed to believe that our presence was for some sort of testing of him."

"To determine the truth of something he had previously stated, perhaps?"

"That is of course possible, but I am further disturbed by his remark when he made the request concerning his wife. As you recall, he said, 'When this is over'. That suggests that he is aware of the duration of this affair, and that he is unashamed of his conduct. I believe that, either Mycroft has been deceived, or he is withholding some aspect from us."

"Are we to visit your brother, perhaps after lunch?"

"I think not. I may consult him later. This afternoon, I think we will keep my promise to Faber."

The remainder of the journey passed swiftly, because Holmes embarked on a tirade about the Trojan War, which interested me because I had read something of it. On our arrival at Paddington, a hansom swiftly presented itself, and so we returned to our lodgings in time to prevail upon Mrs. Hudson for a late midday meal.

As always, she made no complaint, and I had the impression that she had exercised that unerring instinct that she seemed to possess regarding our departures and arrivals. A good meal of fresh trout was served long before I could have reasonably expected it to appear. When it was over, and I had consumed my dessert alone, Holmes put down his coffee cup and rose from the table.

"When you have ceased your rather excessive feeding habits, Watson, we will make our way to Highgate."

I resisted the temptation to give an acid reply. "You have Mrs. Faber's address?"

"Mycroft's written details and instructions are most comprehensive," he said with a scowl.

Less than ten minutes later, we found ourselves in a cab. We left the city on a road that was soon surrounded by green fields and farmer's cottages. Presently we approached the outskirts of the district and, after passing a few shops and stables, our driver turned into a pleasant avenue of red-brick houses.

The hansom left us and we peered at the doors before us.

"This could be difficult," I said. "The houses aren't numbered."

He smiled briefly. "So I have observed. However, I would wager that the fifth residence from that rather neglected house to our right is the one that we seek."

"How could you know that?"

"You will recall Faber's appearance. He had managed to make himself presentable, despite his confinement. That suggests that he is a person of order and tidiness. Also, this isn't a very affluent part of the district, yet the house that I have indicated presents an immaculate sight, with a flower bed and well-swept path. Faber can doubtless afford such maintenance on the adequate sum that his employment provides."

I was by no means convinced of the accuracy of my friend's deductions, until the door was answered by a young woman of startling beauty. She looked at us, uncomprehending at first. Then it must have dawned on her that we must have some connection with her husband's situation and she gave a thin smile as she bade us enter.

We found ourselves in a pleasant living room, well-decorated and with new furniture and several large pots containing flourishing aspidistras. As expected, Mrs. Faber wore a concerned look which seemed to me also confused. She wore a plain blue frock and a string of pearls about her neck.

"Gentlemen, I can only hope that you have brought me good news," she began when we were seated. "I have been almost out of my mind with worry. What my Matthew is accused of I cannot tell, but I know him to be a good and honest man. Perhaps you can enlighten me: Why was he suddenly arrested and transported to Dartmoor Prison? That is the only information I've received regarding his fate."

"We're here," Holmes answered, "first to convey to you a message from your husband. He wants you to know that he is well and optimistic about an early release. The other news we have for you is that there is thought to be some doubt about his guilt. Forgive me for not introducing ourselves. I am Sherlock Holmes, and my friend is Doctor John Watson. We are investigating the circumstances surrounding your husband's arrest, in the hope that the truth may be brought to light. To that end, will you permit us to ask questions that may clear things up?"

She sat forward anxiously in her chair. "Of course! I would do anything to save him."

"Thank you." Holmes sat upright, his eyes never leaving her. "Please tell us what you know of your husband's work."

"Very little. I'm aware that he's employed in a building in Whitehall, but little else. His work is never discussed between us, and he discourages references to it. I formed the impression that he is concerned with overseas trade."

"Quite so. Do you know of any incident, however small, that could explain his arrest. Pray think carefully, in terms of now and however long he has held his present position."

"There is nothing," she replied without hesitation. "We are close. Anything untoward would have affected Matthew, and I would have known."

Holmes nodded. "It is necessary then, to ask you but one more question: Are you acquainted with a colleague of Faber's, a man called Thomas Ollshaw?"

"Why yes, Matthew has known him for years." She twirled a stray lock of dark hair around a finger, remembering. "He and his wife used to visit here often, as we did to their home. Sadly, his wife passed away about two years ago, even more so because their union was short. In fact, Mr. Holmes, had you arrived half-an-hour earlier, you would have met him. He has been here several times since this trouble began. He is a kind and sympathetic man."

"Thank you for your valuable assistance," my friend concluded. "I'm certain that things will be put right before long."

I put away my notebook, the writings therein my only contribution to the proceedings, and we took our leave.

We came upon Highgate High Street as a hansom deposited two young ladies near a milliner's shop, and procured it immediately. After stating our destination, Holmes was initially silent, and I was giving consideration to what we had learned.

He was staring at the passing trees, and the fields of cows and sheep, when I asked him, "Do you believe Faber to be guilty? Your brother indicated that the charge was a serious one. Were this a time of war, he would undoubtedly meet the hangman if convicted. At best, he will be imprisoned for many years."

"I should be surprised if he is guilty of anything. However, I shall be able to confirm this when we meet Ollshaw tomorrow. As it will be Sunday, we should find him at home."

When our dinner, a bulging steak-and-ale pie, followed by stewed apple, was consumed, we settled into our usual chairs. Both Holmes and I were weary from the day's exertions, and after less conversation than was our custom for evenings, we retired. I passed a fitful night. An image of Mrs. Faber in complete distress on learning of her husband's guilt wouldn't leave me, despite Holmes's assurance.

The kippers at breakfast were excellent, and we both ate with relish. Holmes surprised me by appearing to be in no hurry. He sipped his coffee slowly and seemed to be in a jovial mood.

When I asked him about his good spirits, he gave a thin smile and said, "What would you think are the main reasons why crimes are committed, Watson?"

"Money, I suppose. That has been the cause of many in our experience."

"That is correct. What else would you say?"

I considered for a moment. "Revenge?"

"That too, but there is one other cause that is by no means rare."

"Something driven by lust or emotion, I would think."

"You have it. Passion is a powerful instigator indeed."

"But what has that to do with Faber's alleged crime?" I thought back, to our visit yesterday. "Ah, I see. You suspect that this man Thomas Ollshaw has designs on Mrs. Faber."

He nodded. "It is, for the moment, no more than a supposition. It will doubtless be proved or disproved when we meet him later."

"Where does Ollshaw live?"

"According to Mycroft's rather extensive notes he resides in Mayfair, which is of course a further indication when applied to the present situation."

"How so?"

"We have just discussed the various causes that incline a man towards crime. If Ollshaw is behind this affair, it may not be for profit because he must be quite affluent to live in Mayfair. In addition, Mycroft's notes suggest this. As for revenge, it is unlikely, since Mrs. Faber spoke of their long and friendly association. That leaves only passion, so we will see

243

what this morning reveals to us." He then replaced his coffee cup and rose to peer through the half-open window. "Ha! I see that two hansoms have discharged their fares in Baker Street, and their drivers are conversing as they wait for further custom. If we're quick about it, we may be able to interrupt their chatter."

With that he seized our hats and coats. I hurriedly struggled into mine as we descended the stairs at a fast pace. We boarded the nearest cab and in moments were rattling away from our lodgings as soon as Holmes had instructed our driver. As we approached Mayfair, our surroundings changed significantly. The houses were larger and clearly more given to style. Long gardens bloomed between the frontages and the pavement, where rows of dwarf pines often defined the border. Our hansom came to rest outside one such residence, a three-storey building with high chimneys, and we alighted.

I paid the cabby and we waited until his conveyance had turned the corner, before setting off along a level path. As we approached the house it took on a formidable look, and the door opened to reveal a uniformed butler who asked us to state our business.

"We are here to see Mr. Thomas Ollshaw," Holmes replied.

The butler regarded us suspiciously. "I am not sure if he is at home, sir."

"Pray inform him, if he is, that Mr. Sherlock Holmes would like to discuss the future of Matthew Faber with him. Here is my card."

We were left alone for a few minutes. Then the butler returned, stone-faced so that I expected a refusal.

"Please come in, gentlemen," he said tonelessly.

We were shown into a high-ceilinged room decorated in green. Tall windows faced us, with long curtains that were restrained by silken ropes. Before the fireplace stood a tall young man, dressed immaculately in a grey morning-suit. His full beard enclosed thin lips and his eyes, I noticed, were those of a man much grieved.

The butler announced us and withdrew.

"Good morning, gentlemen," Ollshaw began. "My superior, Mr. Mycroft Holmes, has often spoken of you both. I am aware that you are taking some part in establishing the guilt or innocence of my colleague, but I cannot see how I can add further to what you must already know."

I noticed that there was no shaking of hands.

When we had accepted his invitation to sit, he pointed questioningly to the bottle of sherry that stood on a tray with glasses near to him. We both declined, as it was still early.

"We have in fact interviewed Mr. Faber at Dartmoor Prison," said Holmes. "He was unresponsive to our questions, and so it is imperative that we seek information from any other sources to hand. I understand that it was you who first drew my brother's attention to Mr. Faber's apparent disloyalty."

"That is correct. One of my informants in Germany reported forthcoming events of which he should have been unaware, doubtlessly gleaned from others in the same trade as himself. According to your brother's subsequent statement to me, only he and Mr. Faber were known to be privy to the information. Since Mr. Mycroft Holmes is naturally above suspicion, it can be no other but Faber who divulged it. I'm afraid this doesn't look favourable for him."

"No, indeed. I am mystified though, as to his reluctance to speak in his own defence."

"Perhaps he has no defence, or is unable to concoct a sufficiently convincing falsehood. I have known him for a good while, and have never thought of him as a very complicated or deceptive character."

As he spoke, a suggestion of a blush appeared on his face. It struck me as embarrassment, but I couldn't see why Holmes's statement would cause this.

"Were you at school together?" I enquired.

"He was in the year after me, at Eton."

It seemed as if my friend was losing interest in the conversation, since the focus of his attention appeared to be, not our host, but a framed photographic portrait of a remarkably beautiful woman with long blonde tresses which stood upon a side-table. It struck me for a moment that I had met her, but then I dismissed the notion as highly improbable. After all, hadn't Mrs. Faber mentioned that this lady was deceased?

"My brother was taken aback by Faber's actions. I take it that he never heard to remark, or hint in an odd moment, anything that could lead you to believe that he harboured any sympathy with the Kaiser?"

"Not at all, but I cannot imagine why he would allow information entrusted to him to be known elsewhere, otherwise."

Holmes nodded. "Well, Mr. Ollshaw, you have, after all, cleared up one or two things that had puzzled me about this affair." He rose and I did also. "Thank you for allowing us to intrude upon your Sunday respite."

Shortly afterwards, Holmes raised his stick to flag down a passing hansom. He sat with his head upon his chest for a while, as I watched the magnificent homes of the rich give way to lesser residences once Mayfair was left behind.

"Watson," he said suddenly, with the tone of a man awakening from a dream, "I can feel your curiosity. You are wondering why I didn't ask many more questions. But why would I, when the confirmation I sought was in front of my eyes, and I had been supplied with indications that I

245

hadn't even looked for."

"What confirmation? I don't recall . . . Ah, the photograph."

"Precisely. You will have realised that the image was that of Ollshaw's departed wife."

"I had surmised so. A woman of great beauty. The effects of her loss were still plain to see on her husband."

"Perhaps, but were you reminded of someone?"

"It did strike me that she looked familiar, but it cannot be."

"True, it cannot. But picture her in your mind, if your memory of the photograph is sufficient. Give her dark hair and make it shorter, so that it curls in at the neck. Take away the over-reddened lips and rouged cheeks."

I closed my eyes and attempted to comply. I strained to bring back the likeness that I had seen for no more than a few minutes. Then Holmes's meaning became clear.

"Good Heavens!"

"You see it?"

"She, if her appearance were altered like that, would closely resemble Mrs. Faber!"

"Indeed. There then, we have the purpose of Faber's contrived removal which was primarily intended to be from his household, rather than his work."

"Holmes, this is monstrous! Do you think Ollshaw is capable of ruining his friend's career and causing him to be imprisoned because he desires his wife?"

"I believe that Mrs. Ollshaw's death had a greater effect upon her husband than is usual. But it could be that he had unknowingly transferred his affections to Mrs. Faber beforehand, rather than looking upon her as a substitute afterwards. At any rate, we still have work to do since, to Ollshaw, all this has been for nothing unless Faber's absence is made to be permanent."

"But Faber is still in Dartmoor Prison."

"If my hypothesis is sound, then he is safe as long as he remains there. However, our visit to Ollshaw provided the last piece of the puzzle and my case is complete. That's how I know that it is imperative that we return to Dartmoor this afternoon. I recall from my *Bradshaw* that we have time for a hurried luncheon, but we must without fail catch the afternoon train."

So it was that we incurred Mrs. Hudson's displeasure by the speed with which we disposed of an excellent meal. No sooner had I pushed away my empty teacup than Holmes, already clad in his ulster and ear-flapped travelling cap, again thrust my own garments towards me. We picked up our bags, hastily packed once more, and secured a hansom after five minutes of my friend's growing impatience.

The afternoon and early evening passed much as before. Holmes had telegraphed ahead to Crout, and so we were expected. The stout doors swung open to admit us, and we were quickly conveyed to the governor's office.

"Gentlemen," the acting governor seemed in a pleasant mood. "I'm surprised to see you again, especially so soon. Am I to understand then, that you have made some headway in the peculiar case of the prisoner, Faber?"

"I'm confident that I can now put matters in their proper perspective," Holmes assured him. "If you would be so good as to allow us to see him again, everything will become clear."

"Very well, but it's fortunate that you didn't arrive later."

This I couldn't understand, but Holmes wore a look of satisfaction, as if his supposition, or part of it, was proven.

"I would think that you have received word from Whitehall."

Crout plucked a telegram from a cluster of papers, and slid it across his desk. "This was delivered an hour ago."

Holmes read it, and passed it to me.

To Dartmoor Prison, The Governor.

The matter of Matthew Faber has been decided. He is to be allowed to escape from custody at midnight tonight. This is an official request. Kindly ensure that it is effected efficiently and punctually.

Mycroft Holmes

"If this were genuine, I would certainly have been informed," my friend said. "but we will deal with it later. I would be obliged, Mr. Crout, if we could repair to Mr. Faber's cell now."

The governor nodded and got to his feet. He opened the door and shouted something into the corridor, whereupon a burly guard, different from before, appeared promptly.

"Pickthorne, take these gentlemen to Matthew Faber's cell," he ordered. The guard saluted smartly and led us along the dismal passages, quieter now and echoing with the tread of our boots on the stone floor.

We were admitted and the heavy door closed behind us. The guard had assured us that a single cry would summon him from nearby, in the event of trouble.

Faber lay on his bunk, staring at the ceiling until we entered. At the sight of us he quickly sat up, his cheerfulness giving way to a puzzled

247

expression.

"I hadn't expected visitors this evening."

"I'm aware of the plan for your escape," Holmes told him. "and I am here to impress upon you: If you venture out, you will be killed shortly afterwards."

"What can you mean?"

"I'm attempting to make you understand that you have been the victim of a deception that caused your incarceration here, and will claim your life if we do not speak frankly."

He shook his head. "You speak in riddles, Mr. Holmes."

"Then allow me to explain. To begin, let me first give you my solemn word of honour that what I am about to tell you is the absolute truth, and not a means to trap or test you. I am aware that you have been warned against discussing your situation. Mr. Ollshaw, I am certain, told you that any such conversation would be such as you implied during our previous visit. In fact, is it not true that all communication regarding this affair was with Mr. Ollshaw, and never directly with Mycroft?"

He considered, and suddenly appeared less sure of himself.

"I haven't seen or heard from Mr. Mycroft Holmes since Thomas Ollshaw and I were summoned to his office."

"That is because Mycroft had no hand in the proceedings, other than to have you sent here temporarily at Ollshaw's suggestion. Since then, having misgivings about your guilt, Mycroft requested that I see you and conduct an investigation. This I have now completed."

The prisoner's expression changed. He appeared, to some extent, to have been won over.

"I could not understand why Ollshaw would bring unfounded charges against me," he said then. "He accused me of divulging certain facts to agents of the Kaiser. I swear to you, Mr. Holmes, on my life, that there is no truth in this. I am, and always have been, loyal."

"So my enquiries have revealed. You can therefore be sure that you will indeed be leaving this place before long, though not in the way Ollcroft intends. It was suggestive from the beginning that he was responsible for the information making its way to Germany, for if you were innocent, who else can it have been? Doubtless he was somehow able to gain sight of a confidential dossier or message without the knowledge of Mycroft or yourself."

"But that is impossible!"

"That being the case, it may be that the information was never divulged at all, that Ollshaw somehow arranged with an accomplice in Germany to make it appear so. The end result, to cause you to be imprisoned, would be the same."

"All this time, Mr. Holmes, I have believed Mr. Ollshaw's assurance that Mr. Mycroft colluded with this – with the intention of allowing me to escape to keep an arranged meeting with the Kaiser's agents to whom I was to furnish false information. That's why I was able to remain in good spirits while detained in this place, knowing that my escape was already planned and that, afterwards, I would be returning to London."

"Ollshaw was careful to convince you of that. You wouldn't have survived for long."

Faber looked more perplexed than ever.

"But why? I have known Thomas for years. We were friends. Has he come to support the Kaiser?"

"That, as I inferred, has yet to be definitely established. Doubtless, Mycroft will attend to it after your reappearance at Whitehall. Ollshaw's reason, for causing your misfortunes at least, concerns your wife."

"Iris?" He was visibly shocked. "How is she concerned in this?"

"We theorise that Ollshaw wishes to marry her, to replace his dead wife. That is why his scheme was set in motion."

"Does she reciprocate?" He asked in a voice that shook.

"Not at all. Ollshaw has visited her several times since your removal from the capital, but she is unaware of his intentions other than to recognise them as kindness."

"During our interview with her," I added to hurriedly reassure him, "she spoke only of you and with much concern."

"But if he has received no encouragement, what reason can he have? If he is ready to remarry, why does he not seek a new wife elsewhere?"

"Because he isn't ready to remarry," Holmes answered. "He remains obsessed with his deceased wife. I believe he looks upon your wife as a replacement, because of a physical resemblance."

Faber's face lit up, as a man's does when an old memory brings realisation.

"I recall an occasion when Mrs. Ollshaw identified such a similarity. I couldn't see it myself, and we laughed about it before it was forgotten as the conversation moved on. It was at a dinner that the four of us attended at Claridges."

"Evidently Ollshaw didn't forget, or of he did, it came back to him after his wife's death."

"I could feel sorry for him," Faber admitted, "had he not deliberately endangered my life."

"Ah yes, that is the remaining aspect that must be resolved, before you return to London with Doctor Watson and myself. We will leave you now, but I can assure you with confidence that you will not be a prisoner for much longer."

249

When this was explained to Crout, he took on an incredulous look. "This is a strange business, and no mistake. What do you intend to do now, Mr. Holmes?"

My friend leaned forward in his chair. "From what I have just related, it's apparent that Ollshaw has arranged for some harm to come to Mr. Faber, for he cannot allow him to live for long after the arranged 'escape'. It is essential that he dies, not only to justify the accusations against him – I imagine the reason that Ollshaw would give to his superiors would be that the traitorous meeting somehow went wrong, perhaps that Mr. Faber's intended new masters wanted only information – but to satisfy Ollshaw's desire for Mrs. Faber. At this moment, Ollshaw knows exactly where to send an assassin, but only until Mr. Faber leaves here. I therefore believe that such a person lies in wait not far from the prison, in order to accomplish his work quickly. I suggest that Watson and myself reserve rooms at The Flag and Anchor as before, then return here close to midnight. If you would be so good as to allow two of your men, armed as we are, to accompany us in a search of the immediate area, it may be that we can capture the assassin. Finally, I'll telegraph Whitehall in the morning to obtain permission for you to release Mr. Faber. Is that agreeable to you?"

The temporary governor sat very still. After a moment he nodded. "On the face of it, I can raise no objection. When you return, I will have Pickthorne and another ready with firearms. It's likely that the situation will be complicated – " He consulted his pocket watch. " – by the mist that often appears at this hour, so extreme care must be taken."

Less than half-an-hour later, Holmes and I had taken rooms as before. In the short time available to us, we ensured that our weapons were loaded and well-oiled before prevailing upon the innkeeper for a late meal. This the man provided without complaint, and so we were well-fortified when we once more entered that dark citadel.

Crout was as good as his word, and Pickthorne and another guard, whose name we learned was Renning, stood armed and waiting. After a short discussion, Crout wished us well as we departed.

The mist engulfed us at once. Before us lay the moor, in the opposite direction to the small settlement of Princetown.

We reached the coarse earth at the edge of the hidden expanse, finding ourselves in the midst of huge boulders that appeared and then disappeared from our sight in the enveloping cloud. Holmes gave instructions for the two guards to make off in a different direction before we ensured that our quarry wasn't concealed somewhere around us. We moved cautiously, the strange sounds of the moor disquieting and those of our movements a dull echo. We could hear nothing of the others. Indeed, it had been thought better not to call to each other for fear of giving away our positions to the waiting killer.

It had begun to enter my head that Holmes's reasoning might be at fault when a sound of a shot from not far ahead preceded a flash of sparks near my face. We became still at once, and I realised that the bullet had struck one of the boulders that towered above us, indistinct in the swirling mist. We listened, but there was nothing.

"I heard running footsteps, further away," Holmes said in a low voice. "I think we should continue slowly, with our ears pricked."

We trudged on in silence, ever wary of each shadow that dimly crossed our path. Once I was startled by the sudden appearance of a tall shape reaching out towards me, but I lowered my revolver, as I identified the naked branches of a stunted tree. Holmes put a hand on my arm, and again we were both still as we strained our ears for direction. I barely saw that his indistinct form had the alert look of an animal that had scented its prey. For a moment there was complete silence. Then an owl or some other nightbird gave a shrill cry and I heard the flapping of wings as the creature responded to our disturbance. I felt my nerves release some of their tension, but then the sound of two reports came to us through the fog, accompanied by a scream of terror.

"This way!" Holmes broke into a run, somehow avoiding obstacles that appeared before us, and I followed. We paused once, hearing faint voices, and then we hurried on until at last we came upon the two guards standing over the body of a man.

"I got him, sir," Renning said with some relief, "but I swear he nearly did for both of us."

I saw that a double-barrelled shotgun lay on the ground nearby, and reflected that they had indeed narrowly missed death. The assassin had had no chance of survival, for the bullet from Renning's pistol had struck his chest near the heart.

Holmes conducted his observations. "One barrel discharged without finding its target, fortunately, and you fired before the other could be brought into play." He turned to Renning. "You are to be commended."

"I was top marksman in my regiment, sir. Some years ago, now."

"Clearly your skill hasn't deserted you."

The guards carried the body between them, until we found ourselves in the prison yard. It would now be stored in some convenient place until the local police could be informed of the events of the night. Holmes mentioned that it would come as no surprise to him to learn that the dead man already featured in their files.

After relating our adventure to Crout, we returned to the inn, where we both passed a peaceful night. After an early breakfast, I accompanied

251

my friend to the local Post Office, which opened for the day as we arrived. He sent the promised telegram to Mycroft, with a shortened account of his discoveries and the subsequent happenings, as well as a request that a message be despatched to the temporary governor to secure Faber's release from custody.

"The unfortunate thing is," he said as we came to the edge of the moor and took in its vastness under a clear sky, "that we shall probably never know whether Ollshaw's scheme involved the Kaiser's spies or not. It could have been entirely his invention to discredit Faber and have him disposed of before, after some little time had passed, setting out to woo his wife."

"Clearly, the assassin, whoever he was, can throw no light upon that now."

"Or will ever ply his trade again. Renning is an excellent shot. No, the only remaining chance of learning the roots of this matter lies with Ollshaw, but I doubt if he will further incriminate himself unless it is under duress."

I nodded my agreement. "I must confess that I was greatly relieved to leave the moor last night. The atmosphere of the place, and that mist that could have hidden all manner of things, lay heavy on my nerves."

"The memory of the Hound, bounding towards us out of the fog, still haunts you, I perceive. Take heart, Watson. Those are the ghosts of yesteryear, gone forever, and the evil with them.

"What do you say to a walk along this well-used path to enjoy such beauty as our surroundings afford until the time for luncheon arrives? From the aromas that emanate from that coffee shop that we passed after leaving the Post Office, I would say that we can expect a reasonable meal there. After that, we can return to the prison once again, where a representative of the local force may then be in evidence. Also, by then enough time will have surely elapsed for Mycroft to have given Crout permission to release Faber. Then it is simply a matter of the three of us taking the next train back to the capital, where a very relieved Mrs. Faber will doubtless be pleased to receive us."

"Some of my most interesting cases have come to me in this way through Mycroft."

– Sherlock Holmes
"The Greek Interpreter"

The Adventure of the Tired Captain
by Naching T. Kassa

July of 1889 was a particularly busy month for my friend and colleague, Mr. Sherlock Holmes, bringing several important cases to Holmes's door, "The Naval Treaty" and "The Second Stain" among them. And though both of these were quite important and involved espionage, matters which could have destroyed the very fabric of England as we know it, neither was quite as fantastic or strange as the one I am about to relate.

My wife had gone to visit a friend on the 17th, and I, finding myself at a loose end, decided to visit my friend, Sherlock Holmes. The summer heat had been most disagreeable that particular evening, and when I arrived at 221 B Baker Street, I found Holmes just stepping out the door. We exchanged greetings and he invited me out to find some respite.

Our constitutional had taken us to Gloucester Place and as we ambled along the street, we chanced upon a strange sight: A man lay stretched out upon the cobblestones, facing the darkening sky.

At first, upon seeing him, I thought he had been knocked down and had suffered some sort of injury. I rushed to his side, but to my great surprise, found him not only unhurt, but fast asleep. He snored softly as Holmes hurriedly joined me.

I shook the fellow by the shoulder in order to rouse him. His eyelids fluttered, but he did not wake.

Holmes leaned in close to the man. "He has not been overcome by drink. In fact, his very nature rebels against the consumption of liquor."

Without asking how Holmes knew this, I stated, "From his manner, it seems to me he has been drugged." I lifted his eyelid and peered at his left eye. The pupil was small and would not dilate, even in the dim light.

"Let us move him out of the street so that you may continue your ministrations in a safer locale. The steps of that house there – they will do."

We lifted the man off the cobbled street and toward the steps, which led to a brown, brick dwelling. He stirred and woke just as we reached the third step, and so we sat him upon it.

"Who – who are you?" he asked.

"I am Dr. John Watson, and this is Mr. Sherlock Holmes. We – "

"Sherlock Holmes!" the fellow cried. "Why, I was on my way to see you, sir. And by a happy coincidence, you have found me. How did I come to be here? I left my home not ten minutes ago. At least, I believe that it was . . . ." He reached into his waistcoat pocket and removed a gold watch. "Dear God!" he cried. "It has happened again! I left not ten minutes, but *thirty* minutes ago." He made as though to rise, but fell back upon the step instead.

"Perhaps you should rest a moment," I said. "I have some brandy here. It may fortify you."

The captain held up a hand. "No thank you, kind sir. I'm afraid I do not imbibe. I am a firm believer in Temperance."

"As you can see, Watson, he wears the blue ribbon on his lapel," Holmes murmured with a smile. "And aside from his dislike for drink, I see that he is a captain in the 42nd Royal Highland Regiment of Foot, has been to the Gold Coast, and is newly married."

The captain's blue eyes grew wider. "I have read of your abilities, Mr. Holmes. But I must confess, I do not see how you could know these things."

"It is quite elementary. When you glanced at your watch just now, I noticed the insignia of the 42nd Regiment upon the case. Your regiment, also known as the Black Watch, fought at the Battle of Amoaful on The Gold Coast. The inscription inside the watch identifies your rank as captain."

"Ah," the captain replied. "But how did you know I was newly married?"

"The skin beneath your ring is bronzed by the sun. If you had been married for sometime, the skin beneath would've been pale."

"Amazing," the fellow breathed. "My wife was right. You are the only man who can aid us." He held out a hand. "My name is Captain Cyril Jeffries."

Holmes shook it.

"Would you accompany me to my home?" the captain asked. "We are close by and, in my present condition, I am unsure of whether I can go further."

Holmes agreed and quickly hailed a cab.

The journey to Captain Jeffries' home took but a few moments. When we arrived, we found ourselves before a modest house on Marylebone Road.

Captain Jeffries had recovered somewhat from the strange condition which had affected him. He led us into the house and greeted the maid upon entering.

"Has Mrs. Jeffries returned, Elsie?" he asked.

254

"She has, sir," the young woman replied, averting her gaze from us as she spoke.

"Good. Please tell her that I'm back and that we have guests. She will find us in the study."

As the maid rushed off to inform her mistress, Jeffries led us down the hall to his study. There, we seated ourselves in chairs before the empty fireplace and he began his story.

"You gentlemen have no doubt witnessed part of the problem I must set before you. You found me asleep, did you not?"

"We did," I said. "In the street, beneath a streetlamp."

"It has grown worse then," the captain said, shaking his head. "You must understand, gentlemen, that for the past three days, I have suffered from a strange malady – one which was only humiliating at first, but has now turned into a danger. As you have seen, I tend to . . . lose consciousness at odd moments."

"This seems to be a case for my friend and colleague," Holmes said, motioning to me. "I am not a medical man."

"I assure you, Mr. Holmes, this is a case for your particular talents. You see, I believe there has been an attempt on my life."

A soft knock came upon the door, and Jeffries quickly rose to answer it. He escorted a woman into the room, and we rose to our feet.

"Gentlemen, this is my wife. Addy, this is Mr. Sherlock Holmes and Dr. Watson."

The woman who greeted us was, perhaps, the loveliest I have ever seen. Her remarkable eyes revealed a kind and intelligent soul, while her smile brightened the room the moment she entered it. She wore her dark and luxuriant hair in the latest style, and it complimented her warm, brown skin.

"Mr. Holmes, I am so pleased to meet you at last," she said in a slightly accented tone.

"I am amazed you know my name, Madam. It isn't every day that one meets such an accomplished musician as yourself. Watson, we are standing in the presence of greatness. This is Addai Ashanti, the noted pianist."

"Mrs. Jeffries, if you please," she said, holding up a hand. "At home, I prefer my married name." She seated herself in a chair beside her husband. "As you know, Mr. Holmes, I am the second woman of African descent to attend the Stuttgart Conservatory. I know you by way of my favorite professor at the Stuttgart Conservatory, Herr Franz Steiner. He speaks most highly of you. Two years ago, you were of some help to him."

"Ah, yes. An interesting case. He returned to Germany following the unfortunate circumstances."

255

"He is most grateful to you. You stopped him from making a terrible mistake. It was he who recommended us to you. And, I must admit, it was not this alone that brought my husband to your door. We have also read of the Lauriston Gardens case, the one which Dr. Watson has so aptly titled *A Study in Scarlet*. The manner in which you solved the case – Well, it only strengthened our confidence in you. I am glad my husband could persuade you to come. We were unsure of whether you would believe us."

"There was no need to persuade them," Jeffries said gravely. "They witnessed one of my attacks and rescued me from the street."

"From the street? They found you in the street?" The lady clutched her husband's hand. "Oh, Cyril, you should never have gone alone!"

"All is well now, my dear. I will not do such a foolish thing again."

"Your husband says an attempt was made on his life," Holmes interjected. "Do you believe this to be the case as well?"

"I am sure of it," Mrs. Jeffries said.

"What has led you to such a conclusion?"

"We were warned," she said. Jeffries reached into his pocketbook then and withdrew a scrap of paper. He handed it to Holmes, who studied it for some time before handing it to me.

The foolscap looked to have been torn from a larger sheet. It was the handwriting, however, which struck me as strange. It seemed rather large and childish. *"he hates Cyril and has threatened to poison him. Go to the police, before it is too late."*

"Do you recognize the handwriting?" Holmes asked.

"No," Mrs. Jeffries said. "I have never seen it before."

"How did you come to possess this note?"

"Elsie, our maid, brought it to us four days ago."

"I would speak with her."

Mrs. Jeffries rose and rang the bell. The young woman appeared a few moments later. Again, she refused to look in the direction of my friend and myself.

"Elsie," Mrs. Jeffries said gently, "would you tell us the circumstances under which you found this note?"

"I 'eard the knock, Ma'am," the maid said in a soft voice. "When I opened the door, I found it on the step."

"Did you see who may have left it?" Holmes asked.

Elsie glanced up at the sound of Holmes's voice, her eyes like that of a frightened doe.

"It's all right, Elsie," Mrs. Jeffries said. "Please, answer Mr. Holmes's query."

"No, sir. I saw no one."

256

Holmes stared at her for several moments. "How long have you been in the captain's employ?" he asked.

"A little o – over a month, sir."

"And this is your first situation. How did you come by it?"

The young woman turned to Captain Jeffries, as though the answer might somehow lie in his face.

"My sister hired her," he said at last. "She lives here – That is, she *lived* here, until I married Addy."

"She didn't wish to live with a married couple," Mrs. Jeffries explained.

"I wish that were the case," the captain said. "But I can no longer make excuses for her simply because she is my flesh and blood. Barbara did not approve of our match and said so on many occasions. When I did not heed her or her advice, she left."

Mrs. Jeffries sighed. "I suppose I should not be surprised. Many people disapprove of our marriage."

"So much the worst for them," the captain replied. "I have never known a truer and kinder woman than you, Addy."

Mrs. Jeffries did not reply, but continued to grasp her husband's hand.

"Do you have any further questions for Elsie, Mr. Holmes?" the captain asked.

"No," Holmes said. "She may go."

Jeffries dismissed the maid, who curtsied and rushed from the room.

"Have you seen a doctor?" Holmes asked.

"I have seen my own doctor, and he claims that I am fit as a fiddle. He says there is nothing wrong that a little sleep cannot fix. With such a diagnosis, I said nothing of my suspicions. But you yourselves have seen what has happened to me."

"Have you any other symptoms?" I asked.

"None. I have had no distress other than this fatigue."

"I have an extensive knowledge of poisons," Holmes said. "And there are several which may cause the exhaustion you have mentioned. The question is, if it is poison, how was it introduced?"

"We have considered food and drink," Jeffries said. "When the first attack came upon me three days ago, Addy assumed the duties of cooking for me. She eats all of the same meals with me and has suffered no ill effect."

"Then it must be introduced in another manner," Holmes said. He leaned back in the chair and steepled his fingers before him. "Have there been any changes in the household in the last three days? Have you any new staff?"

"Elsie is our only servant. Our housekeeper, Mrs. Flint, took her leave after the departure of my sister. She is the housekeeper in my sister's home now."

"And you have admitted no workmen nor messengers?"

"None."

"And yet," Holmes muttered, "your symptoms grew worse today." "Tell me, what did you do just before you left the house this afternoon?"

"Addy and I had tea. She is to perform at the Royal Albert Hall next Thursday and had to attend rehearsal, so she left immediately after. I came here to the study so that I might collect some of my sister's things, papers she had left behind and asked me to return. I was to stop there on the way to see you . . . ." He trailed off and began to search his pockets.

"My God," he whispered. "Where have they gone? I had them here in this pocket before I left."

"They are missing?" Holmes said.

"They are the *only* thing missing," the captain cried. "I have my wallet and my watch, but the documents my sister asked for are gone! How could I have forgotten them?"

"Perhaps they fell into the street when you were overcome," I suggested.

"No," Jeffries said, shaking his head. "They were within my coat pocket. Nothing could've fallen from there. Someone has taken them."

"Perhaps you were mistaken," Holmes suggested. "You may have left them here."

The captain hurried to his desk. He rifled through papers, tossing a pen there, a bottle of ink there. Holmes crossed to the desk and stood beside him.

"May I ask what the papers contained?" he asked.

"It was my sister's *Last Will and Testament*. I can't imagine why anyone would take such a thing." He shrugged his shoulders. "I suppose it is of little consequence. She had left everything to me, but I'm sure that will change now."

"An odd occurrence indeed," Holmes mused. He too searched the desk, lifting a box of chocolates from Whitaker's before setting it down again. When the quest proved fruitless, he shook his head and returned to my side.

"It seems the papers are lost. However, as you said, it is of little consequence now." He retrieved the note from my hand and examined it once more.

"This note speaks of a '*he*'. Do you know of anyone who would wish to poison you, Captain?"

258

"One man," said the captain with a frown, "has threatened to kill me for marrying Addy. His name is Edgar Chamberlain."

"He is a former suitor of mine," Mrs. Jeffries said, "though now, I wish I had never laid eyes upon him. He seemed a good fellow when first we met, but he became churlish and jealous. I never saw him as anything more than a friend and told him so. When I met Cyril, he became quite disagreeable. He said he would kill any man who tried to take me from him."

"On the day of our wedding," Jeffries added, "he accosted me. I gave him a good thrashing. Before he fled, he vowed that he would kill me, and that the police would never know he did it. That was but a month ago."

"Could you describe this Chamberlain?" Holmes asked.

"He is a tall man, handsome in his way, I suppose. He has a scar on his forehead that extends into his dark hair. It has caused his hair to have a large white patch above his left eye."

"Has he threatened you since?"

"We haven't heard from him since our wedding."

Holmes rose to his feet. "I shall investigate the matter under one condition."

"You have but to name it," the captain said. "If it is a fee – "

"You must not leave this house until I have completed my findings."

"Very well."

"I shall stay with you," Mrs. Jeffries said. "And cancel my engagement."

"No, Mrs. Jeffries, it is imperative you continue as though nothing has happened," Holmes said. "Attend your rehearsals and continue to cook for your husband. We shall find the culprit soon enough."

Holmes and I took our leave. We didn't leave the house, however. Instead, Holmes led me around to the kitchen. There we found the maid, Elsie.

"Good evening, Elsie," Holmes said.

The young woman nearly dropped the china cup she held. She stared at Holmes with wide and frightened eyes.

My colleague, who possesses a most ingratiating way with women, soon assuaged the maid's fears. Within ten minutes, she had forgotten my presence entirely and had answered my friend's questions with a candor one would reserve for a favorite uncle. Holmes listened in a most sympathetic manner as he handed her several china cups to wash.

"That Chamberlain fellow? He was a 'orrible one, that one was. Did 'e ever eat dinner here? No, never did. The master wouldn't let 'im, would 'e? Not with 'im wearin' the blue ribbon and Chamberlain – Well, 'e was given to drink. Miss Barbara, if she'd been 'ere, she would've 'ad a fit and no mistake. Yes, she's a teetotaller, too. Never lets a drop past 'er lips. Miss Barbara's address? Yes, I can write. My mum taught me, she did. I just need a pencil and paper. The paper in your notebook will do. There. She lives at 310 Malden Road. I wouldn't visit 'er 'til morning though. She'll be asleep by now."

Holmes took the scrap of paper upon which Elsie had written the address. "One more question, if you will indulge me: Who does the shopping for the household?"

"Why I do, of course. I 'ad to after Mrs. Flint departed."

"And you shop at Whitaker's?"

"Oh, no. I never go there. The missus has certain tastes. She don't like most of what they carry."

"Then . . . how do you account for the box of Whitaker's chocolates on the captain's desk?"

"What – Oh, that! That was delivered to the 'ouse."

"Do you remember when?"

She paused as though deep in thought. "Three days ago. And I remember, because it was a boy what delivered it. I remember now, because 'e 'ad a finger missing on 'is right 'and, and I couldn't stop staring at it."

"Was there a note with the box?"

"Not that I could see. Might 'ave been in the box. The master must 'ave 'ad it delivered. 'E's quite fond of chocolate."

Holmes nodded. "Thank you, Elsie. You have been most helpful."

"Are you leaving now?"

"I'm afraid we must."

"Shall I show you to the door?"

"That won't be necessary." Holmes put on his hat, tipped it, and together we departed.

A cab returned us to Baker Street. Holmes remained reticent during our journey, and I didn't trouble him with idle banter. It seemed he'd had enough of that in the Jeffries' kitchen.

When we arrived at 221, we found Mrs. Hudson waiting at the door. She seemed somewhat perturbed as she handed Holmes a calling card.

"There is a lady here to see you, Mr. Holmes. I told her the hour was late and to come back tomorrow, but she insisted on seeing you."

Holmes raised an eyebrow as he read the card. He handed it to me.

"'*Miss Barbara Jeffries*'," I read.

"She said her business was most urgent," Mrs. Hudson said.

"Then we should see her at once," Holmes replied.

260

A rather handsome woman rose from the settee as we entered our rooms. The manner in which she carried herself, along with the white threads which streaked her blonde hair, gave her a rather distinguished air.

"Mr. Holmes?" she asked.

"I am he," Holmes replied. "How can I be of service?"

"You have my card?"

"I do."

"Then you know I am the sister of the unhappy Captain Jeffries."

"Unhappy?" I interjected.

The lady turned an icy glare upon me. "Who is this person?"

"This is my friend and colleague, Dr. Watson," Holmes said. "He is the soul of discretion."

"Soul of discretion or not, I will not speak before him."

"Then I am afraid I must bid you goodnight, Madam," Holmes said. "Perhaps your business can wait until the morning. You may return then, but I assure you, Dr. Watson will still be present."

Miss Jeffries stared at Holmes for several minutes and then resumed her place upon the settee. "The welfare of my brother far outweighs such trivialities," she sniffed. "Very well. I shall tell the story straight out. My brother's life is in jeopardy. I believe his wife is trying to kill him."

"What evidence leads you to this conclusion?" Holmes asked.

"This," she said, and reached into her purse. She pulled forth a piece of foolscap and handed it over to Holmes. I stood at his side and read the missive. To my great surprise, the message and handwriting were the same as the note which I had observed at Captain Jeffries' home – with one important difference. This particular note read, "*She hates Cyril*" instead of "*he*".

"My housekeeper found it on my doorstep four days ago," Miss Jeffries said. "She brought it to my attention immediately."

"And you think the '*She*' in this note refers to the captain's wife?"

"Who else could it be? I have it on good authority that my brother's wife has suddenly begun cooking all of my brother's meals. She won't allow Elsie near the kitchen, save to wash the dishes." She leaned forward conspiratorially. "I also heard that she has a lover with expensive tastes, and that her own earnings are not enough for him. That is why she married my brother."

"For his money?" Holmes said.

"No. For *my* money." She reached into her purse once more and withdrew an envelope. "I received this letter last week. It is from my brother's wife, and it reads thus:"

Dearest Barbara,

Let me begin with an apology. I do not know what I may have done to earn your dislike and distrust. A mutual acquaintance of ours has implied that it is Edgar Chamberlain who has driven this wedge between us. If that is the case, then I am most heartily sorry. Cyril is most upset by this matter, and I would be most grateful if you did not mention it to him in future.

I implore you, not for my sake but for Cyril's, to reconsider your decision. He is quite saddened by your departure. Please, do not punish him by taking your legacy from him.

Addy

"There – Do you see? She has written it in her own hand." Miss Jeffries said, handing the letter to Holmes. "Her only interest in my brother is the money I would leave him. And she asks that I keep the identity of her lover a secret."

"That is not necessarily the case – " I began, but Holmes raised a hand and silenced me.

"Have you shared this with your brother?"

"He will not hear a word against her. I intended to tell him this evening, but he did not come to my home as he had promised. I've no doubt he has fallen prey to that woman's machinations. That is why I have come to you. If you investigate her, you may be able to convince him, as I have not."

Miss Jeffries spoke this last as an impassioned plea. For a moment, I thought she might drop to her knees before my friend and beg him for his help.

"Never fear, Miss Jeffries. I shall look into the matter," Holmes said. "It would be best if you return home. I shall come there in the morning, if you will be so kind as to give me your address."

He handed the woman a sheet of notebook paper and a pencil, just as he had the Jeffries' maid. She wrote upon the page and handed it to Holmes with her right hand.

"May I keep the note as well?" Holmes asked.

"Please. Perhaps, you can somehow convince my brother with it."

As the woman rose to leave, she pulled a handkerchief from her sleeve and dabbed at her eyes. "I will await your word, Mr. Holmes." She then turned to me and offered a faint smile. "Please excuse my rudeness before, Doctor. I did not mean it."

I nodded.

When Miss Jeffries had gone, Holmes turned to me and said, "A pretty problem, isn't it? And yet the solution may be quite within our grasp. You noticed the similarities between Miss Jeffries' note and that of her brother's, did you not?"

"They were identical, save for the words '*he*' and '*She*'. They had been juxtaposed."

"That is the least interesting detail about it. Come now, you know my methods. What did you observe?"

"Both had been written in the same hand."

"True."

"And they were torn from a sheet of foolscap."

"Ah! There is the clue! Not just *a* sheet, Watson. The *same* sheet. Look here." He pointed to a large "*S*" near the ragged edge of the foolscap. "The word on Captain Jeffries' note was not supposed to be '*he*'. It should've been written '*She*', just as this note was. The '*h*' is lower case."

"Then both notes were written at the same time, by the same person, and delivered to the two homes?"

Holmes nodded. "How did the handwriting appear to you?"

"It looked as though a child had written it."

"Or a young and uneducated woman. It is the reason why I asked Elsie to write Miss Jeffries' address upon the page of my notebook. As you can see, the handwriting does not match, and I was forced to discard that theory once I saw it."

"Ah, then that's why you had Miss Jeffries repeat the action. But she is not a child. Surely her handwriting did not match."

"Not exactly but see here: The letters in the address and in the note."

"There are similarities . . . many similarities."

"That is because the letter was written by Miss Jeffries – *with her left hand*. And why would a woman write a letter in her left hand instead of her right?"

"To disguise it from those who would know it!" I exclaimed. "Then Miss Jeffries is the one who poisoned her brother?"

Holmes stuffed his cherry-wood pipe with tobacco from the Persian slipper and settled down among his commonplace books. "That I do not yet know. It's a capital mistake to theorize without facts."

"But what of the captain? Should we alert him to the danger he may be in?"

"Watson, it seems you have far less confidence in your abilities as a doctor than I. Captain Jeffries was never poisoned. You hit the nail upon

263

the head the moment you laid eyes upon him. Do not allow the deception to dissuade you from your first diagnosis."

"The man *was* drugged."

"And left in the street."

"By whom? I must confess, I do not believe that Mrs. Jeffries could do such a thing, no matter what her sister-in-law says. She seems utterly devoted to her husband."

"In this case, you would be correct. Obtaining a sample of the maid's handwriting was not my only reason for visiting the kitchen. I also examined the tea things before she washed them. None of them contained the drug in question." He peered at me. "As a medical man, you should have some inkling as to what that drug is."

I considered the symptoms for a moment, remembering the captain's inability to wake and the condition of his left eye.

"Laudanum!" I cried.

"Excellent! I found no traces upon the dishes."

"Then how was it administered? The captain does not drink, and when taken alone, the taste of laudanum is easily distinguishable."

Holmes pulled from his pocket a wadded handkerchief and proceeded to untie the little bundle. Inside was a small brown fragment which seemed to have smeared on the white linen.

"Chocolate?" I cried. "The laudanum was in the chocolate? How did you know?"

"I don't suppose you observed the stain on the cuff of the captain's shirt? Or the small fragment near the corner of his mouth when we found him?"

I shook my head. "No, I did not."

"It is the trifles, Watson – the trifles which put the correct thread within our grasp." He lit his pipe, and the fragrant scent of tobacco filled the air. "Whitaker's is the best shop in London for such confections. They may know who purchased the chocolate for the captain. I shall visit them on the morrow."

The hour had grown late and I knew my time had come to depart. I left Holmes beneath a pall of tobacco smoke and resolved to return the next morning.

Unfortunately, my practice kept me from seeing Holmes for much of the day. A parade of patients passed through my door, and it would be evening before I could visit him. When I arrived in Baker Street, Mrs. Hudson informed me that Holmes had been out and had only just returned. I entered and found him, dressed as a workman, his hands covered with dirt. He vanished into his room, and when he reappeared, he was his old self.

"It is well you have come, Watson," said he. "We shall have a visitor soon, and once he has joined us, we shall make our way to Malden Road. I have my hunting crop. Do you, by chance, have your revolver?"

"I was not sure you would need use of it, but I brought it, nonetheless. Are we to visit the home of Miss Jeffries?"

"We are, for it is there that the solution to this case lies. I have spent a most profitable day among the tombstones."

"Among the tombstones?"

"As a gravedigger."

A knock came upon the door at that moment, and I hurried to answer it. Inspector Lestrade stood upon the threshold.

"I received your telegram, Mr. Holmes," the inspector said, looking past me. "What's this all about?"

"All will be revealed in due time, Lestrade. Come. We've not a moment to lose, and I have a cab waiting."

We piled in and set off for Malden Road. Holmes quickly related the details of the case to Lestrade and then launched into an explanation of his adventure.

"I visited Whitaker's this morning," said he, "where a polite inquiry revealed that Miss Jeffries had ordered the chocolate. It had been delivered to her house four days ago."

"A day before it was delivered to the Jeffries' home," said Lestrade.

"Quite right. Having learned this, I made my way to the captain's house. I questioned him as to why he had eaten from the box and whether there had been a note. He said that there had been no note, and that he had simply assumed his wife had ordered them. You see, when the captain surrendered his habit of drinking, he acquired a new one. Now, when he is tempted to drink, he takes a bite of chocolate instead. It is his custom to eat chocolate before he leaves the house, just in case he should be tempted while out and about."

"That is why he appeared as he did on the street?" Lestrade asked.

"Indeed. Only three people knew this to be the captain's practice: His wife and his sister, of course."

"Who was the other?" Lestrade said, leaning forward.

"Last night, I asked his sister to write her address on a scrap of paper. She did so, and I showed it to the captain. He was quite shocked."

"He was surprised that his sister had come to Baker Street?" I asked.

"No. The handwriting did not belong to his sister."

I was surprised. "Then to whom did it belong?"

"To the housekeeper, Mrs. Flint – the only other person who knew he ate chocolate before leaving the house."

"The housekeeper was impersonating her employer?" Lestrade cried. "For what purpose?"

"A most reprehensible one, I assure you," Holmes said. "I cautioned the captain concerning the remaining chocolates, and then with the help of the Irregulars, I located the whereabouts of Edgar Chamberlain. In the underworld of London, he is not a difficult man to find."

"Edgar Chamberlain?" Lestrade mused. "I don't think I know the name."

"Mrs. Jeffries' former suitor. Perhaps you know him under one of his aliases. He has several, though I think 'Beckett Perkins' suits him best."

Lestrade's eyes widened.

"Yes, I thought you might know that name," Holmes continued, a slight smile on his lips. "The description Captain Jeffries gave of Chamberlain struck a chord. During a foray into my commonplace books, I uncovered his alias. And, today, I ventured out as a gravedigger and made a few discrete inquiries. Workmen of such a low profession do not require much to share information. A few pounds and a bottle are often sufficient payment. They told me where I might find Perkins this evening."

"Where might I lay my hands upon him?" Lestrade asked. "That grave-robber has eluded us for far too long."

"You may find him here," Holmes said, as the cab came to a halt.

We stepped out into the street before a small and lonely house. Darkened windows looked out on the street like the eyes of some somber sentinel. A hush seemed to emanate from the place, increasing my sense of foreboding. I slipped my hand into my coat pocket and gripped my revolver.

Holmes, with hunting crop at the ready, crept toward the dark house. Lestrade and I followed at his heels.

A horse knickered as we rounded the left side of the home. Holmes paused at the sound, and Lestrade and I drew to a halt. We waited in the dark, hardly breathing, as the sound of muted voices drifted toward us. I couldn't make out their words.

After a few moments, Holmes led us forward.

We reached the back of the house and found the doorway awash with lantern light. Two men approached the back of the wagon, carrying what appeared to be a heavy bundle wrapped in linen. The first, a tall man with a patch of white in his hair, cursed at the smaller fellow, a young man with a missing finger on his right hand. The horse stamped its feet as they loaded their cargo.

A woman entered the doorway a moment later, and I recognized her as Mrs. Flint, Miss Jeffries' impersonator.

"You're a right fool, Edgar," she said, addressing the taller of the two men. "Giving her too much the way you did. If you'd listened to me, we wouldn't be in this fix."

"How was I to know she had a bad heart?"

"Because I told you, you cloth-eared idiot! Why do you think she left her brother's house in the first place? She didn't want to be a burden to them. That's why."

"She was too stubborn. She never would've signed it."

"Well, I guess we'll never know now, will we? It's a good thing you can still sell the body. It'll make up for some of what we'll lose on this deal."

"I still don't know why we can't bring Pendergast in on this. We should've hired him in the beginning."

"If you remember, he does have a fee and it would be all the higher if he knew Sherlock Holmes were about."

"How much higher?"

"Three-hundred pounds."

"The amount has increased, then," Holmes said, stepping forward. "Last I heard, Pendergast's forgeries were two-hundred in addition to his usual fee."

The group froze as they looked upon Sherlock Holmes, and then, with a snarl, Chamberlain charged him. The younger accomplice turned on me, while Lestrade hurried after the woman who had vanished back into the house.

I had little time to draw my revolver from my pocket as the younger man grasped hold of me. His attack was clumsy at best. I heard the crack of his knuckle as it struck my cheek and knew that he had broken his hand. A quick jab to the chin and another to his stomach soon dropped him to his knees. I withdrew my revolver from my pocket and held it upon him.

Chamberlain had rushed Holmes, who easily side-stepped him. The larger man fell, sprawling into the dirt. And when he rose to his knees, Holmes brought his hunting crop across the fellow's head. This time, he fell and did not move.

Lestrade emerged a second later, his face bearing the claw marks of the woman he had subdued. He held her, hands behind her back as he walked her out the door.

Holmes turned to the wagon and examined the bundle inside, tearing the linen apart to reveal a pale face. He turned to Mrs. Flint, his face grave.

"There is a good stout rope in this wagon," said he. "We should tie these villains together until the good inspector can return with a constable or two."

I quickly retrieved the rope while Holmes held the villains at bay with my revolver. Lestrade and I bound them, and after we had done so, the inspector rushed off.

Mrs. Flint glared up at us from her place in the dirt.

"It was a very clever plan," Holmes said. "If it had been executed correctly, it might have proved flawless."

"Not for you," the woman sulked. "You knew from the first, else you wouldn't be here."

Holmes gave a slight nod.

"I know what you want," she said, her tone cold. "But you'll not get it from me."

"You are not the author of this plan?"

The woman turned away.

"Ah, I see," Holmes said. "There is another – 'behind the scenes', as it were. I'm afraid he has left you and your grave-robbing younger brother to the hangman's noose."

The woman turned. "How did you know he was my brother?"

"There is a slight family resemblance in the nose and chin. That, and your attitude toward him, led me to this conclusion. He was not so deferential to Addai Ashanti – Mrs. Jeffries, that is."

"Edgar is a clod!" she said bitterly. "I wanted the money. All he wanted was revenge."

"And the the author of the plan, this spider at the center of the web, he made it possible. For a price."

She nodded.

"Let me be clear upon the details. You knew of Miss Jeffries' illness and intended to exploit it for your own gain. It was the money from her legacy that you were to use to entice the Spider. He suggested you write the note to Captain Jeffries, telling him he would be poisoned. He told you to use your left hand, so your handwriting would not be recognized, and he told you to write two notes, so it would seem a secret ally knew of the plan and wished to reveal it.

"With your information regarding the chocolates, he suggested poisoning them with laudanum. I suppose you used a syringe? Ah, yes, I can tell by your expression, you did. The eventual aim was to put the blame on Mrs. Jeffries, so that if her sister-in-law and her husband died of laudanum poisoning, her life would be forfeit.

"In the meantime, you would force Miss Jeffries to sign a new will made in your favor. And when she and her brother died, you would inherit.

268

As I said, a pretty plan, but there were difficulties from the first. The tearing of the note changed the meaning of the message, implicating Chamberlain as a killer. Then, the captain left the house to visit his sister and to see me. Your brother had been watching the house and saw him fall upon the street. He nearly killed the captain by leaving him there after he had robbed him of the will – "

"I told him we didn't need the will, but he insisted on taking it. He thought the will favoring me would be better believed if he did, the great lummox!"

The woman cast a venomous look upon her unconscious brother, and I believe, had she been free, she might have throttled him. "Then he had to go and kill her." She ground her teeth together. "Killed the golden goose."

"There is a possibility that you will live if you can give me the name of the man who planned this," Holmes said gently. "Tell me the Spider's name, and I shall do all that I can."

She offered us a mirthless grin. "No, Mr. Holmes. I would rather swing on the gallows than betray him. It will be a far kinder fate. You will never hear his name. Not from my lips. Not ever."

Lestrade arrived with three constables then. They took charge of the prisoners while Lestrade joined us by the wagon. We looked upon the face of Miss Jeffries and I shook my head.

"Poor woman."

"She will be cared for, Doctor," Lestrade said. "And returned to her family."

"Who we must inform." Holmes said. "Come, Watson."

"Mr. Holmes," Lestrade said, as we turned away.

"Yes?"

"Thank you."

Holmes nodded and Lestrade hurried off.

"A most unusual occurrence," I remarked.

"Indeed," Holmes said.

We returned to the street to await a hansom cab. Holmes's face seemed grim.

"Miss Jeffries should not have perished in such a manner. And I must blame myself. If I had acted sooner, she might yet be alive."

"If anyone is to blame, it should be Chamberlain, his sister, and the mysterious man behind all of this despicable business."

"I have considered that as well. One day, I shall discover the spider as he sleeps in his web. And I shall crush him."

269

The July which immediately succeeded my marriage was made memorable by three cases of interest in which I had the privilege of being associated with Sherlock Holmes, and of studying his methods. I find them recorded in my notes under the headings of "The Adventure of the Second Stain", "The Adventure of the Naval Treaty", and "The Adventure of the Tired Captain".

– Dr. John H. Watson
"The Naval Treaty"

A Dreadful Record of Sin
by David Marcum

When recording the investigations of my friend, Mr. Sherlock Holmes, I have attempted to strike a balance between those cases which best illustrated his unique and well-honed abilities and events that would capture the interest of the reader – even if, in some cases, they will never be seen by the public. Still, even when knowing that some cases cannot be publicly read, I've still made the attempt to transcribe them in an engaging manner.

As I've become more practiced and experienced over the passing years at which type of narratives generate the most reading interest, as well as the ways in which they can be constructed so as to tell a pleasing tale, I've also had to make certain that I didn't stray over several different well-defined lines and inadvertently provide too much information. Certain matters of State have needed to be disguised so that Holmes's methods could be displayed without giving away government secrets. Examples of this include the curse of the Burmese bicyclist, and also the affair of the Godolphin Street murder, and the secret document that was hidden at and then stolen from the premises. Had it not been recovered, then the country might have been plunged into war. But there was no need to name specific figures involved, when I could instead identify the principal actors by other designations and lose nothing in terms of showing how Holmes brilliantly handled the matter. Likewise, I have no qualms about adjusting other names, dates, and locations to protect those individuals who need not suffer from unnecessary public exposure while I describe the manner in which Holmes effectively finds his solutions.

The following adventure took place in the years just before Holmes was presumed dead, although neither the exact date, nor the specific identifies of those involved, need be related in order to describe Holmes's accomplishment. In this instance, hiding the identity of those involved will be additionally accomplished by consigning this document to my tin dispatch box, which holds so many of my other records of Holmes's cases, some simply because they are finished but have not been offered for publication, and others because they hold secrets, often dangerous or destructive, that have no business being held up for public scrutiny. It has been noted to me on more than one occasion, by more than just Sherlock Holmes, that making any kind of record at all of some of these cases is indiscreet at best, and that their very existence as a written record is a menace to the national interest should they be revealed. However, I insist that an accurate and complete record of

Holmes's cases be recorded as best as possible, and therefore I'm including the affair of the Kilworth investigation.

But be warned: The matter was disturbing, greatly so, and this account shall remain locked away for at least a century.

– JHW

"It's my own fault," Mycroft stated, wiping his damp face with a handkerchief. "I decided to save time by visiting you directly, instead of asking you to join me at the Diogenes Club."

"You've just come from an important meeting," said Sherlock Holmes. "So important that you didn't want to wait to seek our help."

Mycroft barked a laugh. "Now I know how strangers at the receiving end feel when we seemingly read their minds." He glanced down at his stout frame. "No tell-tale papers protruding from my pockets. No ink stains of a unique hue on my fingers, indicating that I was recently writing with a leaky pen in a Cabinet member's office. No crumbs on my waistcoat from the unique refreshments served there. How did you know, Sherlock?"

"There were no physical clues. Only urgency could have diverted you in this heat from scurrying directly straight along to the club at this time of evening. What could be so serious?"

"Brian Kilworth's wife is missing – and with her, a number of most-secret state documents. Serious is far too insignificant a word for what might happen should their contents be revealed."

I may have given the impression that Mycroft Holmes ran entirely on fixed rails, as based upon Holmes's own description of him as related in the matter of Mr. Melas's encounter with the captive Greek. In that account, I have recorded, based on Sherlock Holmes's initial revelation of Mycroft's existence, that he was a man who went from his Pall Mall lodgings to his work in Whitehall, and from there to his Pall Mall club directly across the street from his rooms, and then back home again at the end of the day, and doing it all over again on the next. While this description certainly defines someone of eccentric behavior, in truth, Mycroft Holmes was not so rigid as all that. Many men at his level of responsibility had much the same pattern – home to work to club, and then repeating the following day. When someone asks me about it, I point out that in the same narrative describing Mr. Melas's unfortunate adventure, Mycroft departed from his club, the Diogenes, just after we left, and he beat us back to Baker Street, where he was waiting when we finally arrived, placidly smoking one of his brother's best cigars, apparently not put off at all by having to retrieve it from the coal scuttle.

In our dealings with Mycroft over the years, he was far more active than many would like to believe, and while not a frequent visitor to Baker Street, it wasn't entirely unusual for him to arrive, often unannounced, if some urgent and confidential matter needed Sherlock Holmes's efforts, and it needed to be discussed either in the greatest confidence, away from the Diogenes Club or Whitehall, or sooner than if Holmes went around to Mycroft's office during business hours.

This was just such a visit.

The specific date isn't important, but for clarity, I'll mention that the weather was hot, and when Mycroft finished climbing the steps to the sitting room, he was red-faced, winded, and damp. He wiped his scowling countenance with a handkerchief, asked for a tall glass of water, and then another, and then finally accepted some whisky. When he had found an acceptable level of comfort upon our settee, for the room was nearly as hot as the outdoors and there was no breeze from the open windows, he began to speak.

Holmes frowned in response. "Brian Kilworth? Isn't he the fellow who recently returned from Berlin with a trade agreement in his pocket – hailed in the press as an important step toward cementing further peaceful ties between Germany and Britain?"

"The same," agreed Mycroft. "He arranged it on his own. He's always been something of a rogue agent. He believes that he's allowed greater leeway because of his father, and he has no hesitation at taking it."

Holmes rose and circled around the settee to reach the shelf where his scrapbooks were kept, to the left of the mantel and behind my chair. He had first claimed that spot on the day he moved in, the third of January, 1881. I myself had brought my own things 'round from a Strand hotel the evening before, but hadn't had the foresight of the boldness to start marking territory, and therefore I lost any right to those shelves before I'd even given any thought about them. However, I had no objections to Holmes taking the space, as the door to his bedroom was just beside the shelves in question, while my own room had been located upstairs, and it seemed somehow appropriate for him to have those shelves because of that proximity. In any case, those early days were quite uncertain, as I'd only agreed to share the rooms because of the dangerous and poorly managed condition of my finances, and I had no set plans as to how long I'd stay. I certainly didn't do very much to make myself completely at home, at least not at first, in spite of the mothering I received from Mrs. Hudson as she took it upon herself to help accomplish my return to health.

In 1881, Holmes's scrapbooks were already formidable accomplishments, created over the previous years with notes and clippings related to countless individuals, events, and places. Holmes knew the contents of the multiple volumes forward and backward, and he spent a great deal of time keeping them caught up by regularly butchering our newspapers and then using the glue-pot to affix the clippings into the volumes, or making extensive notes in the margins. Many was the time he'd come in from some errand and, first thing, rush to one or another of the commonplace books to jot down some fact that he'd learned while out, unrelated to his current inquiry, before he lost track of it.

Now, almost a decade later, the shelves that we'd found mounted upon the wall when we'd moved in had been augmented by others, and there were many more books as well, all fat with data, and still referenced in Holmes's mind so that he could lay a hand on just what he needed at a moment's notice.

"'*Lord Benton Kilworth*'" read Holmes. "A bit before our time. Born in 1812 near High Roding." He looked up, his eyebrows raised curiously.

"A village and civil parish in the Uttlesford district of Essex," Mycroft explained.

Holmes shrugged. "I don't recall why I noted the fact. The ink is quite faded – apparently I wrote it down a long time ago, thinking there was something important about Lord Benton." He scanned the entry further. "Is he still alive?" he asked, glancing up.

Mycroft nodded. "He turns seventy-eight later this summer. Of course, he's been withdrawn from public life for quite a while, although he's still remembered with great fondness for his numerous accomplishments."

"Family made a fortune in shipping," Holmes continued to summarize. "Lord Benton made his name in politics, married late, had one son – Brian, in 1849. The lad's mother died when he was but two, and – Ah, this is why Lord Benton was of interest." He closed the book and replaced it on the shelf, saying, "He has had *four* other wives since the death of the first. Possibly more than that, since it's been a while since I first wrote this notation, over ten years ago. Possibly that's why I felt the need to make mention of him then. *Five wives?* That seems a bit excessive – and suspicious. And of those five wives, the first four all died before he married the fifth – there were no divorces, and each marriage only lasted for a few years before being . . . terminated." Holmes resumed his seat. "And Wife Number Five? Is she still alive?"

Mycroft shook his head. "Number Five passed nearly ten years ago – while you were jaunting across the ocean during your so-called career as an actor. Even if you had been here, however, it's unlikely that the fact would have made much of an impression. Lord Benton had long since retired from public life by then, returning to his reclusive estate near High

274

Roding. His son, Brian, however, who is now in his early forties, has become the public figure, filling the role his father used to hold."

"And the wives?" Holmes pressed. "Did Lord Benton marry a sixth after the fifth – to make a round half-dozen?"

"He did not remarry. Five seems to have been enough. And his son, Brian, has made do with just the one wife for the past five years. He, too, married late, and has yet to produce an heir."

"And you say that Brian Kilworth's wife is missing?"

"She is. With important papers."

Holmes leaned back. "Tell us about it."

Mycroft never needed much time to collect his thoughts, and he continued immediately.

"Brian Benton's wife, Katherine, is now twenty-three years old. Her father was Simon Rackford, who made a fortune through property management in the East End. The girl's parents were both killed in a carriage accident when she was seventeen, and their affairs were managed by a cadre of lawyers. Katherine was the sole heir. A year after her parents died, she was married off to Brian Kilworth.

"I don't know the specific details, but I have the sense that the affair was managed with legal slickness by the attorneys – more like an arranged marriage of old than for love. However, that is no more than gossip upon my part as – contrary to what some would believe – I don't hold every thread in my hand, and the marriage of one girl to one older man more than twice her age does not often fall within my purview. The only reason I knew anything about it at all was because there was some discussion concerning the economic aspects of the absorption of the Rackford fortune into the Kilworth family. As is so often the case, the Kilworths are already quite wealthy, so it's no surprise that they have now become wealthier. Such is the way of things. Money begets more money."

"And Katherine Kilgore has disappeared," prompted Holmes. "What are the circumstances?"

"The Kilgores live in Mayfair, in the family home that initially belonged to Lord Benton, before he retired to Essex. It's where Brian grew up – him, his father, and his succession of short-lived step-mothers." Mycroft raised a hand. "No, I'm not adding emphasis to that fact, asking you to investigate the deaths of these women, or implying that there was some sort of nefarious plot by Lord Benton to remove them, one by one. I was just making note of the fact that the young man has lived in the house his whole life, and he remained there when his father left, and it's there that he took his new bride, Katherine.

"By all accounts, she has fulfilled her role adequately in all aspects, if without enthusiasm, except for producing an heir. Her duties have been

275

slight, for the Kilgores do not entertain – at least not to the standard that many living in Mayfair expect. They do not participate in the general social cycle, instead having occasional visits and dinners with long-time family friends, many of whom have had connections with Lord Benton since his youth.

"Other than maintaining the household – duties that are apparently carried out in actuality by the long-time servants – Katherine Kilgore has led a rather typical tedious existence for the last five years, while her husband has risen from professional triumph to triumph. She doesn't appear to have any friends. She doesn't travel, and does not even leave the house very often – that according to her husband, who reluctantly sought help when she vanished.

"She disappeared exactly one week ago today, June 14th. It was another typical day at home, and according to the servants that Kilgore questioned, his wife had been seen reading in the morning room around ten o'clock. When a maid went to tell her that lunch was ready, she could not be found. The best guess was that she had simply slipped out of the house and vanished.

"The servants were initially uneasy, and grew more so, but no one sent word to the lady's husband, and he was told when he arrived home that night at six. Strangely, he didn't immediately notify the authorities, instead sending word to some of his friends, asking if Katherine was with them. When she couldn't be located, he widened his circle of inquiries, but still without positive results. It was only today that he felt moved to seek outside assistance – not from the police, but within the Government."

"Because of the important missing papers."

"Yes. Throughout his wife's absence, Kilgore has continued to come to work, while in the meantime leaving the search in the hands of the butler, Hollins. It was only this morning, as Kilgore prepared to leave for the day, that he went to his safe to retrieve one of the important documents related to his recent German work – only to find all of them missing, along with a number of other similarly confidential papers, and all of his cash reserves."

"Were there any signs that the safe had been tampered with?"

Mycroft shook his head. "None. It was at this point that Kilgore acknowledged that the situation was beyond the small efforts he and his staff had been making, and he realized it had crossed into the realm of national security. He sent word for one of my trusted agents, who went and made an examination. I don't say that you couldn't have found more than he, Sherlock, but he is thorough and skilled, and he saw no signs that the safe had been forced. It was locked when Kilgore went to open it, using the combination as he always does."

"Clearly, the wife has chosen to vanish on her own, and went to the safe to obtain funds to do so. Did she have the combination?"

"Kilgore says that she did not – but he admits that he had written it down and kept it in a box upon his dresser, and that she could have easily found it. 'She has all day to putter and prowl around the house!' he snarled when asked about it."

Holmes pinched his lower lip. "One can understand that she would take the money. But the documents? Of what use could those be?"

"None, if what we hear is true. According to the servants, who had her in sight every day – "

"Apparently not entirely," Sherlock Holmes interrupted.

Mycroft nodded. " – who *mostly* had her in sight every day, she had no friends or visitors. She made no calls upon people. When she shopped, it was always in the company of one or another of the servants, and they say she had no interactions of significance with anyone, other than when friends of her husband visited. She had no correspondence. Her only social life was with her husband's rare visitors, and they are all associated with him – people he grew up with, friends from Essex, and so on. He never invites anyone from work over for social gatherings."

"She sounds like a lonely princess locked in a tower," I said, offering my own small opinion. "Perhaps it's no wonder that she felt the need to escape."

"Possibly," said Mycroft. "Probably. But she seems to be helpless and without resources – other than the funds she took from her husband. He estimated it to be around two-thousand pounds."

Holmes whistled softly. "With that amount, she can purchase enough resources to get by for a while."

"If," I added, "someone doesn't take it away from her first."

Holmes nodded. "I suppose that you immediately checked the hospitals and morgues to see if such a woman has turned up."

Mycroft nodded. "That was my first thought – especially considering the nature of the documents that were taken. Some of them – Well, suffice it to say, Brian Kilgore had no business keeping that most-explosive material so carelessly in his home, but it's typical of how his arrogance and carelessness have increased over the years. At least if he didn't have sense enough to immediately seek help finding his wife, he knew to admit that the documents had been taken."

"I wonder," said Holmes. "You said that he opened the safe to retrieve one of the German-related documents – that he was taking it to work. Was it necessary that it be brought today?"

"It was. It needed to be reviewed by the Ministry."

"So, if he hadn't had to take it, then one would think that it might have been even longer still before he opened the safe and discovered the money and documents missing. But look at it a different way: Perhaps he actually learned on the day that his wife left that she had opened the safe and took the contents. He waited a week to report that his wife was missing. Perhaps he would have waited indefinitely, if his hand hadn't been forced by needing the German document today. What is it about her disappearance that has caused him to make his own private investigation, without involving the authorities? There's something about this that doesn't smell right."

Mycroft agreed. "Thus my detour to see you immediately. I'm not sure what this is about, but I want you to act as an independent agent – and you as well, Doctor, if you're willing – to see what you can determine. Why is Brian Kilgore willing to let the disappearance of his wife continue for a full week, until he had no choice but to report it? You both know that in my work, there's a danger of seeing plots where none exist, and reacting to something that is merely unusual as if it has great weight and dangerous importance. I have a sense that there's something here, something that needs to be understood, but possibly it needs to remain unofficial."

"I suspect," added Sherlock Holmes, "that it would be best not to alert Brian Kilgore of our involvement – which is another reason that it was wise for you to stop here, Mycroft, instead of summoning us to the Diogenes. Silence is the watchword within its walls, but that doesn't stop gossip from occurring when visitors arrive or depart, and if news was spread to someone that knows of the missing Kilgore documents that Watson and I were summoned there just after you learned about it, the connection wouldn't be a difficult one to make."

He frowned and reached for his pipe. "Clearly, we'll need to locate the wife, without any help from Kilgore or the servants. It's quite a three-pipe problem, and I hope that you'll both excuse me while I ponder it." And he began to pack tobacco into the bowl, dismissing us as if we had both already departed.

Mycroft wasn't surprised, and with a nod in my direction, he rose and walked out. I heard him lumber down the stairs, pausing halfway at the landing to turn back toward the street door, which I heard open and close a moment later. I too departed upon my own business, and Holmes was still seated, considering his options.

I arose fairly early the next morning, as the temperature was already becoming too warm to stay abed. As I went upon my rounds, I stopped by Baker Street to see if Holmes had anything to share, but he had already departed. There was no note, either informing me where he'd gone, or of any task that I might carry out for him before he returned. Since I'd known him, he'd had many cases that might initially be classified the same as this one – to find a missing woman. But each had presented different challenges and, based on what Mycroft had told us, this one had more than most.

The woman had no friends, so there was no one of that class to question as to Katherine Kilgore's state of mind, or her intentions, or what plans she might have made. There was no one to whom she might have turned for assistance, or for a place to hide. Worse, it seemed as if her husband had some secrets of his own, for he had kept her disappearance concealed for a week, only prompted to seek help when it could no longer be hidden that she had taken an important document that he needed at work that day.

I had much to keep me busy, but as mid-day turned to afternoon, my calls were complete and, dulled by the heat, I wandered my way slowly north and west, working toward 221b by tarrying in a bookstore in Marylebone, and then taking a turn through the Paddington Street Gardens, considering as I always did that a substantial portion of the place had once been a cemetery. With the stones long-since removed before it was turned into a park, I had to wonder upon whose graves I was treading. Surely they knew that visitors there meant no disrespect – or so the small boy still in me sometimes hoped.

I hadn't been back in the Baker Street rooms for more than ten minutes before Holmes also returned, dressed as a rather shabby laborer, but not of the sort that accumulates deeply staining grime, and not carrying the telling odors of a groom or someone who works in an abattoir. He nodded and disappeared into his room. I noted that he carried a rather full carpet bag, and I knew what that was about.

Since long before I'd met him, Holmes had taken a great deal of time to create for himself a number of other identities. Over the years, I've never been quite certain just how many of them there were. Some he assumed as needed, building the character by way of clothing and theatrical makeup for a specific purpose – an urgently sincere clergyman, perhaps, or a drunken groom. But others were more artfully and deliberately contrived: Leonard Stoke, for instance, a shifty gambler with irritatingly nervous hand gestures (which served as a distraction for anyone speaking with him), or Hobbes Bates, a surly dock laborer who drank much and spoke very little – and who stood around various dives of terrible reputation, listening to conversations around him long after anyone who should have known better had stopped paying attention to him.

To help establish these and other invented personas, Holmes maintained rented rooms for them at different spots in London, making sure to keep the landlords paid, and stopping by to visit just enough, in character, to be certain that these created individuals' varied existences were re-confirmed. These rooms, barely furnished and less livable, were not to be confused with those that he called his "hidey holes", also at a number of other locations across the capital. These, sometimes no larger than a big closet, were where Holmes kept disguises and changes of clothes so that he could drop in and hurriedly become someone else. He maintained all sorts of disguises, and also some his own "Holmes" clothing, so that he could instantly shed a disguise and re-emerge as himself, as needed. Sometimes, when he did too much visiting and identity-switching at any one place, the clothing of the different characters became unbalanced between different spots and had to be redistributed.

Holmes worked at maintaining these false identities and hiding places as hard as he did at keeping his scrapbooks caught up, and the re-balancing of clothing between them was something that he had to undertake on a semi-regular basis. Thus, him arriving that afternoon with a carpet bag, while in disguise, told me that he'd finished his day with some hidey-hole maintenance, and that he had returned home toting some of Sherlock Holmes's apparel. Soon he re-entered the sitting room as himself, pouring a drink at the sideboard, and then sinking into his chair across from me before the empty fireplace.

"Sometimes an ounce of luck is worth a pound of skill," he said, stretching out his feet before him on the worn bear-skin rug. I recalled when we had received the unwieldy thing, in lieu of a payment back in the early days when assistance toward accumulating that month's rent was much more important than having a rather inconvenient carpet. Now, a year after I had moved out, I found that I missed the thing.

"I take that to mean," I replied, "that in spite of the absolute lack of initial threads to pull, you reached forward and found one to pull anyway."

He nodded. "Years of throwing bread upon the water, so to speak, means that there are a number of individuals scattered about with whom I've had the opportunity to interact – some in positive ways, and just as many negatively. In nearly every case, I have some sort of leverage, where someone feels that they owe me for doing them a good turn, or conversely, that I have some influence because of knowledge of a past transgression."

I nodded. "And which type did you find with knowledge of the Kilgore situation?"

"No one within the Kilgore residence – but just one house away, as my disguised self sought any little job that might be tossed in my direction, I was happy to meet Emmy Hayes, now in her early twenties. Do you recall when we met her?"

I nodded. I did recall. The simple acknowledgement of that fact could not encompass all that was involved with her rescue from Dr. Ernest Hazelton's locked cellar in the house by Clapham Common, nor the horror when we discovered the two other girls also there who were beyond saving. My attendance at Newgate on the morning of Hazelton's hanging was not required . . . but I attended nonetheless.

"When I recognized Emmy," continued Holmes, "I surreptitiously introduced myself. She was surprised, but not as much as one might expect. She has seen a great deal, as you know, and it has sadly hardened her. She made an excuse with the very-tolerant cook, introducing me as an old family friend, and we talked for several minutes in the rear garden.

"She told me that the Kilgore house is a strange one. The servants there are very withdrawn, all having been brought down from the family's Essex estate in High Roding. They're all country folk with little inclination to get to know anyone not of their circle. The Kilgore servants step out in twos or threes, never alone and, except for rare instances in passing, the neighbors know nothing about them.

"'I believe that they're very religious, though,' Emmy told me. 'Several times when I've passed them on their way to some errand, I've seen that they've been clutching Bibles, the way someone else might hold a knife as defense when walking down the worst street in London.'

"While this was interesting, it didn't help me toward discovering where Katherine Kilgore might be found. But then, Emmy continued, her expression wise and knowing.

"'You're fortunate that I'm curious, Mr. Holmes,' she said. 'They're just a little *too* secretive over there, and since I've seen things in my life, I wanted to know *why*. You know about what happened at Hazelton's – it was only someone becoming curious that led you to save me. One of the girls at the Kilgore house– her name is Lizzy Boles – hasn't been in London for very long, and one day when she was in the back of the garden, alone and depositing the refuse, I spoke to her from our side of the fence and said hello. She was surprised, but she didn't shy away – I guess there's still some of the country girl in her. I saw her again a day or so later, in the same place, and after a few weeks, we were making time to visit, even if just for a moment or two. She seemed to need a friend, for she's an uneasy sort of girl, and there's something about that house that unnerves her, although she doesn't want to say why.'

"I considered whether to visit the Kilgore house in my own clothes, by way of the front door, and to find an opportunity to question the servants in order to speak to Lizzy alone, but I decided that she would probably be too unnerved, realizing as she would that the members of the

281

household would know that she had been questioned. Instead, I asked when Emmy might next expect to speak with Lizzy.

"'Why, later this afternoon – about two o'clock. Do you want to join us?'

"I did, and two o'clock found me waiting with Emmy in the mews by the refuse cans, out of sight of the Kilgore house. It was an unlikely opportunity, Watson: I had only minutes to not only meet the girl and gain her trust, but after doing so, to hear whatever she could tell me – all before she had to return to the house before suspicion was raised. It was seemingly impossible, and would have been, if not for the good will that Emmy had built up with Lizzy over the previous months. The poor girl's need for a friend is desperate, and thank Heavens she was willing to cooperate.

"Lizzy Boles is thin, with large dark eyes. She reminded me of a skittish fawn. When she saw me waiting with Emmy, I thought she'd turn and run, but Emmy called to her, and something in Emmy's tone calmed her. She stepped closer, looking back to make sure she was out of sight of the house, and then waited while Emmy introduced me under my true name. I knew that I only had a moment to make my case.

"'I don't know if you've heard of me,' I explained, 'but I'm a detective. I've helped Emmy in the past, and now I've been asked to look for Mrs. Kilgore after she disappeared last week. I've been asking around the neighborhood to see if anyone can tell me something that will help.'

"Emmy nodded encouragingly, and I saw that Lizzie paid close attention. I continued.

"'I had planned to visit the house next, fancied-up to call by way of the front door, but when I heard from Emmy that she could introduce us, I thought of speaking to you this way.' I took a step closer, lowering my voice even more from the soft tone I'd already been employing. 'I've heard that Mrs. Kilgore was unhappy. Did you see that? Do you have any idea where she might have gone?'

"My question about the lady's unhappiness presumed more than I specifically knew, but it became the new basis of investigation when the girl softly nodded her agreement. Then I struck gold when she began to speak, in a soft hurried rush, as if she could only say it once before time to turn and flee back to the house.'

"'She and I are distant cousins,' she said. 'Way back. My people served her people for ages. It shocked us where her parents died – and even more when she was suddenly married off to Mr. Kilgore.' Then she looked at Emmy. 'Are you sure that I can trust him?' she asked.

"Emmy nodded. 'He saved my life once. He'd do it again if I ever need it.' This was no time to show any false humility, so I simply nodded in agreement and did my best, disguised as I was, to look trustworthy. After the shortest bit of hesitation, Lizzy continued.

"'When I came here, Miss Katherine needed someone – anyone – that she could trust. She's . . . she's so alone, sir, and she doesn't know what to do! She was in the house all day, and they watched her – all of the other servants. They came down from Essex, too, but they're people that have always worked for the Kilgores. They're all members of the True Ones. They think that I am too, but I'm not. When I came to London, I didn't come alone – My young man followed after me. I manage to see him sometimes, when I go with Mrs. Abrams, the cook, to market. I slipped him a note, and he found out what to do – who could help us. It was he who found a place for Miss Katherine to go when she left.'

"She looked again at Emmy, her gaze once again seeking reassurance, even if the words remained unuttered. Emmy nodded, and Lizzie spoke one final time before fleeing back to the house.

"'Michael Naughton,' she said. "That's him. He found a job working the stables near the Langham Hotel. If he trusts you, then he'll get a message to Miss Katherine. That's all I can tell you. I don't know where she went – only that Michael found a place for her that he felt would be safe, and that it was better if she went alone. That's why I'm still here – for now." She glanced over her shoulder toward the house. "I have to go! Don't make me regret this, Mister Detective!' And she turned and was away without another word.

"Emmy told me that she had no knowledge of Michael Naughton, so after thanking her, I immediately worked my way toward the Langham. I observe, Watson, that you had a call this morning in Queen Anne Street – no, the signs are numerous, and not worth recounting – but you had no idea that I probably passed not three-hundred feet from you as you unknowingly went about your business.

"Naughton was easily found in the stables just south of the hotel – a fellow of about Lizzie's age, strapping and straight-forward and capable-looking. Just the sort to entrust with a lady's rescue. I explained who I was and what I was about, and then emphasized that I had been given his name by Lizzie Boles. I was emphatic to establish that I was not involved in some mission to drag Mrs. Kilgore back to her husband – especially if there was a good reason for her to have left him. I dearly wanted to ask him about the members of 'the True Ones', as mentioned by Lizzie, but I felt that it was more important to simply stick to the point of finding the lady, as once I've done so, the details can then be painted in.

"Naughton weighed my request for some minutes, a stern expression on his face as he did so. Then, without explanation, he told me to wait there in the mews, leading to the hotel. He was back in less than ten minutes, with instructions: I'm to be at the corner of Goulston Street and Whitechapel High Street tomorrow morning at eight. If all appears above-board, I'll be taken to a spot where more information will be revealed. Are you free to accompany me?"

The question was unexpected, but I indicated my agreement.

"Excellent. Be here at seven."

"Do you fear some sort of trap?" I asked.

"I always expect a trap, even if I don't fear it, but in this case, I doubt it. Rather, they are being especially careful, and while I don't know why, I sense that they have reason to be." He glanced at the clock and stood up. "I'm going back out. It pays to have as many cards in one's hand as possible, and a bit of further research into the Kilgores, along with whatever I can find about these 'True Ones', may prove to be invaluable."

"Do you think that my presence will prove to be objectionable?" I asked, rising as well, but Holmes stated that after all these years, it would be expected to have me at his side.

"In any case," he added, "if the lady or her protectors are fearful, your participation might serve to calm their nerves and do something toward gaining their trust. You are a most dependable fellow, Watson."

The following morning was overcast, but the heat remained. The air felt charged, as if a storm was brewing. There was a smell to the air, some warning for the deep and primitive part of the brain, carrying a message to stay close to shelter, for danger was near.

If Holmes felt it, it made no difference. He hurried me into the third hansom we found – after first confirming that I had my service revolver. That was how I knew he wasn't as calm as he might seem, for he knew that I'd long-ago learned to keep my weapon close at hand when venturing out anywhere. After so many years, we both had enemies.

As we drove east, Holmes was mostly silent, but he did explain that he'd been unable to find much else about the Kilgores or the "True Ones" since the night before. "When people truly keep to themselves," he explained, "it's difficult to find a way to breach their defenses. Hopefully we'll learn more this morning."

We were at the corner in central Whitechapel ten minutes before the appointed time, and we were still standing there at ten minutes after the hour as well. Holmes had done nothing to disguise himself, and he was wearing his noted fore-and-aft cap, making identification a certainty. From the time I'd known him, and from what I'd learned about his days long before that, he wore that had at all times, except when in disguise. Some have argued over the years that it had no place in the city, being a country hunting cap, but such thoughts had no validity or importance for Sherlock

284

Holmes. Social convention didn't matter to him whatsoever. This was the same man who had once shot the Queen's initials into the sitting room wall with a hair-trigger target pistol – to the high consternation of our landlady. That someone would forcefully state that he was improperly wearing a country hat and expect Holmes to care was ludicrous and meant nothing. For him it was functional, but I also believe that there was some memory associated with that type of hat which made him choose it. And most of all, he liked it, the way some chaps prefer a bowler.

Whatever the reason, wearing that hat made Holmes recognizable when he wished to be recognized. After another five minutes, when I was beginning to believe that we hadn't passed muster and that we would learn nothing new, a tall fellow in his early twenties approached by way of a nearby alley, bringing with him a short matronly woman closer to Holmes and my ages. She was dressed practically, nothing showy, but rather functional in a plain way. The young man, who I assumed to be Naughton from Holmes's description and recognition, spoke, saying, "This is Mrs. Smith."

He nodded toward the woman, with just enough emphasis on her name to indicate that it was likely false – and also that the young man was not given to comfortably uttering falsehoods. The woman glanced at both of us and said, "Mr. Holmes. And Dr. Watson, I take it?" Then she looked us up and down for another minute before glancing around.

"You both seem to be alone. We've been watching to verify it, but I still must ask upon your word of honor: *Are you? Are you both alone?* If we take you with us, can you guarantee, as gentlemen, that we will not be followed afterwards?" Then she awaited her answer.

"I promise this," said Holmes.

"I do as well," I said, adding, "Upon my honor."

She nodded, appeared to take one more instant to fully decide, and then said, "Very well. Come with me. Michael, you stay behind, to keep an eye out and make sure that no one comes along after us." Then she turned and walked toward the alley from which they'd initially appeared, moving without any hurry, apparently to avoid any increased attention.

Once she led us away, she moved with direct purpose, showing no inclination to look back to make sure we were keeping up. We turned this way and that, moving deeper into the warren of streets. I had no doubt that Holmes knew just where were at during any given moment, but I was thoroughly lost. If it had been a sunny day, I might have beheld some clue from the morning shadows to tell me our direction, but in the dim light, growing dimmer with every moment as some sort of atmospheric crisis approached, the inconclusive morning dusk was no help at all.

Finally, we stopped at a door in the rear of some anonymous and dilapidated two-story building. I had no doubt that if I followed the alley in which we found ourselves far enough to one side or the other, I'd discover a passage that would take me through to a street where I could determine our address, but that wasn't why we were here. Mrs. Smith seemed to read my thoughts.

"It will do you no good to remember where this building is located when we're done," she said. "This is just a place we've arranged for today's meeting. We'll never return here, and the people who run it know nothing." Then she opened the heavy metal door, which was unlocked, as if prepared for us. "Follow me." And she went inside.

As the door closed firmly behind us, she paused for a moment while our eyes adjusted. We were at the foot of a stairway leading up to an open doorway above us on the first floor. The light spilling down was just enough for us to see where to place our feet. There were no other doors at the foot of the stairs. The entrance through which we passed had only one terminal point: The room to which we were now climbing.

I was surprised when we entered it to see that it was mounded with all sorts of cloth. The air had the smell of fabric, blended together with many dyes into a strong scent that weighed heavily and tickled one's nose. There were bolts of all sizes and hues, piled and stacked everywhere. Across the opposite side of the room were a number of tall windows, high enough to see both the upper floors of the buildings across the street and the sky above them, now quite dark with an approaching storm. Even as I watched, the first heavy drops of rain hit the glass.

The room was lit by four equally spaced lanterns. I was glad to see that they were carefully arranged to stay away from both the bolts of cloth, and the many scraps and threads and pieces of fabric that littered every inch of the wooden floor, and most of the tops of the four large tables that were spaced around the room. On top of each table, beside the lanterns, were several large pairs of shears, all well-aged and missing paint from the handles. Beside them were a number of long straight-edges and wide-leaded pencils, apparently used for lining out and measuring and marking the cloth.

But all of that was seen in an instant and then ignored as Mrs. Smith crossed the room, leaving us facing her, another elderly lady, and between them one of the most beautiful women I have ever encountered.

Katherine Kilgore, for certainly it was she, was just a few inches over five feet. She was wearing a plain blue dress that only accentuated her female charms, and highlighted the lovely and healthy tone of her skin. Her face was round, and while her nose might not have been classically shaped, it fit perfectly with the arch of her dark brows, her wide-set and

286

direct-gazing eyes, and the bow of her lips. All of this was framed by the richest and darkest red hair I've ever seen, worn loose and down to her shoulders. In that rough and unswept setting, the room seemed to rearrange itself around her, and her presence was made more dramatic by the high windows which framed her, illuminating from the rear with the odd light of the coming storm.

My first impression was of the woman herself, and the striking beauty which had not been conveyed to us as a factor in the case. Then I saw two other things: One was that she had a terribly sad expression that, once noticed, could not be unseen, and which colored the perception of the rest of her. I was moved upon instinct alone to feel that she needed my help, and that I was the only one who could provide it. It was a unique effect, and I wondered if Holmes noticed it too.

The other thing that came to my attention, as my focus returned to the room around us, was that the elderly lady to Katherine Kilgore's right, opposite Mrs. Smtih, was someone that I recognized – a woman from one of Holmes's cases in the early 1880's who we had rescued from an abusive husband. She saw that I knew her, and she shared a small secret smile at my understanding, but then she shook her head, as if to say that I shouldn't acknowledge her previous troubles, or even speak to identify her. Somehow I knew from that look that she was telling me today's meeting should concern only the troubles of the younger woman at her side. I barely nodded that I understood as Holmes began to speak.

"Mrs. Kilgore," he began, and even from a distance of ten feet, it was obvious that the woman winced with discomfort upon hearing that name. "We appreciate that you have come from your place of hiding to speak with us. I want to assure you that Watson and I are not here to find you for your husband, or to drag you back. Neither of us have ever spoken with him, and he doesn't know that we're acting in the matter. Rather, we were asked by a representative of the Governement to find where you were, so that the documents you removed from your husband's safe can be retrieved." He paused for a few seconds, and then continued. "However, whatever my original intention was in that direction, I perceive that you need my assistance – our assistance. Are you willing to share with us your story? So that we might understand, and see what can be done?"

Mrs. Kilgore looked at Mrs. Smith, and then the woman beside her, as if to see if they had any advice or opinion to offer, but all she received was a small nod from the latter. Then she looked back at us, weighing the decision as if she were considering the wisdom of taking a step off a cliff. Finally, with a sigh, she spoke, her voice rich and low and tinged with heavy weariness.

"May we sit?" she asked. "My story – what I have to tell you will take a few minutes."

We all moved to arrange some of the work stools, the two camps facing one another but still separated, as if attending a wary negotiation. I could see that even though we were trusted to a certain degree, it was not absolute, and that Mrs. Smith and the other woman, whom I shall call *Mrs. Jones*, were both tense and alert, as if they might need to spring into action at any signs of treachery in order to hustle Mrs. Kilgore away to safety, should Holmes and I prove untrustworthy after all.

It was only Holmes's reputation that had earned this meeting, but their well-earned distrust of men in general, as we were to find out, overwhelmed any other goodwill.

"You must understand," began Mrs. Kilgore, "that I knew very little about anything of the world when my parents died. I've had a good education. I'm curious and well-read and keep up with the news, but in terms of real life – ? I knew that my parents were wealthy, but I didn't know how wealthy. I still don't. Men that I didn't know managed their affairs before their deaths, lawyers and accountants and supervisors and foreman, and they continued to do so after. I meandered through my days in ignorant bliss, and when they died, I was told where to go and what to sign, and then I was told that I was to be married – a business arrangement to blend two fortunes.

"Brian – my husband . . . It was already arranged that I would marry him by the time I met him. I was . . . it was medieval – in so many ways. I know that now – " She turned to look at Mrs. Smith, who patted her hand. "But I knew no better, and I married him, and only after did I meet his family. Then I was swept to London and placed into a fine house with servants who did whatever I asked – as long as that was no more than choosing what I wanted to eat, or which dress to lay out for the day. But the servants had come down from Essex, and had been with the Kilgore family for their whole lives, as had their parents before them, and it didn't take long for me to realize that I was now part of something most peculiar, and far beyond my small experience."

She was silent for a moment, as if considering how to proceed. Both of the older women watched her intently, but she didn't glance at either of them, instead marshalling her thoughts to continue.

"Since you've found me," she finally said, "then you must know something about the Kilgores by now – the facts, the history. The fame of Lord Benton, and all that he accomplished so many years ago. He still gets by on the credit that he earned as a great man in past generations. I've learned all of this as the dutiful wife, educated about the family into which I was abruptly placed. Lord Benton, Brian's father, is a famed man – or so

I've been told. I'd never heard of him until just before I was married. Have you met him? No? In person, he's terrifying. I found him so from the very beginning, and that was just a fraction of the terror I feel now . . . now that I know. He is nearly eighty years old, but he still has the size and vitality of a man half that age. He's tall and broad – much taller than Brian, his only child – and he has long white unkempt hair and a thick and tangled white beard. His fierce dark eyes are always angry, glaring out from under low and tangled white brows, and when he speaks, it's with the rumble of some dark raging Biblical patriarch bringing down God's curses from a mountaintop. His view of life . . . his view is one of rage and punishment and vengeance. I gather that he was once a person of great influence, but viewpoints changed and left him behind, and for that he's become much more bitter and hateful than when he was younger.

"He . . . Brian told me of his father's wives, how Lord Benton waited until middle-age to marry, and that his first wife was too weak to survive much past Brian's birth. Brian has always been a disappointment to his father. Smaller, less forceful. In spite of Brian's many successes, he has not impressed his father. And Brian . . . he might not have been a bad man, on his own, but he never had the spine to stand up to his father. Or the True Ones.

"Brian . . . Ah, Brian. He is so weak. In spite of our age difference, he and I have grown closer than I would have thought. We are confidantes in a way, but not like a true man and wife. He's never mistreated me, not once. No, it's his weakness that doesn't let him defend me."

She swallowed and took a deep breath, and I had an inkling that what was to follow would be even more disturbing than I'd expected.

"When I first met Brian, he was distant, awkward. I soon realized that he didn't want to marry me any more than I wanted to marry him. He was told to do so by his father, so he did it. I don't love him, and he doesn't love me, even now that we've known each other for five years, but he can talk with me, a luxury something that he never had before. After we married, he began to share things with me, gradually revealing the life in which I was now plunged. About the True Ones.

"That's what his father, Lord Benton, calls them – his followers. That's what they call themselves. I see that you've heard of them – or at least that you've heard that phrase. Does it mean anything to you? No? Then I must explain them, or the rest of the story – of why I had to escape – will have no meaning.

Lord Benton . . . he is a deeply religious man, very knowledgeable of the Bible and other ancient texts after a lifetime of intense study. But what he believes, supposedly associated with the Christian God, has very little to do with Christianity. The only part of the New Testament that he favors are the times in Jesus' ministry where punishment was a factor – such as when Jesus took a whip and chased the moneychangers from the Temple. Lord Benton looks upon other aspects of Christ's teachings as degenerate puniness. Love for the hurt and injured is just weakness and moral failure. Compassion? He feels that the weak and downtrodden don't deserve it, and that Jesus was a fool to instruct us to care for the poor.

"He favors the Old Testament, and the God of bitter vengeance and harsh punishment, instead of forgiveness and tolerance. According to Brian, this was molded by events in his life. As Lord Benton's influence grew within the government, he seemed to be unable to find what he wanted in his personal life. His first wife produced Brian, who he has always considered unworthy. Then she died, and he remarried several other times – and these women died young as well, all too soon and before they could produce another heir. By then, Lord Benton had used his influence to set Brian up on a path to success, but already Lord Benton's own star was falling, and that only made him more bitter. He retreated to his estate in High Roding and began to brood – that, and to fall deeper and deeper into his twisted Biblical studies.

"He began to formulate his own interpretations, and to share them with those around him – preaching to the captive servants who had been in the family for generations, and who were beholden to him with nowhere else to go, and who were overwhelmed by his certainty and his forceful and dramatic presence. With no one to tell them different, Lord Benton's beliefs took root, reinforced with each succeeding generation. His estate became more and more isolated, as he convinced everyone within it that they were following the only path toward salvation, as interpreted by him, while the world outside was racing toward irredeemable sin and destruction. But inside the estate, under the guidance and teachings of Lord Benton, they would be safe, following the truth. His truth. They would be the *True Ones*.

"He allowed Brian to remain in public life, and to live in London, feeling that he would be Lord Benton's agent, fixed in a place to affect public policy in the directions Lord Benton wishes it to go. Brian is completely under his father's thumb, and any State secret to which Brian has access is immediately shared with his father. Heaven only knows what the old man does with them, but he has remained in contact with people that he knew during his own public career – foreign diplomats from countries who are no longer friendly to Britain, but who take the time to curry Lord Benton's good will so that he will gullibly share information. They recognize him for what he is, an old fool, but they tell him what he wants to hear.

"Brian knows all of this – he himself is no fool, and he's seen it time and time again. And he's told me, and it has frustrated him to no end, but there's nothing that he can do about it, nor is he willing to oppose it. I listened as Brian shared all of these things, dutiful as I supposed that I should be, but for the longest time none of it meant anything to me – none of it seemed real or important. But then . . . Lord Benton began to take an interest in *me*!"

She swallowed, and Mrs. Smith patted her hand once again. She then left her hand in place, squeezing lightly. Katherine Kilgore seemed to have reached the crux of her story – the turning point that I already dreaded without knowing any of the terrible details.

"Brian and I have been married for five years," she finally said, her voice even lower and strained, "and we have yet to produce an heir to what Lord Benton considers his *dynasty*." She said it with distaste. "It . . . it became more and more of an issue, to the point . . . to the point . . . ."

It was here that Katherine Kilgore fell completely silent, unable to relate what happened next. But she had already told Mrs. Smith, who took over, quietly filling in the next part of the story.

"Are you gentlemen aware of the ancient custom of *prima nocta*?"

Holmes and I were silent, both struck dumb with simple shock at the implications of what had just been introduced into the conversation. When we nodded, Mrs. Smith stated, "Lord Benton has exercised that right. Repeatedly, declaring his son to have failed him, and casting him aside. Lord Benton has inflicted himself upon Katherine, and now she is with child – Lord Benton's child. She is to be the mother of her own husband's half-brother. She did not reveal to her husband or her father-in-law that she has been impregnated. Instead, she chose to flee."

"They do not know," Katherine whispered. "If Lord Benton finds out, and he gains control of my baby . . . ."

This information was staggering. In just a few moments, we had gone from hearing how the innocent girl found herself literally sold into marriage with an older stranger, and how a respected elder statesman had transfigured himself into the leader of his own harsh cult while sharing State secrets with foreign powers, all with the collusion of his spineless but also well-respected son. But the implications of this outrage upon the gentle and helpless woman now before us was too harsh to imagine. I realized that my fists were clenched in rage, and forced myself to loosen them and breathe deeply, as that anger had no place in that current setting. But I could find it again when needed – and I would find a way to make use of it soon. This I promised to myself.

291

Glancing at Holmes, I found that his jaw was clenched, and his lips so tight that they had vanished, leaving a thin white line. He nodded, as if understanding.

"As you know," he said, his tone low and steady but vibrating still with a kind of electric menace, "I spoke with Lizzie Boles, who told me how she came to London to be with you, Mrs. Kilgore, and how she worked with Michael Naughton to arrange for your escape." He looked toward Mrs. Smith. "I assume that he asked around until he found you and your group. He knew enough to gain your interest, and you decided that you could trust him. Then you worked to make safe arrangements for when Mrs. Kilgore managed to leave."

Mrs. Smith nodded. "I and some other women operate an organization for abused women – helping to spirit them away, and hide them, and find new lives for them. There are a number of us, more than you know, with many well-placed to accomplish our work. We move in secrecy, and most of us have been abused ourselves, so we understand how a woman feels in that situation – the helplessness, and the anger, and the desperation most of all. We understand, and we have learned how to do what needs to be done. Working in the shadows as we do, we can bring pressure to bear. I'm not ashamed to say that we use blackmail and coercion and threates when necessary to force the abusive men – usually husbands – to provide funds, and to release their wives from their bondage.

"Michael Naughton had passed a message to Mrs. Kilgore, by way of Lizzy, to bring what she could to help with any coercion that might be necessary. When I saw what she'd carried away – government documents of the greatest importance – I'll confess that I was a bit intimidated. These weren't simply letters or diaries filled, as we usually receive, with embarrassing accounts of men's nasty secrets that can be used as leverage. No, we had something far more weighty in our hands – and dangerous. Far too much for us. Frankly, I wasn't sure what to do, and it was almost a relief to find that you were inquiring about the matter, Mr. Holmes, for we wish to put the documents into your hands and be done with them.

"But the question that still must be asked is: Will that be the end of your involvement? Will you return the documents to the proper authorities, and then step away? I know you are too honorable to try and drag Mrs. Kilgore back to her husband and that wicked family – more wicked still than you yet know – but will you do anything else to help? Will you stand up to this evil, and help put a stop to it?"

If Holmes hadn't replied immediately, I would have, but he spoke for both us by saying, quietly and decisively, "Of course we will put a stop to it."

Mrs. Smith nodded firmly. "Good. Good. Then there's more that you need to know." And then she proceeded to relate what else she had learned, both from Katherine Kilgore, and then by way of her own subsequent investigations, once she knew where to look and what questions to ask.

"Over the last twenty years or so, as Lord Benton Kilgore has entrenched himself deeper and deeper into his own self-based religion – for that's what it's become – he has apparently come to believe that he is something between an Old Testament Prophet and the Hand of God. His bizarre sect consists of forty or fifty people, all living on his estate, and becoming more insular by the year. If he wasn't passing government secrets to foreign powers, he and those who follow him would probably only be hurting themselves, for they don't recruit, and they don't go forth and rain violence on their neighbors. Yet the harm he's doing to those who follow him is a just as much of a crime as if he has attacked his neighbors – a crime against society. Even if those in his cult are willing participants, it cannot be allowed to continue. You see . . . this is difficult to say and hear, gentlemen . . . Mrs. Kilgore is not the only victim of Lord Benton's exercise of *prima nocta*. Any woman on the estate, within the influence of his self-declared kingdom, is subject to the same violations. Women, teenage girls. Even . . . even children . . . ."

At that, Katherine Kilgore spoke, the last words I would hear her say: "I fear . . . I am afraid . . . that if I stay – that if he finds me – and if I have a daughter, that she too might be . . . She might be . . . That her own grandfather would . . . ."

More need not be related, although there was more, much worse, to be heard before we had finally seen the true portrait of Lord Benton Kilgore. When Mrs. Smith was finished relating all that she had learned, she looked at Katherine Kilgore, who simply nodded that it was all true. Meanwhile, Mrs. Jones quietly wept, overcome by the terrible visions that had been painted for us.

At the conclusion of our discussion, Katherine Kilgore handed us the missing government documents. Holmes promised that the situation would be "cleaned up" in a suitable fashion, and quickly.

"Best you don't worry about the details," he said. "It's time that a little Old Testament Justice be visited upon a certain blighted spot in Essex."

We thanked the three women, and they turned to leave, asking that we allow them some time to depart safely before we went back downstairs. As they walked past us to the door, Katherine Kilgore looked up and nodded toward us. Her eyes locked with mine, for only a second. It was a connection of some sort, one person to another, but if she was trying to convey a message, none that I could understand passed between us –

293

nothing except, perhaps, an infinite sadness at what she had been forced to endure at such a young age. Then, with almost an imperceptible nod, she turned away and passed through the door.

I never saw her again, and can only hope she and her unborn child, with the aid of Mrs. Smith and Mrs. Jones and their able band of like-minded women, found the good life that they both deserved.

Holmes and I waited ten minutes before descending. No doubt the ladies had hurriedly vanished within seconds, but I think that both of us, so lost in our dark thoughts, were in no hurry to precipitously rush forth.

Perhaps if we had, we would have been able to be in a cab and on our way by the time the impending storm was fully unleashed. As it was, the rain was well and truly falling when we reached nearby Liverpool Street Station, where we were fortunately able to hail a hansom almost immediately.

"Whitehall," said Holmes in a clipped tone, providing the address of Mycroft's office.

We settled into motion, and I could only pity the poor driver and his beast as the torrent dropped upon them. I thought about discussing what we'd heard, but the rain was too loud, and in any case, I could see that Holmes was deep in thought, the recovered papers clutched protectively under his Inverness.

As quickly as the violence of the rains had started, it rolled away, and the heat of the late June day enveloped us again before we reached our destination. The pavement steamed, and suddenly I felt as if I were back in the tropics. I was glad to reach our destination, the massive governmental structure where Mycroft Holmes's office was located. Inside it was cool, and soon we were ushered in to Mycroft's sanctum.

If Holmes's brother was surprised at the quick return of the Kilgore documents, he didn't show it. He was quite matter-of-fact, and seemed ready to perfunctorily thank us and then return to whatever was occupying his time, showing no interest in how the pages had been recovered. But Sherlock Holmes was not ready to be dismissed, and proceeded to insist on relating what we had learned from Katherine Kilgore.

Mycroft listened without speaking, his level gaze devolving into a scowl.

"I won't ask if you're certain," he said, "for it's the unsubstantiated testimony of one woman who feels that she is wronged, supported by two anonymous ladies who run a shadowy organization ostensibly dedicated to taking the side of other wronged women."

I started to protest, but Mycroft raised his hand. "Hold, Doctor. I'm not saying that I don't believe you. This actually explains a good deal about how certain information has been leaking to both our enemies and our friends. This path has not been considered, and if it's true, it's easily verified – and fixed."

"But the women?" I said. "And the children! What of that crime?"

Mycroft's lips tightened. "You know the age of consent in this country, Doctor, and how hard it is to prove something when relying on testimony of people like Lord Benton's followers, who don't believe that what he's doing is wrong, and wouldn't give him up to the law in any case."

Even as I started to cry out about the injustice, Mycroft and Sherlock Holmes both began speaking at the same time, each talking over the other.

"However," said Mycroft, "I hold a great deal of discretionary power to – "

"If you don't do something about this," growled Sherlock Holmes, "then I will be forced to – "

They stopped and looked at one another, their thoughts communicating back and forth faster than I could follow. Then Sherlock Holmes nodded. "How can we help?" he asked.

"Be at Liverpool Street Station at six o'clock. Armed, and in dark clothing. Sadly, daylight comes late this time of year, but my men will simply have to be more careful not to be seen while they fix the nets. You say there are fifty people at the Kilgore compound?"

"Approximately. So we were told."

"Then I'll have a special train made up accordingly to bring them all back to London for interrogation. Ostensibly, this is an espionage investigation directed toward Lord Benton, but our interrogators will certainly be on the lookout for other crimes.

I had more questions, and I'm sure that Holmes did as well, but we were dismissed, and so went to make preparations for our Essex campaign.

The special train from London to Chelmsford took seventy minutes. Mycroft had made sure that it had priority. There were five cars, but during the down trip, two were empty, to be used later when the entire population of Lord Benton Kilgore's estate, the "True Ones", were rounded up a brought back to London. The rest of the cars held a combination of Mycroft's agents and soldiers who would do what they were told, providing security while the agents sought evidence of Lord Benton's treachery and perversion. The interviews with the believers would scrape loose the additional charges.

Joining us was Michael Naughton, whom Holmes had gone out to find not long after we'd returned to Baker Street. The young man didn't say anything, other than to nod when he saw me, and none of Mycroft's men questioned Holmes about an addition to the troops.

At Chelmsford, we found dozens of cabs, wagons, carriages, and even vehicles borrowed from the nearby prison, all waiting to carry us swiftly north, the ten miles or so to High Roding, which straddled the road to Grand Dunmow. We never entered the village proper, however, before we veered east onto a narrow farm road, which the local driver on the lead cab assured us would run directly to the Kilgore lands. This was swiftly proven correct as we approached a great wall which led off in each direction. The road took us to a closed gate, which seemed to be unguarded. On the wrought-iron archway which spanned it from side to side, worked into the design, was the word *Naqam.*

"'*Vengeance*' in Hebrew," whispered Holmes. He gave one of his silent laughs which always boded ill for someone. "A word he'll understand after tonight!"

All of the wagons pulled to a stop, dozens of them, lined up behind us. Except for the whickering of horses and the occasional small ring of metalwork upon the tackle, or the soft landing of many man climbing down and taking formation, there was no sound. Even when the lock on the gate was cut, I heard nothing. Then the men slid by us like dark ghosts, infiltrating the grounds and vanishing into the darkening gloom.

I realized that Michael Naughton was not with us. Apparently he had gone on ahead.

Over the next fifteen or twenty minutes, with occasional outbursts of yelling or indination, the occupants of the estate were rounded up – men, women, and children. All that we found were servants of all levels – farmers, grooms, household cooks and maids, footmen and a butler of sorts. As Holmes and I moved among the various searches that were occurring throughout the house, we saw that Mycroft's men were accumulating quite a haul of documents that had no business being there. They had been left unsecured on Lord Benton's desk, and his night table, and in less-likely spots throughout the house. This was an egregious violation of the Official Secrets Act of the previous year, and I couldn't help but wonder if the presence of so many secret documents at this location, without any sort of permission, wasn't a capital offense. It turned out that it was.

Our search found the other evidence we sought, and members of the True Ones as well – some of whom were already ranting about their religious mania as if it were a defense against their seizure. All that we couldn't find was Lord Benton Kilgore.

It wasn't until all of the discovered documents and the estate staff were being loaded for the return to Chelmsford, where further questioning would begin, that we saw Michael Naughton walking toward us from the darkness behind the great house. He had his hand on what appeared to be a tall woman, shuffling along in a long dress, a bonnet pulled up over her head and a scarf wrapped over her lower face. She would occasionally fight him or try and pull away, and Naughton would stop, cuffing her on the head with a riding crop until she resumed walking. As they approached, I could hear her deep voice cursing, an unceasing litany of offenses and promised punishments.

Holmes stepped forward and ripped off the bonnet and scarf, and when Lord Benton – for it was he – lurched forward as if he was going to attack, still spewing forth his venom, I stretched forth my arm, showing him my service revolver, aimed toward his head.

"Be quiet," I stated, carefully enunciating, but it only made the old man curse all the more. He was a curious specimen – tall and fat, probably close to three-hundred pounds, his eyes red and pig-like, his white hair long and unkempt, and his unnatural carrot-tinted skin reflective of a lifetime of bilious and wicked habits.

My command to silence himself only served to make the repulsive old man angrier, and he lurched toward me in a rage. I swung my pistol, ensuring that he went to the gallows without most of his teeth.

"You've killed him," breathed one of Mycroft's men, standing nearby, shocked and staring down at the fallen man. The others pretended to look elsewhere.

I bent to check, and Kilgore was still breathing. But not for too much longer.

The damage that Kilgore had already caused by his indiscreet dissemination of information was severe, but it would have been much worse had some of the documents provided by his son been given to agents of other countries. That was enough to bring about a quiet capital conviction of espionage and treason. His son received the same sentence, and I could feel no sorrow for him either, as he'd known what he was doing, even if he'd been too weak to resist his father's influence.

In consideration for his efforts, and how this successfully concluded investigation did so much to prevent any number of security disasters, Holmes was offered a knighthood – not for the first time. And like the other occasions when he'd had no use for it, he quickly turned it down. "Art for art's sake," he told Mycroft and me when the subject came up. "And in any case, should I ever choose to accept such an honor, I wouldn't want it to be in association with this seamy affair. I'd never be able to hear of it without being reminded of that vile old sinner's terrible crimes."

Of more importance – at least in my opinion – was that it didn't take very long for one member, and then another, of the evil man's congregation to turn and reveal the terrible activities that had been going on at the remote estate. I was reminded of Holmes's dictum from the previous year that the smiling and beautiful countryside had a much more dreadful record of sin than the vilest London alleys. "Look at these lonely houses," he'd told me as we passed through a remote area, watching the lovely scene outside our train window. "Each in its own fields, filled for the most part with poor ignorant folk who know little of the law. Think of the deeds of hellish cruelty, the hidden wickedness which may go on, year in, year out, in such places, and none the wiser."

And none had been the wiser. – at least for the longest time – about what was occurring at that remote estate outside of High Roding. If not for the courage of Katherine Kilgore, finally forced to engineer her escape to protect an unborn child, how much more horror would have been visited upon those foolish people who had been convinced to submit to Kilgore's vile passions so that they could arrogantly and stupidly consider themselves the "True Ones"?

"Some of my most interesting cases have come to me in this way through Mycroft."
– Sherlock Holmes
"The Greek Interpreter"

"It is my belief, Watson, founded upon my experience, that the lowest and vilest alleys in London do not present a more dreadful record of sin than does the smiling and beautiful countryside."
"You horrify me!"
"But the reason is very obvious. The pressure of public opinion can do in the town what the law cannot accomplish. There is no lane so vile that the scream of a tortured child, or the thud of a drunkard's blow, does not beget sympathy and indignation among the neighbours, and then the whole machinery of justice is ever so close that a word of complaint can set it going, and there is but a step between the crime and the dock. But look at these lonely houses, each in its own fields, filled for the most part with poor ignorant folk who know little of the law. Think of the deeds of hellish cruelty, the hidden wickedness which may go on, year in, year out, in such places, and none the wiser."
– Sherlock Holmes and Dr. John H. Watson
"The Copper Beeches"

ur, also known as *prima noctis* or *ius primae noctis*, was a
in medieval Europe wherein feudal lords were allowed to
with subordinate women, in particular on the wedding nights

st: Back in the 1980's and 1990's, in my previous life as a
ator employed with a small little-known agency that's long
nvestigated two cases that had some coincidental similarity
t began as a routine background check to update the security
hose wife had left him. Digging deeper, I found that he had
rrelly and abusive habits, including cleanliness phobias
. When I finally tracked the man's wife down to interview
dition that she be accompanied by two anonymous women
ization that was keeping her hidden, for fear of retribution
vas lucky to get permission to speak with her at all, and the
out in the neutral territory of the upstairs floor of a sewing
day.
nvolved renewing the security clearance of an old man who
uclear defense industry since the days of the Manhattan
emely religious, and considered himself to be an amateur
ith his massive extended family on a farm/compound in a
vestigation revealed that he was a child molester of the
naving convinced all of those who were under his cult-like
ight to rape any of the women that lived there, including his
anddaughters.
the world. As Holmes knew, there is hellish cruelty and
l around us, year in, year out, and none the wiser.

299

Mathews of Charing Cross
by Ember Pepper

After the dark, blood-soaked winter of 1888 had passed, lightened only by the happy start of my blissful matrimony to my dear Mary, Mrs. Hudson once remarked to me on one of my sporadic visits to Baker Street that Holmes's routine had become strangely quiet. He was abed before eleven at night and up before eight in the morning. It was not a condition of his boarding agreement, but on those days of inactivity he often descended to the kitchen and spoke to our doting landlady while helping her here and there as she put together one of her hearty and serviceable breakfasts. I knew that Holmes, with my constant urging, had made a valiant effort to put away those appalling tendencies I so lamented when we resided together. We never spoke of it at length, but after he was free from the inevitably crushing weight of that dreaded morphine and cocaine concoction that had threatened to derail his illustrious career (and, frighteningly, his mind) in those dark years after 1888, it seemed he was aware that he needed to stay busy in whatever capacity he could, no matter how trivial, lest he slip back in to harmful habits.

It was thus very surprising to feel his hand shaking me awake a little after two in the morning on a chill Wednesday in the early spring of 1891. My wife had left for an extended stay in the country with Mrs. Forrester to see her previous charge through a mild illness, so I was once again taking up bed in the room of my bachelor days. I admit to feeling an initial surge of irritation at the sight of his shadow looming over me, considering I had a long day of patient visits ahead of me and needed to be well rested and ready in only five hours.

Holmes, ever prescient, sensed my annoyance. "Very sorry to knock you up so early. Lestrade felt this was an appropriate time to pay us a visit."

I blinked up at him blearily. "Is it regarding a case?"

"I cannot imagine he'd come to us at this ungodly hour if he didn't deem the matter to be of some urgency. You aren't obliged to sit in, of course, but I thought it best to give you that choice."

The blissful warmth of the soft mattress pulled me down, but I fought off my bed covers and shook my head, too tempted by the possibility of adventure.

Holmes left me to get dressed, and I shucked on some trousers and wrapped myself in my own worn out dressing gown.

Lestrade was seated in the wicker seat, drinking from his small hip flask.

Holmes stretched his bare feet towards the newly lit fire in the grate as I took my customary chair across from him.

"My apologies," Lestrade started, looking rumpled but wide awake. "Your landlady wasn't quite pleased to see me."

"That was readily deduced by how loudly she pounded on my bedroom door," Holmes responded ruefully.

Lestrade looked embarrassed. "Yes, yes. She made a hardy effort to be polite to me, so I worried she might redirect her anger towards you. I trust you have experience smoothing her ruffled feathers."

"You didn't come here from Scotland Yard," Holmes observed abruptly, as was his wont. "You came to us from your home."

Lestrade took the observation in stride, nodding. "True, though I had been at Scotland Yard late into the night." He fell silent, looking pensive.

Holmes cast me an amused but tired look after a protracted silence. "Not to rush you, Inspector, but the dear doctor here must decide if he needs to ask Agar to take on his patients."

Lestrade cleared his throat. "Did you read about the accident near St. James's Square yesterday?"

Holmes frowned. "No, there was nothing in the papers."

Lestrade hummed. "Might show up on the morning edition, if even then. On the face of it, the whole thing is a simple tragic accident, hardly worth reporting, I'm sure. Around nine in the evening, Mrs. Clara Mathews stepped in front of a four wheeler and was trampled to death." He cringed and then continued, "An unpleasant way to exit this world."

"Unpleasant and tragic, but I fail to see the mystery."

"Well, some in her social circle say that her behavior has been erratic the past few weeks."

Holmes cocked his head curiously. "Erratic in what way?"

"Speaking to herself – or rather, speaking as if to voices only she could hear. Paranoia and apparent hallucinatory incidents."

"Hallucinations and paranoia?" I interjected. "Those symptoms often indicate mental deterioration of the sort that could explain the action, whether accidental or purposeful, that led to her death."

"Indeed, indeed," Lestrade murmured, falling into pensive silence once again, pulling absently at the ends of his neglected mustache.

"Inspector," Holmes urged with startling gentleness considering his usual nature and the unpleasantly early hour, "who precisely is in this 'social circle', as you call it?"

"Mrs. Mathews' stepdaughter spoke to me." He hesitated. "As did my wife."

301

"Ah, I see. And how does your lovely wife know the late Mrs. Mathews?"

"They are friends from the Somerville Club. They met almost a year ago and got on immediately."

"And are you here seeking my help at your wife's behest?"

Lestrade, apparently sensing some censure in the detective's tone, flushed up defensively. "I'm here, and this may be difficult for you to understand, because I have come to trust my wife's instincts. And, yes, scoff all you wish, but her concern is my concern, and I wish to address it for her peace of mind."

Holmes stared impassively at him for a long while before speaking, his voice flat and carefully measured, "I didn't scoff, Lestrade." He looked into the roaring fire, his expression lit by the orange flames and the angles of his face sharply shadowed. He seemed deep in thought.

"Tell me about the Mathews' household," he said at last.

"Mr. Felix Mathews is from a decidedly middle class family from Horley. He's now some hoity-toity textile importer specializing in materials from China, since that's all the rage right now. He has a daughter, about thirteen, from his first marriage. The first wife died fairly soon after the birth of the child, I believe. He married Mrs. Mathews seven years ago, and they now live in a nice bijou flat in King Street."

"In wedded bliss?"

"As far as I know, but I'm more familiar with the lady than the couple."

"Have you spoken to Mr. Mathews since her death? Does he seem affected?"

"Gregson handled the case. He said Mathews seems affected, though he has admirable control over himself."

This time, Holmes did scoff. "Of course, I forget that it is difficult to gauge the depths of a gentleman's grief, seeing as he is expected to conceal it. Did the child have a good relationship with her stepmother? Did she seem affected?"

"She was a right mess, clearly in shock."

Holmes straightened, clapping his hands with resolved finality. "Very well then. I'm not sure what can be mined from this incident, but if it is sufficient enough to worry your better half, than it is sufficient enough for me to take a look. After all, if you cannot call on your friends for favors, who can you rely on?"

Lestrade flushed in surprise at being elevated to so high a status and stood quickly, coughing to cover the moment. "Many thanks, Mr. Holmes. Would you like to see the site of the accident?"

"Was this accident witnessed?"

302

"Yes, by approximately twenty people."

"Then, no. I don't think that's a priority. I likely don't need to prove she walked in front of the horses, but I do need to deduce *why*. I assume she hasn't been buried?"

"No, she's still at the morgue."

"We'll start there. We – " He gave me a questioning glance which I answered with a quick nod. " – will visit the morgue at ten. Perhaps the Good Doctor and I can get in a bit more sleep."

"That should do nicely," Lestrade agreed. "The funeral will not be for a few days. Thank you again, Mr. Holmes. I didn't know the lady beyond the few friendly visits she bestowed on my wife, but she seemed a nice, gentle-hearted sort, and if there is any trickery here, I'd like to get to the bottom of it."

Holmes steadfastly ignored my suppressed yawns on the way to the Westminster Coroner. I don't believe he went back to sleep after Lestrade left Baker Street, but he somehow looked impeccable in his smart morning coat and expensive embroidered waistcoat. I brushed self-consciously at the slight wrinkles in my hastily knotted cravat, but my friend didn't seem to notice, lost deep in thought as he stared out of the carriage window at the passing bustle of the London streets.

The recently built three-story brick building smelled of rotting flesh and the strange pickle-like odour of formaldehyde. Mrs. Mathews' body was behind a curtain on the second story. If I had forgotten the manner of her death, I was cruelly reminded of it when the sheet was pulled back to reveal her face and upper body. Even Holmes took a pause to gather himself before moving forward to examine the body in that minute but efficient way of his that was still so comforting after all these years.

From what I could tell from her bruised and disfigured face, she had been a wispy, delicate blonde. Her collarbones were starkly defined in a way that spoke of recent loss of weight. I noticed a strange look to the pinna of her ear and moved closer in my curiosity.

"Holmes," I said, "she has necrosis here."

The detective stepped next to me with his magnifying glass, his shoulder brushing mine. He hummed under his breath as he analyzed the blackish dead tissue dotting her ear. He scurried down the slab to gently raise her hands to peer at her fingertips and then raised the sheet from her feet and did the same to her toes.

"Did you conduct a full *post-mortem*?" he asked the coroner, Doctor Braxely, as he worked his way systematically up her leg with his face bent close to her skin.

303

Braxely, a seasoned medical man, gave me a disbelieving look and gestured towards the woman's crushed body. Holmes missed the expression and looked up expectantly.

"I did a cursory examination, of course," the man answered patiently. "The actual cause of her death was injury to her head. Her lung was also collapsed, but she passed before that injury could kill her. Her death was blessedly quick and hopefully painless."

"But you didn't examine her organs for any external toxins or for any diseases?"

"I did not think it likely that she expired due to poison at the exact time her head was being crushed by a horse's hoof," the man riposted with irritation.

Holmes let out a quiet, oddly pacifying chuckle and raised the corpse's hand up from the slab once more. "You notice the peculiar gangrene of her fingers and toes?"

Braxely frowned. "I did, and I noted it in my report but, clearly, it isn't related to her death."

"Not directly," Holmes murmured. "And, as the observant Dr. Watson pointed out, the necrosis affecting both her ears? Did you make note of that as well?"

"Young man, I make note of every detail I see during my *post-mortems*. Is there a point to this? You clearly suspect some correlation between these details and her existence here on my autopsy table."

"I do." Instead of elaborating, my friend gave me an expectant look which caught me by surprise. I floundered, wracking my brain for whatever response he was looking for. I settled on a vague but safe speculation.

"I imagine you believe that Mrs. Mathews was exposed to some sort of toxin." As the words left my mouth, the gears of the much slower and less-precise machinery of my own mind began to turn. "And you believe this toxin is responsible for her erratic and ultimately tragic behavior."

Holmes fairly beamed. "Spot on, Watson! The process by which your brain arrived at that conclusion may have been painfully plodding, but you arrived nonetheless to an extremely obvious deduction. Now, what toxin causes hallucinations, paranoia, gangrene, and possibly necrosis of some extremities?"

Braxely and I stared once again at one another. I was admittedly not an expert on rare poisons or natural toxins as Holmes was. Much of that esoteric knowledge was merely peripheral to my main general medical practice. From my acquaintance with Holmes, I was familiar with the common poisoning agents such as arsenic, and the more-recently discovered ricin, but these didn't have mental effects. Certain mushrooms,

I knew, could cause some vivid hallucinations. I was on the cusp of venturing forth that hesitant guess when Braxely saved me.

"Ergot poisoning," he asserted. "Of course."

"Ergot poisoning?" I echoed. "The fungus that can decimate livestock if they consume affected barley and wheat?"

"Precisely," Holmes confirmed. "The fungus *Claviceps purpurea*, which can grow on many food crops and often eaten by unfortunate animals can cause, among other things, visual and auditory hallucinations, paranoia and disturbed behavior, as well as gangrene of the fingers and toes. Necrosis of pigs' ears has also often been seen in affected animals."

"How would she have been exposed to ergot poisoning?"

Holmes shrugged. "It can grow on bread, particularly rye. She may not have known what it looks like. You know, there are some who speculate that the witch trials of Salem and Norway were caused by consuming ergot-infested bread. The women affected suffered convulsions and unsettling behavior that was interpreted by the highly superstitious and religious communities as being bewitched."

"All those brutal executions, and they may have simply been infected? How horrible," I sympathized.

"One man was pressed to death over the period of three days."

"I'm not sure I'd like to know the details of that."

Holmes smirked. "Fascinating process, actually. But inarguably gruesome – but Hullo! Here is Lestrade! Good morning!"

The official inspector stepped around the curtain, hat in hand, and attired in a somber black suit. He gave the body on the table a long, sad look before collecting himself.

"I told my wife that she did not suffer, but it is hard to imagine that is the truth when one looks on damage such as this," he murmured, almost as if to himself. He looked up at Holmes. "What's up, then? You look strangely satisfied for one standing in a morgue."

"I believe we have discovered some important details," Holmes announced with some relish.

"Do you care to share them with us mortals?" Lestrade snarled impatiently. He clearly had suffered a fitful few hours of sleep after departing Baker Street.

Holmes graced him with a patently patient look. "I'm endeavoring to help you, Lestrade," he reminded with gentle firmness. "You and your dear wife are evidently very distressed, so I won't bandy the usual barbs with you. But I urge you to remember that, in this case, I am on your side."

The inspector flushed with embarrassment and only nodded brusquely.

"As I was saying," Holmes continued, "Watson and I found some curious details while examining the late Mrs. Mathews' body. You'll notice the ears, as well as the fingers and toes."

Lestrade took a closer look. "Why, they're all black," he said, grimly.

"Dead tissue," Holmes replied in his languid fashion, but I could sense the undercurrent of excitement he was attempting to keep under rein.

The official looked at them with a puzzled expression. "I am no medical man, but an accident such as this wouldn't cause that." He glanced towards me. "Poison?"

I nodded. "It seems very likely."

"So she was drugged, panicked, and that's why she walked in front of the horses?"

Holmes frowned. "Not quite as simple as that. She may have been hallucinating, but we cannot be sure exactly why the accident happened. Furthermore, and more importantly, we cannot be sure how she ingested the poison to begin with."

"Well, clearly, someone fed it to her!" Lestrade exclaimed.

"This particular poison," I interjected, "could possibly be ingested accidentally. Perhaps in bread or some grains."

Lestrade ran an exasperated and tired hand across his face. "So we've circled back around to merely an accident."

Holmes shook his head. "As I said, we cannot be sure. It might be educational to meet the family. Do you believe they would be willing to speak with me?"

In my association with Holmes, I had often followed him into the dark underside of London. This experience had noticeably changed my perspective of the fine, expensive flats of Mayfair, St. James, and the like. The beautiful white-washed villa, the front built right to the kerb with a lovely little garden in the back, struck me with a strange deflated sense of sadness when I thought of all the dim, grimy little hovels populated with hordes of unfortunates in Whitechapel.

On closer inspection, however, I noticed signs of neglect as we stepped from the pavement up the small porch steps and rang the bell. The parts of the garden I could see were marred by a few freshly grown weeds, and the tall windows looking into the sitting room had a thin layer of dust that any respected butler or housekeeper would find unacceptable.

Servant issues became even more evident as the door was opened, not by a doorman, but a young girl wearing a clean, smart black dress and collar. Her eyes were red from weeping. I guessed this to be the deceased's stepdaughter.

Lestrade removed his hat hastily. "Maddie! I'm not sure if you will remember me, but your mother brought you to our home once –"

"Of course I remember you, Mr. Lestrade," she answered. Her voice was small and tremulous, but her manner was strangely confident for one so young. "Mama brought me to visit your wife a long time ago when I was still at the girl's school. She gave us lemon scones with clotted cream."

Lestrade forced a light chuckle. "Yes, my wife's scones are certainly memorable."

"Are you here because of what happened to Mama?"

Lestrade pressed her shoulder comfortingly. "Yes. This is my colleague, Sherlock Holmes, and our friend, Dr. Watson."

"Oh, Mama was so fond of following you in the newspapers," she told Holmes with wistful sadness. "She always boasted that she shared a mutual friend with the famous detective. I do think she was hoping to meet you."

Holmes blushed, as he was wont to do when unexpectedly praised. "I see. I admit I regret that meeting never happened."

"That's quite all right. I'm sure she would be just tickled to know you were here looking into her death." That same sad wistfulness marred her face. "You may enter, sirs, if you'd like." She stepped aside, and we shuffled into the wide hall.

"Maddie, why are you answering the door to guests? Where is your doorman?"

"Oh, Papa let all the servants go."

Lestrade started with surprise and hung up his hat. "All of them? Why ever for?"

"He said he didn't trust them not to gossip about Mama's . . . moments of distress."

"How long ago?"

"Approximately three weeks."

"You've been without servants for that long?"

She waved her hand airily. "I know how to cook and make tea, and Papa made sure everything in the house was in order." She brought us into a large sitting room and bid us sit as she bustled to make tea, despite our protestations.

She returned a few moments later with some fragrant tea and a small assortment of finger sandwiches. Holmes forwent the food, but sipped on the tea dutifully. I, on the other hand, never passed up some fortifying nourishment and chomped appreciatively on the cucumber sandwiches.

"This is very good tea," Holmes complimented.

"Papa makes his own blends. He says the Chinese know tea even better than we do."

"So I've heard," Holmes agreed. "May I ask you some questions about the days before your mother's death?"

She folded her hands primly across her lap. "I've already told the other inspectors everything, but I'll answer any of your questions, sir."

"Were you close to your stepmother?"

Grief suffused her innocent features. "Yes, we were very close. I don't remember my own mother. She died when I was a baby. Mama – my stepmother – took care of me and loved me as her own."

Holmes gave her a gentle smile. "She sounds lovely. Inspector Lestrade here tells me that you spoke about some strange behavior of hers recently."

She pressed a fretful hand to her forehead and stood, pacing behind the settee as she spoke. "Oh, it's terrible to remember, but she would sometimes talk to herself, even argue with herself."

"With herself or possibly with voices she was hearing?"

"Is there a difference?"

"A minute one, but yes."

"It seemed she was talking to someone else. Once or twice, she was convinced there was a monster in the house. She kept saying, 'Don't you see it, Maddie?' and trying to hide. It was horrible to watch because she was normally so sensible. She was often dizzy, as well, and complained about her muscles aching."

"Did she ever faint or convulse?"

"Once, during tea, she began to shake violently. I also thought that maybe I was to be a sister soon because she was often sick in her stomach." She flushed a bit. "If you understand . . . ."

"It's all right," Lestrade reassured. "You're doing very well and being very helpful. Now, think carefully: Did anything else strange happen?"

"Well, one time right before bedtime, I caught her trying to leave the house in her dressing gown. It was odd because she seemed distressed, as if she didn't want to leave, but couldn't stop herself. I pleaded with her and finally told her she simply couldn't go outside dressed as she was – " She made a firm chopping motion with her hand looking so much older than her tender years. " – and she immediately listened to me. Like I was the mother. It was strange and upsetting."

Holmes gave me an intent look. "Extreme compliance? That doesn't fit the pathology of ergot, as far as I know."

"Ergot?" the young girl queried.

"It is a toxin," I explained.

Holmes nodded in confirmation. "We suspect your mother may have been ingesting it, perhaps in something she was eating or drinking accidently. You say your father blends his own teas? May we look at them?"

All colour drained from the girl's face. "Do you mean to say we may have been inadvertently poisoning her this whole time?"

"That isn't exactly what we mean," Holmes assured her, already standing, "but I would like to take a peek to be sure."

Following behind her, I could see one of the small pearl buttons that clasped the high neck of her collar was undone, likely overlooked as she had attempted to dress herself without the aid of a lady's maid. There was no appropriate way to inform her. I saw Holmes's own look catch on the detail, but he had enough common sense to leave it be as well. Such a small thing made me feel a surge of sympathy for the girl, now all alone with her father and no female presence to guide and support her.

"Do you have any other family?" I asked.

"My grandmother – my father's mother – is still alive. She lives where my papa used to live – in Horley, out in the country – and he sends her money. My stepmother has a sister that lives in Bristol whom I love very much. She has asked me to come stay with her for a short while, but I can't think of leaving my father while he is grieving."

She brought us into the large kitchen and opened a cupboard, removing an ornate floral tea caddy. Inside, were five matching tea containers, tightly capped.

Holmes pulled them free without asking, opening each and sniffing them carefully. He went so far as to shake a few leaves free from each, poking and separating them with his finger and examining them with his lens. Young Maddie watched patiently, a curious but worried expression on her face.

"There is no ergot here," Holmes declared at last. "Only a very interesting mix of Assam and fruit leaves. Also green tea – it seems your father is highly influenced by the East." He smiled at the girl and brushed the leaves into the waste bin.

Maddie looked understandably relieved to hear this.

"Did your mother have a favorite café or bakery? Some establishment she frequented often?"

"No, sir. We often ate at home. She would occasionally go to the A.B.C. Tea Shop by her club, but that wasn't often. I went a few times with her, both to the shop and the club. I had a lovely time with all those bright women!"

309

A key turning in the latch of the front entryway brought us up short. Holmes quickly rearranged the tea caddy and returned it to its spot. He pressed a finger to his lip conspiratorially.

"Now, Maddie, let's keep this little tour between us for now. No need to upset your father any more than he already is."

By the time we retook the sitting room, her father was opening the door from the hall and entering. Naturally, he looked startled to see three strange men in his home.

Holmes broke the ice by striding forward with that casual charm he could adopt like a second skin.

"Mr. Mathews, I presume? My name is Sherlock Holmes. This is my friend, Dr. Watson, and Inspector Lestrade of Scotland Yard. Your lovely daughter here was just about to tell us when we could expect you home."

Even though Holmes's manner managed to put him a bit at ease, Mr. Mathews still clasped his outstretched hand with guarded weariness. "Is that so? You're the private detective?"

"Consulting detective," Holmes corrected smoothly. "Your wife was acquainted with Inspector Lestrade's wife. We're merely here in assurance to her."

"I see," our host responded carefully. He was a man of middle age and wore a face that, from certain angles, made one wonder what any woman could see in him, and from other angles, could pass by without attracting any special notice. His dark hair was thinning, and I could see that he was contemplating combing it forward in order to disguise it – an ill-advised choice. His clothes were expensive, though a few years out of trend, and his waistcoat cut from fine, Chinese floral silk.

"Inspector Lestrade, you say?" he continued. "I dealt with your colleague about this . . . accident. Gregson, I believe his name was."

"And we mean to cast no aspersion on Gregson, believe you me," Lestrade said clumsily. "He is, in fact, a superior detective. But he did mention in his report that your wife had been demonstrating some odd symptoms in the last few weeks."

"Of course she was," Mathews responded testily. "She obviously suffered from a mental break. After all, gentlemen, she killed herself."

I gently touched Maddie's arm and suggested she leave us alone. While I didn't want to think too harshly on a man who had recently suffered such a great loss, such a blunt statement shouldn't be uttered in the presence of a young lady. Maddie's face had gone white, but she nodded with admirable equanimity and left the room.

"Forgive me, sir," Holmes began quietly, "but the symptoms described don't align with one in a suicidal state of mind."

"What does it matter? One could hardly stage horses stomping her to death or the twenty or so witnesses who saw it when it happened." The man's voice was angry, and I felt this interview wasn't going to be productive.

"Who said anything about staging her death?" Holmes asked sharply, his gaze like a hawk.

"No one did, sir, but you are clearly implying that the events weren't so cut and dried. And if they aren't cut and dry, then they are complicated. I won't have you filling my daughter's head that her mother's death was anything but a tragic accident. Nelda was unwell, and I curse myself that I didn't get her help in time. Now, I'm a very busy man, so if you don't mind?"

A few moments later, we found ourselves on the small porch, the black mourning wreath rattling against the closed door.

"Hmm," Holmes grunted under his breath and took off down the street without a word. Lestrade and I followed quickly.

"Well, Mr. Holmes," Lestrade demanded, "what are you thinking?"

"He is responsible for his wife's death," Holmes responded simply. "It was no tragic accident, but a premediated murder. And I will find out how he did it, mark my words."

"I can't say I disagree, but what makes you so certain?" Lestrade demanded.

"Her symptoms indicate that she was poisoned consistently over a period of time. It's only logical to conclude that it was someone in consistent close contact with her. Her only company the past few weeks had been her stepdaughter and her husband. Now, I highly doubt young Maddie is capable of such a dastardly deed."

"There seems to be no motive," Lestrade mused. "He is obviously doing well financially, if the material of his suit is any indication."

"Eh? I didn't realize you had an eye for high-end fashion, Lestrade," Holmes riposted good-naturedly.

"Well, clearly not as much an eye as you do." It was meant as a slight, but the barb had the opposite effect on Holmes, who pressed an exaggerated hand to his chest and smiled.

"My dear Lestrade! I had no idea you held my attire in such high regard."

Flustered, Lestrade struggled to regain control of the interaction. "Stop fishing for compliments, Mr. Holmes."

"I have to fish," Holmes waved off airily as he continued down the street. "Watson is frugal with his praise, always scolding me about this or that."

"I can't imagine why."

"Ha! In any case, my suits benefit greatly from a well-skilled tailor. I did some work for a prominent figure, who shall remain unnamed, and of the many gifts I received for my services was free access to his tailor. I have his card here. Tell him Mr. Sherlock Holmes sent you, and you'll likely get a free fitting." Holmes pulled out a card and held it between two fingers.

Lestrade took it, red-faced. "Huntsman?" he exclaimed. He cocked a curious eyebrow at my friend. "A prominent figure, hmm? I suppose I know better than to ask."

Holmes tapped his nose conspiratorially. "One lesser-known advantage to my chosen career, Inspector."

After lunch, Holmes emerged from his room and, after gulping down a cup of coffee, departed without a word.

I put my notes on the matter of the three beryls case in some sort of rudimentary order, and then settled down to catch up on the newspapers before dinner.

Holmes returned a moment before the clock struck four o'clock.

"Try to guess what I discovered, Watson!" he exclaimed, barging into the room and startling me into an unmanly gasp of surprise.

I straightened my copy of *The Times* with a huff. "That the Earth revolves around the Sun?"

He drew up short, giving me a wickedly amused glare. "We'll have that debate for a later time. No, I discovered that our dear Mr. Mathews is in dire financial straits." He plopped himself on his favourite armchair and propped his feet up on the raggedy footstool. "I made a quick visit to his import warehouse and it was – " He made cutting motion across his neck. " – dead. Empty. There is no importing going on there. It appears to have been derelict for at least a year."

"But his clothing is very expensive," I protested.

"And who knows how much coin he spends to keep up that façade. You may not have the 'eye' that I am accused of having, but surely you noticed that his waistcoat had been mended more than once and was a season out of style. Of course, to a casual observer, those small details are easy to overlook. I doubt many people know the reality of the state of his business. And I unearthed more salient details. Someone – I'll give you one guess as to who – recently took out a life insurance policy on Mrs. Mathews from the Bank of England – for one-thousand pounds!"

"So we have motive."

"And I think I have a clear idea of the means, thought it may require a trip to Horley, if you're up to it."

"Horley? Mathews' childhood home?"

312

"I began to wonder when I saw the empty warehouse: Where does Mathews go every day if he isn't going to his job? He could be spending time at a club or engaging in some pleasurable activity, but I also checked at Charing Cross Station and discovered that a person of Mathews' description regularly purchases a ticket to Horley."

"How regularly?"

"At least three times a week for the past two months. One ticket seller took particular notice of the Chinoiserie style of his clothing."

"How does this help if you think he poisoned his wife with the tea?"

"I need to get my hands on that tea to prove my hypothesis. Perhaps he has stored it somewhere safe when not in use. Check the copy of *Bradshaw* for the earliest train, please."

We were in Horley as the sun began to dip close to the horizon, spilling pinkish hues across the sky. The older Mrs. Mathews lived in a little two-story brick house that seemed to embody Mathews' modest upbringing. There was an enclosed garden in the back that gave way, through a small waist-high stone wall, to an expansive field of wildflowers. Holmes stared at it for a long moment before nodding to himself and opening the small little gate to enter the front yard.

An older woman, clearly the housekeeper, answered with a gruff greeting, her voice marred as if she had spent her whole life drinking hard spirits.

"Good evening," said Holmes jovially, "My name is Peterson, and this is my associate, Mills. We're horticulturalists visiting your town to view the spring wildflowers. We noticed your beautiful yard and wondered if we could take a closer look. Is your master or mistress at home?"

"Eh?" the woman barked as if hard of hearing. "The flowers?"

"Yes, ma'am."

"Come in, then. I'll get the mistress and see if she wants to bother coming down to speak to you."

Holmes smiled brightly. "Many thanks."

We were shown into a small drawing room dotted with plants and an old sheep dog that only lifted its heavy head at us before rolling over and going back to sleep.

The minute the door was closed behind us, Holmes was up and pressing his ear to it. Apparently satisfied that the wizened housekeeper was out of the hall, he opened the door and gestured for me to follow him.

I was fairly certain that the only ones in the house were Mathews' mother and the elderly housekeeper, so I felt no mortal fear at being caught sneaking around, but as a gentleman, I still felt a spike of panic at the idea of being detained by the local constabulary who, I'm sure, wouldn't look too kindly on two men skulking about a widow's home uninvited.

313

Holmes headed straight for the back of the house, and we swung through the green baize door into a small, serviceable kitchen. Holmes immediately began opening and closing cabinets, and I followed suit, desperate to be back in the drawing room before we were caught in this embarrassingly inappropriate behavior.

"Holmes!" I whispered urgently, kneeling down to the cabinet near the sink. "Look at this." I pulled out a small tea container that was the exact same floral design as the one we'd seen in Mr. Mathews' kitchen.

"Hullo!" Holmes said excitedly, snatching it from me. He made to open it when his movements were arrested by a shuffling in the room above us and a creak of an unstable step. He shoved the tea into a pocket of his morning coat and rushed me out of the room.

By the time the drawing room doors were opened to let in the mistress of the house, Holmes and I were posed respectably in our chairs.

Mrs. Mathews and her housekeeper made an apt pair, both a bit haggard and distrustfully puzzled by our appearance in their quiet home.

Holmes introduced himself under our assumed names once more, ever the gentleman even in the face of the lady's irritation and disbelief.

"We don't get many visitors up here," she squinted at us. "You're horologists, you say?"

"Horticulturalists. We merely request permission to walk about your garden and beyond to look at the flowers."

"Bit odd, isn't it?" She snorted in the most unladylike way. "Never heard of men eager to frolic in flowers."

Holmes laughed in that light manner that was efficient at putting people at ease. "It's our specialization, ma'am."

"Well, if you want to traipse around the foliage, go right ahead. Just mind the rose bushes near the back door because they're delicate, and I don't want you ruining my hard work."

"Of course, Madam." Holmes tipped his chin, and we were shown around the back and let into the garden like two schoolboys let out to play.

"Ergot doesn't grow on flowers," I commented as we passed through the walled fence and into the field.

"No, it does not," Holmes agreed, "but I thought I saw something interesting . . . ." He trailed off, and we waded through the brightly spotted field until we came to the side of the house where stood an odd tree with upside-down little trumpet flowers drooping towards the ground.

"What is that?" I asked.

Holmes pressed a finger to one of the buds, his face furrowed in concentration. "Angel's Trumpet, I believe. They are usually native to the South American continent, though it can also grow in China."

"I've never seen it before. What an odd-looking tree."

314

"It's also called Devil's Breath. When ingested, it can cause a host of symptoms, including a loss of free will. I wasn't expecting this, but it certainly adds shape to the mystery."

He glanced back at the house, noting the curtains closed tightly, and removed the pilfered tea container to look at it closely. He smelled the contents carefully and shook a few leaves into his palm, his face scrunching in both distaste and satisfaction at what he had evidently found.

"Look at this," he directed me, pointing to a small scratch on the side of the container. "I saw the same scratch on one of the tea containers in Mr. Mathews' kitchen. It must be a small defect in the tea caddy. When the container is pulled from it, some imperfection nicks its side. It's an easy enough thing to check. Come, we'll wire Lestrade at the train station."

We sent a telegram for the inspector to meet us in London at the Mathews' townhouse. On the train, I asked Holmes what he found in the tea. He once again shook some of the very fragrant leaves into his hand, and I leaned over as he delicately shifted them with an elegant finger. "Here, that black long grain? That's ergot. But here – also smell this." He offered me a small, dried flower petal.

"It's very musky," I confirmed.

"That's Devil's Breath."

"So ergot *and* this other poison? But Holmes, that tree was old. Either he has great foresight, or he conveniently had that poison already on hand at his mother's home."

"Mmm," Holmes murmured, deep in thought, "It makes me wonder if another look into the first Mrs. Mathews' death isn't in order as well. I wonder if there was any financial benefit to her passing."

"You think he's done this before? He marries women and then murders them for their life insurance?"

"I don't know if he plans it, but once you get away with a crime, you may be tempted to try your luck twice. His business is failing, he's on the brink of economic humiliation. Perhaps he leaned back on old tricks."

"First, we have to convince Lestrade that he's the villain behind this death."

"That won't be hard. The tea is clearly made to be exchanged without notice. It contains poison. Any amateur chemist could prove that, and I'm no amateur. A confrontation is in order, and the confrontation is the most exciting part of our work, wouldn't you agree?"

The confrontation ended up being delayed. Our trio was invited into the Mathews' home by a newly hired doorman who, with much more dignity than the housekeeper in Horley, escorted us back into the clean sitting room. Like before, Holmes waited a brief moment before herding us with stealth into the kitchen.

"*Déjà vu,*" I murmured.

"Eh?" Lestrade queried as we entered the kitchen, doing our best to be quiet. "What is that?"

"It means '*already seen*' in French," I explained. "A philosopher speculated recently that a long forgotten perception can trigger a feeling a reliving a moment."

Lestrade chuckled. "Odd. It's usually the other one explaining these intellectual concepts to me."

The "other one", Holmes, was busy opening the tea caddy. He beckoned Lestrade to him with some impatience and demonstrated that the two containers had identical scratches, fitting perfectly into the tea caddy.

"This one," he held it up, "contains harmless green tea. This one contains multiple poisons that cause hallucinations, compliance, and overall mental deterioration."

Lestrade sighed. "It's always the husband, isn't it?"

"Patterns are patterns for a reason," Holmes confirmed wryly. "Come, let's see what Mr. Mathews has to say for himself." He pushed the caddy and the extra tea container further back on the counter, clearly setting it up for the *denouement* of the whole affair, and we reentered the sitting room to await our prey.

Our prey remained elusive. After the clock had ticked by a quarter-of-an-hour, little Maddie once again received us with that restrained grace that I found so admirable.

"My dear," Holmes greeted kindly, "we were expecting to speak to your father."

"I'm afraid he isn't here," she apologized. "A telegram came through about an hour ago, and he left in a hurry."

"He didn't tell you where he was going?"

"No, not a word. He seemed very worried." An anxious look crossed her face, and I felt a surge of sympathy for this girl whose recent loss was about to be compounded.

"Do you have the telegram?" Holmes asked eagerly.

"He shoved it into his pocket as he left. Is something the matter?"

He waved off her concern with practiced ease. "No, not at all. Do you mind if we wait for a little longer to see if he returns?"

"Of course. Would you all like something to eat? Some tea?"

Holmes gently took her shoulder and, with a skill that I could never quite understand, managed to herd her towards the door without her realizing she was being herded. "No, no, dear. We have no wish to inconvenience you. Please, feel no need to keep us company."

She looked undecided for a moment before nodding, her tiny hand going to the door handle as if directed by a higher power. That higher power being Holmes, of course. "I'll be just upstairs. If you need me, ring for the doorman."

"Ah, we noticed you have expanded your household."

"Yes, father hired Mr. Hardy yesterday. I predict we'll have a full staff again very soon."

"That will be well for you," I commented gently, "to have a lady's maid and a governess to rely on"

Sadness marred her face and tears filled her eyes. She blinked them away valiantly. "Yes," she agreed hastily. "Good evening, gentlemen."

"Dear Heavens," I lamented after she had gone. "I didn't mean to upset her."

"I don't think your words have pained her any more than her recent loss, Watson," Holmes reassured.

"Does she have somewhere to go?" Lestrade asked, retaking his seat. "I mean, when this is all said and done, her father will likely get the noose."

"She has an aunt by marriage," I said. "I hope she will take her in."

"That telegram was from his mother," Holmes announced, crossing his ankle over his knee. "She must have been sharper than I gave her credit for and wired him that two men were looking about the house. She may have even noticed the missing tea."

"Are you saying she is an accomplice?"

"I wouldn't be surprised," Holmes shrugged. "I'm not so sure how we could prove it."

"So, was the trampling merely an accident?" Lestrade asked. "He may have been poisoning her, but I'm not sure what evidence I can bring against him for murder."

Holmes scowled. "He routinely induced her to take mind-altering substances, one of which makes a victim extremely compliant, and likely ordered her to wander outside at a danger to herself. I don't think it mattered much to him exactly how she met her fate, but in that state, time was working against her. A fall, a rough villain in a dark alley, or horses' hooves – in the end, he would have his money and a chance to restart his business. People have gotten hanged for less."

"If he rushed to Horley, we likely passed him on our way back," I grumbled. "If he left an hour ago, as Maddie said, we have a bit more of a wait on our hands."

A faltering thud from the other side of the sitting room door drew us all up short.

317

Holmes stood and flung the door open. Maddie stood at the bottom of the stair, gripping the balustrade with a grip so tight her knuckles were white.

"My dear! What ever is the matter?" Holmes asked.

She pressed a hand to her stomach. "I do not feel well, sirs. I think I may need a doctor."

As a doctor, I moved forward and steadied her. "How are you feeling? What's bothering you?"

She looked very pale. She licked her lips a few times. "I feel sick to my stomach and shaky. I think I may faint."

Holmes circled a supporting arm around her waist as I checked her pupils and pulse, which was beating frantically and erratically. She faltered, only staying upright with our help.

"When did you start feeling this way?" I asked, pressing my hand to her forehead to gauge her temperature.

"Just now. I was sitting at my desk, writing, and the room spun." She held out a hand as if she had never seen it before. It was shaking terribly.

Holmes made a sudden grunt, a distressed sound that I had never heard from him before. "Maddie," he asked calmly, though I was familiar enough with him to hear the undercurrent of urgency in his tone, "did you make yourself some tea?"

"Yes, I brought a cup to my room. It tasted funny, but I put more milk in . . . ." She trailed off, swaying.

Panic stabbed at my chest. "Holmes – !"

"All right, my dear," he interrupted, his voice soothing. "Perhaps a brief stop at the hospital may be in order. Don't you agree, Watson?"

I took her other arm as Lestrade hurried outside to fetch a cab. Holmes darted to the kitchen for a moment before returning.

"Am I in trouble?" the young girl wailed, clearly sensing that she was in dire straits.

"No, no, not at all," I replied, guiding her down the hall. "But perhaps a bit of antimony and a few hours of observation are in order."

She followed with a malleable passivity that was troubling. It was fortunate for her that she was in the company of trustworthy men. We bundled her into a cab and headed towards Charing Cross Hospital. She put her head against my lapel and lapsed into a dumb silence that I couldn't break her out of. Her pulse was still racing, and I wondered if she was even aware of what was happening any longer.

"Mr. Holmes," Lestrade whispered, "will she be all right?"

"She should be. Prolonged use is when it becomes more dangerous, but Watson is right. She should be carefully observed for a few days." He clenched his fist. "I'm such an imbecile!" he castigated himself. "I never

318

should have been so offhand with whole thing while a young lady was in the house. You know I'm fond of the dramatic finale, Watson, but please remind me from now on that it isn't the most important consideration."

"Let us not focus on fault," I murmured, "Let's get her seen to."

The waiting room of Charing Cross Hospital in Agar Street was habitually crowded, but upon relating the nature of our predicament to the nurses, the young lady was immediately escorted into the inner room full of curtains and beds. I accompanied her to the private area, removing my coat and helping the nurse administer an emetic, the results of which were always unpleasant.

After the contents of her stomach were expelled. I sat with her for a few moments, monitoring her pulse. She began to stir, asking for water and answering my questions with admirable calm. Once I was relatively sure she was out the woods, I left her to the fine care of the nurses and retreated to the waiting room.

Holmes had disappeared into the administration office and was just retaking his seat when I returned. "I dashed off a telegram to Mathews' home in London and another to his former home in Horley. I imagine he'll be here soon. I also sent a wire to the aunt in Bristol. I foresee she may be needed."

After roughly a half-of-an-hour, a small-statured, bespectacled doctor approached us, thanking me for my help and reassuring us that the young patient seemed to be doing better, but they wished to keep her for observation for at least a day.

"We aren't her family," I explained as we introduced ourselves. "Her father should be here soon – "

"Speak of the devil, and he shall appear," Holmes murmured, looking over my shoulder.

I turned to see Mathews stalking towards us through the mass of waiting patients.

"What is this?" he demanded of Holmes. "Why are you sending me urgent telegrams about my daughter being ill?" He was red-faced and breathing heavily from his exertions to hurry here. It was clear, at least, that his feelings for his daughter were genuine, even if he discarded wives like used napkins.

Holmes held up a conciliatory hand. "Nothing to be alarmed about," he comforted. "She had a bad reaction to something she ingested." He pulled the tea container from his jacket and handed it to Lestrade. "Is there some ingredient in this homemade tea of yours that may have caused an adverse effect?" he asked with exaggerated innocence. "It seems she drank it and immediately felt ill."

319

Mr. Mathews' eyes had gone wide at the sight of the tea caddy. "Did – did you – ?" he stammered. "Did you feed my daughter that tea? Is that my tea from my mother's house? Is that why you were snooping about?"

There was unmistakable accusation in his voice, and Holmes tilted his head with curiosity. "Why do you ask that? Is there something wrong the tea?"

Mathews threw his hat and coat onto a nearby chair in a fit of anger. "You know good and well, sir, what is in that tea! You dared to give that to my Maddie! You would do that to a child!"

All pretense of innocence fell from the detective's face. He stepped to the fuming man with a piercing gaze. "So, you admit that there is something amiss with the tea, sir?"

Mathews looked from Holmes to Lestrade to the tea and back again. It was clear he knew the game was up. I tensed, wondering if he would run, or if concern for his daughter would keep him here.

"What is wrong with the tea?" Holmes asked, punctuating each word carefully and forcefully.

Our quarry was well and cornered. I flexed my hands, aware of the whispering spectators surrounding us, viewing our tete-a-tete with concerned fascination. Mathews also seemed to be aware of the many witnesses who had just heard him essentially confess to knowing the tea the inspector held was poisoned. A nurse was standing nearby, in habitual readiness and attention for whatever would follow.

What followed, no one really expected, not even Holmes. Instead of running or slumping in wearied resignation to his fate, Mathews pulled back quickly and delivered an unexpected punch to my friend's face. The detective, in a rare moment of being caught off guard, knocked over a smattering of chairs as he doubled over from the force of the blow.

"That's less than you deserve for poisoning my daughter!" he roared as Lestrade and I rushed forward to restrain him. The few waiting patients nearby had scattered with loud gasps and murmuring, giving the scene a wide berth.

Holmes was bent over, holding the side of his face. Once we had Mathews under control, helped by the irons Lestrade clapped on his wrists, I noticed Holmes shaking.

Both the nurse and I rushed to his side in concern. He stood to his full height, and I saw with relief and some irritation that he was laughing. "By Jove!" he declared, "I wasn't ready for that!" He seemed absolutely delighted to have been struck, wiping the blood from his chin and then gracelessly digging around his mouth until he pulled out a tooth. "The man knocked my canine out!" he commented, as if it were an exciting surprise.

The nurse tried to lead him away for medical aid, but he brushed her off. "No, no, ma'am. I'm afraid my only hope is a speedy visit to my dentist." He gently shoved the tooth back into its spot, flinching in pain. "Watson, let's be off, eh?" he suggested wryly, his words mumbled by the effort of keeping his tooth in place. "If we do not hurry, this tooth may not re-reoot and end up in my box of mementos instead of in my mouth!"

"My collection of M's is a fine one. Moriarty himself is enough to make any letter illustrious . . . and Mathews, who knocked out my left canine in the waiting room at Charing Cross."

– Sherlock Holmes
"The Empty House"

The Grey Lama
by Adrian Middleton

It was in the dying days of summer, 1894 – not long after his return from the dead – that my long-lamented friend, Sherlock Holmes, called upon me to assist with the restoration of his – our – Baker Street rooms. Much of the hard work had already been carried out by the indefatigable Mrs. Hudson, leaving us to restore those items displaced by myself or stored elsewhere.

Among these items were various boxes of correspondence, most of which involved long expired requests for help by those oblivious to the events which kept my friend away for the best part of three years. One such box, recently transferred from Greenhough Smith's Burleigh Street office – home of The Strand *– sat waiting to be opened for the first time.*

The Strand *had begun publishing my accounts of Holmes's adventures only a few weeks after he had disappeared, and my expectations for anything other than letters of criticism and praise were low. Unsealing the postage tape, I prised open the chest in which the correspondence rested, and my nostrils were immediately assailed by a pungent odour that began to fill the room, its cabbage-like smell urging me to find the offending object and remove it to a well-vented location. The dustbin came to mind.*

The object was easy to spot, its wrapping paper split by the small grey twig that protruded from its otherwise well-bound packaging. On closer inspection, I could see that it was a budding branch – quite unusual for something kept in complete darkness for so long.

*"A-ha!" said Holmes from across the room. "*Unicum lignum de montibus. *One of a kind."*

"You've never seen this before, and yet you know what it is? How is that possible?"

"In this case, Watson, the simplest explanation will suffice."

"That you have seen this before?"

"Not quite that simple, but close. It would be better if you were to fully explore the evidence before arriving at a preliminary conclusion."

"If it didn't stink so much, I'd happily oblige," I retorted, turning the parcel around in my hands for a closer inspection. "The paper is stained and, from the look of it, roughly handled. Probably runners or a courier beyond the borders of the Raj. From the markings, it would appear to have passed through a border outpost – Paro – in the care of the Indian Army,

arriving in the Chamba district under the local post before receiving a British India stamp. Carriage was overland, followed by a Home Line Steamer from Calcutta. All told, that indicates a five-month journey from Lhasa in Tibet."

"Bravo, Watson!" Holmes clapped appreciatively. "You are off to a wonderful start. All correct!"

"How would you know that?" I asked. "You haven't yet examined the package yourself – Oh!"

"The simplest explanation."

"You sent this parcel?" My heart sank. The package had arrived several weeks before Holmes's return, and if I had only seen it sooner, I might have been more prepared.

"It was sent on my behalf on the orders of the High Lama himself. But don't despair! It was a memento, not an announcement. It could also have been a clue, I suppose."

"A clue as to what?" I asked.

"My whereabouts, although I had little confidence in your ability to decipher its meaning. Not even my cleverest enemy could have worked out what it meant."

"Not even your cleverest enemy is as familiar with you as I am. Surely I might have deduced something."

"Very well," said Holmes, excitedly clapping his hands together. "Let's put you to the task. Have at it! Examine what lies within and tell me what you can deduce."

Carefully, I pulled the package open. Thankfully the odour of rotten vegetation was quickly masked by a different smell.

"Stale incense," I said, sniffing more intently. "This was wrapped by someone in a room where incense was burned. I can smell jasmine and camphor, blended with ash and resin."

"Wonderful. And the object within?"

Tied into shape with waxed string, the plant seemed to be wrapped in a bundle of filthy grey cloth.

"Some local rags used to wrap up whatever lies within," I ventured, pulling on the binding to unroll the cloth. "Some fragment of Buddhist tapestry or other," I added, noting colourful swirls of paint on the inside of the cloth. "Old paintings of men and mountains, no doubt depicting a mythic journey significant only to some local legend."

The rank smell of vegetation returned as I exposed the thing that lay within.

"It's a kernel – a seed or nut that has split and grown. Fibrous weeds have become attached to the cloth, perhaps soaking up any moisture that may have been absorbed in transit. The branch has no leaves, nor sign of

leaves, and contains but a single bud beneath its tip. Had I seen this earlier, I might have sent it to Kew for further inspection."

"Excellent, Watson. Correct in all areas but one: The seed was indeed to be passed on to Kew for further inspection. I knew you would work that part out, but the memento, and the clue, lies in the wrapping. That 'local rag' was a fragment of my own clothes, the Glen Urquhart check supplied by the Regent Street draper that we have both frequented. It is, in fact, a swatch cut from my clothes, intended as a template for Tibetan weavers, and later used as a canvas for the painting."

"So not old at all?"

"Far from it. The cloth serves two functions: As a map it depicts one man – me – and the journey that I took from England to Tibet, and as a t'angka, it shows my divine ancestry, as determined by the High Lama himself, in the form of a mandala."

"Divine ancestry?"

"I make no claims of godhood, Watson. In Tibetan culture, only an enlightened tsul'sku may interact with the Great Lamas of the region."

"And what, precisely, is a tsul'sku?"

"The reincarnated soul of a great teacher. In my case, an Imperial Magistrate of the Tang Court whose capacity for enlightened deductions is celebrated across the Orient. Despite his Chinese origin, his effective and impartial judgements received high praise in Lhasa. Flattering, but quite ludicrous."

"And how could I possibly have known any of that?"

"You could not – not without spending a month or two on the streets of Limehouse. My friend, just because you are sometimes ignorant of the facts, it doesn't follow that you are in any way stupid. You are brave, intelligent, resourceful, and more capable than most of the so-called detectives we have seen come and go over the years. It is your impatience that lets you down."

I harrumphed loudly, returning to the object of our attention.

"So why did you send this, and why to the offices of The Strand?"

"As I said, I didn't send it. I asked for it to be forwarded on to me. In most cases that would mean sending it to Baker Street, or at the very least into the care of Dr. Watson, but the High Lama knew of me only through your stories. He is . . . a subscriber."

"You're serious?"

"Completely," said Holmes, politely ignoring that I had turned a shade of crimson. "In Lhasa, your works are second only to Kipling. In fact, I think we should make a gift for the High Lama. Get some pen and ink, and I shall recount the story of how he and I met . . . ."

It was on the Roof of the World, beyond the eastern edge of Zanskar, that I first came across him. It had been two weeks since I had left the monastery at Likir, home to another Lama, Tenzin Rinpoche, for whom I had resolved the enigma of the whispering silence. Travelling along an ice-hardened trail one day, and through sun-blessed crop-fields the next, my yak and I meandered along narrow tracks, passing out from the hidden valley and into its neighbouring kingdom, Tibet.

I didn't recognise him at first. His identity was unknown in the West, and there had been no formal recognition. Until his enthronement, he lived anonymously among several other candidates being groomed for high office, each sponsored by opposing interests, secretly backed by the Great Powers – China to the east, the British Raj to the south, from whence I had come, and Russia to the northwest. They each disputed the territory without a thought for the people, and they were each desperate to exert political influence over whomsoever should be anointed as the one true incarnation of the High Lama.

All that I saw was a young man on his knees, a yak at his side, toiling in the dry and frozen earth beneath the shadow of a great barren tree. Draped in prayer flags and propped up by *mani* stones that were colourfully painted in remembrance of those who had died, it loomed over us like a great statue, dwarfing even Lady Liberty in New York. Its bole was wider, its trunk taller, its spindly canopy broader, and its bare roots were longer than any tree I had ever seen. Its impenetrable bark was so thick and hard that it was indistinguishable from the bare rock that surrounded it.

As I approached, I could see that the man was chanting, his lips moving as he pruned a single thin green branch that protruded outwards. The cluster of closed buds that hung from the branch confirmed to me that the old tree was, in fact, alive.

"Observe this tree," he said, without looking up from his task. I am no groundskeeper, so I cannot say why he was doing this, but I deduced that he was encouraging a single bud to bloom. "How old would you say that it was?"

"Perhaps the oldest in the world," I said. "Certainly, the largest I have ever seen. I followed one of its exposed roots for the last three or four miles, and it would appear that the track follows the root, and not the other way around."

"As old as the mountains," he agreed. "Perhaps older. It is said that the tree beneath which the Buddha found enlightenment grew from a seed of this very tree. As you have observed, its roots spread far and wide. Some have been seen protruding from the mountain slopes, thousands of yards below us. Perhaps they reach down into the bowels of the earth itself."

"'The Tree of Life'," I said. "In the West, there are tales of a great world tree so large that it connects nine separate worlds. I would have little time for such nonsense, but I recently found myself investigating a hoax – a book purporting to be ancient in origin, whose fabrication was so obvious, but whose narrative was so compelling that a dozen experts deluded themselves into wishing it were real."

"This is no myth," said the young man, "nor any kind of fabrication. It might better be called 'The Tree of Death', or 'Time', and its doom is said to herald the end of the current age, to be followed by centuries of chaos. This is why the High Lamas have tended to this tree for more than a thousand years. It is a sacred duty."

"Just the High Lamas," I asked, "or can anyone muck in?"

"That is an interesting question, in and of itself." He smiled thinly. "Our truths are revealed by our words and our deeds."

"And by our appearances," I added, "and from its appearance, I would say the tending hasn't been productive." There were cracks in the rock surrounding the tree, and I saw no evidence of pollination. A book by Darwin sprang to mind, on the effects of pollination in flora. As I began to explain the science to the young man, he cut me short.

"I am familiar with Darwin and his theories," he said. "One of my tutors is an Englishman, and he has made many such books available."

"I see. Then you will know that you need bees. I encountered a *genus* of giant cliff bee roaming wild on my way here. The locals risk life and limb to harvest their honey from the mountainside."

"Yes. Red honey. It is an interesting suggestion, and while the honey-hunters left our kingdom centuries ago, taking the great bees with them, we still trade for remedies and to enhance our tea. Perhaps the bees could be encouraged to return."

"If it isn't too late."

"Appearances can deceive, can they not?"

"To the untrained mind such deception is rare, but yes, we are all fallible, Your Holiness."

"You speak as one well versed in discerning the truth. You have the air of an investigator about you."

"Is that an observation or an informed guess?"

"It is the job of a lama to recognise those of his own kind. *Tsul'sku*. The reincarnate. Sometimes revelation is spontaneous, and other times there is much meditation involved."

"And tea drinking?" I asked.

"Of course. Butter tea is our national drink."

"You speak English well."

"It seems that language is important to your people. I speak the four languages of my four foreign tutors, each supplied by those keen to curry my favour. I sense, though, that this isn't your goal. You have a different objective, Mister – ?"

"Sigerson," I said, keen to maintain my anonymity.

"If you insist," said the boy, "although I see the spirit of another. A restless man. A seeker of truth. As much a Lama as any of my fellows, and in spite of your older age, I sense your latest death was very recent. Metaphorical, perhaps, or spiritual."

I was intrigued by the boy's natural skill, pressing for him to explain his deduction.

"Your name is Scandinavian, yet the cut of your clothes bears no trace of the West, except one: The grey fabric you wear is a tweed from the British Isles. It is common for a traveller to retain some fragment of their true identity and this, I believe, is yours. This, your reference to Darwin, and your accent, which is clearly that of an Englishman."

"Excellent powers of deduction," I replied.

"It is a method I have recently learned from stories about Sherlock Holmes, a London detective."

"Stories?" Unaware that my adventures were being serialized, I enquired further.

"In *The Strand Magazine*," he replied. "My English tutor brings copies when he visits. The accounts by Doctor Watson are quite enthralling, and he describes you to a tee, Mister . . . *Holmes*. Your diction is quite distinctive."

"I suppose he must if you are able to identify me from such scant evidence."

"You may also bear a striking resemblance to a picture that appeared in your obituary."

We journeyed to Lhasa together, and along the way we forged an unlikely friendship. I learned much about the culture of the Tibetan Buddhists, while Thub – his birth name – explained that he could do with my help.

"You're a smart young man," I said. "Why would you need that?"

"I may be allowed to carry out some duties, but the regimen at the Potala Palace is harsh and the rules are strict. The *tsul'sku* candidates are segregated from the other monks, and from each other. We are watched closely, and those who do get close to us are keen to impose their political views upon us. Until I am enthroned, which happens next year, there is no guarantee that I will become the next *Rgyalba Rinpoche*."

"But if you have been recognised – "

"Recognition means nothing until I am invested. If I die before I am invested, then another candidate will be sought out and recognised in my place. That is why my life is in so much danger, and why someone less-politically exposed must investigate on my behalf."

"Investigate?"

"You saw the prayer stones scattered around the Great Tree?"

"The *mani* stones? Yes."

"They are in memory of the lost lamas, those who were identified and recognised, but who died before they could be enthroned. History will not record their names, and two of them were, like me, recognised as the *Talai Lama*. The twelfth died the year before I was born, but I wasn't chosen for another two years. In that time two others were chosen but died as infants. Poisoned."

"That is horrific."

"It is the way. A dark consequence of our importance to our neighbours. I want to know who is killing all of these *tsul'sku*, and I want to know how."

Of course, I agreed to help, but it wasn't going to be an easy task. There had been dozens of *mani* stones at the Great Tree, each of them representing a child below the age of ascension, killed before or during their training as a monk, either at the hands of the Great Powers, or else by someone who had the means and motive. There were thousands of monks in Lhasa alone, with hundreds having the required access. It could, I explained, take quite some time.

Thub made my assimilation into *tsul'sku* culture very easy in the time that I was in his company. I was formally tested and recognised as the *tsul'sku* of Di Renjie, Duke of Liang, a seventh-century magistrate immortalised in Chinese folk tales. Using a swatch of my hiking clothes, Thub had new robes made for me as I was initiated into the Yellow Hat school of Buddhism and continued my study of Tibetan culture. My *faux* tweed quickly earned me the name "The Grey Lama", and my new position gave me access to a wide circle of suspects, and an even larger number of motives and murder methods.

Contrary to my belief that Buddhists abstained from intoxicating drugs and alcohol, I discovered that "traditional medicines" weren't considered to be either. The red honey, for example, often had hallucinogenic properties, and was regularly served up to the monks at bedtime in a concoction known as "night milk". And then there was the humble yak – source of wool, milk, meat, and bone – the most important resource in the kingdom. An examination of yak dung confirmed that this was sometimes contaminated with hallucinogenic toxins. There were hallucinogens in the incense, and even the local beer, made from highland barley grain and fermented ginseng, was regularly used in pastries consumed by the monks. The opportunities to poison were so common and so diverse that no two murders would be the same.

The answer to the High Lama's question: Who killed the lost lamas? Everybody.

I set about solving all the murders one by one, starting with poisonings which quickly began pointing to different perpetrators. An officer of the Raj was implicated in one, a Russian-born monk in another, and several Chinese monks with known sympathies to the Qing Dynasty were similarly implicated. The reputation of the Grey Lama improved with each passing investigation, but the impossibility of my task became obvious. To illustrate this, I persuaded Thub to let me look into three of the most intriguing cases. Should each be committed by a different perpetrator, he agreed that his safest course of action would be to seek refuge until his enthronement the following year. In the time remaining to me, I selected the poisoning of a boy, Tenzin Gyaltzen, the murder of a *tsul'sku* on the snowy slopes of the Red Mountain, and the bloodiest and least typical murder of all, that of the chosen Khanpo Rinpoche.

The death of Tenzin Gyaltzen was a straightforward case that relied upon my prior knowledge of what Thub had called "Red Honey". The boy had died in 1890, well before my arrival in Tibet, so I was unable to examine the location of the crime. By all accounts, the boy had arrived at Potala seeking refuge from an unknown threat. All that he possessed was a simple cup which remained in his possession until his death a few days later. In the intervening time, his name was placed in a Golden Urn, which was used to identify the *tsul'sku* of a recently deceased lama. Following a period of dizziness and nausea, the boy died of a seizure, choking on his own vomit. According to various accounts, his lips had been blue.

The boy's body had been mummified and encased in the statue of the ascetic Gautama in the form of a child. The cup that he bore had been placed in the Buddha's hand. My initial request to break open the statue and examine the child's corpse was refused, but an examination of the cup revealed that it had contained a highly toxic concentration of the Red Honey.

Not having been in Lhasa long, and coming from a village to the north, it was unlikely that the boy had developed a tolerance for the honey, and that such a large dose would easily have killed him.

Before I had convinced Thub to plant rhododendrons around the Great Tree and to reintroduce the giant bees in its vicinity, access to the honey was limited. Its sparse availability ruled out an accidental overdose, leading me to look into suspects connected to the village from which the

329

boy had come. This exposed a small group of monks who believed that the cup was a relic. Of these, only one – the eldest – had access to Red Honey. On being confronted this monk, Lobsang, confessed that the boy had thwarted an attempt to steal the cup. Tenzin's recognition as a *tsul'sku* had given him a credibility that would see Lobsang and others exposed as thieves. Ironic, then, that I exposed them as murderers instead.

The second of the three cases was that of an older boy, a monk named Jampa Namgyel. This young man had been a chosen *tsul'sku* for some years, and was fifteen years old. Like Thub, his enthronement would have happened on his eighteenth birthday, and he was being educated by tutors in advance of his formal recognition. He died in the winter of 1891 on the slopes of Mount Marpori, the Red Mountain upon which the city of Lhasa was located.

Jampa's lifeless body was found by locals, his robes stained with crimson and his prayer-beads scattered on the snow-covered ground. The murder had shaken the entire region, and was initially blamed on a mythical creature, a great black-haired man-bear called a *mirdred*. There had been no sighting, but claw-like wounds and the presence of large footprints in the snow had persuaded the locals of the creature's guilt. *Dob-dobs*, the monk-guardians who police Lhasa, had found traces of man-bear hair in the vicinity of the murder, and had made no further enquiry.

Thub, of course, suspected that Jampa had been murdered because of his position, and not by some random monster that crossed his path. My own investigations revealed that a British Army Officer, Captain Edward Montgomery of the Argyll and Sutherland Highlanders, had been seen out on the slopes on the fateful night of the murder. Montgomery, stationed in Bhutan, had been conducting business in Lhasa, and had left the city the next day. Upon examining the so-called man-bear hair, I discovered that it was, in fact, black horsehair. This prompted me to forward a message to the British fort at Paro. A response from the commanding officer there confirmed that the tassels of Montgomery's sporran, made of black horsehair, had been clipped, and that under interrogation he confirmed that he had used his bayonet to place claw marks on the boy's face, and that he had been bribed into murdering the young monk over religious differences between Tibetan and Bhutanese Buddhists.

My third and final investigation involved Khanpo Rinpoche. This lama was a seventeen-year-old boy just months away from his investment and, unlike the other deaths, his had been unnecessarily violent, the result of his throat being slashed with a sacred dagger, known as the *Kalachakra* Blade. This blade had been in the lama's possession on the night before he died, but was the only item missing from his meditation chamber the next morning.

As with many legends in the Himalayas, the sacred dagger wasn't only important to those of the Buddhist faith, but also to the Hindoo, to whom the blade was a symbol of great spiritual power connected to their death goddess, Kali.

Revisiting the location of the crime some months after the lama's death, there was little surviving evidence, with no marks on the door or windows that might have suggested forced entry. According to witnesses, the Khanpo's body, which had been laid out in a ritualistic manner, had had a curious mark on the forehead. Relying on conflicting accounts, I managed to determine that the mark wasn't – as had originally been assumed – a wound, but rather a *tilaka* – a symbol painted at the location of the third eye. Its shape was sufficiently unusual for me to identify it as a Hindoo sect-mark, a symbol used by Kali-worshipping pansolar until their extermination by the Indian Army decades earlier. The flight of the *phansigar* out of the Raj had resulted in survivors finding refuge in neighbouring kingdoms, and it seems that the *Kalachakra* Blade was a *Katar*, a weapon sacred to the cult and its rituals. The inevitable conclusion was that there were *phansigar* among the lama's disciples, and that the cult continued to exist among the villages surrounding his monastery.

I had suspected that the murderer was focused on recovering the dagger, and not to intentionally kill Khanpo Rinpoche. Determining that the murderer's intent was to carry out a ritual important to the *phansigar*, it was a simple matter to identify the time, place, and other requirements for such a ritual to take place. Some miles away from Lhasa, at a secluded space well hidden by an overhanging cavern devoted to Kali and Bhairava, we disturbed the ritual, scattering the *phansigar* with a charge of a dozen white horses ridden by myself and a number of *dob-dobs* warrior monks who traditionally protected their monasteries. While the monks engaged the *phansigar*, I took it upon myself to seize the dagger and ride away, pursued by a handful of murderous cultists.

I took the track that I knew, taking me through the blooming rhododendron fields I had persuaded my friend Thub to plant. This brought me under the shadow of the Great Tree, where I had hoped to lose my pursuers and double back towards Lhasa. Unfortunately, the phansigar were close behind, and I committed an act I have come to regret to this very day. Clustered around the tree were the transplanted hives of Himalayan bees, whose presence had already helped new growth on the Great Tree. In my haste, I failed to consider the consequences of my actions, striking at the hives with a riding crop as I was forced to ride downwards, passing alongside the roots of the Great Tree.

A cloud of giant bees buzzed angrily around the based of the tree as my pursuers rode into and through them. Jumping the numerous cracks and crevices, I paid little heed to what ensued behind me, kicking up dust as my horse's hooves loosened the ground beneath its feet. Blindly chasing me, the *phansigar* were less cautious, their steeds stumbling and plunging forward with little control, kicking up clouds of thick dust as their movement slowly pulling at the already widening fissures. Unknown to me, they were tearing the ground apart. As my pursuers showed no sign of stopping, my horse and I plunged further down the mountainside. The thunderous echo of hooves shook free the dirt that had held tree and mountain together for a thousand years, and "The Grey Lama" disappeared as a great rolling rockslide pulled the great calcified tree down into the valley below, plumes of scree and dust enveloping my pursuers and forcing me to ride on and on. A thousand yards below, I settled under the shade of a protruding bluff, lamenting the catastrophe that had brought a mountain and possibly the world's oldest tree down upon our heads. As I gazed up through the settling dust, I could see that the way back had been lost, and that my return to Lhasa had been thwarted . . . .

Dusting off my faux-tweed robes, I shook my head in disgust. It might take months to return, I wished that I could explain my actions and beg forgiveness for the loss of the Great Tree. I consoled myself only in the knowledge that I had asked my friend Thub to forward a seed from the tree to London, where the botanists of Kew might at least cultivate its successor. Taking the reins of my horse, I led it down into the neighbouring Kingdom of Nepal.

The bones in my hand ached as I wrote down Holmes's last words. I was grateful he had spared me the many of the Tibetan names that should have filled his account, and with no decent dictionary, I cannot be sure the few that he used were properly rendered.

"An intriguing account," I said at last, "but I thought you had been in pursuit of Moriarty's agents?"

"I did encounter one during my time with the High Lama, Watson," he replied, *"but that is another story for another day."*

"I travelled for two years in Tibet, therefore, and amused myself by visiting Lhassa, and spending some days with the head lama. You may have read of the remarkable explorations of a Norwegian named Sigerson, but I am sure that it never occurred to you that you were receiving news of your friend."

– Sherlock Holmes
"The Empty House"

Appendix:
The Untold Cases

The following has been assembled from several sources, including lists compiled by Phil Jones and Randall Stock, as well as some internet resources and my own research. I cannot promise that it's complete – some Untold Cases may be missing – after all, there's a great deal of Sherlockian Scholarship that involves interpretation and rationalizing – and there are some listed here that certain readers may believe shouldn't be listed at all.

As a fanatical supporter and collector of pastiches since I was a ten-year-old boy in 1975, reading Nicholas Meyer's *The Seven-Per-Cent Solution* and *The West End Horror* before I'd even read all of The Canon, I can attest that serious and legitimate versions of all of these Untold Cases exist out there – some of them occurring with much greater frequency than others – and I hope to collect, read, and chronologicize them all.

There's so much more to The Adventures of Sherlock Holmes than the pitifully few sixty stories that were fixed up by the First Literary Agent. I highly recommend that you find and read all of the rest of them as well, including those relating these Untold Cases. You won't regret it.

David Marcum

A Study in Scarlet

- Mr. Lestrade . . . got himself in a fog recently over a forgery case
- A young girl called, fashionably dressed
- A gray-headed, seedy visitor, looking like a Jew pedlar who appeared to be very much excited
- A slipshod elderly woman
- An old, white-haired gentleman had an interview
- A railway porter in his velveteen uniform

The Sign of Four

- The consultation last week by Francois le Villard
- The most winning woman Holmes ever knew was hanged for poisoning three little children for their insurance money

- The most repellent man of Holmes's acquaintance was a philanthropist who has spent nearly a quarter of a million upon the London poor
- Holmes once enabled Mrs. Cecil Forrester to unravel a little domestic complication. She was much impressed by his kindness and skill
- Holmes lectured the police on causes and inferences and effects in the Bishopgate jewel case

The Adventures of Sherlock Holmes

"A Scandal in Bohemia"
- The summons to Odessa in the case of the Trepoff murder
- The singular tragedy of the Atkinson brothers at Trincomalee
- The mission which Holmes had accomplished so delicately and successfully for the reigning family of Holland. (He also received a remarkably brilliant ring)
- The Darlington substitution scandal, and . . .
- The Arnsworth castle business. (When a woman thinks that her house is on fire, her instinct is at once to rush to the thing which she values most. It is a perfectly overpowering impulse, and Holmes has more than once taken advantage of it

"The Red-Headed League"
- The previous skirmishes with John Clay

"A Case of Identity"
- The Dundas separation case, where Holmes was engaged in clearing up some small points in connection with it. The husband was a teetotaler, there was no other woman, and the conduct complained of was that he had drifted into the habit of winding up every meal by taking out his false teeth and hurling them at his wife, which is not an action likely to occur to the imagination of the average story-teller.
- The rather intricate matter from Marseilles
- Mrs. Etherege, whose husband Holmes found so easy when the police and everyone had given him up for dead
- Windibank, who will rise from crime to crime until he does something very bad, and ends on a gallows. *(An Untold Case previously unlisted and newly identified for this volume by David Marcum.)*

"The Boscombe Valley Mystery"
NONE LISTED

"The Five Orange Pips"
- The adventure of the Paradol Chamber
- The Amateur Mendicant Society, who held a luxurious club in the lower vault of a furniture warehouse
- The facts connected with the disappearance of the British barque *Sophy Anderson*
- The singular adventures of the Grice-Patersons in the island of Uffa
- The Camberwell poisoning case, in which, as may be remembered, Holmes was able, by winding up the dead man's watch, to prove that it had been wound up two hours before, and that therefore the deceased had gone to bed within that time – a deduction which was of the greatest importance in clearing up the case
- Holmes saved Major Prendergast in the Tankerville Club scandal. He was wrongfully accused of cheating at cards
- Holmes has been beaten four times – three times by men and once by a woman

"The Man with the Twisted Lip"
- The rascally Lascar who runs The Bar of Gold in Upper Swandam Lane has sworn to have vengeance upon Holmes

"The Adventure of the Blue Carbuncle"
NONE LISTED

"The Adventure of the Speckled Band"
- Mrs. Farintosh and an opal tiara. (It was before Watson's time)

"The Adventure of the Engineer's Thumb"
- Colonel Warburton's madness

"The Adventure of the Noble Bachelor"
- The letter from a fishmonger
- The letter a tide-waiter
- The service for Lord Backwater

337

- The little problem of the Grosvenor Square furniture van
- The service for the King of Scandinavia

"The Adventure of the Beryl Coronet"
NONE LISTED

"The Adventure of the Copper Beeches"
NONE LISTED

The Memoirs of Sherlock Holmes

"Silver Blaze"
NONE LISTED

"The Cardboard Box"
- Aldridge, who helped in the bogus laundry affair

"The Yellow Face"
- The (First) Adventure of the Second Stain was a failure which present[s] the strongest features of interest

'The Stockbroker's Clerk"
NONE LISTED

"The "Gloria Scott""
NONE LISTED

"The Musgrave Ritual"
- The Tarleton murders
- The case of Vamberry, the wine merchant
- The adventure of the old Russian woman
- The singular affair of the aluminum crutch
- A full account of Ricoletti of the club foot and his abominable wife
- The two cases before the Musgrave Ritual from Holmes's fellow students

"The Reigate Squires"
- The whole question of the Netherland-Sumatra Company and of the colossal schemes of Baron Maupertuis

The Crooked Man"
NONE LISTED

The Resident Patient"
- [Catalepsy] is a very easy complaint to imitate. Holmes has done it himself.

"The Greek Interpreter"
- Mycroft expected to see Holmes round last week to consult me over that Manor House case. It was Adams, of course
- Some of Holmes's most interesting cases have come to him through Mycroft

"The Naval Treaty"
- The (Second) adventure of the Second Stain, which dealt with interest of such importançe and implicated so many of the first families in the kingdom that for many years it would be impossible to make it public. No case, however, in which Holmes was engaged had ever illustrated the value of his analytical methods so clearly or had impressed those who were associated with him so deeply. Watson still retained an almost verbatim report of the interview in which Holmes demonstrated the true facts of the case to Monsieur Dubugue of the Paris police, and Fritz von Waldbaum, the well-known specialist of Dantzig, both of whom had wasted their energies upon what proved to be side-issues. The new century will have come, however, before the story could be safely told.
- The Adventure of the Tired Captain
- A very commonplace little murder. If it [this paper] turns red, it means a man's life . . . .

"The Final Problem"
- The engagement for the French Government upon a matter of supreme importance
- The assistance to the Royal Family of Scandinavia

The Return of Sherlock Holmes

"The Adventure of the Empty House"

- Holmes traveled for two years in Tibet (as) a Norwegian named Sigerson, amusing himself by visiting Lhassa [*sic*] and spending some days with the head Llama [*sic*]
- Holmes traveled in Persia
- . . . looked in at Mecca . . .
- . . . and paid a short but interesting visit to the Khalifa at Khartoum
- Returning to France, Holmes spent some months in a research into the coal-tar derivatives, which he conducted in a laboratory at Montpelier [*sic*], in the South of France
- Mathews, who knocked out Holmes's left canine in the waiting room at Charing Cross
- The death of Mrs. Stewart, of Lauder, in 1887
- Morgan the poisoner
- Merridew of abominable memory
- The Molesey Mystery (Inspector Lestrade's Case. He handled it fairly well.)
- Three undetected murders in one year. Lestrade wants want a little unofficial help. *(An Untold Case previously unlisted and newly identified for this volume by Alan Dimes.)*

"The Adventure of the Norwood Builder"
- The case of the papers of ex-President Murillo
- The shocking affair of the Dutch steamship, *Friesland*, which so nearly cost both Holmes and Watson their lives
- That terrible murderer, Bert Stevens, who wanted Holmes and Watson to get him off in '87

"The Adventure of the Dancing Men"
NONE LISTED

"The Adventure of the Solitary Cyclist"
- The peculiar persecution of John Vincent Harden, the well-known tobacco millionaire
- It was near Farnham that Holmes and Watson took Archie Stamford, the forger

"The Adventure of the Priory School"
- Holmes was retained in the case of the Ferrers Documents
- The Abergavenny murder, which is coming up for trial

340

"The Adventure of Black Peter"
- The sudden death of Cardinal Tosca – an inquiry which was carried out by him at the express desire of His Holiness the Pope
- The arrest of Wilson, the notorious canary-trainer, which removed a plague-spot from the East-End of London.

"The Adventure of Charles Augustus Milverton"
- Milverton paid seven hundred pounds to a footman for a note two lines in length, and that the ruin of a noble family was the result. *(An Untold Case previously unlisted and newly identified for this volume by Chris Chan.)*

"The Adventure of the Six Napoleons"
- The dreadful business of the Abernetty family, which was first brought to Holmes's attention by the depth which the parsley had sunk into the butter upon a hot day
- The Conk-Singleton forgery case
- Holmes was consulted upon the case of the disappearance of the black pearl of the Borgias, but was unable to throw any light upon it

"The Adventure of the Three Students"
- Some laborious researches in Early English charters

"The Adventure of the Golden Pince-Nez"
- The repulsive story of the red leech
- . . . and the terrible death of Crosby, the banker
- The Addleton tragedy
- . . . and the singular contents of the ancient British barrow
- The famous Smith-Mortimer succession case
- The tracking and arrest of Huret, the boulevard assassin

"The Adventure of the Missing Three-Quarter"
- Henry Staunton, whom Holmes helped to hang
- Arthur H. Staunton, the rising young forger

"The Adventure of the Abbey Grange"
- Hopkins called Holmes in seven times, and on each occasion his summons was entirely justified

- The woman at Margate. No powder on her nose – that proved to be the correct solution. How can one build on such a quicksand? A woman's most trivial action may mean volumes, or their most extraordinary conduct may depend upon a hairpin or a curling-tong

The Hound of the Baskervilles

- That little affair of the Vatican cameos, in which Holmes obliged the Pope
- The little case in which Holmes had the good fortune to help Messenger Manager Wilson
- One of the most revered names in England is being besmirched by a blackmailer, and only Holmes can stop a disastrous scandal
- The atrocious conduct of Colonel Upwood in connection with the famous card scandal at the Nonpareil Club
- Holmes defended the unfortunate Mme. Montpensier from the charge of murder that hung over her in connection with the death of her stepdaughter Mlle. Carere, the young lady who, as it will be remembered, was found six months later alive and married in New York

The Valley of Fear

- Twice already Holmes had helped Inspector Macdonald

His Last Bow

"The Adventure of Wisteria Lodge"
- The locking-up Colonel Carruthers

"The Adventure of the Red Circle"
- The affair last year for Mr. Fairdale Hobbs
- The Long Island cave mystery

"The Adventure of the Bruce-Partington Plans"
- Brooks . . .

- ... or Woodhouse, or any of the fifty men who have good reason for taking Holmes's life

"The Adventure of the Dying Detective"
   NONE LISTED

"The Disappearance of Lady Frances Carfax"
- Holmes cannot possibly leave London while old Abrahams is in such mortal terror of his life

"The Adventure of the Devil's Foot"
- Holmes's dramatic introduction to Dr. Moore Agar, of Harley Street

"His Last Bow"
- Holmes started his pilgrimage at Chicago ...
- ... graduated in an Irish secret society at Buffalo
- ... gave serious trouble to the constabulary at Skibbareen
- Holmes saves Count Von und Zu Grafenstein from murder by the Nihilist Klopman

The Case-Book of Sherlock Holmes

"The Adventure of the Illustrious Client"
- Negotiations with Sir George Lewis over the Hammerford Will case

"The Adventure of the Blanched Soldier"
- The Abbey School in which the Duke of Greyminster was so deeply involved
- The commission from the Sultan of Turkey which required immediate action
- The professional service for Sir James Saunders

"The Adventure of the Mazarin Stone"
- Old Baron Dowson said the night before he was hanged that in Holmes's case what the law had gained the stage had lost
- The death of old Mrs. Harold, who left Count Sylvius the Blymer estate
- The compete life history of Miss Minnie Warrender

343

- The robbery in the train de-luxe to the Riviera on February 13, 1892

"The Adventure of the Three Gables"
- The killing of young Perkins outside the Holborn Bar
- Mortimer Maberly, was one of Holmes's early clients

"The Adventure of the Sussex Vampire"
- *Matilda Briggs*, a ship which is associated with the giant rat of Sumatra, a story for which the world is not yet prepared
- Victor Lynch, the forger
- Venomous lizard, or Gila. Remarkable case, that!
- Vittoria the circus belle
- Vanderbilt and the Yeggman
- Vigor, the Hammersmith wonder

"The Adventure of the Three Garridebs"
- Holmes refused a knighthood for services which may, someday, be described

"The Problem of Thor Bridge"
- Mr. James Phillimore who, stepping back into his own house to get his umbrella, was never more seen in this world
- The cutter *Alicia*, which sailed one spring morning into a patch of mist from where she never again emerged, nor was anything further ever heard of herself and her crew.
- Isadora Persano, the well-known journalist and duelist who was found stark staring mad with a match box in front of him which contained a remarkable worm said to be unknown to science

"The Adventure of the Creeping Man"
NONE LISTED

"The Adventure of the Lion's Mane"
NONE LISTED

"The Adventure of the Veiled Lodger"
- The whole story concerning the politician, the lighthouse, and the trained cormorant

"The Adventure of Shoscombe Old Place"
- Holmes ran down that coiner by the zinc and copper filings in the seam of his cuff
- The St. Pancras case, where a cap was found beside the dead policeman. The accused man denied that it is his. But he was a picture-frame maker who habitually handled glue.
  - "Is it one of your cases?" Merivale of the Yard asked Holmes to look into it

"The Adventure of the Retired Colourman"
- The case of the two Coptic Patriarchs

About the Contributors

The following contributors appear in this volume:
The MX Book of New Sherlock Holmes Stories
Part XLI – Further Untold Cases (1887-1892)

Tim Newton Anderson is a former senior daily newspaper journalist and PR manager who has recently started writing fiction. In the past six months, he has placed fourteen stories in publications including *Parsec Magazine*, *Tales of the Shadowmen*, *SF Writers Guild*, *Zoetic Press*, *Dark Lane Books*, *Dark Horses Magazine*, *Emanations*, and *Planet Bizarro*.

Brian Belanger, PSI, is a publisher, illustrator, graphic designer, editor, and author. In 2015, he co-founded Belanger Books publishing company along with his brother, author Derrick Belanger. His illustrations have appeared in *The Essential Sherlock Holmes* and *Sherlock Holmes: A Three-Pipe Christmas*, and in children's books such as *The MacDougall Twins with Sherlock Holmes* series, *Dragonella*, and *Scones and Bones on Baker Street*. Brian has published a number of Sherlock Holmes anthologies and novels through Belanger Books, as well as new editions of August Derleth's classic Solar Pons mysteries. Brian continues to design all of the covers for Belanger Books, and since 2016 he has designed the majority of book covers for MX Publishing. In 2019, Brian received his investiture in the PSI as "Sir Ronald Duveen." More recently, he illustrated a comic book featuring the band The Moonlight Initiative, created the logo for the Arthur Conan Doyle Society and designed *The Great Game of Sherlock Holmes* card game. Find him online at:
www.belangerbooks.com and
www.redbubble.com/people/zhahadun and
zhahadun.wixsite.com/221b

Mike Chinn's first-ever Sherlock Holmes fiction was a steampunk mashup of *The Valley of Fear*, entitled *Vallis Timoris* (Fringeworks 2015). Since then he has written about Holmes's archenemy in *The Mammoth Book of the Adventures of Moriarty* (Robinson 2015), appeared in three volumes of *The MX Book of New Sherlock Holmes Stories*, and faced the retired detective with cross-dimensional magic in the second volume of *Sherlock Holmes and the Occult Detectives* (Belanger Books 2020).

Barry Clay is a graduate of Shippensburg University with a BA in English. He's dug ditches, stocked grocery shelves, tutored for room and board, cleaned restrooms, mopped floors, taught cartooning, worked in a bank, asked if you'd like fries with that (and cooked the fries to boot), ordered carpet for cars, and worked commission sales at Sears, and most recently a long-time veteran of the Federal employee workforce. He has been writing all his life, in different genres, and he has written thirteen books ranging from Christian theology, anthologies, speculative fiction, horror, science fiction, and humor. He volunteers as conductor of a local student orchestra and has been commissioned to write music. His first two musicals were locally produced. He is the husband of one wife, father of four children, and "Opa" to one granddaughter.

Martin Daley was born in Carlisle, Cumbria in 1964. His thirty-year writing career has seen over twenty books and numerous short stories published. Inevitably, Holmes and Watson remain his favourite literary characters, and they continue to inspire his own detective writing. In 2010, Martin created Inspector Cornelius Armstrong, who carries out his police work against the backdrop of Edwardian Carlisle. With the publication of the first Inspector Armstrong Casebook (published by MX Publishing), Martin became a member of the Crime Writers' Association. He lives with his wife Wendy, in Kirkcudbrightshire, in Southwest.

Sir Arthur Conan Doyle (1859-1930) *Holmes Chronicler Emeritus.* If not for him, this anthology would not exist. Author, physician, patriot, sportsman, spiritualist, husband and father, and advocate for the oppressed. He is remembered and honored for the purposes of this collection by being the man who introduced Sherlock Holmes to the world. Through fifty-six Holmes short stories, four novels, and additional Apocryphal entries, Doyle revolutionized mystery stories and also greatly influenced and improved police forensic methods and techniques for the betterment of all. *Steel True Blade Straight.*

Steve Emecz's main field is technology, in which he has been working for about twenty-five years. Steve is a regular speaker at trade shows and his tech career has taken him to more than fifty countries – so he's no stranger to planes and airports. In 2008, MX published its first Sherlock Holmes book, and MX has gone on to become the largest specialist Holmes publisher in the world with over 500 books. MX is a social enterprise and supports three main causes. The first is Happy Life, a children's rescue project in Nairobi, Kenya, where he and his wife, Sharon, spend every Christmas at the rescue centre in Kasarani. They have written two editions of a short book about the project, *The Happy Life Story.* The second is Undershaw, Sir Arthur Conan Doyle's former home, which is a school for children with learning disabilities for which Steve is a patron. Steve has been a mentor for the World Food Programme for several years, and was part of the Nobel Peace Prize winning team in 2020.

Mark A. Gagen BSI is co-founder of Wessex Press, sponsor of the popular *From Gillette to Brett* conferences, and publisher of *The Sherlock Holmes Reference Library* and many other fine Sherlockian titles. A life-long Holmes enthusiast, he is a member of *The Baker Street Irregulars* and *The Illustrious Clients of Indianapolis.* A graphic artist by profession, his work is often seen on the covers of *The Baker Street Journal* and various BSI books.

Paul D. Gilbert was born in 1954 and has lived in and around London all of his life. His wife Jackie is a Holmes expert who keeps him on the straight and narrow! He has two sons, one of whom now lives in Spain. His interests include literature, ancient history, all religions, most sports, and movies. He is currently employed full-time as a funeral director. His books so far include *The Lost Files of Sherlock Holmes* (2007), *The Chronicles of Sherlock Holmes* (2008), *Sherlock Holmes and the Giant Rat of Sumatra* (2010), *The Annals of Sherlock Holmes* (2012), *Sherlock Holmes and the Unholy Trinity* (2015), *Sherlock Holmes: The Four Handed Game* (2017), *The Illumination of Sherlock Holmes* (2019), and *The Treasure of the Poison King* (2021).

John Atkinson Grimshaw (1836-1893) was born in Leeds, England. His amazing paintings, usually featuring twilight or night scenes illuminated by gas-lamps or moonlight, are easily recognizable, and are often used on the covers of books about The Great Detective to set the mood, as shadowy figures move in the distance through misty mysterious settings and over rain-slicked streets.

Arthur Hall was born in Aston, Birmingham, UK, in 1944. He discovered his interest in writing during his schooldays, along with a love of fictional adventure and suspense. His

348

first novel, *Sole Contact*, was an espionage story about an ultra-secret government department known as "Sector Three", and was followed, to date, by three sequels. Other works include seven Sherlock Holmes novels, *The Demon of the Dusk, The One Hundred Percent Society, The Secret Assassin, The Phantom Killer, In Pursuit of the Dead, The Justice Master*, and *The Experience Club* as well as three collections of Holmes *Further Little-Known Cases of Sherlock* Holmes, *Tales from the Annals of Sherlock* Holmes, and *The Additional Investigations of Sherlock Holmes*. He has also written other short stories and a modern detective novel. He lives in the West Midlands, United Kingdom.

Stephen Herczeg is an IT Geek, writer, actor, and film-maker based in Canberra Australia. He has been writing for over twenty years and has completed a couple of dodgy novels, sixteen feature-length screenplays, and numerous short stories and scripts. Stephen was very successful in 2017's International Horror Hotel screenplay competition, with his scripts *TITAN* winning the Sci-Fi category and *Dark are the Woods* placing second in the horror category. His three-volume short story collection, *The Curious Cases of Sherlock Holmes*, will be published in 2021. His work has featured in *Sproutlings – A Compendium of Little Fictions* from Hunter Anthologies, the *Hells Bells* Christmas horror anthology published by the Australasian Horror Writers Association, and the *Below the Stairs, Trickster's Treats, Shades of Santa, Behind the Mask*, and *Beyond the Infinite* anthologies from OzHorror.Con, *The Body Horror Book, Anemone Enemy*, and *Petrified Punks* from Oscillate Wildly Press, and *Sherlock Holmes In the Realms of H.G. Wells* and *Sherlock Holmes: Adventures Beyond the Canon* from Belanger Books.

Roger Johnson, BSI, ASH, PSI, etc, is a member of more Holmesian societies than he can remember, thanks to his (so far) 16 years as editor of *The Sherlock Holmes Journal*, and thirty-two years as editor of *The District Messenger*. The latter, the newsletter of *The Sherlock Holmes Society of London*, is now in the safe hands of Jean Upton, with whom he collaborated on the well-received book, *The Sherlock Holmes Miscellany*. Roger is resigned to the fact that he will never match the Du
ke of Holdernesse, whose name was followed by *"half the alphabet"*.

Naching T. Kassa is a wife, mother, and writer. She's created short stories, novellas, poems, and co-created three children. She resides in Eastern Washington State with her husband, Dan Kassa. Naching is a member of *The Horror Writers Association, Mystery Writers of America, The Sound of the Baskervilles, The ACD Society, The Crew of the Barque Lone Star*, and *The Sherlock Holmes Society of London*. She works in Talent Relations at Crystal Lake Publishing and was a recipient of the 2022 HWA Diversity Grant. You can find her work on Amazon.
https://www.amazon.com/Naching-T-Kassa/e/B005ZGHTI0

David MacGregor is a playwright, screenwriter, novelist, and nonfiction writer. He is a resident artist at The Purple Rose Theatre in Michigan, where a number of his plays have been produced. His plays have been performed from New York to Tasmania, and his work has been published by Dramatic Publishing, Playscripts, Smith & Kraus, Applause, Heuer Publishing, and Theatrical Rights Worldwide (TRW). He adapted his dark comedy, *Vino Veritas*, for the silver screen, and it stars Carrie Preston (Emmy-winner for *The Good Wife*). Several of his short plays have also been adapted into films. He is the author of three Sherlock Holmes plays: *Sherlock Holmes and the Adventure of the Elusive Ear, Sherlock Holmes and the Adventure of the Fallen Soufflé*, and *Sherlock Holmes and the Adventure of the Ghost Machine*. He adapted all three plays into novels for Orange Pip Books, and also wrote the two-volume nonfiction *Sherlock Holmes: The Hero with a Thousand Faces*

349

for MX Publishing. He teaches writing at Wayne State University in Detroit and is inordinately fond of cheese and terriers.

David Marcum plays *The Game* with deadly seriousness. He first discovered Sherlock Holmes in 1975 at the age of ten, and since that time, he has collected, read, and chronologicized literally thousands of traditional Holmes pastiches in the form of novels, short stories, radio and television episodes, movies and scripts, comics, fan-fiction, and unpublished manuscripts. He is the author of over one-hundred Sherlockian pastiches, some published in anthologies and magazines such as *The Best Mystery Stories of the Year 2021* and *The Strand*, and others collected in his own books, *The Papers of Sherlock Holmes, Sherlock Holmes and A Quantity of Debt, Sherlock Holmes – Tangled Skeins, Sherlock Holmes and The Eye of Heka,* and *The Collected Papers of Sherlock Holmes.* He has won first place fiction awards from *The Arthur Conan Doyle Society* and the Nero Wolfe *Wolfe Pack.* He has edited over eighty books, including several dozen traditional Sherlockian anthologies, such as the ongoing series *The MX Book of New Sherlock Holmes Stories,* which he created in 2015. This collection is now at forty-two volumes, with more in preparation. He was responsible for bringing back August Derleth's Solar Pons for a new generation with his collection of authorized Pons stories, *The Papers of Solar Pons* and *The Further Papers of Solar Pons.* Pons's return was further assisted by his editing of the reissued authorized versions of the original Pons books, and then several volumes of new Pons adventures. He has done the same for the adventures of Dr. Thorndyke, and has plans for similar projects in the future. He has contributed numerous essays to various publications, and is a member of a number of Sherlockian groups and Scions, as well as *The Mystery Writers of America.* His irregular Sherlockian blog, *A Seventeen Step Program,* addresses various topics related to his favorite book friends (as his son used to call them when he was small), and can be found at *http://17stepprogram.blogspot.com/* He is a licensed Civil Engineer, living in Tennessee with his wife and son. Since the age of nineteen, he has worn a deerstalker as his regular-and-only hat. In 2013, he and his deerstalker were finally able make his first trip-of-a-lifetime Holmes Pilgrimage to England, with return Pilgrimages in 2015 and 2016, where you may have spotted him. If you ever run into him and his deerstalker out and about, feel free to say hello!

Kevin Patrick McCann has published eight collections of poems for adults, one for children (*Diary of a Shapeshifter,* Beul Aithris), a book of ghost stories (*It's Gone Dark,* The Otherside Books), *Teach Yourself Self-Publishing* (Hodder) co-written with the playwright Tom Green, and *Ov* (Beul Aithris Publications) a fantasy novel for children.

Tom Mead is a UK-based author and Golden Age Mystery aficionado. His debut novel, *Death and the Conjuror,* was an international bestseller, and named one of the best mysteries of 2022 by *Publishers Weekly.* The sequel, *The Murder Wheel,* was published in July 2023, and described as "compelling" by *Crimereads* and "pure nostalgic pleasure" by the *Wall Street Journal.* His short fiction has appeared in *Ellery Queen's Mystery Magazine, Alfred Hitchcock Mystery Magazine,* and *The Best Mystery Stories of the Year,* edited by Lee Child.

Adrian Middleton is a Staffordshire-born independent publisher. The son of a real-world detective, he is a former civil servant and policy adviser who now writes and edits science fiction, fantasy, and a popular series of steampunked Sherlock Holmes stories.

Will Murray is the author of some 75 novels, including some 20 posthumous Doc Savage collaborations with Lester Dent, and 40 books in the long-running Destroyer series. Other

Murray novels star the Executioner, Tarzan of the Apes, The Spider, Pat Savage and the Mars Attacks characters. His book, *Nick Fury, Agent of S.H.I.E.L.D.: Empyre* (2000) foreshadowed the 9/11 terrorist attacks. Murray has penned more than 45 Sherlock Holmes short stories. Twenty of Murray's Holmes short stories have been collected as *The Wild Adventures of Sherlock Holmes*, Vols 1 and 2. His novelette, "The Adventure of the Vengeful Viscount", in which Tarzan of the Apes, otherwise Lord Greystoke, hires Sherlock Holmes to solve a mystery, was approved by both the Estate of Sir Arthur Conan Doyle and Edgar Rice Burroughs, Inc. Murray is the author of the non-fiction book, *Master of Mystery: The Rise of The Shadow*, which is an exploration of the famous radio and magazine character, and a sequel, *Dark Avenger: The Strange Saga of The Shadow*. *The Wild Adventures of Cthulhu* Vols 1 & 2 collect Murray's Lovecraftian short stories. For Marvel Comics, Murray created the Unbeatable Squirrel Girl with legendary artist Steve Ditko. Website: *www.adventuresinbronze.com*

Sidney Paget (1860-1908), a few of whose illustrations are used within this anthology, was born in London, and like his two older brothers, became a famed illustrator and painter. He completed over three-hundred-and-fifty drawings for the Sherlock Holmes stories that were first published in *The Strand* magazine, defining Holmes's image forever after in the public mind.

Ember Pepper was born and raised in San Diego, CA. She has an M.F.A. degree in Creative Fiction Writing. She has been a fan of The Great Detective since she was a pre-teen and her greatest artistic enjoyment is challenging herself to write quality pastiches of Sherlock Holmes and his stalwart biographer and friend, John Watson.

Margaret Walsh was born Auckland, New Zealand and now lives in Melbourne, Australia. She is the author of *Sherlock Holmes and the Molly-Boy Murders*, *Sherlock Holmes and the Case of the Perplexed Politician*, *Sherlock Holmes and the Case of the London Dock Deaths*, *The Adventure of the Bloody Duck and Other Tales of Sherlock Holmes*, *Sherlock Holmes and the Curse of Neb-Heka-Ra*, and *Sherlock Holmes and the Hellfire Heirs*, all published by MX Publishing. She is currently working on her seventh book, *Sherlock Holmes and the Deathly Clairvoyant*. Margaret has been a devotee of Sherlock Holmes since childhood and has had several Holmesian related essays printed in anthologies, and is a member of the online society *Doyle's Rotary Coffin*, as well as being *a member of Sisters of Crime Australia*. She has an ongoing love affair with the city of London. When she's not working or planning trips to London. Margaret can be found frequenting the many and varied bookshops of Melbourne.

Emma West joined Undershaw in April 2021 as the Director of Education with a brief to ensure that qualifications formed the bedrock of our provision, whilst facilitating a positive balance between academia, pastoral care, and well-being. She quickly took on the role of Acting Headteacher from early summer 2021. Under her leadership, Undershaw has embraced its new name, new vision, and consequently we have seen an exponential increase in demand for places. There is a buzz in the air as we invite prospective students and families through the doors. Emma has overseen a strategic review, re-cemented relationships with Local Authorities, and positioned Undershaw at the helm of SEND education in Surrey and beyond. Undershaw has a wide appeal: Our students present to us with mild to moderate learning needs and therefore may have some very recent memories of poor experiences in their previous schools. Emma's background as a senior leader within the independent school sector has meant she is well-versed in brokering relationships between the key stakeholders, our many interdependences, local businesses, families, and staff, and all this while ensuring Undershaw remains relentlessly child-centric in its approach. Emma's energetic smile and boundless enthusiasm for Undershaw is inspiring.

*The following contributors appear
in the companion volumes:*
The MX Book of New Sherlock Holmes Stories
Part XL – Further Untold Cases (1879-1886)
Part XLII – Further Untold Cases (1894-1922)

Mike Adamson holds a Doctoral degree from Flinders University of South Australia. After early aspirations in art and writing, Mike secured qualifications in both marine biology and archaeology. Mike has been a university educator since 2006, has worked in the replication of convincing ancient fossils, is a passionate photographer, master-level hobbyist, and journalist for international magazines. Short fiction sales include to *Metastellar*, *Strand Magazine*, *Little Blue Marble*, *Abyss*, and *Apex*, *Daily Science Fiction*, *Compelling Science Fiction*, and *Nature Futures*. Mike has placed some two-hundred stories to date, totaling over a million words. Mike has completed his first Sherlock Holmes novel with Belanger Books, and will be appearing in translation in European magazines. You can catch up with his journey at his blog "The View From the Keyboard"
http://mike-adamson.blogspot.com

Tim Newton Anderson is a former senior daily newspaper journalist and PR manager who has recently started writing fiction. In the past six months, he has placed fourteen stories in publications including *Parsec Magazine*, *Tales of the Shadowmen*, *SF Writers Guild*, *Zoetic Press*, *Dark Lane Books*, *Dark Horses Magazine*, *Emanations*, and *Planet Bizarro*.

Hugh Ashton was born in the U.K., and moved to Japan in 1988, where he remained until 2016, living with his wife Yoshiko in the historic city of Kamakura, a little to the south of Yokohama. He and Yoshiko have now moved to Lichfield, a small cathedral city in the Midlands of the U.K., the birthplace of Samuel Johnson, and one-time home of Erasmus Darwin. In the past, he has worked in the technology and financial services industries, which have provided him with material for some of his books set in the 21st century. He currently works as a writer: Novelist, freelance editor, and copywriter, (his work for large Japanese corporations has appeared in international business journals), and journalist, as well as producing industry reports on various aspects of the financial services industry. However, his lifelong interest in Sherlock Holmes has developed into an acclaimed series of adventures featuring the world's most famous detective, written in the style of the originals. In addition to these, he has also published historical and alternate historical novels, short stories, and thrillers. Together with artist Andy Boerger, he has produced the *Sherlock Ferret* series of stories for children, featuring the world's cutest detective.

Deanna Baran lives in a remote part of Texas where cowboys may still be seen in their natural habitat. A librarian and former museum curator, she writes in between cups of tea, playing *Go*, and trading postcards with people around the world.

Donald I. Baxter has practiced medicine for over forty years. He resides in Erie Pennsylvania with his wife and their dog. His family and his friends are for the most part lawyers who have given him the ability to make stuff up just as they do.

352

Thomas A. Burns Jr. writes *The Natalie McMasters Mysteries* from the small town of Wendell, North Carolina, where he lives with his wife and son, four cats, and a Cardigan Welsh Corgi. He was born and grew up in New Jersey, attended Xavier High School in Manhattan, earned B.S degrees in Zoology and Microbiology at Michigan State University, and a M.S. in Microbiology at North Carolina State University. As a kid, Tom started reading mysteries with The Hardy Boys, Ken Holt, and Rick Brant, then graduated to the classic stories by authors such as A. Conan Doyle, Dorothy Sayers, John Dickson Carr, Erle Stanley Gardner, and Rex Stout, to name a few. Tom has written fiction as a hobby all of his life, starting with *The Man from U.N.C.L.E.* stories in marble-backed copybooks in grade school. He built a career as technical, science, and medical writer and editor for nearly thirty years in industry and government. Now that he's a full-time novelist, he's excited to publish his own mystery series, as well as to write stories about his second most favorite detective, Sherlock Holmes. His Holmes story, "The Camberwell Poisoner", appeared in the March-June 2021 issue of *The Strand Magazine*. Tom has also written a Lovecraftian horror novel, *The Legacy of the Unborn*, under the pen name of Silas K. Henderson – a sequel to H.P. Lovecraft's masterpiece *At the Mountains of Madness*. His Natalie McMasters novel *Killers!* won the Killer Nashville Silver Falchion Award for Best Book of 2021.

Chris Chan is a writer, educator, and historian. He works as a researcher and "International Goodwill Ambassador" for Agatha Christie Ltd. His true crime articles, reviews, and short fiction have appeared (or will soon appear) in *The Strand*, *The Wisconsin Magazine of History*, *Mystery Weekly*, *Gilbert!*, *Nerd HQ*, Akashic Books' *Mondays are Murder* web series, *The Baker Street Journal*, *The MX Book of New Sherlock Holmes Stories*, *Masthead: The Best New England Crime Stories*, *Sherlock Holmes Mystery Magazine*, and multiple Belanger Books anthologies. He is the creator of the Funderburke mysteries, a series featuring a private investigator who works for a school and helps students during times of crisis. The Funderburke short story "The Six-Year-Old Serial Killer" was nominated for a Derringer Award. His first book, *Sherlock & Irene: The Secret Truth Behind "A Scandal in Bohemia"*, was published in 2020 by MX Publishing. His second book, *Murder Most Grotesque: The Comedic Crime Fiction of Joyce Porter* will be released by Level Best Books in 2021, and his first novel, *Sherlock's Secretary*, was published by MX Publishing in 2021. *Murder Most Grotesque* was nominated for the Agatha and Silver Falchion Awards for Nonfiction Writing, and *Sherlock's Secretary* was nominated for the Silver Falchion for Best Comedy. He is also the author of the anthology of Sherlock Holmes stories *Of Course He Pushed Him*.

Barry Clay *also has stories in Part XLII*

Alan Dimes was born in Northwest London and graduated from Sussex University with a BA in English Literature. He has spent most of his working life teaching English. Living in the Czech Republic since 2003, he is now semi-retired and divides his time between Prague and his country cottage. He has also written some fifty stories of horror and fantasy and thirty stories about his husband-and-wife detectives, Peter and Deirdre Creighton, set in the 1930's.

Brett Fawcett is a humanities and Latin teacher at the Chesterton Academy of St. Isidore in Sherwood Park, Alberta. He lives with his wife and son in Edmonton, where he is a member of The Wisteria Lodgers (The Sherlock Holmes Society of Edmonton). He vividly remembers the first time he finished reading the Sherlock Holmes stories in Grade 6, and has been a student of Holmesian literature and scholarship since then. He is also a frequent author of columns and articles on topics like theology, education, and mental health, as well as the occasional mystery story.

Arthur Hall *also has stories in Parts XL and XLII*

Paula Hammond has written over sixty fiction and non-fiction books, as well as short stories, comics, poetry, and scripts for educational DVD's. When not glued to the keyboard, she can usually be found prowling round second-hand books shops or hunkered down in a hide, soaking up the joys of the natural world.

Paul Hiscock is an author of crime, fantasy, horror, and science fiction tales. His short stories have appeared in a variety of anthologies, and include a seventeenth-century whodunnit, a science fiction western, a clockpunk fairytale, and numerous Sherlock Holmes pastiches. He lives with his family in Kent (England) and spends his days taking care of his two children. He mainly does his writing in coffee shops with members of the local NaNoWriMo group, or in the middle of the night when his family has gone to sleep. Consequently, his stories tend to be fuelled by large amounts of black coffee. You can find out more about Paul's writing at *www.detectivesanddragons.uk*.

Kelvin I. Jones is the author of six books about Sherlock Holmes and the definitive biography of Conan Doyle as a spiritualist, *Conan Doyle and The Spirits*. A member of *The Sherlock Holmes Society of London*, he has published numerous short occult and ghost stories in British anthologies over the last thirty years. His work has appeared on BBC Radio, and in 1984 he won the Mason Hall Literary Award for his poem cycle about the survivors of Hiroshima and Nagasaki, recently reprinted as "Omega". (Oakmagic Publications) A one-time teacher of creative writing at the University of East Anglia, he is also the author of four crime novels featuring his ex-met sleuth John Bottrell, who first appeared in *Stone Dead*. He has over fifty titles on Kindle, and is also the author of several novellas and short story collections featuring a Norwich based detective, DCI Ketch, an intrepid sleuth who investigates East Anglian murder cases. He also published a series of short stories about an Edwardian psychic detective, Dr. John Carter (*Carter's Occult Casebook*). Ramsey Campbell, the British horror writer, and Francis King, the renowned novelist, have both compared his supernatural stories to those of M. R. James. He has also published children's fiction, namely *Odin's Eye*, and, in collaboration with his wife Debbie, *The Dark Entry*. Since 1995, he has been the proprietor of Oakmagic Publications, publishers of British folklore and of his fiction titles.

Susan Knight's newest novel, *Death in the Garden of England* (2023) from MX publishing, is the latest in a series which began with her collection of stories, *Mrs. Hudson Investigates* (2019), the novel *Mrs. Hudson goes to Ireland* (2020), and *Mrs. Hudson Goes to Paris* (2022). She has contributed to many recent MX anthologies of new Sherlock Holmes short stories and enjoys writing as Dr. Watson as much as she does Mrs. Hudson. Nine of these stories comprise a new collection of hers, *The Strange Case of the Pale Boy and Other Mysteries* (2023). Susan is the author of two other non-Sherlockian story collections, as well as three novels, a book of non-fiction, and several plays, and has won several prizes for her writing. Susan lives in Dublin.

David Marcum *also has stories in Parts XL and XLII*

Tracy J. Revels, a Sherlockian from the age of eleven, is a professor of history at Wofford College in Spartanburg, South Carolina. She is a member of *The Survivors of the Gloria*

354

Scott and *The Studious Scarlets Society*, and is a past recipient of the Beacon Society Award. Almost every semester, she teaches a class that covers The Canon, either to college students or to senior citizens. She is also the author of three supernatural Sherlockian pastiches with MX (*Shadowfall*, *Shadowblood*, and *Shadowwraith*), and a regular contributor to her scion's newsletter. She also has some notoriety as an author of very silly skits: For proof, see "The Adventure of the Adversarial Adventuress" and "Occupy Baker Street" on YouTube. When not studying Sherlock, she can be found researching the history of her native state, and has written books on Florida in the Civil War and on the development of Florida's tourism industry.

Roger Riccard's family history has Scottish roots, which trace his lineage back to Highland Scotland. This British Isles ancestry encouraged his interest in the writings of Sir Arthur Conan Doyle at an early age. He has authored the novels, *Sherlock Holmes & The Case of the Poisoned Lilly*, and *Sherlock Holmes & The Case of the Twain Papers*. In addition he has produced several short stories in *Sherlock Holmes Adventures for the Twelve Days of Christmas* and the series *A Sherlock Holmes Alphabet of Cases*. A new series will begin publishing in the Autumn of 2022, and his has another novel in the works. All of his books have been published by Baker Street Studios. His Bachelor of Arts Degrees in both Journalism and History from California State University, Northridge, have proven valuable to his writing historical fiction, as well as the encouragement of his wife/editor/inspiration and Sherlock Holmes fan, Rosilyn. She passed in 2021, and it is in her memory that he continues to contribute to the legacy of the "*man who never lived and will never die*".

Dan Rowley practiced law for over forty years in private practice and with a large international corporation. He is retired and lives in Erie, Pennsylvania, with his wife Judy, who puts her artistic eye to his transcription of Watson's manuscripts. He inherited his writing ability and creativity from his children, Jim and Katy, and his love of mysteries from his parents, Jim and Ruth.

Jane Rubino is the author of *A Jersey Shore* mystery series, featuring a Jane Austen-loving amateur sleuth and a Sherlock Holmes-quoting detective, *Knight Errant, Lady Vernon and Her Daughter*, (a novel-length adaptation of Jane Austen's novella *Lady Susan*, co-authored with her daughter Caitlen Rubino-Bradway, *What Would Austen Do?*, also co-authored with her daughter, a short story in the anthology *Jane Austen Made Me Do It, The Rucastles' Pawn, The Copper Beeches from Violet Turner's POV*, and, of course, there's the Sherlockian novel in the drawer – who doesn't have one? Jane lives on a barrier island at the New Jersey shore.

Fifteen of **Brenda Seabrooke**'s Sherlock Holmes pastiches have been anthologized in MX Publishing and Belanger Books, six in *Best Crime Stories of New England*, one in *Destination: Mystery* and *Mystery Tribune*, and twelve in literary reviews such as *Yemassee, Confrontation*, and one in *Redbook*. Twenty-two of her books for young readers have been published at Penguin, Clarion, etc., and won awards such as a Notable from the National Council of Social Studies, Junior Literary Guild, Hornbook Honor, an Edgar finalist, etc. She received a grant from the National Endowment for the Arts, and The Robie Macauley Award from Emerson College. In 2022, MX published her collection, *Sherlock Holmes: The Persian Slipper and Other Stories*.

Liese Sherwood-Fabre knew she was destined to write when she got an A+ in the second grade for her story about Dick, Jane, and Sally's ruined picnic. After obtaining her PhD, she joined the federal government and worked and lived internationally for more than fifteen years. Returning to the states, she seriously pursued her writing career, garnering such awards as a finalist in the Romance Writers of America's Golden Heart contest and a Pushcart Prize nomination. A recognized Sherlockian scholar, her essays have appeared in newsletters, *The Baker Street Journal*, and *Canadian Holmes*. She has recently turned to a childhood passion: Sherlock Holmes. *The Adventure of the Murdered Midwife*, the first book in *The Early Case Files of Sherlock Holmes* series, was the CIBA Mystery and Mayhem 2020 first-place winner. *Her latest book is a young adult fantasy Wilhelmina Quigley: Magic School Dropout*, which is available through all major booksellers. More about her writing can be found at *www.liesesherwoodfabre.com*.

Robert V. Stapleton was born and brought up in Leeds, Yorkshire, England, and studied at Durham University. After working in various parts of the country as an Anglican parish priest, he is now retired and lives with his wife in North Yorkshire. As a member of his local writing group, he now has time to develop his other life as a writer of adventure stories. He has published a number of short stories, and he is hoping to have a couple of completed novels published at some time in the future.

Award winning poet and author **Joseph W. Svec III** enjoys writing, poetry, and stories, and creating new adventures for Holmes and Watson that take them into the worlds of famous literary authors and scientists. His *Missing Authors* trilogy introduced Holmes to Lewis Carroll, Jules Verne, H.G. Wells, and Alfred Lord Tennyson, as well as many of their characters. His transitional story *Sherlock Holmes and the Mystery of the First Unicorn* involved several historical figures, besides a Unicorn or two. He has also written the rhymed and metered Sherlock Holmes Christmas adventure, *The Night Before Christmas in 221b*, sure to be a delight for Sherlock Holmes enthusiasts of all ages. Joseph won the Amador Arts Council 2021 Original Poetry Contest, with his Rhymed and metered story poem, "The Homecoming". Joseph has presented a literary paper on Sherlock Holmes/Alice in Wonderland crossover literature to the Lewis Carroll Society of North America, as well as given several presentations to the Amador County Holmes Hounds, Sherlockian Society. He is currently working on his first book in the *Missing Scientist Trilogy, Sherlock Holmes and the Adventure of the Demonstrative Dinosaur*, in which Sherlock meets Professor George Edward Challenger. Joseph has Masters Degrees in Systems Engineering and Human Organization Management, and has written numerous technical papers on Aerospace Testing. In addition to writing, Joseph enjoys creating miniature dioramas based on music, literature, and history from many different eras. His dioramas have been featured in magazine articles and many different blogs, including the North American Jules Verne society newsletter. He currently has 57 dioramas set up in his display area, and has written a reference book on toy castles and knights from around the world. An avid tea enthusiast, his tea cabinet contains over five-hundred different varieties, and he delights in sharing afternoon tea with his childhood sweetheart and wonderful wife, who has inspired and coauthored several books with him.

Kevin P. Thornton was shortlisted six times for the Crime Writers of Canada best unpublished novel. He never won – they are all still unpublished, and now he writes short stories. He lives in Canada, north enough that ringing Santa Claus is a local call and winter is a way of life. He has contributed numerous short stories to The MX Book of New Sherlock Holmes Stories. By the time you next hear from him, he hopes to have written more.

DJ Tyrer is the person behind Atlantean Publishing and has had fiction featuring Sherlock Holmes published in volumes from MX Publishing and Belanger Books, and an issue of *Awesome Tales*, and has a forthcoming story in *Sherlock Holmes Mystery Magazine*. DJ's non-Sherlockian mysteries can be found in anthologies such as *Mardi Gras Mysteries* (Mystery and Horror LLC) and *The Trench Coat Chronicles* (Celestial Echo Press), and on *Mystery Tribune*.

DJ Tyrer's website is at *https://djtyrer.blogspot.co.uk/*

DJ's Facebook page is at *https://www.facebook.com/DJTyrerwriter/*

The Atlantean Publishing website is at *https://atlanteanpublishing.wordpress.com/*

I.A. Watson great-grand-nephew of Dr. John H. Watson, has been intrigued by the notorious "black sheep" of the family since childhood, and was fascinated to inherit from his grandmother a number of unedited manuscripts removed circa 1956 from a rather larger collection reposing at Lloyds Bank Ltd (which acquired Cox & Co Bank in 1923). Upon discovering the published corpus of accounts regarding the detective Sherlock Holmes from which a censorious upbringing had shielded him, he felt obliged to allow an interested public access to these additional memoranda, and is gradually undertaking the task of transcribing them for admirers of Mr. Holmes and Dr. Watson's works. In the meantime, I.A. Watson continues to pen other books, the latest of which is *The Incunabulum of Sherlock Holmes*. A full list of his seventy or so published works are available at: *http://www.chillwater.org.uk/writing/iawatsonhome.htm*

The MX Book of New Sherlock Holmes Stories
Edited by David Marcum
((MX Publishing, 2015-   )

"This is the finest volume of Sherlockian fiction I have ever read, and I have read, literally, thousands." – Philip K. Jones

"Beyond Impressive . . . This is a splendid venture for a great cause!"
– Roger Johnson, Editor, *The Sherlock Holmes Journal,*
The Sherlock Holmes Society of London

Part I: 1881-1889; Part II: 1890-1895; Part III: 1896-1929

Part IV: 2016 Annual

Part V: Christmas Adventures

Part VI: 2017 Annual

Eliminate the Impossible
Part VII: (1880-1891); Part VIII: (1892-1905)

2018 Annual
Part IX: (1879-1895); Part X: (1896-1916)

Some Untold Cases
Part XI: (1880-1891); Part XII: (1894-1902)

2019 Annual
Part XIII: (1881-1890); Part XIV: (1891-1897); Part XV: (1898-1917)

Whatever Remains . . . Must be the Truth
Part XVI: (1881-1890); Part XVII: (1891-1898); Part XVIII: (1898-1925)

2020 Annual
Part XIX: (1882-1890); Part XX: (1891-1897); Part XXI: (1898-1923)·

Some More Untold Cases
Part XXII: (1877-1887); Part XXIII: (1888-1894); Part XXIV: (1895-1903)

2021 Annual
Part XXV: (1881-1888); Part XXVI: (1889-1897); Part XXVII: (1898-1928)

More Christmas Adventures
Part XXVIII: (1869-1888); Part XXIX: (1889-1896); Part XXX: (1897-1928)

2022 Annual
Part XXXI: (1875-1887); Part XXXII: (1888-1895); Part XXXIII: (1896-1919)

"However Improbable . . . ."
Part XXXIV: (1878-1888); Part XXXV: (1889-1896); Part XXXVI: (1897-1919)

2023 Annual
Parts XXXVII (1875-1889), XXXVIII (1889-1896), and XXXIX (1897-1923)

Further Untold Cases
Part XL: (1879-1886), Part XLI: (1887-1892) and Part XLII: (1894-1922)

In Preparation *. . . Part XLIII (and XLIV and XLV as well?)*
and more to come!

360

The MX Book of New Sherlock Holmes Stories
Edited by David Marcum
(MX Publishing, 2015-   )

<u>*Publishers Weekly*</u> says:

Part VI: *The traditional pastiche is alive and well . . . .*

Part VII: *Sherlockians eager for faithful-to-the-canon plots and characters will be delighted.*

Part VIII: *The imagination of the contributors in coming up with variations on the volume's theme is matched by their ingenious resolutions.*

Part IX: *The 18 stories . . . will satisfy fans of Conan Doyle's originals. Sherlockians will rejoice that more volumes are on the way.*

Part X: *. . . new Sherlock Holmes adventures of consistently high quality.*

Part XI: *. . . an essential volume for Sherlock Holmes fans.*

Part XII: *. . . continues to amaze with the number of high-quality pastiches.*

Part XIII: *. . . Amazingly, Marcum has found 22 superb pastiches . . . his is more catnip for fans of stories faithful to Conan Doyle's original*

Part XIV: *. . . this standout anthology of 21 short stories written in the spirit of Conan Doyle's originals.*

Part XV: *Stories pitting Sherlock Holmes against seemingly supernatural phenomena highlight Marcum's 15th anthology of superior short pastiches.*

Part XVI: *Marcum has once again done fans of Conan Doyle's originals a service.*

Part XVII: *This is yet another impressive array of new but traditional Holmes stories.*

Part XVIII: *Sherlockians will again be grateful to Marcum and MX for high-quality new Holmes tales.*

Part XIX: *Inventive plots and intriguing explorations of aspects of Dr. Watson's life and beliefs lift the 24 pastiches in Marcum's impressive 19th Sherlock Holmes anthology*

Part XX: *Marcum's reserve of high-quality new Holmes exploits seems endless.*

Part XXI: *This is another must-have for Sherlockians.*

Part XXII: *Marcum's superlative 22nd Sherlock Holmes pastiche anthology features 21 short stories that successfully emulate the spirit of Conan Doyle's originals while expanding on the canon's tantalizing references to mysteries Dr. Watson never got around to chronicling.*

Part XXIII: *Marcum's well of talented authors able to mimic the feel of The Canon seems bottomless.*

Part XXIV: *Marcum's expertise at selecting high-quality pastiches remains impressive.*

Part XXVIII: *All entries adhere to the spirit, language, and characterizations of Conan Doyle's originals, evincing the deep pool of talent Marcum has access to. Against the odds, this series remains strong, hundreds of stories in.*

Part XXXI: *. . . yet another stellar anthology of 21 short pastiches that effectively mimic the originals . . . Marcum's diligent searches for high-quality stories has again paid off for Sherlockians.*

Part XXXIV: *Mind-bending puzzles are the highlight of Marcum's fully satisfying 34th anthology, which again demonstrates that multiple authors are capable of giving Sherlock Holmes and Watson innovative mysteries to tackle while staying in character. Marcum's inventory of canonical pastiches shows no signs of being exhausted any time soon.*

The MX Book of New Sherlock Holmes Stories

Edited by David Marcum

(MX Publishing, 2015-   )

An Investees' Anthology
Edited by David Marcum
(MX Publishing, 2022)

Selected Contributions to
The MX Book of New Sherlock Holmes Stories
by Members of
The Baker Street Irregulars

*All royalties from this collection are being donated
for the benefit of the preservation of Undershaw,
a school for special needs students located at
one of the former homes of Sir Arthur Conan Doyle*

Stories, Forewords, and Poems in this volume
have previously appeared in Parts I – XXXVI of
The MX Book of New Sherlock Holmes Stories

Featuring Contributions by:

Mark Alberstat, Marino C. Alvarez, Peter Calamai, Catherine Cooke, Carla Coupe, David Stuart Davies, John Farrell, Lyndsay Faye, Sonia Fetherston, Jayantika Ganguly, Jeffrey Hatcher, Roger Johnson, Leslie S. Klinger, Ann Margaret Lewis, Bonnie MacBird, Stephen Mason, Julie McKuras Nicholas Meyer, Jacquelynn Morris, Otto Penzler, Christopher Redmond, Tracy J. Revels, Steven Rothman, Nancy Holder, Mark Levy (and Arlene Mantin Levy), Nicholas Utechin, and Sean M. Wright (and DeForeest B. Wright, III)

MX Publishing

MX Publishing is the world's largest specialist Sherlock Holmes publisher, with over five-hundred titles and over two-hundred authors creating the latest in Sherlock Holmes fiction and non-fiction

The catalogue includes several award winning books, and over two-hundred-and-fifty have been converted into audio.

MX Publishing also has one of the largest communities of Holmes fans on Facebook, with regular contributions from dozens of authors.

www.mxpublishing.com

@mxpublishing on Facebook, Twitter, and Instagram

Printed in the USA
CPSIA information can be obtained
at www.ICGtesting.com
LVHW091653210324
775156LV00001B/8